The
Summer
of Yes

ALSO BY COURTNEY WALSH

The Summer of Yes

COURTNEY WALSH

THOMAS NELSON
Since 1798

The Summer of Yes

Copyright © 2024 by Courtney Walsh

Published in Nashville, Tennessee, by Thomas Nelson. Thomas Nelson is a registered trademark of HarperCollins Christian Publishing, Inc.

Thomas Nelson titles may be purchased in bulk for educational, business, fundraising, or sales promotional use. For information, please email SpecialMarkets@ThomasNelson.com.

Publisher's Note: This novel is a work of fiction. Names, characters, places, and incidents are either products of the author's imagination or used fictitiously. All characters are fictional, and any similarity to people living or dead is purely coincidental.

Any internet addresses (websites, blogs, etc.) in this book are offered as a resource. They are not intended in any way to be or imply an endorsement by Thomas Nelson, nor does Thomas Nelson vouch for the content of these sites for the life of this book.

Library of Congress Cataloging-in-Publication Data
Names: Walsh, Courtney, 1975- author.
Title: The summer of yes / Courtney Walsh.
Description: Nashville, Tennessee : Thomas Nelson, 2024. | Summary: "A near-death experience catapults workaholic junior editor Kelsey Worthington into changing her life--one yes at a time"--Provided by publisher.
Identifiers: LCCN 2024003867 (print) | LCCN 2024003868 (ebook) | ISBN 9780840713698 (paperback) | ISBN 9780840713728 (epub) | ISBN 9780840713865
Subjects: LCGFT: Christian fiction. | Romance fiction. | Novels.
Classification: LCC PS3623.A4455 S86 2024 (print) | LCC PS3623.A4455 (ebook) | DDC 813/.6--dc23/eng/20240202
LC record available at https://lccn.loc.gov/2024003867
LC ebook record available at https://lccn.loc.gov/2024003868

Printed in the United States of America

24 25 26 27 28 LBC 5 4 3 2 1

For my father-in-law, Bill Walsh.
The last time we spoke, he told my boys,
"You've got lives to live, so get on the road and start livin' 'em."
Truly words to live by.

Chapter 1

KELSEY

BEEP. BEEP.

Click. Drip.

Whirrrrr.

Click. Drip.

My eyes flutter open, from murky to gray to light and back to gray, like the shutter on a camera taking pictures in the dark.

Head spinning. Voices muffled. Low, steady beeping persists.

Am I . . . in a hospital?

I force my eyebrows up, hoping they help crack my eyes open. The movement sends a searing pain through my head, splitting it like an axe.

I try shifting my position and a sharp spasm cuts through my side. I gasp.

"Welcome back."

My eyes struggle to focus, but eventually I see a nurse who looks approximately fifteen years old fussing with a tube.

The tube that I now see is attached to my arm.

What in the world . . . ?

My mouth is crusty and dry, and my voice croaks out, "Am I . . . ?"

"You're in the hospital." She smiles. "I'm Cecelia, and I'll be taking care of you."

Thanks to my parents, her name triggers an automatic Simon and Garfunkel response, and I find myself trying hard not to get down on my knees to beg her please to come home.

Flashes of coffee. And a car.

A car. But . . . did it? I can't remember . . .

I try to sit up, suddenly alarmed. The room spins and I slump back on the bed.

She lays a hand on my shoulder. "It's okay. Take it slow," she says.

Slow. Yeah, right. This child doesn't know me at all.

She gently fluffs a stiff pillow behind my head. It's one of those plastic ones with a pillowcase that does nothing to stop it from feeling like I'm lying on a bag of potato chips.

"Um . . . water?" I whisper-croak. "How am I here?"

"I'll tell you what I know." She pours water from a pink plastic pitcher into a Styrofoam cup and sticks a bendy straw in it. "You were in an accident. You were brought here unconscious with head trauma two days ago."

Two days ago? Head trauma?

Another flash of a car. *I was hit by a car.*

My first thought is: *I don't have time to get hit by a car.*

My second thought, which I speak out loud, is: "Wh-what?"

She leans over and holds the straw to my lips. "Take it slow. Drink this."

I take a sip, struggling to swallow, and to remember. It seems like being hit by a car would be imprinted on my brain, but I'm foggy. The last thing I remember is walking out of Starbucks toward the office. And the only reason I was in Starbucks at all was because one of the assistants, Tess, called in sick.

"It was a car accident," she says, confirming my hazy memory. "The vehicle jumped the curb and ran right into you." Cecelia takes the cup back and sets it down on a rolling tray. "It was all over the news." Then, after a pause, "You're really lucky."

"I don't feel lucky," I say, my sense of humor struggling to stay intact. "I feel like I got hit by a car."

My head throbs. I instinctively reach up to rub it, dragging along the tube from my IV, which I realize now stings up my arm like icy fire.

Her hand rests on my shoulder again. "Is there someone you'd like us to call?" she asks.

I feel strangely soothed. This teenager has some incredible bedside manner.

"No, I . . ." My head is killing me, and I shut my eyes, wincing through the pain. "There's no one."

It's odd—that is my first thought. It's not exactly true, and yet, for some reason, I feel so detached.

When I crack my eyes open enough to glance at Cecelia, I find her watching me, pity in her stare. "I mean, I have *people*, you know. Friends. Family. Just"—I close my eyes and sink into my bag of chips a bit farther—"no one I want to see me in the hospital."

"Well, having someone here may help," Cecelia says. "It would be better not to be alone."

"Oh, I'm not alone," I say. Though something about it doesn't ring true. Sitting here, in this hospital room, I feel weirdly alone. For some reason, I don't want to surround myself with anyone, not even Ravi. I know I've been bad about communicating with him, and it feels wrong to reach out now that I'm in a bit of trouble.

Wait . . . *two days*?

"Two days? You said I've been here . . ." I try to sit up again, and Cecelia is over to my bed quickly, hands on me to slowly back me down from trying to vault out of the room.

"No sudden movements."

"I have to go," I plead.

"I'm afraid that might not be possible," she answers. "Not yet."

"But . . ." Trying to focus with this headache is like trying to read *War and Peace* through the bottom of a root beer float glass. "But I have a meeting. An important one."

Chase Donovan will not wait. She has other offers. We aren't the only publishing house courting her.

Cecelia pushes a button on the wall and shakes her head at me emphatically. "You're here at least another night. Maybe two. You're concussed, major subcutaneous contusions on your left side, and the doctor wants to evaluate to make sure it's not something more serious."

"I'm fine," I lie firmly, vision cloudy and a weird metallic taste in my mouth. "Where's my bag?"

I need my phone. I need to reach out to Chase's agent. And my boss, Charlie.

What time is it?

What day is it?

I have a fleeting thought that waking up after an accident should be more *While You Were Sleeping* and less *A Quiet Place*.

Cecelia takes my non-IV hand. "Miss Worthington, you have to take it easy."

These words don't compute. I laugh and then wince—hard. "You're breaking my heart, Cecelia. Chase Donovan will not wait. And please call me Kelsey."

"Chase Donovan? From TikTok?"

I slowly nod, my head a buoy in rough seas. "She's got two other publishing houses interested. If I stand her up . . ."

There goes everything I've worked for.

"I'm sure once you explain that you're in the hospital because you got hit by a car, she will understand." Cecelia takes on a firm tone, and I want to applaud her for it. She may look young, but she's obviously no pushover.

"I'll grab your phone. Tell her you're sorry, but you'll have to reschedule."

I know Chase is in the city meeting with other publishing houses. I know I have one shot to convince her that I'm the best person to edit her book. I know I cannot be stuck in this bed with this stupid tube jabbed into my hand for another second.

Before I can protest any further, though, a doctor comes into the room. Maybe he'll have better news.

"You're awake. That's great." He's holding a clipboard with a folder attached to it, and he opens it up and starts flipping through pages.

"I am," I say, even though I feel like my head has a spear sticking out of it.

He smirks. "How are you feeling?"

"I feel great. I think the accident even fixed my lower back problems."

He chuckles. Sense of humor. Also good. "Okay, follow this with your eyes."

He pulls a pen from his coat pocket and holds it vertically in front of my eyes. I focus on it, but when he moves it from side to side, the room tilts and my vision goes fun-house mirror, and I grab the sides of the hospital bed to keep from falling out of it.

"Yeah, you're not going anywhere anytime soon."

He flips the pen around, which turns out to be a flashlight, then he shines it in and out of my eyes. It makes my head sway and nausea wash over me.

"We'll wait for the CT scan to make sure there's no additional swelling," he says, finally clicking the light off. "You were involved in a serious accident. Plus, there's an officer outside waiting to get your statement."

I frown, blinking away the phantom spots left in my eyes from the light. "What? Why?"

"He has a few questions."

"I'm fine, really, I—" But before I can finish whatever it was I planned to say, the nausea worsens. Cecelia might look fifteen, but she recognizes immediately what's about to go down . . . or out. She sticks a plastic container under my mouth and stands there patiently, holding my hair back while I puke my guts out.

"I'm so sorry," I sputter and spit, hoping I didn't get anything on her.

I lay my head back and Cecelia holds the cup for me again. I swish some water and spit it into the container, which she then whisks out of the room like a magician's assistant.

"I have work." I mutter this half-heartedly, because at the moment I can't imagine being able to convince anyone that I'm the best person to work on anything.

"No screens for you, I'm afraid. Work will have to wait," the doctor says. "It'll be there when you're better."

"But Chase Donovan won't be."

The doctor starts. "From TikTok?"

I feebly open an eye and raise a thumbs-up.

"Well, as cool as that sounds, what you need is rest. Is there someone else you want us to call?"

I should probably let the office know where I am. I should probably text Tess and tell her that, while she might have a stomach bug, I shook hands with a Toyota. I should probably call Ravi and my parents and let them know that I'm not dead. Everyone will be concerned.

But that's just it. Everyone will be concerned. And they'll fuss over me. And this is not a big deal. I'll be out of here in no time.

So I don't do any of those things.

Instead, I lean back, the pillow crunching as I do, and shake my head no.

"Very good." He nods. "You sit tight. Cecelia will be back to prep you for the scan. I'll let the officer know you're not able to talk right now. Get some rest."

"I really do need to get out of here, Doc—" But the thought goes unfinished and the world fades to black.

Chapter 2

KELSEY

I DON'T WANT to go in here!"

I must've dozed off, but at the sound of a woman's angry voice, I'm awake. And I think I have a new roommate.

"I'm paying you thousands of dollars—the least you can do is consider my needs!"

My eyebrows shoot up, but I quickly learn the woman isn't finished. I don't want to sit up and stare, but I'm very curious who they are wheeling into my room.

"You mean to tell me there is nowhere else in this entire hospital for me to rest comfortably? Alone?"

"I'm so sorry, but every room is occupied tonight. We're hoping we can move you tomorrow when something else opens up." That sounds like Cecelia.

"Get someone in here who can actually *do* something. You look like a child." *Definitely Cecelia.* "I cannot believe they're entrusting my care to a *child.*"

"I'm twenty-five, ma'am," she says.

"Like I said," the woman says. "A child. Where's Dr. Fisher?"

"I'll see if he's on call." Cecelia turns and looks at me. When she sees I'm awake, her eyes go wide, and I can almost feel her apologizing to me. "Oh, Kelsey, you're awake. You kind of fainted."

"How does a person *kind of* faint?" the older woman on the other side of my room barks. "You either faint or you don't faint. I would think nursing school would've taught you that."

Cecelia closes her eyes in what appears to be a calming exercise, then opens them and focuses on me. "Dr. Fisher will want to know you're awake. How are you feeling?"

"Thirsty." I press a hand to my temple. "And my head hurts."

"Okay, just stay still."

At that, a police officer appears in the doorway. "Miss Worthington, do you mind if I ask you a few questions?"

"I'm sorry," Cecelia says. "She just woke up."

"I'm in a room with a criminal?!"

I shift my position and see the woman, sitting up in a bed identical to mine on the opposite side of the room. She's wearing a silk robe and her hair is perfectly styled, her face made up like she's got a date to the opera.

And I recognize her instantly.

"Oh. My. Goodness." I sit up fully now. "You're Georgina Tate."

She raises a neatly manicured brow at me but says nothing until she directs her attention to Cecelia. "Are you getting Dr. Fisher or do I need to make a call?"

Cecelia makes a face like she deals with this kind of thing every hour of every day, and leaves as the officer steps inside and smiles at me.

"This won't take long, Miss Worthington," he says. "I'm Officer Truman. I just need to know what you remember about the accident."

I shift my position in the bed, feeling slightly self-conscious. "I don't remember much of anything."

"Maybe something prior to the accident? Where were you headed?"

"I remember walking out of Starbucks and then . . . waking up here."

"Okay, good. That's a start. What did you order at Starbucks?"

"What difference does that make?" Georgina barks.

I'm starting to get the sense that, like a large boulder dropped in a pool, when this woman jumps in, everything else just kind of gets pushed out of the way.

Our circles likely never would've intersected if it weren't for this accident, and it's strange that my life is the pool to her boulder.

Everyone in New York knows Georgina. She's a legend.

"Ma'am, I apologize; this is a private conversation," the officer says.

She leans forward. "We're literally in the same room. The only way to make it private is to take up sign language or *take me to my own room*!" She shouts this last part at the door.

This doesn't feel like a good time to smile, but I'm struggling not to. I wonder if this ability to say whatever the heck you're thinking is something that comes with age.

I hope so.

And maybe not *everyone* knows Georgina Tate. Officer Truman obviously doesn't realize he's talking to one of the most successful women in the country. Georgina started her cosmetics company back when women didn't do such things, and now people are writing books about her. Business professors are studying her. She hasn't met an intact glass ceiling.

I'm wondering if a little bit of that devil-may-care attitude could rub off on me. I'm a thirty-two-year-old assistant editor at a New York publishing house with a small client list and a whole lot of insecurity. I want to be Georgina when I grow up.

We all want to be Georgina when we grow up.

And yet, I didn't *always* want to be Georgina . . . I used to have different dreams altogether.

The thought startles me. Where it came from, I have no idea.

Officer Truman turns back to me. "I asked what drink you ordered in case it jogs your memory."

"Ah. Makes sense." I furrow my brow, which hurts, and try to remember. "I ordered a skinny vanilla latte for Charlie . . ."

He starts to write. "Charlie?"

"Goldfarb," I say. "My boss."

Truman scribbles something in a notebook. "What do you do for Mr. Goldfarb?"

"Basically whatever he tells me," I say without thinking.

"Are you Mr. Goldfarb's assistant?"

"No, I'm an editor," I say, then correct myself. "Assistant . . . editor." I pause, and maybe it's Georgina's tilted glare, but I suddenly feel like I have to shine up my story. "I'm working my way up." I tap his notebook where he's writing his notes. "Make sure that gets in there."

He looks at me funny.

"So you're not his assistant, but you do certain duties an assistant would perform?"

"Yes, but not an errand-running assistant," I say, trying to laugh it off and wincing instead. "That's what Tess does."

"And Tess is . . ."

"His assistant."

Georgina cackles one singular "Ha!" and we both turn to look at her. "Goldfarb doesn't need two assistants. He needs a better toupee artist and some Nicorette gum."

We turn back to each other, and it's not lost on me that she described my boss to a T.

"Then why were you getting the coffee, and not Tess?"

"Because she called in sick," I say.

Georgina flicks a perfectly manicured hand in the air. I'm not sure what she's getting at, but the police officer doesn't give me time to interpret it.

"Is your boss, Mr. Goldfarb, a well-known person? Would anyone have a grudge against him for any reason, former employee or . . . ?"

"Nobody mowed me down on the sidewalk to try to get to Charlie, if that's what you're thinking. I work in publishing, and nobody's spilling trade secrets—" Then I frown. "Wait, are you asking me questions because you don't know who did this?"

"It's an ongoing investigation," he says. "We've got a few leads, but the car was stolen. The driver left it at the scene."

"Wow," I say. "So I'm, like, a victim."

"Or a criminal," Georgina says.

"Ma'am, please," Officer Truman says. Then back to me. "You don't remember seeing a person behind the wheel?"

I shake my head, looking down, trying to visualize things. It's all so hazy. "I was on the phone confirming my meeting. I wasn't paying attention. I guess I . . ." I shut my eyes, willing myself to remember the details, but . . . nothing.

And then another wave of nausea and I have to rest my head back on the bed. Things start to go swimmy, and it takes all my willpower not to lose it on the nice officer's uniform pants.

"You're very lucky," the officer says. "The doctor said you don't even have any broken bones."

"Oh yeah," I muse, smacking my dry mouth. "Lucky."

"Your guardian angel must be worn out." He chuckles.

"Her guardian angel must be taking the week off," Georgina quips.

"Ma'am"—he turns to Georgina—"with all due respect, she could've died."

"I could've died," I repeat. And if I'd died right there on Forty-Second Street, who really would've cared? It would've been one of those *can you believe what happened?* stories people share at parties, but without my name attached.

Because nobody knows my name. Not even Charlie half the time.

I suddenly realize that in all of my thirty-two years of being on this planet, I've never done anything remarkable at all.

I haven't been out of the country. I haven't taken a road trip or skipped out on work just for fun. I've never gone skinny-dipping or skydiving or horseback riding. I've never had a margarita. Or had dinner with a stranger. Or gotten the courage to write again. Or . . .

A long list of things I've never done races through my mind as Officer Truman snaps his notebook shut. He pulls out a card and hands it to me. "If you remember anything else, give me a call. Unfortunately, it's pretty rare that we find the perpetrator of a hit-and-run, but we'll do our best to catch whoever it was that did this to you."

I take the card, the tube of the IV pulling against my skin as I do. "Okay."

He glances over at Georgina, then back at me. "And . . . um . . . good luck." Then he walks out.

The two biggest thoughts I'm left with are: *Georgina Tate is in my room* and *I could've died.* Oddly, these things are equally hard to believe.

I can't keep my eyes open, and that's a good thing, because frankly I don't know what to think about either one of those thoughts right now.

Chapter 3

KELSEY

I'VE NEVER DONE anything.

That's all I'm thinking about as Cecelia wheels me down the hall for a CT scan.

It's all I'm thinking when she rolls me back into my room afterward. And it's all I'm thinking now, as I lay in this stiff bed, staring at the ceiling.

Of course, I always planned to have a big, full life—more than just work—but I know I have to pay my dues before I get there. Earn the right to time off.

Across the room, Georgina is propped up on pillows that don't look crunchy—the kind she probably brought from home. Why didn't I think of that?

Oh. Right. I woke up here.

And I have very few friends.

I wonder what she's here for. She doesn't look injured. Or sick.

Outside the room, a nurse is telling another nurse about "the time her one brother shot her other brother in the privates with a BB gun." They're laughing and joking and being all *normal* while I'm in here contemplating my place in the world and wondering when I'm going to get out of here.

How did I let this happen to me? Not the accident but the rest of it. My life rolls out in front of me like an art film that nobody understands.

It wasn't supposed to go like this.

Plus, my head still feels like the Lord of the Dance took up residency there.

"Time to go back in."

"Ugh, already?"

I tune in to the conversation just outside my room. Apparently, the nurses are done talking about "the BB in the PP" and are now back to talking about work. I can hear the dread in their voices.

Is that because of me? Or my surly roommate?

"I have to check her vitals," the other one says. "I can't believe she's back already."

"I know," a voice says. "It's really sad, isn't it? And nobody's come to visit her. I think that's why they put her with the car crash victim."

I blink three times. Now they're talking about me.

"No visitors for either one of them."

"I know, I feel sad for them."

A sigh. "Okay. Wish me luck!"

The door to our room opens and I quickly slam my eyes shut, like a tween caught flashlight reading after bedtime. The nurse enters and walks over to Georgina's bed. The older woman must be sleeping because there's no angry berating going on.

I resist the urge to snag my phone and text everyone I work with to come in and make me look popular.

See? I have people! I have visitors!

I want the nurses to know I'm not a charity case. I'm not some loner.

I'm an editor.

Well, *assistant* editor. I'm working my way up. It's officially in a police notebook.

I know I'm trying to convince myself. Hopefully I'll be gone tomorrow, and I can put this whole stupid experience behind me.

And maybe I can work a little harder on getting a life.

....

Georgina

Another morning and I'm still alive.

Another morning and I'm back in this godforsaken hospital. Would it kill them to change the curtains once in a while?

My criminal roommate is clicking away on her laptop like she's just cracked the code to solve world hunger. And I know for a fact she's not supposed to be looking at screens because I've heard the nurse tell her so every time she's asked.

I've been in the hospital so many times this past year, you'd think they could've at least found me my own room.

JP, my assistant, has a call to make to Michael at McKenzie Capital Management, the company that owns this particular hospital.

Someone's going to lose their job.

I sit up in the bed, still attached to that ridiculous machine.

Still waiting to die.

It's not unlike that period between 5:00 p.m. and bedtime, where you're just waiting for sleep to take you so you can be done with the day.

Still waiting. *Still full of regret.*

I glance at the young woman across the room. "What in the world are you doing?"

She stops typing and looks at me. There's something familiar about her. Not familiar like I've seen her before—familiar because she reminds me of me.

Though a little self-confidence and some makeup would go a long way.

"Working," she says. "I really don't have time to be sitting in this stupid bed."

I understand that on a spiritual level.

I'm not going to wax poetic about my being here, though. Unfortunately, it's given me more than my fair share of time to think. More time than I wanted.

Regrets are more in focus when hindsight is twenty-twenty.

Her gaze flits back to her laptop, a line of worry etched deep in her forehead.

I know that look.

I'm confronted with a memory of a younger version of myself, moments after giving birth, barking orders at my then assistant because *"I cannot fall behind."*

There was always another deal to be closed. Another meeting to lead. Another point to prove. I didn't have the luxury of relaxing, something Dylan never understood. In the early years, I let him whisk me away for a day on the boat, a weekend up north, anything to, as he called it, "help me recharge."

When he left, I thought I was finally free to spend my time as I saw fit. I told myself that was a good thing.

But now, with the benefit of a lot of years and Death peeking at me through the curtains, I'm starting to see things differently.

Even now. This whole waiting thing is a complete waste of time.

If only my kidneys would fail already.

The woman's phone buzzes beside her.

"I thought they told you no screens," I say.

"Work won't wait," she says, her tone defensive. "And I texted my parents and work and a friend that I'm here."

"You don't have to tell me," I say. "I'm not your doctor."

She frowns. Her phone is still buzzing.

"Are you going to answer it?"

The woman pauses for a split second, then picks it up and presses a button. "Tess." A pause. "You saw it on the news?" A sigh. "I was just drafting an email to explain to Charlie that I'll be out for a few days." She presses her fingers into the bridge of her nose. "I don't know—I hope later today?"

A nurse walks in. Her name is Belinda. She's a tall, heavyset Black woman, and I know they've sent her here to deal with me because she is the only one who doesn't put up with my attitude.

"You're back," Belinda says, busying herself with one of the machines.

"Disappointed?"

"That depends," she says. "Did you find me a Rum Berry lipstick in your stash?"

Regardless of how much I like her, I wish I didn't have a familiar relationship with this woman. I'd rather be known by the barista in my neighborhood coffee shop, but JP always gets my coffee, and here we are.

I nod toward my Kate Spade bag. "It's in there."

"Ooooh! You remembered!" She puckers her lips. "You are so good to me, Miss Tate."

I pretend to be annoyed, but really, I like Belinda. I like that I can count on her to dish back whatever I give her. Very few people in my life have the guts to do that.

She picks up my bag and brings it over to me.

"It's in the inside pocket."

She starts rummaging through it, then pulls out the gold tube. The packaging on my cosmetics really is top-notch. I want my customers to feel like they have something elegant, something that will make them feel a little richer than they are.

"You really did me dirty discontinuing this color." She opens the tube and presses the lipstick on her lips. "Bring it back?"

I raise a brow. "I'll think about it."

"Bring it back but rename it . . . *Belinda Berry*." She laughs that loud, hearty laugh.

"You've been thinking about that one for a while, haven't you?" I try not to let on that I'm amused.

She responds with a fake air-kiss, then tucks the tube into the pocket of her scrubs and finds the blood pressure cuff that's hanging on a machine behind my head. "Did you call your son?"

I glance across the room, aware that my roommate is now off the phone and pretending *not* to listen. "You're nosy," I say to Belinda.

She waits for the cuff to tighten on my arm and flashes me a look. "And you're stubborn."

"There are things about my life you can't possibly understand."

She pulls the Velcro apart and rolls her eyes. "I understand you almost scared our new night nurse into quitting last night."

"She needs a thicker skin," I say. "The world I live in would eat her alive."

"We're not in your world, are we?"

"No, we are not," I say. "My world isn't nearly so *beige*."

"At least you brought your own pillow this time." Belinda rolls a little tray toward me. "They're bringing you breakfast. And you're going to eat it." She points a finger in my face. "Or I'll force-feed you."

"I'll have JP bring me something," I say. "This could be my last meal—I am not eating powdered eggs."

"You're so high-maintenance." Belinda rolls her eyes again. "And so dramatic."

I glance up at the clock. It's after eight and JP isn't here yet.

I hope he didn't also get hit by a car on the sidewalk.

Belinda turns to my roommate. "And how are you today, Miss Worthington?"

The younger woman wears a pained look. "I'm fine. I just need to get out of here. Do you know when I can go?"

"The doctor needs to come see you," Belinda says. "Did you fill out your breakfast preferences?"

I study the girl. I can't remember her first name. Kailey? Carrie? Something with a *K* sound. Her dark hair falls past her shoulders, and her nails are manicured and bright red. I have a feeling she's as hard on herself as I was all those years ago, and for a fleeting moment, I want to tell her it's okay to relax once in a while.

Which would be completely hypocritical. Relaxing is the last thing on my mind. Contrary to my wishes, this trip to the hospital won't be my last. However, it is the most recent interruption to what I really need to be doing—choosing a successor and ensuring that everything I've built lives on long after I'm gone.

My thoughts turn to Hayden. I wasn't delusional enough to think that he'd want to take over my company, but I thought maybe he'd at least want a piece of it.

Being my son and all.

Belinda finishes with my roommate and leaves the room. The woman glances over at me. She knows who I am, which means there's a danger of my illness getting out once the woman is discharged. Which would be a disaster.

Better play nice.

"You know me," I say without looking at her.

"Yes," she says. "I do."

"How?"

"I saw the profile a few months ago in *New York Magazine*. But also, I use your entire skincare line."

"That's why you have a flawless complexion."

She blushes. "Thanks."

I eye her. "More of a compliment to myself."

Her face falls.

"You work in publishing."

She presses her lips together. "Yes."

"And some talented person is off your hook now that you're laid up?"

"We're trying to reschedule."

"I see," I say. "And this is someone important?"

"Could be," she says. "I'm trying to prove to my boss that I have what it takes to recognize talent. Instead of just managing people he brings in, which is all he's really let me do."

"Waiting for a man to let you do anything is pointless."

She stops moving and looks at me.

"If I'd waited for permission, do you think I'd have my own company today?"

"Probably not."

I look at her.

"Definitely not," she amends.

I nod.

"Can I ask you something?" she asks.

"That depends." I sigh. "I'll only answer if I feel like it."

She seems to be working up the courage for a moment, then finally asks, "Is it worth it?"

Well now.

I didn't expect *that* question.

I fold my hands in my lap, realizing I need to cancel my manicure this week, unless Belinda can spring me from this prison. Maybe I can find someone to come here to do my nails. If there's any chance of me dying this week, I'm not doing it with chipping polish.

I must have stayed silent for too long, because she adds, "The profile I read said you'd had to give up a lot to get where you are."

"Success comes with a price," I say, refusing to think about what success has cost me.

"So?"

I look over, and she's watching me.

"Was it worth it?"

A short man pushes a tray into the room, saving me from having to confess anything real to this perfect stranger.

"Good morning, ladies," he says. "Breakfast."

"Breakfast implies edible," I say. "That is not breakfast."

"I know it's not gourmet," he says, trying to smooth things over, "but it's what we have. And you still have to eat it." He puts a plate covered with a plastic dome on the woman's tray, then walks one over to me.

"You can take that away. I told the nurse I would have my meal delivered."

"Apparently, she ignored you." The man smiles, lifting the dome off the plate. "Biscuits and gravy! That should be nice and filling."

"That would kill me even quicker," I say. "If you think I'm eating that, you're as big an idiot as you look."

The man smiles without so much as a flinch. "Take it up with your nurse."

He's good. He might be tolerable.

"Believe me, I will."

After he walks out, the doctor comes in to talk with the crash test dummy in the bed across from mine. She's likely only got a few more hours locked up in this place—lucky stiff. Meanwhile, I'm here indefinitely with cursed food and offensive decor and contemplating what's-her-name's question.

Is it worth it?

I really, really wish I could say that it was.

But given my current circumstances, I'd be lying to myself if I did.

Chapter 4

KELSEY

I DON'T EXPECT Georgina Tate to have a real conversation with me.

But as I stupidly lie in this stupid bed, I find myself full of questions.

And I *want* her to have a real conversation with me.

How did she do it? How *does* she do it? How did she start? Did she always want to run a big company? What does she see at the end?

Can I get a peek at next year's line?

And the one question I managed to ask—is it worth it?

My revelation is that I'm two years into my thirties and I've got nothing to show for it.

I'm not even a real editor.

Yet.

And, if I'm honest, I don't even know if I like my job.

Around noon, a thin man in a neat suit rushes in. He looks straight past me to Georgina, and I have to wonder if anyone *out there* knows she's here.

I'm curious what's wrong with her. Is she sick? And where is the son the nurse was talking about? The magazine profile didn't mention him, which makes me think that the journalist didn't do his due diligence. Or Georgina paid someone off.

After a few minutes of business, the man, whose name is JP, glances at me then back at Georgina. "Roommate?"

She ignores his question. "Paperwork?"

He pulls a few sheets of paper from his satchel and walks over to me. "Miss . . . ?"

I'm confused. "Kelsey."

"Miss Kelsey. We're prepared to offer you financial compensation in exchange for your signature."

I frown. "For what?"

"Standard nondisclosure." JP points to the papers. "Liability release form, non-circumvention clause, it's all there. Sign here, here, and initial here and here, and sign here."

I just stare.

He sighs, as if I should automatically understand everything he's saying. "These are legal documents stating that you won't tell anyone that Miss Tate is in the hospital."

I glance at the older woman, who is watching me with that trademark pursed lip, uplifted brow look. Somehow, even though her chin is perfectly straight, it's still clear she's looking down her nose at the world.

I suppose no woman gets to be in her position by being nice.

I look back at JP. "Should I get a lawyer, or . . ."

"It's important to Tate Cosmetics."

"I don't need to sign anything," I say with a nod toward the papers. "And I don't need money. I'm not going to tell anyone."

"Great!" Then he adds, lower in tone, "Then you won't mind making it official."

I eye him. I don't want money, but I do want something. "I'll think about it."

JP looks as intimidating as a five-foot-tall substitute algebra teacher. He doesn't realize that while I may not have reached Georgina Tate status, I'm no pushover.

Okay, that's not true. I'm actually nothing like Georgina. She would probably point that out if I gave her the chance. She'd probably also tell me that's why I'm still an assistant editor.

Too soft. Too insecure. I don't play dirty.

She wouldn't be wrong. Sometimes I feel like I'm walking around in someone else's life, wearing someone else's clothes.

I'm cosplaying as a boss lady.

"I really must insist—"

"I said I'll think about it." I give him a pointed look, and he glances helplessly at Georgina. She waves him off, and he walks away from my bed and over to hers.

They whisper something, probably about me, and then JP walks out.

She clears her throat, announcing to the room that she's about to speak. "I'm sure you can appreciate why I need your silence on this matter," she says. "Shareholders get nervous. People assume things and that's how rumors get started."

The door to our room opens, and Belinda strolls in, this time with my discharge papers. "Good news, Miss Worthington. You get to go home."

Home.

My bed. My stuff. The thought has me anxious to get moving already.

The more I think about it, it's not exactly "home," though. Home is not what I have. I have an apartment with blank walls and moving boxes stacked to the ceiling of the bedroom closet. I have a bed, and I have a kitchen I don't use.

It's a place to sleep, but it's not a home.

That never bothered me before, but today it does. Which also bothers me. I'm not one for navel-gazing.

Who knew near-death experiences bring that out in a person?

I don't like it.

I like having a singular focus—becoming an editor. Sure, it wasn't what I thought I'd be doing—or even what I necessarily want to be doing—but it's what made the most sense for me. I could still work with words and books and stories, even if I wasn't the one writing them.

It's safer this way.

Why am I dwelling on this? Editing suits me. It's good to be behind the scenes.

It's where I belong. People who would know have told me so.

All at once, everything about my life feels unsure.

And I don't like it.

Everything that seemed so important before my accident has lost urgency. All I can think about is all the things I haven't done, or accomplished, or seen, or experienced.

It's a very long list.

I've never been in love. I've never been in the ocean. Or even on a boat. I've never had a conversation with a woman as successful as Georgina Tate.

Belinda is going over discharge instructions with me, but I'm thinking about Georgina's life. She's gutsy in a way I've never been. Fearless in a way I can't fathom.

I'm now wondering if it was fate that brought us together. Me, having a mini crisis of conscience, and her, a woman who has accomplished more than I could hope to in a lifetime.

She's sitting right there.

Belinda leaves (I didn't hear a word she said), and I look at Georgina.

"I'll sign your papers," I say.

"Good choice." She seems unfazed. "So what do you want?"

"I want you to answer my question," I say.

"What question is that?"

I know she knows what question—I've only asked her one since we've been here. I swing my legs over the side of my bed, taking a moment to grimace at the weird, uncomfortable purple booties that I only now realize I'm wearing. At the moment, my head throbs again, and I wonder if Belinda gave me instructions about that.

I should've paid attention.

"Tell me if it's worth it," I say, facing her. "Because in the two days we've been here, the only person who's visited either of us appears to be a paid employee. And I'm wondering if you're really okay with that."

"I'm fine with that," she says.

"You are," I say, only half questioning.

She purses her lips and narrows her eyes, almost as if she's deciding whether to be truthful with me, sizing me up for trustworthiness.

"I made a choice to put my career first," she says, and then adds with arms spread, "and look how well that worked for me." I notice there's a simple diamond bracelet dangling from her wrist. It probably cost more than I make in a month.

She most likely has designer clothes and shoes and purses hanging in the hospital room closet.

She has power and wealth and a title.

And yet, she's here. Alone.

Just like me.

I don't have to be. She probably doesn't either. I do have people, but they all feel so far away right now. And while I'm not willing to admit it yet, I have a lurking suspicion that it's my fault.

How did it work out for her? What did she give up when putting her career first?

I can't help but think again about all the simple adventures I was supposed to have but didn't. Things that seemed frivolous at the time, distractions at best.

The time my group of college girlfriends invited me to go backpacking through Europe. I said no.

The time my parents wanted me to enter my short stories in a local competition *just to see*. I said no.

Trivia night with Ravi and his girlfriend, Sasha. No.

Vacation anywhere. No.

Scuba diving along a reef. Judging a local celebrity dance competition. Riding a mule in the Grand Canyon.

But not just big things . . . little things too.

Taking off in the middle of the day because I need fresh air. Trying new hobbies. Trying new food. Spending time with people for any reason at all.

No. No. No.

I haven't seen or done anything notable since I was a kid, and then, only because I had no choice. I was dragged along by parents who were much freer and more open to adventure than I am.

Unlike them, or maybe because of them, I crave stability. Security. Predictability. I learned the value of those things the hard way.

Did Georgina go on adventures? Did she use her money to take trips and see the world? Did she ever take off in the middle of a workday just because she could? Or has she spent most of her adult life sightseeing within the walls of her office building?

I stand. "I know you had to give up a lot to get where you are, and I just wondered . . ."

"Yes," she says flatly. "Of course it's worth it."

I hold her gaze for a three-count, and then she looks away.

"But that's not to say"—she sighs—"that I don't have regrets."

I don't move, and I don't respond because I want her to keep talking.

After a beat, she says, "I wish I'd said yes more." She looks at me. "To the fun things of life, you know? I always chose work over everything. It suited me. But it cost me too. Nothing comes without a cost, young lady, and only you can decide if you're willing to pay it."

The moment, and what feels like my entire life, hangs there, frozen in time, like someone hit Pause on the DVR.

She is a picture of what my future could be.

Is it worth it?

"You should go," she says. "Get back to your life."

"Right," I say. "My life." I had goals—big, shiny, pretty goals. I've been working toward something, the thing I've told myself I've wanted ever since graduation. I'm close, I can feel it.

But do I really have a life?

Did Georgina have a life?

"Sign the papers before you leave," she says. "I'm looking forward to having my own room."

I narrow my gaze, but she's not looking at me. I scribble my signature on the paperwork, then set it on the table beside her bed.

"I'll come back and visit you," I say.

"Please don't," she says. "Don't get sentimental simply because you caught me in a rare reflective moment."

"Right," I say. "Well, it was good to meet you, Miss Tate."

"It was good to meet me, was it?"

I pick up the plastic bag Belinda left on the end of my bed, pull my clothes out of it, and disappear into the bathroom. I hurry and get dressed, and by the time I'm walking out, Georgina has turned over and is now sleeping or pretending to sleep.

So long, Georgina Tate. I hope what's left of your life is happy.

I stare at her for a long moment—she looks so small in that bed, all by herself.

That thought floats back to me: *She is a picture of what my future could be.*

While I've never hoped to achieve her level of wealth and power, this life she's built for herself is exactly the one I've been after.

And at what cost?

I shake the thoughts away and walk out.

"Will somebody be driving you home?" Belinda asks as I close the door to the room behind me.

"Uh, no," I say. "I'm good. I can get myself home."

She shakes her head. "You and Miss Tate are two peas in a pod. Never wanting help from anybody."

"I have . . . people," I protest lamely. "I just didn't want to bother them."

She muses. "Mm-hmm. Then you don't have the right kind of people."

I like Belinda. And she's right. It's just that it's not my people who are the problem. It's me. I texted my parents and Ravi to let them know about the accident. I downplayed the whole thing and told them I'd call as soon as I got home because I don't want them fussing over me.

But I'd found a way to talk to Tess. To make sure work was okay. What does that say about me?

"What's wrong with her?" I nod toward the door. "Can you say?"

"I can't," Belinda says.

A pause. "Is it bad?"

She looks around, then leans toward me. "Well, it's not good."

I have no idea why, but the words make me sad. It's not like I know Georgina or even like her as a person, and yet, for everything this woman has accomplished, it definitely seems like she still has more to do.

Amends to make, maybe.

"A cautionary tale, for sure," Belinda says. "Work too much and end up sick and dying and all alone."

"Wait, she's dying?"

Belinda looks caught but quickly says, "I'm speaking hypothetically. We're all dying, Miss Worthington. Now promise me you're going home to get some rest."

"I will—I have to get back to work," I say.

Belinda shakes her head. "Two peas in a pod."

Chapter 5

KELSEY

I REALLY SHOULD hang some things on the walls. A painting of a landscape, a cat clock, something.

Later that night, I'm quietly resting in the safety of my bare little apartment, thinking about my accident, about the hospital, about the fact that I could've died. All the things.

And Georgina.

Seeing someone I only know as a powerful, strong, competent person felled by an illness is just another reminder of my mortality.

In the end, time is undefeated.

People, movies, billboards, all hawk the "life is short" mantra. It's a sentiment I often reject. I guess that people my age often feel immortal in a way, especially if nothing life-threatening has ever happened to them.

For years, I'd hear old women lamenting the speed of things as they looked at photos of years gone by. That babies grow up in a blink. They turned around and—boom!—it was thirty years later.

I don't want life to go by in a blink. Not anymore. Because some guy jumped a curb, I'm now realizing that life *is* short. And you get one shot. All the clichés, it turns out, are true.

And I'm not sure how to process that.

I tend to overthink, but not about things like this. I've accepted there are things about life I can't change—how quickly it moves, for instance. How working for someone else often determines how high you climb.

How long your success lasts.

There's a knock at my door.

Ravi is my only friend outside the office, and I know he's out of town at some math convention (can you think of anything more boring?), and there's nobody else who would pop over unannounced.

"Kelsey? Are you in there?" The knocking grows more insistent. *Mom.*

My parents live about four hours from the city in Upstate New York. The house where I grew up is an old Victorian that's actually on the National Register of Historic Places, and honestly, I'm shocked my parents haven't started public tours of the place yet. It took years to restore it, and even though they painted it sage green with coral-colored shutters and cream trim, it really is beautiful.

And the perfect place for two theatre professors to live.

But not the perfect place to grow up, I learned after I left for college. Yes, it was a childhood of wonder and borderline chaos, but I quickly discovered I can't make a living making up stories for the kids in my neighborhood. That boundaries and rules and structure aren't always a bad thing. That creativity doesn't always pay the bills.

I open the door and find her standing there. My mother. Charlotte Rose Worthington. Once upon a time, she was a renowned actress who gave up the stage in favor of raising a family.

Did she regret that, I wonder? I've never asked her.

She gasps, grabs my arms, and pulls me into a hug. I smell the musky fragrance of cedarwood incense mixed with some herbaceous essential oils.

I wonder if the neighbors have complained lately about her chickens.

"Mom, what are you doing here?"

"Kelsey! What a thing to say!" she says, waving her hands as if this budding conversation were an orchestra. "I get a text that you 'had a little accident,' you go radio silent, and you don't think I'm going to drop everything and see for myself that you're okay?" She steps back and studies me, eyes landing on the cut above my eye. She reaches out and lightly touches it. "Oh, sweetie. I just needed to know that my darling child is okay."

"It was . . . something." I offer a weak smile. She means well, I know she does. But as with most moms for most kids, concern and fretting are equal parts comforting and annoying.

I turn and walk back into my apartment, where my mother hasn't been in literal years. Our visits are rare but always upstate. Weekends occasionally, holidays mostly.

I've been bad about prioritizing people. Looking at her now, I'm ashamed at that thought. She might be quirky and even a little wacky, but she loves me fiercely. And just because I've decided to take my life in a direction that makes no sense to her doesn't mean she can't understand me anymore.

She *is* still my mother.

"I should've called," I say weakly. "But I'm fine." I plop down onto the couch while Mom closes the door and steps fully into my apartment.

She looks around, and I know what's coming.

"Well, this is certainly spartan."

Translation: Call a decorator—I'm staging an intervention.

"Darling, it doesn't even look like you live here." She drops her bag onto the armchair and does a quick tour of my space. "Is this where you live?"

I drop my head to one side. "Yes, Mom, this is where I live."

She's behind me, but I can feel her looking at me. "Oh, Kelsey." Then she walks over to the opposite end of the couch and sits down, pulling my feet in her lap.

I can't look at her because if I do, every emotion I've been holding in will come flooding out like a dam breaking. That's how it's always been with her. She's artsy and hooty and granola and a little *too* in tune with her daughter.

And I'm not sure I can handle that right now.

"What happened?" she asks. "I tried calling. You didn't answer."

"I know," I say. "I'm sorry."

"You can't do that to a mother, Kelsey," she says. "I worried the entire train ride down here."

I see the pain on her face, and I realize that my typical "I can do it myself" attitude has caused someone I love a lot of grief. What is wrong with me?

"I wasn't supposed to look at my phone," I tell her. As if that's an excuse.

"Why?" she asks. "Do you have a concussion? I might have something for that actually. Nothing pharmaceutical, of course— they're only out to make money, those people. This is all-natural and honey-flavored, and . . ." She starts rummaging through her slouchy bag.

I reach over and put a hand on her arm.

"Mom. It's okay. Honestly."

"I feel like you downplayed the seriousness of your accident," she says.

"I didn't want to worry you," I say. And also, I was contemplating every life choice I've ever made.

"The lack of information worried me more." She sets her bag back down, places both hands on my feet, still on her lap, and just looks at me.

And I spill.

I tell her the entire story—leaving out everything about Georgina—and she listens like she always does.

It feels good to talk. Good to vent. Good to have someone listen.

Why I thought I needed to deal with this accident by myself, I have no idea. Independent doesn't have to mean alone, right?

Growing up, I was always a bit . . . different. I never thought of myself as odd, but looking back on it now, I think I might've been.

I lived in the world of my imagination, and for the most part, the other kids would've rather played in the real world. I was constantly making things up, acting out imaginary TV interviews, sketching out scenes for plays I would act out in my head.

I liked my world. And because my parents were both creatives, they let me live there.

Somewhere, though, between the wonder and imagination of childhood and the worries and responsibilities of adulthood, I weaned myself off that world.

The imaginary world isn't suitable for adults. Having Mom here in my apartment makes me miss it for the first time in ages.

That world was passionate and unpredictable and colorful.

And strangely safe.

If something wasn't going right, I could yell, "Plot twist!" and change it all. Not so in real life. Real life needs a Ctrl+Z.

Mom pats my feet twice, then stands and walks into my kitchen. "Tell me you have a teakettle."

To my mother, tea heals everything.

"I think I do," I say. "Somewhere."

She starts banging around my kitchen, and I can't lie—I like it. It's nice not to be alone. And it's nice to be taken care of. I've been DIYing my life for years. And, I'm realizing, backing myself into a very lonely corner.

About forty-five minutes later, because my mother is a wizard, I'm being served comfort food—blueberry pancakes with blueberry syrup and hot green tea.

"Where did this come from?" I ask, knowing I do not have fresh blueberries in my kitchen.

"I brought the berries from home." Then she smiles. "I grew them myself."

"Blueberries? Wow. I'm impressed." I sit up and let her prop a tray in front of me.

"Do you want whipped cream too?"

I laugh. "Um, *yes*. Is that even a question?"

I have vivid memories of her "bombing" my sister, Rosie, and me with shots of whipped cream straight from the can into our mouths. We were like little birds, clamoring for more, and Mom never said no.

How did she do that?

And more importantly, how did she raise a daughter who almost exclusively tells herself no?

Short answer: she didn't. I'm the one who changed.

While I eat, Mom cleans. It's like she can't help herself. She may thrive in a loose, creative kind of world, but there is still order and she's still my mother and dirty dishes can't exist in the sink.

When I finish, she's right there to take my plate off to the kitchen, where she washes it and puts it away.

And when she's finished, she sits. And she looks at me. It's like she's waiting for me to open up about something more. Something I have no interest in talking about. Like a therapist with a patient who's been ordered to be there by the court.

"How are you doing?"

I laugh lightly. "I'm good. Still alive, so you know, that's good."

"This was a traumatic experience," she says.

I shrug. "I mean, sort of."

"No, not sort of," she says. "It was. And whether or not you look at it that way, your body went through a trauma. It is going through a trauma. It's okay to take some time with that."

Time. The one thing I'm not usually willing to give.

"I have work," I say. "A big client. A possible promotion."

She reaches over and puts a hand on my foot. "Work can wait. It'll be there once you heal."

"No offense, Mom, but I don't have tenure. That's not how things work in my world."

"Well, you can't rush back. Not when you're still recuperating."

"I'm fine," I say again. "I didn't even break a bone. I was very lucky."

She narrows her eyes in a way that only she can do. Looking straight through me. "Kelsey, maybe this is a wake-up call."

I frown. "I'm plenty awake."

"In my experience, when things like this happen, it's for a reason. I call it a disruptor."

I can feel the lecture coming.

I'm curious, though, what she has to say. I wonder if it will solidify the feelings I had while sitting in that hospital bed.

I could've died.

Is it worth it?

I've never done anything remarkable.

Two peas in a pod.

"The universe sends disruptors along when we've gotten into a pattern that's too comfortable," Mom says.

I roll my eyes. "The universe? The universe cares?"

She waves me off. "Well, I personally think it's God who sends them, but I don't know where you stand on that matter these days."

I don't say anything because, honestly, I don't know either.

"Regardless, something comes along and wakes you up."

"Like a car jumping a curb."

She makes a face. "Well, not *always* that painful or scary, but yes. Like that."

I shake my head and throw up my hands. "I don't know what I'm supposed to learn. I'm doing what every other young professional my age is doing. Working. Hard, in fact. Trying to get ahead. I've got bills to pay. People to meet. Things I'm responsible for."

"True," she says. "But is that really a life? Is this really the life you want?" She pauses. "Because it didn't used to be. Growing up, I never heard you talk about entering this merry-go-round and calling it a life."

I want to correct her. Because people *do* have to work for a living. We can't all subscribe to her loosey-goosey way of life. Some of us have to pay the bills.

But then, just as before, mental clarity falls into place like a cog.

What if I can do this another way?

Kelsey . . . what are you doing?

I let my head fall back on the cushion of the couch and think of Georgina's outline curled up in her hospital bed.

For years, I'd been aspiring to a life just like hers, keeping everyone at arm's length, striving for more, more, more.

Yet somehow, the world (*the universe? God?*) leveled the playing field, putting us side by side in that hospital room.

There, she wasn't one of the most powerful businesswomen in the country. There, she wasn't directing photo shoots or meeting with designers.

She was simply another patient.

Just like me.

No visitors. Only an assistant.

And a lot of work.

"You're not a child anymore, Kelsey," Mom says. "And as an adult, you get to decide what kind of life you want to live."

"You make it sound so easy," I say. But what I mean is: *What if I want to change my life? How do I even start? What if all the choices I've made up until this point were the wrong ones? Do I even have the capacity to love another human, and if so, will anyone ever love me back?*

Do I start over?

Was that all just wasted time?

I'm paralyzed with questions, and my mother must sense this because she moves from the chair back to the couch, draping an arm along the back of it and staring at me.

"Changing your life is never easy, sweetie," she says.

I know she speaks from experience. Once upon a time, she lived and worked here. "Why did you leave New York?"

A wistful smile lights up her face. "I had you and then your sister. And I realized I wanted something different for you. I wanted you to grow up surrounded by nature and art. And I didn't want to leave you every night to perform."

"We were your disruptors," I say, realizing.

"The very best disruptors." She scrunches her nose. "Changed my entire trajectory. My whole life."

Is it really that easy?

"I was so content to have you two around, letting you see the beautiful world, basking in creativity."

I smile nostalgically. "We made a lot of messes, didn't we?"

She leans in. "And I loved every second of it."

Wildflower bouquets. Acting out fake newscasts about the science of bubble blowing. I learned to shoot an arrow and French braid in the same afternoon, then wrote a story about a heroine who helps her sister win the archery contest by getting her hair out of her face.

For what it's worth, it was a pretty amazing childhood. Even in the midst of chaos.

When did I lose that sense of wonder?

A memory stings me from the inside, like I swallowed a bee. I know exactly when. *Words have so much power.*

"And you know," she continues, "I've hoped for a long time that you might come back to the creative side of yourself."

I groan. "Not this again."

"I still have the stories you wrote."

I cringe. "You should burn them."

"Not a chance."

"Writing won't pay my bills," I say. Especially if I stay here.

"But will it set your soul on fire?"

So melodramatic.

But a fair question.

I shake my head, not exactly in a "no" but in an "I can't fathom it" sort of way.

My mother doesn't exactly live in the real world. She's married to my hopelessly romantic father, who dotes on her so terribly they could single-handedly make the world's biggest cynic believe in love again. She raises chickens and runs the community theatre. She teaches acting sessions to a bunch of collegiate hopefuls who haven't had their dreams completely squashed by ill-intentioned mentors yet. She gets all of the gooey cuddles she could possibly want from my sister, Rosie's, little girl, Melody. She gardens and sells farm-fresh eggs at the farmer's market and has pretty much built a world for herself that I simply cannot relate to anymore.

It's so countercultural. She lives her life like a rock in the rapids, letting the tumultuous rush of the race of life flow right on by.

I decided a long time ago, for better or worse, that I wanted something different.

I traded sun-kissed stories for upward mobility.

Is it worth it?

"I worry about you, dear heart."

I laugh. "I'm fine, Mom. I promise."

"Physically, you're probably fine—or will be. But emotionally? Mentally? Spiritually? You're a little stalled out. You don't seem very happy. You don't seem . . . alive."

I hold out my wrist. "Check my pulse."

"You know what I mean. You work. That's all. Some days, I don't even think you eat."

"I eat plenty."

"You don't come home. Melody wouldn't recognize you. I feel like you're missing out on things." After a pause, she adds, "Your father has ear hair now, do you believe that?"

"Okay, so I could've done without knowing that."

"Well, it's true," she says. "Because times change. People change. 'Life moves pretty fast. And if you don't stop and look around once in a while, you could miss it.'"

I grin. She does this thing where she quotes random movies just to see if I'll pick up on it.

I sing-song, "'Ferris Bueller, you're my hero . . .'"

She grins back at me. "I've taught you well."

We sit in that moment and smile.

"You have taught me well, Mom," I say. "Which is why you don't need to worry about me. Yes, I had an accident, but I'm okay now, and I'm not taking that for granted."

She frowns. "If it's meant to change your life, Kelsey, let it."

Let it.

Let it.

How?

Chapter 6

KELSEY

I DIDN'T LET it.

Two days later, I'm back at work.

There's a bit of that "going through the motions" feeling one gets after being gone for a while—readjusting to the routine, participating in cursory conversations with workplace acquaintances about how I'm "so lucky" and I'm "on the mend," trying to make each rehashing of the story sound a little bit different to make it stay interesting.

But through the small talk and the empty promises from colleagues saying, "Whatever you need, just ask," I can't stop thinking about Georgina.

My mother and Georgina.

I returned fully intending to dive straight back into work, but here I am, staring at my blank computer screen, zoning out and accomplishing nothing.

Mom left on an early train—she had to get back for some important reception—but she invited me to come up for the weekend.

When I told her I couldn't, that I needed to get back to work, she put her hand on my cheek and looked at me like she felt sorry for me. "Just once, Kelsey, I wish you'd choose to say yes to something other than work."

Her words stick with me as I stare at my blank computer screen.

And then a final mental cog falls into place, and it's as if a long-dormant, beautifully creative machine whirs and chugs to life.

Say yes.

It hits me like I'm riding a donkey on the road to Damascus.

Say YES, Kelsey.

All those things I haven't done, that long list that rolled through my mind in the hospital—it was *my choice* not to do them.

My choice not to go on vacation.

My choice not to have a relationship.

My choice not to visit my family or get to know my niece or let myself become the writer I'd been meaning to become since I was a little girl having conversations with imaginary people in my bedroom closet.

I haven't done them because my life has been a series of no's.

Purposeful, intentional, forceful no's.

It's been a choice. *My* choice.

I'm sitting at my desk, dazed by the crisscrossing searchlights of revelation, when Charlie gets off the elevator and heads my way. "Heard you got yourself hit by a car," he says. "On the sidewalk." He chuckles. "Only you, Worthington."

In a flash, I see a scene in my mind, set in a workplace drama on TV, complete with stage direction and backstory.

Charlie, in the story of my workplace that I'm suddenly and spontaneously writing in my head, is the man-child boss who lords his authority over his coworkers and drives a hybrid and uses paper straws because he's "concerned about the environment."

In an inspired bit of casting, he's played by James Spader.

It's the whole episode. I can see it all. If I had a half hour, I could write the whole thing, almost like dictation.

I blink back to reality.

Where did that come from?

He continues past my desk, then stops. "Oh, hey, did Tess tell you?" He looks at Tess, who is standing a few feet away. "Did you tell her?"

Tess's eyes are wide, like she's been caught. She shakes her head. "Not yet."

"Tell me what?"

"We sent Daniel to patch things up with Chase Donovan."

I do a mental double take. "Patch things up? What does that mean? Chase was my find!" I say. "I approached her!" She was the first person I'd brought in all on my own.

Or she was supposed to be.

"And then you disappeared." Charlie shrugs, like *whatever*.

Normally, I would sit and take this. Normally, I would stew silently, put on a fake smile, and keep my head down. Be a team player and all that.

I'm not feeling normal. Not even a little.

I stand. "I was hit by a car!"

Tess's eyes widen, a shocked look on her face. And all of a sudden, I've got more in the hopper too—clever retorts and none of them PG.

"It wasn't your fault, but she and Daniel hit it off, and we're really close to making a deal."

"That was *my* deal, Charlie."

"Her agent called when you didn't show, and Daniel had to think fast."

"Think fast? *Think fast?* Daniel couldn't think fast if he was being dragged behind the lead car at the Indianapolis 500."

This is completely unlike me.

I sound like Georgina.

I glance over to the poster on the wall that has "Teamwork Makes the Dream Work" written in a horribly old-fashioned, chalky hand-drawn font.

Yeah, right.

"She was a good find, though, right?" Charlie says, double finger guns a-blazing. "Sounds like this book is going to be *huge*." He says the last word like the former president.

He walks away, leaving me standing there, feeling like I just went seven rounds.

Tess moves toward me. "What. Was. *That*?"

I shake my head, coming down from the high, back to earth, feet on the ground. "I honestly don't know."

She sits on the side of my desk, like we're two friends having a chat. I like Tess, and frankly, she's the only person in this office who has my back.

"Between you and me, I never really wanted Chase Donovan to be your big claim to fame. She's a TikTok influencer, big whoop. I hate to say it, but you can do better."

"What do you mean?"

"Sure, she'll write something. It'll sell, but is that the kind of editor you want to be? The kind that puts more Kardashian-quality garbage into the world?" She eyes me like we're in on a secret.

She's right. And another flash like an old-timey camera goes off in my mind's eye.

"I need to find someone else," I say. "Someone with a lot more to say than a teenage TikTok 'celebrity.'" I hook my fingers around the word "celebrity" because I know full well that after about fourteen minutes, Chase Donovan will be replaced by someone else.

At that moment, Daniel walks back out of the elevator, and the Insult Generator flips on in my head.

A plum fungus. An evangelical crusader of utter mediocrity. A complete Oompa-Loompa.

In my fabricated impromptu screenplay, he's played by Sam Rockwell. Just good-looking and talented enough to put people off their game, but with an unlikable quality that you can't quite put your finger on.

He makes eye contact with me, and I scowl at him. As he walks out onto the floor, I see that he's not alone. Chase is with him, following him around like a little lost puppy. He gives me a thumbs-up and leads her into a conference room.

"I can't stand that guy," Tess says.

I can't stand him either. He's been here a whole year less than me, but this will almost definitely secure him a promotion. *My* promotion.

My head throbs.

"Kelsey, maybe you need a break," Tess says. "You had a traumatic accident. And you need to rest."

"A break. Yeah. I think you're right," I answer, but I'm agreeing for entirely different reasons.

I'm not going to rest. But I'm not going to work either.

This newfound creativity, this unlocking of something that's been buried, or dormant, or boxed up, is bursting at the seams.

I gather my things and leave the office, desperate to say yes to something I've never done before. I don't take the subway back to my apartment.

I take the one that goes back to the hospital.

Because for some unknown reason, I feel drawn back to Georgina Tate.

Chapter 7

KELSEY

I HAVE MORE questions.

And I think Georgina is the only one who can answer them.

When I exit the elevator onto the third floor, I'm struck by that very unique hospital smell, like stagnant water and stale Ritz crackers, and it almost makes me gag. Not because it's alarmingly bad, but because it conjures up the memories of being here only days ago, of throwing up, of contemplating my life.

It's late afternoon, and I have no idea what visiting hours are, but I breeze past the nurses' station with a purpose, convinced that if I look like I belong, nobody will say anything to me.

I reach Georgina's door but pause just outside of it when I hear a man's voice inside.

"He still hasn't gotten in touch with the office, ma'am," the voice says. "I'm sorry. I've left several messages."

"I guess when he said he doesn't want my money, he actually meant it," Georgina says, and I hear her sigh. "That's too bad. There's no one else to leave it to."

I step away from the door. It seems Georgina does have regrets, albeit the kind she doesn't talk about.

JP exits the room and I turn away, not wanting to draw attention to myself. When he disappears down the hall, I slip inside. Georgina is lying on the bed with her eyes closed.

I clear my throat and she stirs, meeting my eyes with a dose of confusion.

"What are you doing here?" Her tone is not friendly.

"I don't really know."

She raises a brow and studies me.

"I almost died," I say, not really knowing where else to start.

"Well, that's a little dramatic. It was a headache and a bruise."

"I got hit by a car. On the sidewalk."

"Yes, I know. I was here for your little interrogation, remember?" She sounds bored.

I muster up a double dose of courage to continue. "It's made me think about my life."

"Oh, for the love, someone just kill me now." She rolls her eyes, like that's the dumbest thing I could've said.

"Hear me out," I say, making this up as I go along. I sit in the chair next to her bed.

"No, no, don't do that," she says. "Don't make yourself comfortable."

"You think this chair is comfortable?" I drop my bag on the floor.

"You're going to want to disinfect the bottom of that bag." After a pause, "Or better yet, throw it away. It's hideously out of style." She folds her hands, letting them rest on her stomach. "Unless you were going for homeless chic."

When I pause for too long, she barks out, "Well, hurry up, Miss Revelation. Tell me so I can kick you out and die in peace."

"Now who's being dramatic?" I volley.

Georgina gives me a pursed-lipped look, as if to say, *"Carry on,"* and I wonder if this is the kind of tone she responds to. "After what you said, I've been thinking about all the things I've said no to in my life," I say. "About the things we have to sacrifice in order to be successful."

"We?" She says this like it was bold of me to categorize us together.

"Women," I say, hoping that we can at least agree we both belong in that category.

"Ah. Right."

A pause.

"I didn't say anything particularly earth-shattering," she says. "It's not like that would be the topic of my Ted Talk."

"I know," I say. "I saw your Ted Talk."

Another impressed eyebrow raise.

"It's more what you didn't say that I've been thinking about," I admit.

Not overtly, but quietly, at the back of my mind, I've been thinking about Georgina, about her life, about regret. For years, I've been striving to be just like her, but the picture of her now, lying in this bed, alone—

"You lost the big deal, didn't you?" She interrupts my thoughts.

"How did you know that?"

"I recognize that look," she says. "Defeat."

"I'm not defeated," I say.

"You're certainly not determined."

"That's true. I'm not. I'm more . . . confused. Frustrated. Annoyed."

Georgina watches me but says nothing.

"It's this overwhelming fear that I'm missing out on everything," I say. "I'm a gerbil in a wheel. I'm the Greek guy who keeps rolling the stone up the hill only to have it roll back down again, day after day, for eternity. I keep telling myself it'll get better once I get this job, this apartment, this promotion, but will it?"

"I don't know," she hits back. "*Will* it?"

I pause. "Are you really dying?"

Her expression holds.

"Because I have an idea." A spark of an idea. It's like a crack of flint against steel, catching tinder and slowly growing from ember to flame to crackling fire.

"I'm listening."

"You don't want to die here, right? In the hospital?"

"I'd prefer not to die at all," she says.

"What's the diagnosis?"

"Kidney disease." She doesn't miss a beat when she says this. "And I only tell you because you signed that NDA." A pause. "That's why I'm hooked up to this *amazing* machine." Her description drips with sarcasm.

"Dialysis?"

"Unfortunately."

"Does it travel?"

She frowns.

"Miss Tate, you said you wished you'd said yes to more things," I say. "But it's not too late."

"It is, Kailey."

I frown.

"Carrie." She says it with absolute certainty.

When I just stare, she flicks a hand in the air. "I can't remember your name."

"It's Kelsey."

"I like Kailey better."

"Take it up with my mother."

"I just might. It's a weird name."

"She raises chickens and teaches theatre. I come from a weird family."

This feels like verbal tennis. And I'm actually holding court.

She smiles, closes her eyes, and pulls a deep breath. The machine beside her clicks.

I point. "Is that thing portable?"

"It depends," she says. "It can be, if I get through this latest roadblock." Then she looks at me. "What are you suggesting?"

"A Summer of Yes."

"Oh please. Who are you, Jennifer Garner?" She drops her head back on the pillow and closes her eyes, an action I'm sure is meant to dismiss me.

"Hear me out." I sit taller in my seat to give off a bit more confidence. "We spend the summer saying yes to all the things we've said no to over the years."

She lifts her head with an incredulous look on her face. "You want me to spend what will probably be my last summer on this earth with *you*? A perfect stranger?"

"I don't see anyone else offering to spend it with you."

She glares at me for a few long seconds, then barks out a laugh. "Touché." Then, after a beat, she adds, "What's in it for you?"

I look away.

"Come on, there has to be something."

I know Georgina will appreciate confidence. It's just, I'm not actually feeling very confident at the moment. "I was thinking you could write a memoir."

Another laugh—this one full of sarcasm and condescension. "And there it is. I suppose you want to publish it? Am I your meal ticket?"

I feel myself rising up, more sure of what I'm proposing. "On its face it looks totally selfish of me, and maybe part of it is, but I think people would want to know who you are, who you *really* are."

We stare at each other for a good three-count.

"And I think people should know what you know. I think"—I lean in slightly—"that there is a whole generation you could fix with a single sentence."

She leans in as well, and half whispers, "Yes, but that generation doesn't read books."

I hold up a finger. "That is not true."

"Well, they won't read one about an old woman like me."

In the lull, I think about this idea. When Tess said she didn't want Chase to be my claim to fame, it got me thinking. Maybe working with someone like Georgina is a better fit.

This idea is about more than a memoir or a book . . . there's this deep, strange yearning inside me. A desire to know what she knows. To learn the lessons she could teach me. To say yes for once in my life to something other than work.

"Do you know there's a whole course at New York College about you? It's called 'The Rise of the Diva Director.'"

She points a look at me. "Well, that's a terrible title."

"I agree."

"And what is it they teach in this course?"

"How to be a girl boss, I think."

She rolls her eyes. "I hate that term."

"So do I."

Something else we have in common.

"So, what, you think you're going to *Eat, Pray, Love* your way to fame?" She straightens her covers.

"No," I counter, "but what I can say with almost one hundred percent certainty is that I have this deep-seated *knowing* that I'm supposed to do this. That *we* are supposed to do this."

"It's also probably a great way to keep your job."

I shrug. "Maybe."

"Maybe losing your job would be a good thing."

I scoff. "I don't think so."

"I lost plenty of jobs," she says. "Then I realized I didn't like the fact that other people had the power to take my livelihood away from me. That's when I started my own business."

I straighten. "See? That's the kind of thing that should go in a memoir. Do you know how inspirational your story is?"

She laughs. "Oh yes, dying alone before my seventy-fifth birthday. Very inspirational."

I pause. I hate that she's this close to dying. I hate that she even has to think about it. But I hate it more that when she does, all of her wisdom and fire will be lost. Forever.

"I have no desire to write a book about my life," she says. "I can't think of anything more boring and trivial and self-serving and narcissistic than that."

I shrug. "I think you know you've had a unique life."

Her eyes dart to mine, then away. I get the impression that very few people in her life ever disagree with her. "No memoir. No books about me at all."

I chew the inside of my lip. If she isn't going to write a memoir, why do I still feel like there is something we're supposed to do? Together?

"What are you still doing here?"

"Waiting to convince you to say yes to the Summer of Yes."

She rolls her eyes. "I have no tolerance for ridiculous games."

"It's not a game," I say. "You said yourself you wish you'd said yes more. This really was your idea."

"I've made my peace, Kimberly."

"Kelsey."

A dismissive flick of her hand that I'm sure is meant to make me feel small. I don't let it.

"So tell me, Miss Tate," I say. "What's something you wish you'd said yes to?"

She rests her head back on her pillow and lets out an annoyed sigh. "I'd love to eat one of those street pretzels."

"Like from the vendors on the street corners?"

"Yes, the big, soft ones with the chunky salt," she says. "I've never had one."

Ooh, I'd love one too. I haven't had one of those in ages.

"Yeah, that doesn't surprise me."

"Oh?"

"You don't seem like you eat a lot of street food," I answer.

"I also don't eat carbs."

"Ever?"

"Ever," she says.

I pause. "But you want to."

She smiles a wicked smile, like she's breaking rules simply by thinking about it. "Now that I'm dying, it is tempting."

"Okay, first of all, if we're going to be partners—"

"We're not partners," she cuts in.

"Well, you're not my boss and we're not friends, so what do you want to call us?"

"Right now, I'd call you a pain in my—"

A nurse walks in. "Vitals check."

Georgina looks at me. "You go wait in the hall. Or just go away."

"Not until you agree." Maybe I can't get her to write a memoir, but she seems a little more open to a Summer of Yes.

She points a finger toward me, then whips it over to the door.

I fold my arms.

She sighs. "You're not going to get any kind of answer from me right now. This nurse is going to prod me in places that I don't talk about at dinner parties. For the love of everything holy, can you just—"

I hold up a hand. "Yes. I can. I'll leave." I stand. "But I'll be back."

"Can't wait," she cracks.

I walk out into the hall and let out a deep breath.

Why do I have the feeling that my whole life is about to change?

Chapter 8

KELSEY

GEORGINA LEAVES ME outside her room for a solid half hour. I don't consider myself a patient person, so I'm basically ready to chew my own arm off out here.

Plus, I'm hungry.

So I do what any self-respecting New Yorker would do and leave. If Georgina wants to string me along, fine, but I'm not going to do it on an empty stomach.

I have to walk three city blocks, but eventually I find a street vendor. He's got pretzels the size of my head, and when he asks if I want salt, I toss him a look and say, "Uh, *yes*. Is that even a question?"

I get a flash of my sister and me with the whipped cream.

This might've been Georgina's wish, but I don't eat street food either, not anymore. Or carbs, unless my mother is in town.

It's just a pretzel.

This will be item one in my Summer of Yes.

Not exactly the most exotic choice, but there is something slightly decadent about saying yes to something I typically don't.

It then occurs to me I have too many rules for myself. Ravi's always said so, and I've always ignored him. He might be my best friend, but he doesn't know everything. Plus, he's a genius, so he doesn't have to work as hard as everyone else to get ahead.

I walk back toward the hospital, carrying the pretzels like they're the Olympic torch. This might be just the thing to convince Georgina to take this crazy leap with me. And if she won't write a memoir, at least I'll benefit from all the things she knows.

And maybe one day, *I* can write about it.

That thought makes me pause. I'm not a writer anymore. I need to stop thinking things like that. And yet . . . is writing just another thing I've said no to?

I make my way back up to her floor, and when I round the corner toward her room, I see a man standing outside—different from the man who was in her room earlier.

He's tall and tan, and he looks a little lost. His hair is sandy colored and wavy, and he's perfected that "I didn't have to try to look like this" look, like a model in a catalog selling camping gear.

And I, holding two huge pretzels like I'm about to flag down Bavarian Airlines, am utterly stopped in my tracks.

He's strikingly good-looking. Unfairly so.

He's a few feet away from Georgina's room, in the opposite direction from the nurses' station, and my reawakened writer's mind goes into overdrive.

The guy (we'll call him Jake because that's a good hot guy name) is here because his father is slowly withering away, stricken with Alzheimer's. The only way Jake can reconnect with his dad is to come to the hospital and meet him, again for the first time, every day—because at the end of every day, his father forgets.

And I, a single, hopeless romantic, just happen to be delivering pretzels to the children's wing (because that's what I do—I save kids with pretzels) when we meet, coincidentally, for the first time.

Jake and I hit it off. I bring my pretzels into his father's room, and it just so happens that it triggers something in his memory that starts him on the path of a miraculous recovery. Jake and I fall in love, his father is cured, we launch our own pretzel business, and we end up spending nights full of passion in our new home on the sun-kissed slopes of the Alps.

It's called Let's Get Knotty.

I shake my head out of the creative blur and focus. This is not the time to fancy myself a romance writer.

Maybe he has a relative on this floor? Maybe he's walking around the hospital because someone he loves is in surgery? Maybe he's my future husband, put directly in my path by God himself so I don't miss him?

If that last one is true, then what a gift. He would almost make getting mowed over on the sidewalk worth it.

I'm staring at a stranger. Giving him a backstory. Wondering, and not for the first time, what it might be like to *not* be alone.

"Admiring the view, are we?" Belinda's voice is loud, and the man looks up at the sound of it.

I shoot daggers at her, but she only laughs. I walk past her, and she says under her breath, "Can't blame you—that boy is yummy."

She's not wrong.

When I stop at Georgina's room, the man looks at me.

I smile.

With my pretzels.

I tell myself to relax my face. "Hey."

He lifts a hand in a slight wave, uncertainty on his face.

"Are you looking for someone?" I glance over at Belinda. "I can get the nurse."

He shakes his head. "Oh, no, thanks. I'm good."

I stand there for a few seconds, then realize I'm staring again. "You visiting someone?"

Well, look at me being nosy . . .

"Uh, yeah," he says.

I should walk away. It's obvious he has no interest in talking to me. And yet here I stand, trying to find a reason to keep talking.

"Okay," I say. "I know my way around this floor pretty well. I got hit by a car a couple days ago."

I'll take "Things Idiots Say" for four hundred, Alex.

He looks visibly shocked. "You . . . what? You got hit by a car?"

I nod.

"Are you okay? You must be okay. You're walking around . . ."

"I was very lucky," I say dryly.

"I see that." He pushes a hand through his hair, and it falls in the most beautiful messy waves. "Were you— I mean, are you hurt? Still?"

"Yeah, subcutaneous contusions, a little bit of brain damage, nothing major," I joke.

"Oh." His face turns somber, and I think that being able to blame my strange behavior on brain damage might come in handy. "I'm sorry."

"Oh no! I'm just kidding," I say, waving a pretzel at him like an oversalted maniac. I try to laugh it off by tapping it against my temple. "Still got my brain! All intact! Though I realize now I shouldn't joke about brain damage."

What is wrong with me?

Now it's horribly awkward, and there's a low buzzing inside me, like a thrum.

It's him. It's this guy. It has to be—it's not the pretzel.

Or maybe it's something else. Maybe I know I'm supposed to know him, the same way I know I'm supposed to do *something* with Georgina.

"Ooookaaaay." He looks properly confused.

"So . . ." I wish I had a reason to carry on a conversation, but I don't. Not without looking even weirder than I currently do. "Good luck."

He stuffs his hands in his pockets and nods. "Yeah, you too."

I lift my pretzels in the air in a salute and push open the door to Georgina's room with my rear end.

As I enter and the door swings shut behind me, she glances in my direction. "You again."

"I bet you hoped I'd given up and left," I say. "But no such luck. I brought you a present."

She adjusts her position, and I notice she's unhooked from the dialysis machine. JP walks out of the bathroom.

"I thought they let you out," he says.

"Well, I came back." I face Georgina and shake a pretzel in her direction. "What do you say, GT? Shall we?"

"GT?" JP asks.

"You're not the only one who can use initials," I say. "What does JP stand for anyway? John Paul? Justin Peter? Just Pterodactyls?" I giggle, aware that my oddness has followed me in from the hallway.

Maybe I do have minor brain damage.

He frowns and ignores me.

Georgina, I notice, is eyeing the pretzels. "Where'd you get those?"

"Street vendor," I say, shrugging nonchalantly, like no big deal. "I swiped some cheese too. It's in my bag."

"You expect *Georgina Tate* to eat street food and"—he shudders—"bag cheese?" He says her name like she's the Dalai Lama. Then, to Georgina: "It's a good thing I'm taking you home and away from all this mess."

But Georgina is still looking at me.

Not me. She's looking at the pretzel.

My mouth crawls into an evil smile. JP fusses with something in his satchel behind me. I take a step toward Georgina and slowly start waving the pretzel in front of her like a mentalist turning an audience member into a chicken. "A whole summer." For effect, I slow down my speech and say, "Say yesss to the pretzellll . . ."

She doesn't so much as twitch.

I slowly move one pretzel toward my mouth, open wide, and take a huge bite, eating it like I'm in one of those Godiva chocolate commercials. With a chewy, bready maw, I manage the words, "Mmmmm . . . this is so good . . ."

She frowns and whips out a hand, palm up.

I hand over one of the pretzels.

"Fine," she says.

"Fine?" I hear the giddiness in my own voice through the wad of pretzel in my mouth.

"What did you just agree to?" JP asks, but we both ignore him.

"Fine." She's firmer this time. "But if you bring up the memoir idea again, the whole deal is off. I'm not interested in cracking myself open and letting everyone crawl around inside."

"Too many regrets?" I ask. "Because there's a lot of wisdom in—"

"A normal amount of regrets," she says. "And . . . things people wouldn't understand." She holds her hand out again and I look at it, unsure what she's asking.

"Cheese." She says this like it should have "comma idiot" tacked to the end of it.

"Oh, right!" I fish around in my bag and find the small lid-covered tubs I threw in.

"You're going to eat that?" JP asks.

Georgina tears off a piece of pretzel and dips it down to the bottom of the cup of cheese. It's a weird dichotomy—food this cheap in the hands of someone wearing that diamond bracelet and two museum-quality rings.

I sit in the chair next to the bed and do the same, ripping off a chunk of pretzel and dousing it in cheese. Then I hold up my piece like I'm making a toast. "To the Summer of Yes!"

"What is even happening?" JP sounds horrified.

"Fine, Cassie."

"Kelsey."

She doesn't miss a beat. "Whatever. And let's not get carried away. I'm not sure I'm agreeing to anything except eating this pretzel."

Behind me, JP lets out a little gasp.

Georgina appears to be holding in a smile.

I tap my pretzel to hers, and we each take a bite. It's so good it should be listed as an eighth deadly sin. When was the last time I had street food? At least two months ago—Ravi took me to a new taco truck. And even then, I thought I was too swamped with work, so I snarfed down two tacos and insisted that was all I had time for.

Ravi ate five.

This is better. This is freer.

This is the Summer of Yes.

We eat in silence for a few minutes, and then I decide to give my idea one more pitch. "Think of how good it feels to do whatever you want."

"I always do whatever I want."

"But you're like me," I say. "You have rules for yourself."

"There's nothing wrong with setting boundaries," JP says.

"Why should I do this with you?" Georgina asks. "I'm perfectly content to let myself die in peace."

I am briefly stopped by the finality of that thought, but then try a different tactic. "I have to say, I'm surprised you're just rolling over and taking it."

JP scoffs. "That's what I said. Especially when she doesn't have to."

I frown and turn to Georgina. "What does that mean?"

"Nothing." Georgina shoots JP a look. "And after some further thought, I've decided I don't want to do a Summer of Yes."

I feel my shoulders slump.

"Your posture is atrocious," Georgina says.

"Miss Tate." I straighten. "I can't explain why, but I feel like we're supposed to do this together."

She frowns. "I'm not interested. I have more important things to do with my time."

I look around the room comically. "Like what? Like this?"

She swallows and looks right at me. "Let me give you some advice, Callie—"

I point a hand at her. "Kelsey."

"Stop caring so much." She locks eyes with me for a long moment, then tears off another chunk of her pretzel and takes a bite.

"You can go now."

I don't move for several seconds, and then Georgina turns on the television, something I'm sure she does only to convey she's through with this conversation.

A dismissal.

Finally, I stand, and as I start out of the room, JP steps forward and discreetly hands me a business card. I glance down at it. Simple white stationery with raised silver lettering. Georgina's name is on one side, and on the other, a phone number and email address scrawled in blue ink.

Then I turn and face her. "You're wrong, you know?"

JP takes a step back, as if removing himself from the line of fire. Georgina turns toward me slowly, an annoyed expression on her face.

"I don't think there's such a thing as caring too much," I say. "Only not caring enough. And I'll never apologize for that."

"Then you'll never succeed in business."

The words conjure a memory. Another strong leader telling me what I will never do. It stings, but I do my best to let it roll off my back. I surprise myself when I lift my chin and retort, "You'll change your mind."

She raises her eyebrows and watches me. I choose to believe she's impressed with my gumption, but it could just be that she's irritated I'm still here.

I turn on my heel and push the door open, walking out into the hallway, where I see the guy from before. Now he's sitting in a chair, looking slightly miserable. He glances up at me, then toward the room as the door closes behind me, almost like he wants to see inside.

I pause and look around. And even though I have no business doing it, I walk over to him. Because the way he's lurking out here, I'd bet money this is Georgina's son.

"Do you want to go say hello?" I ask, trying to focus on reconnecting him with his assumed mother and not on the barely noticeable scar above his right eye. *I wonder what happened there . . .*

He gives me a quizzical look. "Oh no. I'm here for, uh . . . a friend."

"Oh," I say. "I thought maybe you were visiting Miss Tate."

"No." He stands. "I don't even know who that is."

I study him. "Okay . . ."

He starts to say something, but as the door behind me opens, it pulls his attention. I turn toward the sound just in time to see JP leading Georgina out, and when I turn back, the guy is halfway down the hall in the opposite direction.

"Why are you still here?" Georgina asks, sizing me up. Now that she's standing, I see she's a tiny woman. She's bordering on frail, and she's at least four inches shorter than me.

"I literally just walked out of your room," I say.

"And apparently forgot the way to the elevator."

"I'm going now." I nod my head toward the exit. "We can walk out together."

"Oh goody," she says dryly.

We all start down the hall toward the elevator, and when I glance back over my shoulder, I see the man moving out from behind the corner, watching us go.

Chapter 9

KELSEY

DANIEL STRONG IS the male equivalent of a burger from Five Guys.

Great marketing, but up close he's pretty greasy and horribly overpriced.

I'm sitting at my desk procrastinating and working up a Yes List when he slithers over. I click out of my document and slow-roll my eyes at him, and he responds with a smug smirk.

One might think Daniel and I are perfect candidates for an enemies-to-lovers kind of story, but rest assured, we are not.

Daniel is three inches shorter than me, leaves his top buttons unbuttoned on his shirts, and perpetually smells like he bathed in aftershave.

If he had a sweet gold chain, he'd be a ringer for a 1980s professional bowling champion.

"Hey, Kels, I wanted to stop by and make sure everything is, you know, *kosher* between us." He talks with his fingers like a toddler holding a flag at a Fourth of July celebration, which is to say he waves them around a lot.

"Everything's fine, Daniel," I say dismissively.

"Because Chase Donovan—I mean, she's big-time." He claps his hands together and laughs. "Sorry, I know you were hoping to make a mark with that deal."

I raise a brow. "Oh, don't you worry yourself about little old me, Daniel. I've moved on. Bigger fish and all that."

"Was that before"—finger wave—"or after the car ran you over?"

Do any of these people realize my accident is not comedic? *I could have died.* "After, actually."

"Huh." He crosses his arms and leans against my desk. I look away so I don't have to stare at his chest hair.

"That's great for you then," he says.

"It *is* great." I keep my eyes averted. "Definitely going to put my name on the map."

In my peripheral vision, I see him watching me, chin poised upward, yet looking down on me. "Sure it is, Kelsey."

I manage a pained smile at him, wishing he could find out on Ancestry.com what all of us already know—that somewhere in his lineage he's related to the garden variety of slug.

Daniel bops away, finger pointing at Tess as she slides into the space he's just vacated. She waves the air to try to dissipate the fog of cologne left in his wake.

"Ugh. Did you know he asked me out?" she asks.

It doesn't register for a second, until it does. "He *what?*"

She nods, folding her arms. "I haven't given him a straight answer yet, so he probably still thinks there's some chance. I can't believe he . . ."

She keeps talking, but my mind drifts. And just then, as before, an idea clicks into place and feels . . . *right.*

I stand and cut her off. "I'm taking a vacation."

Tess's eyes go wide. "You're . . . what?"

"I've saved up all my vacation time since I started working here." I realize this as I'm saying it. "I'm going to use it." Just saying it out loud is liberating. I feel *free.*

"All of it?"

"Yes. All of it."

"How much do you have?"

I do a quick count in my head. "Paid time? Three weeks."

"Whoa. You really haven't taken any time off, have you?"

I hold up my hands in a gesture of my agreement.

"Okay . . ." Tess looks lost. "What am I supposed to do?"

I start packing things into my bag—an action that is more symbolic than anything, because at the moment, I have no intention of doing any work while I'm off. "I don't know actually." I look at her. "Whatever you want, I guess."

I can't help it. I feel a little giddy.

I always say no to taking time off because I want Charlie to notice all my hard work and promote me. Plus, there's always something to do, to tweak, to make better, to rearrange. But so far, working 24-7 and taking no vacation time has gotten me exactly nowhere on the promotion front.

I think work can take a back seat for the time being.

I'm starting to think the real story I need to be writing is the story of my own life. And honestly, it needs a rewrite.

My mom's question nags at me. *Is this really the life you want?* Why have I never paused to ask myself this question?

"I don't want to be here anymore," I say out loud, but mostly to myself.

"You don't . . . ?" Tess looks a little worried.

"No," I say. "I don't want to think about finding someone bigger and better to replace Chase Donovan. I don't want to think about how I'm going to refocus or make Charlie finally pay attention to my work. Today, I'm saying yes."

"Okay . . ." Tess watches me pack up my things but otherwise appears to be frozen. "What are you saying yes to?"

"I have no idea!" I know I'm not making sense, but at this moment I don't care. I hitch my purse up over my shoulder. "But it's going to be good!"

"Are you sure you're okay?"

"No!" I point a finger in the air. "But I will be!" Ooh, maybe I can get medical leave on top of my vacation time and start the Summer of Yes free and clear.

I sit back down and pound out a quick but polite email to Charlie, letting him know that, given the events of the last few days, I need to take some time off. On top of the medical leave my doctor has recommended, I'll also be cashing in on the weeks of vacation time I've accumulated.

It's not lost on me that my head only started to ache when I started typing.

I add, "Please don't promote anyone while I'm out," with a smiley face, delete it, then hit Send. Then I stand.

Tess is still watching me. "I don't know what I'll do without you. What if they temporarily assign me to Daniel?"

"Start working on a restraining order now."

I start walking. She follows me. "Kelsey, I don't know if I can work here without you."

"You'll be fine," I say as I reach the elevator. "Or maybe you should take a vacation too?"

"Yeah, right," she says, like I've just told her to try skinny-dipping in the Hudson. "Should I keep you posted on everything that happens?"

I give a perfunctory glance around the office, spotting Daniel near the back of the large room talking with one of the new female interns like the creepy pig that he is. I can smell his cologne from here. "No," I say. "I don't really care."

The elevator opens, and I step inside. Again, Tess follows me. "This really isn't like you, Kelsey. Is it the concussion? Are you concussed? I read somewhere that people who get in accidents suddenly wake up having completely different personalities."

Maybe I have. Huh.

"Should we go back to the hospital?"

I smile. "I'm thinking more clearly than ever, Tess."

She frowns. "Doesn't seem like it."

The elevator opens on the first floor. "Listen. I need this. For me. But you'll be okay." I place a hand on her arm, trying to temporarily reassure her. "Take care of yourself until I get back."

If I come back.

That thought startles me. I have no intention of quitting my job. And yet . . . part of me wonders: *What if there is something more for me out there?*

I leave her in the elevator, and the doors slowly close, vertically—and visibly—shutting off that part of my life.

I walk outside and breathe in the warm air. It's the middle of the day, and I don't have a thing on my agenda.

I'm free. Free to do something I wouldn't normally do.

An idea hits me, and I text Ravi.

> **Kelsey:** Hey, what are you doing?
>
> **Ravi:** Have invaders snatched your body? You're texting me in the middle of a workday?

I hit the voice-to-text feature and say slowly into my phone: "I'm taking a vacation. Period. Doctor's orders. Period."

I start walking in the direction of nowhere. I have nowhere to go. Nothing pressing. Normally, that would stress me out—I live to stay busy. But today? I decide that "Take a day off" is going to be the next item on my Yes List.

And I'm going to relish it.

I'm going to do something just for me. Just for fun.

> **Ravi:** Are you unwell? Since when do you listen to doctors?

I click my phone to life and call him.

"And now you're *calling* me? Who even are you?" His voice makes me smile and ache at the same time. He's known me almost as long as my parents and, tacos notwithstanding, it's been weeks since we spent any quality time together.

"I have a concussion, so I can't look at my screen for very long without feeling nauseous."

"Oh. Yeah. That actually makes sense," he says. "Why were you back at work anyway?"

I haven't talked to Ravi since my accident. I texted him the morning after I landed in the hospital, suffered through a series of "YOU'RE JUST TELLING ME THIS NOW?" texts, and assured him I'm fine. We were supposed to meet up tomorrow after work, but as it turns out, I won't be going to work, so maybe we'll have breakfast or go see a show or drink coffee after 11:00 a.m.

All things I normally never do.

"Are you okay?" His voice takes on a more serious tone.

"I am," I say. "I'm saying yes."

"To what?"

"Everything," I say.

There's a pause. "Where are you?"

"Just left the office."

"Okay, meet me at our Starbucks."

I stop walking. "No, meet me at the zoo."

"Huh?"

"Central Park," I say. "Let's spend the day at the zoo."

I can practically hear Ravi frowning as he mutters a long "Ooookaaaay."

And twenty minutes later, I'm standing at the entrance to the zoo when I spot him walking toward me.

Not unlike the misguided interpretation of my working relationship with Daniel, Ravi and I might appear to be perfectly positioned for a friends-to-lovers romance, but let me assure you, we are not.

Ravi and I grew up together, inseparable and thick as thieves. And unlike in romance novels, he and I are not harboring secret feelings for each other. Ravi really *is* like a brother to me. A smart, witty, endearing brother who has an equally brainy girlfriend named Sasha.

She was skeptical of me at first, but very quickly realized that I'm no threat. I won her over with our mutual love for Scrabble.

I'm outside a zoo, waiting for a great friend, and thinking of a complete stranger.

Jake . . . or whatever his name actually is.

I wonder if there's a way to get that man on my Yes List.

Before my inner screenwriter starts typing *that* one out, Ravi comes up the walk.

I half wave by holding up a bag of popcorn I bought from a booth outside the carousel, and fleetingly wonder if I should come up with a diet plan made up entirely of food purchased from street vendors.

Today Ravi is wearing khakis, a button-down chambray shirt, and a sweater vest, looking every bit like the PhD he is.

"Good day, Professor," I say cheekily.

"Good day, weirdo," he says. "What are we doing here?"

"I want to see the penguins." That thought just popped into my brain.

"I'm almost positive that's a line from *One Flew over the Cuckoo's Nest.*"

I respond by shoving a fistful of popcorn in my mouth.

"Why do I feel like if we go in there, there's a risk of you letting animals out?" He eyes me. "Are you on drugs?"

I chomp and scoff and turn toward the entrance of the zoo. "Maybe."

We walk up to the ticket booth. "My treat." I grin at Ravi.

"I would hope so, considering the fact that I'm only here to make sure you don't endanger yourself. Or the animals."

We walk through the gate, and I stop and look around. "I've never been here."

He squints at me. "Okay . . ."

"I've lived in New York for nine years, and I've never even been to the Central Park Zoo. Or the MoMA. Or to see a Broadway show. Can you believe I've never been to see a show?" Then I mutter, "My mom is an actress and I love the theatre, and I've never seen a show . . ."

"What's gotten into you, K?"

"A lot, actually." I pull up a zoo map on my phone, and we start walking toward the sea lions. "And I'm honestly not sure how to process it all."

"Well, I'm here to help." He holds out his hands and shrugs his shoulders, mocking confidence. "It's, you know, kinda what I do."

I smile and offer the popcorn, which he takes a handful of.

"Everyone at the hospital kept telling me how lucky I am."

"You *are* lucky," he says. "Do you realize the mathematical probability of walking away from that accident without a scratch?"

I tap the cut on my forehead and pull back my sleeve to show him the bruise left by the IV.

"You know what I mean," he says. "No broken bones. A concussion, yeah, some bruising, that's expected. But you're going to be, like, totally fine. Back to your normal self."

We're walking as slow as the Gilmore girls on the sidewalks of Stars Hollow. All that's missing is me holding an empty coffee cup to pretend to drink.

"Ravi, what if I don't want to go back to my normal self?" I ask.

I glance at him—my friend who has been with me through all my phases. My creative, imaginative phase. My artsy phase. And now, my workaholic, ladder-climbing, neglect-my-friends-and-family phase.

He knew all about the dreams a younger version of me was determined to make come true, but he accepted my new life.

Accepted the stability-seeking version of me, the girl who shut up all artistic endeavors in an airtight, fireproof box and threw away the key. And now I'm saying . . . what, exactly? That I chose the wrong path?

I imagine this is all pretty confusing for him.

"I almost died, you know?" I say as we reach the sea lions.

We stop.

"Sea lions are so weird," I continue. "I don't know that I've ever actually seen one before."

"You almost died," he says, as if just realizing it now.

"I mean, I could've. Just like that." I snap my fingers. "Everything could've ended."

"But . . . you didn't."

"Right," I say. "I didn't."

I turn to him. "Why is that, do you think?"

He laughs a little to himself. "That's a *bit* outside my purview. Different kind of professor can help you with that one, I think. Or a priest or something."

I turn back to watch the sea lions. They're just lying there, barking and hooting at one another.

"So . . ." He hesitates. "Why are we really at the zoo in the middle of a workday?"

I put both hands on the wooden-framed railing. "Because, Ravi, I've never been at the zoo in the middle of a workday. I've never seen sea lions." I pause. "Because I've never done anything."

He smirks. "Well, that's not true."

"It is."

"Kels, you graduated—with honors, I might add—from Northwestern. Then you moved here, which took a lot of courage."

"It didn't take courage," I say. "I had a job all lined up. I knew exactly how I was going to survive. Plus, you were coming here too."

"Why are you acting like that's a bad thing?"

I turn and start walking again. "The penguins are this way."

"Kelsey," he says. "What's going on?"

I stop. I turn and look at him. "I say no to everything, Ravi. *Everything.* I can't think of anything fun or risky or illegal or border-line inconvenient that I've said yes to. Not in years."

He quietly listens.

I unload more than I thought was there. "I don't take vacations. I don't take days off. I don't go places with a lot of people. I don't make new friends or"—I turn away—"see my old ones." I turn back in time to see him gently smile.

I go on. "I don't sleep in on weekends or ever skip the gym. I don't eat junk food or go to Trivia Night or do anything that's not work." The list is growing. So many things I want to add to my Yes List.

He makes a concerned face.

"What if . . . just, *what if* . . . I've been given a second chance here? What if I'm waking up to where I am, and I don't like it?"

He smiles. "You're not crazy. This is . . . actually kind of awesome."

"And terrifying."

He nods, and we start walking again. "Yeah, that too. But if you could honestly describe what it feels like to get a second chance at life, how would you describe it?"

Without hesitation, I say, "Free."

"Free," he repeats.

"Yeah. And so far, the first forty-eight minutes of being free is amazing."

"So you're taking time off? To do all those things?"

I nod. "It's going to be the Summer of Yes."

He glances at the bag in my hand. "And today you're saying yes to popcorn and penguins."

"And my friend." I give his arm a squeeze.

"A friend who doesn't have months of vacation time," he says.

"No, but it's almost summer," I say. "You'll have some time off then, right?"

"Some." He winces. "But I'm teaching a summer class."

"Lame."

He laughs.

"Can you stay for the penguins?" I ask.

He looks at his watch, then pulls out his phone and sends a quick text. "Now I can stay for the penguins."

I know he just moved something so he could stay. It's so easy for him to say yes to me—I make a mental note.

We enter the exhibit, and I decide I don't need to see anything else in the entire zoo. These little guys are the whole reason anyone should come here. They're funny and quirky and full of personality. Watching them instantly puts me in a better mood.

Today I said yes to penguins.

"So what are you going to do, make a list of things you want to do? Like a bucket list?"

I shrug. "Not exactly. I mean, yes, technically I've already started one. But I'm thinking I just need to be more open to whatever comes my way. No more no. Way more yes."

"Catchy. So, like, if I say, 'Hey, Kelsey, can I borrow a hundred dollars?'"

"I'll say yes, but can it be on a payment plan of one dollar over the next hundred months?"

He laughs. "Well, that's no fun."

I bump his shoulder with my own. "I don't know what it's going to look like exactly, but I'm going to figure it out. I have a partner."

As soon as I say the words, I remember the NDA and snap my jaw shut.

"A partner?"

"A possible . . . partner." I grimace. "Shoot. I signed an NDA."

He starts. "An NDA?"

I hold up my hands. "Yeah, it's this . . . thing I can't really talk about yet, but . . . I'm hopeful that I can convince her."

His brow furrows. "Her?"

I face him. I press my lips together and ultimately decide I can't keep it a secret.

"Okay, Ravi, for real, swear to me that you won't tell anyone this."

He holds one hand over his heart and another up, palm facing me.

"I, Dr. Ravindhar Subramani, do solemnly swear, upon penalty of prolonged payment plans . . ."

I smack him. "Stop it, you bozo."

Did Georgina's legal contract really include my very best friend? Surely not. I have the right to talk about my own experience in the hospital.

Right?

So I tell him.

I tell him about waking up to find Georgina Tate in the bed across the room. It turns out that Ravi doesn't even know who she is, which makes me feel a little safer about blabbing, and I leave out the *why* she was there. For all he knows, she had a nose job. I tell him about JP, about signing the NDA, about pretzels with cheese and the Summer of Yes.

And when I'm done, he just stares at me.

"What?" I ask.

"That's a lot."

"Yeah, I know. But I signed a document," I say. "She probably has a drone listening to this conversation, and I'm probably going to get sued. Or thrown in jail. Can I go to jail for blabbing when I signed an NDA? I never actually read the document."

He shakes his head. "I'm not going to say anything."

"Not even to Sasha?"

"Not even to Sasha," he agrees. "But I want to go on record and say I think this is the most brilliant thing you've ever done."

I feel myself beam. "Really?"

"You work too hard. You never take a day off. You aren't really living, Kelsey. You're just working. You deserve this."

"I do. I deserve this." I feel good saying it out loud. "Now I just have to wait for Georgina to come around."

"You think she's just going to change her mind?"

I reach in my pocket and pull out the business card JP gave me. "I have her phone number."

Ravi shakes his head. "So your plan is to annoy her until she agrees?"

I smirk. "If I remember right, that's how I got you to be my friend."

"That's true," he says. "That or you threatened to beat me up."

"I was a bruiser when I was little, wasn't I?" A penguin dives in and zips underwater past the glass. "You really think it's a good idea?"

He looks away, and I can see there's something he's not saying. "What?"

He shrugs. "It's not important."

"It is," I say. "I can tell by the look on your face."

He sighs. "It's just . . ."

"Just what?"

"It's just good to think that I might get the old Kelsey back." He glances over at me. "The one who made time for her friends."

"Oh, come on, I always make time for you, Rav." But even as I say it, something about it feels false.

He grimaces again.

I frown. "What?"

"You . . . missed my birthday party," he says.

I search my mind for today's date and realize that he's right—his birthday was three weeks ago. And I missed it. I was working and I missed it.

"Your birthday," I whisper.

He chuckles, trying to blow it off like it's no big deal, but I know better.

"I was supposed to bring the cake."

His smile is sad, and I start to see the depth of my mistake. I always, always put work first. Even before Ravi.

"You see? *You see?*" Tears start welling in my eyes. "Something has to change. Something *had* to change. A disruptor."

"A what?"

"Something my mom said that is making more and more sense." I look at him. "I'm the worst."

"You aren't," he says.

"I am." I face him. "Can you ever forgive me?"

"I already have, Kels," he says. "But I'm glad you're taking some time off. Maybe this whole 'yes' thing will help you prioritize what really matters."

That wasn't my intention for making the Yes List, but it absolutely should've been. His words shame me. "I'm so sorry, Ravi."

He drapes an arm around my shoulder and gives me a quick squeeze. "You're missing the penguins."

....

Kelsey: Georgina? It's Kelsey. From the hospital.

Kelsey: Just texting to see if you've changed your mind.

Georgina: Kelsey, it's only been a day. Give her a little more time.

Kelsey: JP?

JP: Yes. You didn't really think I'd give you her personal number, did you?

Kelsey: Can I come visit her?

Kelsey: I really think I can convince her to agree to my plan.

JP: You can't.

JP: She only makes decisions for herself.

JP: Not because someone convinces her.

Kelsey: I'd still like to visit.

JP: . . .

Kelsey: There's a reason you gave me the card.

JP: Fine. But if she asks, you found her address on Google.

Kelsey: Deal.

Chapter 10

GEORGINA

You have a visitor."

JP stands just inside the door to my living room, an apprehensive look on his face.

I frown. A miniscule piece of me is hopeful that maybe, after all this time, Hayden has finally come around. But when the girl appears, my hopes are dashed.

I'd be lying if I said I hadn't thought about this little scrap of a person and her ridiculous plan.

If I want to say yes to things, I'll just say yes. I don't need a list. Or a pact. How childish.

And yet, there's something so naively endearing about her. She's so earnest, like the world hasn't quite sunk its teeth into her yet.

I vaguely remember being the same way. A lifetime ago.

Empowered. Fearless. Determined.

And now, a shell of who I once was.

"What are you doing here?" I ask. "In my home?"

She glances at JP, and then JP glances at me. I give him my best "you're in trouble" glare while mentally scrolling through things within reach to throw at him. But he ducks out of the room.

Lucky, because I'm sitting next to a small lamp.

"He gave you my address?"

"He gave me your card," she says. "And I hounded him for your address."

I fold my hands in my lap. "So. You're a stalker."

She shakes her head. "No, I'm not. You know why I'm here."

She might have some fire. Interesting.

The room goes silent for several long seconds.

I concede and motion for her to sit. She's here; she might as well. A part of me is morbidly curious what she might say. She is the first person I've encountered who doesn't seem to be after my money or my approval.

I'm sure she still has ridiculous delusions about me writing a memoir, but I get the sense that her being here isn't about that at all. Still, I have a feeling my patience for her presence isn't going to last long.

"I went to see penguins yesterday."

"That hardly seems noteworthy."

She crosses one leg over the other, and I take note of her improved posture. There. I've given her the best piece of advice I could've given her: sit up straight. What more does this girl want from me?

"I went in the middle of the day."

I don't respond. If she has a point, I hope she makes it quickly so I can shoo her out and spend my evening in peace—alone.

"I'm taking a few weeks off."

That gets my attention. "From work?"

"Yes."

"Why?"

She frowns. "I think I need to reevaluate. Or reset. Or retire. I'm not sure."

"You do know you didn't actually have a near-death experience, don't you?" I ask. "You're being so melodramatic about the whole thing. Meanwhile, I'm over here, legitimately in my last days, and you don't see me having grand epiphanies about my life."

"Maybe you should," she says.

I narrow my eyes.

"Maybe the fact that your body has alerted you to its . . . issues . . . is a gift?"

I scoff. "A gift? Ulcers in your mouth and blood in your urine— that's a gift?"

She looks hurt, embarrassed even. Maybe what I said is harsh, but what I deal with on the day-to-day is definitely not something you unwrap at Christmas.

"I didn't mean *those* things. Those things are horrible. I'm so sorry you have to deal with that."

I can't stand people feeling sorry for me. I level her with my glare. "Do you have a point?"

She folds her hands in her lap. "I forgot my best friend's birthday."

The words send an unexpected jolt, and I'm transported back decades. Hayden's tenth birthday. I got called into a board meeting as I was leaving for the day. There was a work crisis, and I really didn't have a choice.

That's what I told myself.

"I was supposed to bring the cake," she says. "Ravi—he's my friend—was really sweet about it, but he thinks this break will be good for me." She pauses. "He remembers me before I was like this." Her face falls.

"Kailey, did I give you the impression that I'm interested in your life?" I ask.

"It's Kelsey. And no," she responds. "But I got the impression that maybe you missed a birthday or two in your day."

In a flash, I'm back there, leaving the office to find three angry voice messages from my husband, Dylan.

"Do you know how your son felt today when his own mother didn't show up to his birthday party?"

"I had to lie to all of our friends, trying to come up with any kind of plausible excuse for you missing this."

"Georgina, the look on his face when I told him you weren't coming . . . Can you get here? Please?"

I sat in the back of my car, knowing I was too late. I'd missed the whole thing. And when I got home that night, Dylan had already cleaned up everything from the party.

And the look on his face told me everything I needed to know.

It was the last straw. He was leaving.

And he was going to take Hayden with him.

I couldn't argue. I'd done my best to make it work—*did I, though?*—but society lies to women when it says they can have it all. A family, a career, success at home and success in the workplace.

You can't. At least not all at the same time.

A job? Yes. That I could've had. But that's not what I wanted. I wanted to make my mark. I wanted to build something bigger than myself.

That didn't leave a lot of room for anything or anyone else.

Which, I suppose, is why this woman is now sitting in my living room telling me about missed birthdays.

Maybe she feels some sort of strange, unfounded kinship with me. Maybe she sees me as her future, and she doesn't know how to square that.

Maybe I'm a cautionary tale.

Fantastic.

I didn't have time to wallow in my regrets before, and I certainly don't now that Death is hanging around on my porch, waiting for me to open the door.

I made my choices, and I have to live with them. End of story.

"I tried to go back to work," she says. "It felt . . . wrong. Odd. Almost like . . ." She trails off, circling her hands, seemingly searching for the right description.

"None of it mattered," I say, finishing her sentence.

She looks up, lights behind her eyes. "Yes. Exactly."

"Why are you here?"

"Georgina, *I don't know*." She looks a little lost, and for a flicker of a moment, I don't mind that she's sitting here, invading my space.

And now, because of something I said, she has this harebrained idea that we're partners or something. Because I admitted I wish I'd said yes more, she's turned the whole idea into some sort of quest.

She obviously doesn't know me at all. I'm prepping for the end, not looking to start something new. I have things to put in order. A life to wrap up.

Never mind the pretzel—good grief, that was delicious—and how it made me feel.

Daring. Bold. Rebellious.

Or the fact that there are so very many things I'd still like to do. That time got away from me, and I suppose that's the one thing we can't buy, isn't it?

Nobody's hawking extra years on the street corners in Times Square.

"I suppose you're making a list," I muse. "All the things you want to say yes to, things you've constantly said no to in the past?"

At the slightest interest in her ridiculous idea, she perks up. She seems to be trying to hide a smile, but she's failing miserably.

"I . . . am making a list," she says, like a child who doesn't want to tell you they snuck cookies into bed. "But not a bucket list. These are things that I've specifically said no to before. And I really want to try to say yes to whatever comes my way."

"That sounds like some New Agey malarkey."

"And the word 'malarkey' sounds like something an old person would say."

Now it's me trying not to smile. Fortunately, I'm much better at it than Kailey is.

"You don't want to spend the summer with me, Kailey." I fuss with the throw pillows as she corrects me again that her name is, in fact, Kelsey.

I'm intrigued by this idea of hers, but I'm not sure how to say so. I don't like to go along with other people's plans. Usually, plans are not good unless I've thought of them myself.

"So no grand plan? No map, no direction? You just say yes," I say.

"Just say yes."

"To anything?"

She shrugs. "To anything I'd normally say no to."

"So, going to bed with a stranger? You're just going to say yes to that?" I raise a judgmental brow.

"Of course not," she says.

"Specificity is important, dear."

She draws in a breath. "I'm going to say yes to things that don't compromise my morals."

"It's good to know you have morals," I say. "So many people your age don't."

She frowns. "That's a very broad generalization."

I shrug. Because I really don't care. I make no apologies for having big opinions. Most of the time, I'm right.

"I'm going to say yes when the world gives me opportunities. Like the chance to see the penguins." She smiles at this, like it means something to her. It means nothing to me. I have no interest in penguins.

Then she looks at me. "Or when I want to eat ice cream. Or giant pretzels. Or whatever. Do you know how much time I've wasted trying to make my body look perfect?"

"There's no such thing as a perfect body," I say.

"Says the woman with a perfect body."

I frown. "Oh? A body with failing kidneys is what you're after?"

She goes quiet.

"Thin isn't perfect, Kenzie," I say, knowing full well this is not her name.

At that, she sighs. "If we're going to be friends, could you at least remember my name?"

"We're not going to be friends."

"We could be," she says.

"I don't have time."

"Say yes to making a friend, Miss Tate," she says. "You might like it."

I'm unaffected by her plea, and yet I still say, "What is your name?"

She glares at me. "I just told you two minutes ago."

It's Kelsey. I just like watching her fuss.

"*Kelsey*," she says, clearly annoyed.

"Kelsey," I say. "Like Chelsea but with a *K*."

"Or just like Kelsey," she quips.

"Fine," I say. "I'll do my best to remember."

"Great."

"Kelsey. Kelsey. Kelsey." I'm trying to make it stick. "What's your last name?"

"Worthington."

"Great. Kelsey Worthington. I'll say it a lot and see where that gets us, *Kelsey*."

She doesn't react the way I thought she would—instead, she smiles. "I like that I don't have to guess what you're thinking. I also like that you're not afraid to say what you want. It's refreshing. Most of the people I work with are either sucking up or shutting up."

I pause. "I know exactly what that's like," I say. "People never tell me what they really think, and I can't stand it. I don't want a bunch of sycophants. If an idea is terrible, I want someone to tell me so."

"Yes!" she exclaims. "Finally! Someone who understands that. Just say what you mean—I don't have time to keep guessing!"

There's a moment, just the smallest of moments, where I feel a connection.

It's a strange feeling since I'm typically accustomed to being alone at the top. At the moment, I don't feel like I'm steering this ship; I feel like a copilot.

And I'm not sure I like it.

"I have an idea," she says.

"Oh goody." I barely refrain from rolling my eyes.

"You're going to have to loosen up for this to work."

"I haven't said I want this to work," I remind her.

"True. But at this point, I don't even care about that." She takes a breath. "Here's my idea: let's be tourists in our own city."

"Tourists," I say, unimpressed. "That's what you've come up with?"

"Have you ever been to the top of the Empire State Building?"

"My office is *in* the Empire State Building."

"Oh." Her face falls in the most pathetic way.

So I throw her a bone. "But no, I haven't been to the top."

Now she's a bright light again.

"What about the Statue of Liberty?" she asks. "Have you seen it? Or Ellis Island? Or the FRIENDS Experience?"

I frown. "The FRIENDS Experience?"

"From the TV show?" She says this like I should know what she's talking about.

"Kelsey," I start.

"Thank you for remembering my name."

I flick my hand in the air. "Do you really think I've ever had time for television?"

She scrunches her nose. "Probably not. But I can make a list. All the famous stops. We can ride the carousel in Central Park. I'll even buy you a balloon." She's grinning now. "We're doing this, right?"

I think of my little Hayden, his bright eyes watching me from the back seat of his father's car as they drove away. Out of the city. Out of my life.

So many regrets.

"Fine."

"Fine?" She's practically bouncing up and down, wearing her excitement like a fancy new party dress.

"Stop bouncing."

"Sorry."

"Meet me here tomorrow," I say, uncharacteristically curious where this might lead.

"Yes!" She pumps a fist in the air. "We're doing this."

"All I said was meet me tomorrow."

She points a triumphant finger at me. "But what I heard . . . was a yes."

Chapter 11

KELSEY

THAT NIGHT, AFTER my win with Georgina, I'm sitting in the living room looking around my apartment and feeling very alone.

If it weren't for Ravi, I wouldn't have any connection to the world outside of work, and I haven't even done a good job of staying in touch with him.

I'm not sure how that happened.

I open my laptop and type "touristy things to do in NYC" in the search bar. I scroll past the sponsored ones, which I assume everyone does, and land on "The Best 84 New York Attractions."

Oof. Eighty-four.

After about forty-five minutes, I've got a nice itinerary—a good mix of seeing things from above and tasting things street level—and then my curiosity has me typing Georgina's name into the search bar.

So. Many. Results.

Most of the articles written about her are "Success in Business" or "Women to Watch." There are some puff pieces about her life, which, after a few quick scans, I discover say absolutely nothing. The interviews she gives are full of stock answers that make her sound like she's reading from a script.

Who are you, Georgina Tate?

I click around online and uncover only facts I already know. Some answers she gives are repeated verbatim. Nothing personal. Nothing deep. Georgina Tate is one of the most successful women in the country, and she's managed to keep her private life truly private.

One article calls her "the notoriously private cosmetics mogul." Another says she has the personal life of a ghost. There are fleeting mentions of a son—Hayden—but no photos and nothing to clue me in as to why he and his mother are estranged.

I search and search for a photo of the man, wondering if my hunch about the good-looking guy at the hospital is correct, but come up empty. Either he doesn't use the last name Tate or he has sworn off social media.

Smart guy.

After several minutes of clicking on every Hayden Tate I can find (*A seven-year-old doing reviews about stuffed animals, nope. A family man at a bowling alley in Spokane, nope*), I stumble upon a page by an organization that celebrates women in business. According to a press release, Georgina Tate is set to receive a Lifetime Achievement Award from the organization, which she has been a part of since her early days in business.

I see that there's a ceremony and a gala celebrating this milestone, and I wonder if she's planning to attend.

I add it to my mental list of things to ask her about as a text comes in from Ravi.

Ravi: Dinner with my family?

I grew up with Ravi. I know his parents well. But his extended family of mostly strangers is loud, and they *really* like to ask questions. Ones that require self-reflection, or at least an admission that my life needs work.

It's this that has kept me avoiding and declining his invitations, claiming work and scheduling conflicts for years.

It's not a lie. I *am* always working.

But now I realize that he wouldn't ask if it wasn't important to him. He wants me to be there. Isn't that worth a little social discomfort? Isn't *he* worth it?

I consider it. I'm afraid of being put on the spot.

Strike that. I could've ended that sentence after the word "afraid."

Afraid of what, exactly? I'm not a pushover. I'm not a wallflower.

Afraid of not being in control.

This revelation hits just as hard as the last one.

I'm extremely comfortable when it's me calling the shots, me making decisions, me in control.

But things that are *out* of my control—flying, waves in the ocean, crowds, new places, lots of people—I avoid them because I'm afraid of not being in control, and I'm afraid of the unexpected.

Like a car jumping a curb.

It's not *work* that's kept me from living my life. It's *fear.* Work was just my excuse.

From the time I was very young, I always gravitated toward one-on-one friendships. I thought if I had just one good friend, I'd be fine. For me, that's Ravi. Always. And he's stuck by my side all these years. In spite of missed birthdays and long periods of silence on my end.

Ravi: Ooh, your first YES TEST.
Ravi: Penguins are easy.
Kelsey: Is Sasha coming?
Ravi: No.
Ravi: She's got a bachelorette party.
Ravi: But I promise I won't leave you alone.

My fingers hover. I feel hot. Why is this so hard for me? I don't have social anxiety. I can make adult conversation.

Ravi: Will you come?

I know why it's hard. Because last time, albeit years ago, his mother asked if I was happy with my life.

Simple question.

I couldn't answer it, so I fumbled. This led to more questions, and I felt like I needed to defend my life choices. His family was genuinely interested, and just because I felt put on the spot, I decided not to come over anymore.

It feels so lame in retrospect.

Ravi's family doesn't mess around. They get to the heart of matters. They can tell when I'm not being fully honest, even with myself.

But I have to say yes. It's the deal I made with myself, and now I'm being put to the test.

I double-tap Shift to lock all caps and then tap three letters.

Kelsey: YES

....

On the drive to Ravi's aunt's house, I drill him about, well, everything. He laughs at my questions, but this is important stuff. Dinner for me is usually something microwaved from the freezer, eaten by myself on the floor of my apartment.

"Will your aunt be offended if I don't stuff myself?"

"Yes," Ravi says. And then, as if just remembering, he asks, "Have you made any progress with the spicy food?"

"I sometimes put pepper on my noodles."

He just looks at me. "We'll keep working on that."

"Do I need to know everyone's names before we get there? It's been a while, and I'm not sure . . ."

He laughs. "No, and you won't remember after I tell them to you either. It's a lot of people."

This spikes my pulse. A lot of people. A lot of questions.

"You're good with people," Ravi says, sensing my hesitation. "And you know my parents love you."

"I'm good with people at *work*," I say. "I understand how to do my job. Arm's length. Witty banter. But my personal life? That is a whole other thing."

They've invited me out for things too. My coworkers. And my response has been the same every time.

Trivia night? No.

Happy hour after work with Tess and her friends? No.

Speed dating? Karaoke? Swing dance lessons? No. No. No.

By all accounts, dinner with Ravi's family is low pressure. Yes, there will be people I don't know. Yes, there will be food I've never tried. Yes, there will be probing questions and loud conversations and strangers.

But this is Ravi. And I want to know his family—all of them.

"I'm just glad you're coming," he says. "It's about time. How long's it been?"

I reach across the front seat and squeeze his arm, not wanting to calculate the many, many months. "I'm so sorry I've been such a bad friend, Ravi."

He reaches over and squeezes back. "Don't be dumb. You're not a bad friend."

"I didn't used to be a good friend," I say honestly. "But lately?" I let my shrug finish the statement.

"You've just gotten . . . you know . . . very caught up with work. Plus, you worry about everything now."

That's true. I do. I worry about everything now. I didn't used to.

I didn't used to. Seems to be a recurring theme as of late.

It's like my overactive imagination and my English degree had a fling, and now I come up with possible stories about *everything*.

When I leave for work, I always take a different way home, because *what if I'm being followed by someone who's been casing my workplace, and I get mugged and have my identity stolen?* I always keep an eye on the exit in the subway *just in case it collides with an oncoming train.*

I'm running through the list of other catastrophic events I've worried about when I realize I never once thought: *What if I get hit by a car on the sidewalk?*

Ironic.

And I'm still here.

I'm still here.

Since the accident, life has taken on this whole new meaning for me. It feels like a precious, volatile, sacred, unpredictable, fleeting thing, and I'm holding it in my hands trying not to drop it.

"Paging Dr. Kelsey."

Ravi's voice startles me back to the present, and I realize I've zoned out for a good three minutes. "Sorry."

"You okay?"

I nod.

"We're here." Ravi smiles. "They're so excited you're coming."

We're in a suburb, in a neighborhood, staring at an adorable, albeit small, home, and I wonder how many people are going to be crammed in there. I worry that my heart will race or my palms will sweat and wonder if I'll put myself in the corner, like I used to do on the rare occasion I went out to a college party.

Always observing. Never participating.

And that's my life in a nutshell. I'm an observer. Not an active participant.

Then, a mental pause. Almost like a deep breath, but in my mind.

As before, things settle. I relax, and shockingly, I start to smile.

I'm free to choose *yes.*

And I'm choosing it. I'll say yes to the food, the family, and the questions I don't want to face.

The realization follows me into Ravi's aunt's house, and as soon as we open the door, we're met with the smell of curry and warmth.

A short, plump, dark-haired woman lets out a little squeal when she spots us standing in the entryway. Arms raised overhead, mouth smiling wide and eyes doing the same, like welcoming someone home from overseas, she exclaims, "Ravi! You made it!"

Ravi leans toward me. "She says that like I'm not here every week."

The woman is wearing a bright pink top, and her eyes are wide and beautiful. Her long, dark hair is pulled into a braid at the back of her neck, and when she reaches us, I feel a little like a giant.

"Kelsey," she says, taking both my hands in hers. "Do you remember me? Aunt Nila!"

I smile. "Thank you so much for having me."

"We've been wanting to see you again," she says, swatting my arm three or four times. I awkwardly laugh, and she swats it again. "I started to think maybe you were a ghost."

I smile, and a thought strikes me. And I say it out loud.

"I've been so rude to turn down so many invitations over the years. I let work get in the way, and I am so sorry for not coming sooner." I look at Ravi. "I don't want to do that anymore."

I take stock of my pulse and find it's trying to ramp up, but holding steady.

A little self-revelation goes a long way apparently.

"Oh, stop! People are busy, Ravi is busy, I am busy. You are here now! Welcome, welcome! Let me get you a snack." Aunt Nila scurries off just as a young guy about our age waves at Ravi.

"My cousin Kash," Ravi says, leaning toward me.

But before we've moved, Aunt Nila is back with a tray of appetizers.

"Pace yourself, Kelsey," he says. Then, smiling at Nila, he says, "There's a *lot* of food."

She hits him with a towel and says something in Hindi.

I turn to Ravi, questioning.

"She thinks I need to eat more and that I look like I'm wasting away."

I laugh and pick up one of the skewers as Aunt Nila hands me a napkin. She stands there watching me, like she's waiting for me to try the food. I glance at Ravi, who's already two bites in.

"Don't be shy," Aunt Nila says.

Say yes, Kelsey. Even if it's spicy. Say yes.

I take a huge bite, and the spices explode in my mouth. I have no idea what I'm eating, but it's delicious.

"Oh my *gosh*. This is amazing! What is this?" I ask.

"Paneer tikka," she says. "You like it?"

I take another bite. I've never tasted anything like it. "It's so good."

She smiles and shoots a knowing look at Ravi, and it seems like the small compliment has made her night.

"Come on, Kelsey," Ravi says. "Let's meet everyone."

He introduces (and in some cases, reintroduces) me to everyone, but as he promised, I don't remember all their names. I try, but there are more than twenty people here, and all I can think is, *Where are we all going to eat?*

About ten minutes later, I have my answer: everywhere.

There's a big table in the dining room, which is where Ravi and I go with his parents and his grandmother, who is a tiny woman with graying hair.

Aunt Nila dishes me a plate of food, and I listen to the conversation pinballing around the table—some English, some I'm assuming is Hindi, and some a mix of both. They start on the topic of Ravi and Sasha, and everyone wants to know why he hasn't popped the question yet.

Ravi laughs it off the way only he can do, but even I'm wondering what he's waiting for. Sasha is the love of his life.

Maybe I'm not the only one who's afraid.

After that conversation lulls, they turn to Ravi's cousin Dev, who is sitting *with* his girlfriend, and begin to pepper them with questions about their future plans.

"We all just want some beautiful babies," Ravi's mom says, and the room reacts loudly, the men oohing and the women laughing. Someone shouts over the din, "Then better not let Dev be the father!" And another wave of laughter follows.

"What about you, Kelsey?" Aunt Nila asks.

I'm mid-bite into a brightly colored chicken dish. I'm caught—do I spit it out and talk? Or do I awkwardly sit and chew and *then* answer?

"Oh, Kelsey has sworn off men." Ravi saves me, thank the Lord.

"But you're so young and pretty," his mom says. "You need to get out there."

"Oh, I've been out there." I laugh nervously. This is just what I'd feared—the probing questions that make me the center of attention. But . . . it feels . . . safe somehow.

That's totally foreign. I worry. I hide. I avoid.

But here, now, in the presence of so much kindness, I feel totally at ease.

"The last guy I dated thought that a deep conversation was me helping him with his fantasy football draft. And the guy before that had an Apple Watch to monitor his heart rate—to see if I 'did it for him.' Like, what?"

The room erupts with laughter, and one of the women shouts out, "Men are such pigs!" And one guy responds, "Yeah, too bad we own everything!" And the room is laughing and loud and I secretly love that Ravi was right.

This is *so fun*. Being in a large crowd, even at the center of that crowd, is not at all what I'd imagined in my head.

I needed a little shake-up.

"Honestly, I don't have time for dating because I work a lot," I say.

There's a loud, obnoxious, collective groan around the table, and I think maybe I've said the wrong thing, but Nila jumps in.

"Work will *always* be there," she says. "Your eggs are only good for so long."

"My *eggs*?!" I cough, trying to swallow the bite in my mouth.

"Aunt Nila!" Ravi puts a hand on my arm. "I'm sorry."

"It's fine." I laugh. "My eggs are still workin'"—I pat my stomach—"but I'm not so sure after this meal—this is *spicy* for me!"

A collective protest again, and this time Ravi's mom—bringing in more dishes from the kitchen—says, "We haven't even gotten to the hot stuff yet!"

"You're on the apps, right?" Dev's girlfriend asks me. "That's how Dev and I met."

"Not true," Ravi says. "They met through Aunt Nila."

Aunt Nila taps her nose twice. "I make no apologies for spreading love. It's my duty to be a matchmaker."

"We met through my mom," Dev says. "But we found each other on an app."

"I'm not on any dating apps," I say.

Another groan.

"What? It seems like such a cattle call!" I try not to dwell on all the dinners I've missed over the years. I could've been a part of this my whole adult life, but I told myself a story that kept me on the sidelines. I wish I could take it back. I continue, "Dismiss me by simply swiping left? No thank you!"

"You have to get out there," Aunt Nila says. "I'll help you set up a profile after dinner. I'm very tech savvy!" She stands and starts scooping more food onto my plate.

I want to tell her I'm beyond full, but I get the impression that would be rude, so I do my best to pace myself.

"What are you afraid of?" Ravi's mom asks. "You could meet a lovely man."

"She's dated lovely men," Ravi says. "But never for long."

"What are you waiting for?" Aunt Nila asks.

My face heats, and not from the food. I'm on the hot seat, and these are the kinds of questions that kept me away.

I poke a meatball in a fiery red sauce and lift it up. "A spark, I guess?"

Aunt Nila and Ravi's mom turn to each other and do a little shimmy.

"You want it *spicy*!" Aunt Nila says.

But then Ravi's mom's expression turns serious. "Sometimes you get married and find the spice later." She points at me. "You're not getting any younger." Then she points at Ravi. "That goes for you too."

"Okay, okay, I get it," Ravi says, holding up two surrendering hands.

The conversation lulls, then shifts, and I settle in and survey the scene around me.

My eyes are wide open to the sights, sounds, and smells around me. The world is bright and colorful. It's tinged with sweet and spicy. It's loud and vibrant, and I've been walking around like Dorothy before she lands in Oz— settling for faded black and white.

I internally narrate my revelation, the way I would if I were sitting behind my computer, and I'm struck by how long it's been since I've heard my own voice.

It's so easy to silence.

As I scan the table, my eyes meet the eyes of Ravi's silver-haired grandmother. She's been quiet throughout the meal, and now she just smiles at me.

And I wonder . . . what's her story?

I think about my mother, all that talk of something that sets my soul on fire. I'd rejected the idea because who has time to listen to a soul that's on fire when there are so many deadlines to meet? But now, met with my own curiosity and a new outlook on life, I wonder if I have the courage I need to let my voice be louder in my own head.

To record the thoughts and ideas that have been lying dormant for so long.

Not because of logic or practicality. Not because of work or scheduling.

Because of fear.

Ravi's grandma reaches over and squeezes my hand, as if she senses that I'm on the precipice of a revelation and need a little push to let myself fly.

"Be fearless, *mera priya*," she says. "The world needs your voice."

My voice.

Just say yes, Kelsey.

Chapter 12

KELSEY

I'VE NEVER BEEN hungover from a meal . . . until now.

The mood, the smells, the tastes, the laughter, the new friends who felt like old ones—it's all still with me as I wake up the next morning.

I rise and smile, thinking about some of the mirth and light-hearted banter that went on last night. And then I start to think of the day ahead of me.

I'm out my door in plenty of time to meet Georgina for a full day of touring the city. I've added lunch at the Stardust Diner, a Broadway staple, and if we're lucky, we'll have enough time for dessert at Serendipity 3.

And in between, all the touristy things New Yorkers avoid.

All the things I've never made time for.

Georgina's going to just *love* it.

When JP opens the door, he stares at me like he has no idea why I'm here. As snobbish as Georgina is, her assistant is ten times worse.

If he were a character and I were to cast him, he'd definitely be the maître d' dealing with Ferris posing as Abe Froman, the Sausage King of Chicago.

I suddenly have the overwhelming desire to make him like me.

"Hey, JP," I say, like I'm his long-lost friend.

"Hey?" He eyes me with the disdain of a socialite who was just handed a $10 coupon to Goodwill.

"I'm here to see Georgina," I say.

"Do you have an appointment with *Miss Tate*?" he asks.

"I do," I say.

He tilts his head down at me.

"Sort of." I squirm slightly. "She told me to come over so we can go sightseeing. You were here when she told me to come back . . ."

"Miss Tate doesn't 'go sightseeing.'"

He repeats my words back as though they taste like bad fish.

"Well, my friend, she does today." I smile at him. "If you're sweet to me, I'll bring you back an 'I heart NYC' T-shirt. What's your size?" I give him a once-over, as if trying to determine it for myself.

His right brow rises, but he doesn't crack a smile. He's overtly irritated with me, but I'm not remotely deterred. He did give me her card, after all. I wouldn't even be here if it wasn't for him.

Unfortunately, he's blocking the door.

"Did you want to come with us? I have a whole plan." I pull out my phone and open my Notes app. I turn it around so he can see it, and after he scans it for point-three seconds, he rolls his eyes and steps out of the way.

I walk inside and into Georgina's living room. Then, appearing beside me, he turns and says, "Wait here."

I didn't pay much attention when I was here the day before, but now? Now I look—really look—at Georgina's condo.

It's strange to see anyone with this much space in the city. Georgina lives near Central Park, in a building with tall ceilings, dark hardwood floors, and lots of windows. It's obvious that the space has been professionally decorated—and there isn't a single personal item in the entire space.

It's set up for entertaining. Parties and social gatherings. Events where people go to see and be seen. In my past life (only, like, a few weeks ago), if I'd been invited to such a gathering, I wouldn't have gone.

They're not my people. I would've had *major* impostor syndrome.

I'm wittier on paper.

More interesting via email.

I wouldn't be able to hold anyone's attention long enough to have a single conversation.

I'm realizing that fear was getting a lot of playing time on my team.

Time to ride the bench, buddy.

Plus, I proved that I'm a rock star at getting out of my comfort zone during the dinner at Aunt Nila's.

I had *so* much fun at dinner last night. Sure, I went home with an exploding belly, and I mildly offended Aunt Nila when I couldn't finish my fourth plate of food. But all in all, the questions and the banter and the large crowd of mostly strangers weren't at all what I'd made them out to be. It was *delightful*.

Standing in Georgina's living room, I think how interesting it would be to be a fly on the wall during one of *her* parties. According to my online sleuthing, there have been many.

In one photo, the only one I eventually found as evidence that Georgina has a son at all, there's a small boy standing behind a door, peeking out into the living room full of New York's most notable socialites. And his eyes are drawn straight to his glamorous mother.

Georgina. Wow, she was a knockout.

And she has no idea he's there watching.

Granted, I'm filling in the blanks and concocting a backstory from just one frame, but it's the only picture that seems to give any kind of hint into the life she lived when she wasn't the only one under this roof.

It has my curiosity piqued.

JP told me to wait here.

I don't.

I take a few cautious steps into the kitchen and stop short. The space might've been set up for Wolfgang Puck or Bobby Flay. If I spend enough time here, even I might actually start cooking.

I wonder how often it gets used. Georgina certainly doesn't seem like a "whip up her own meals" kind of person.

Beyond the kitchen is a dining room with a modern, oversized rectangular table and eight chairs. In the corner of that room, a sleek baby grand piano. And when I look out the window, I see the green tops of the trees in Central Park.

It's stunning. The exact kind of place you'd imagine a person like Georgina living.

I retrace my steps, going back the way I came, and when I come through the living room, I notice something.

It's quiet. Not just this room but the whole house.

There's no television. No music. No people.

The whole space seems to lack personality.

Just like my tiny apartment.

I notice an arched opening off the living room and take a peek inside.

It's a library.

I'm struck by the walls of built-in floor-to-ceiling shelves loaded with books. *So many books.* I feel like Belle in Beast's castle, spinning in a circle while the camera pans around me.

I forget where I am and whose house this is and walk straight to the shelves and begin perusing.

I can hardly believe it. First editions, signed copies, fiction, nonfiction—*The Memoirs of Sherlock Holmes* by Doyle, *Poems in Prose* by Oscar Wilde, *On Her Majesty's Secret Service* by Fleming, rows and rows of incredible—

"What are you doing in here?"

I whip around and find Georgina—*in the room and I didn't even notice her*—attached to what I assume is her dialysis machine. I clutch the book I'm holding as if doing so will hold me upright.

"Wow, you're super quiet," I say, trying to laugh away my awkwardness.

"Do you think you could put that incredibly rare and priceless early edition back on the shelf where it belongs?"

I look down and see that I'm holding *Alice's Adventures in Wonderland* by Carroll.

How fitting.

I immediately—and gingerly—put it back on the shelf in its place.

At that moment, JP storms in. "I apologize, Miss Tate. I told her to wait in the living room."

"Obviously, she doesn't know how to listen." Georgina fusses with the machine, flicking it off and silencing its rhythmic clicking. She pushes herself up while JP simultaneously rushes to her side, but as she stands, she shoos him away.

"I'm fine, JP," she barks. "Concern yourself with this intruder."

He clears his throat slightly. "She said you told her to come over."

Georgina closes her eyes and inhales a deep breath. "I've changed my mind. I have to work today."

"No you don't," I say.

Her eyebrows snap up, and she glares at me.

"Today, we're doing this." I tap my phone to life and show her my list.

She takes it. "What is this?"

"Your itinerary."

"Itinerary?" she repeats, handing back my phone. "I'm not a tourist. I live here."

"Really?" I say. "Where's the best place to get a slice?"

"A slice of what?"

I smile. "Exactly my point."

Georgina isn't amused.

I stare.

She stares back.

"Say yes, Georgina. It's the only way to get me to go away."

She looks as if she's pouting for a moment. I shake my phone's screen at her, and she rolls her eyes.

Then, by some miracle, her features soften. She holds out one hand as if to say, *"Fine, lead the way."*

"Woo-hoo!" I hold up a high five to JP, who looks at my hand like I just wiped a five-year-old kid's nose with it.

"We'll work on that," I say to him.

Chapter 13

KELSEY

I REALLY DON'T have time for this, you know," she tells me as we get into a lavish car parked outside her building.

"This is the exact same kind of car I once saw Harry Styles getting out of," I say, as I discreetly tell the driver our destination.

"I don't know who that is."

I frown over at her. "You don't?"

"I don't keep up with who passes for 'celebrity' in your generation, Kelsey." She crosses one leg over the other and rests her hands in her lap.

"You remembered my name!" I grin at her, but she remains stone-faced.

As we drive to the Upper West Side, Georgina begins to pay attention to the view. I know from reading about her that she lived here when she was newly married, and I wonder what kind of memories are racing through her mind.

I wish she was one of those older people who will share their stories ad nauseam with anyone who'll listen, but unfortunately, Georgina is the opposite of an open book.

She's a . . . closed book.

Creativity's a bit slow on the uptake this morning.

The driver, Eddie, parks the car, and Georgina looks at me. "We're getting out here?"

"Uh-huh."

She lifts her chin to look down at me. "If you're going to say yes to something, Kelsey, why don't you say it in proper English?"

I smile and ignore her, sliding toward the door as Eddie pulls it open. It makes me feel fancy. "Thank you, kind sir."

He smiles at me. "Have fun."

We start walking, and in just a few feet, I realize I'm going to have to pick up my pace to keep up with her. Kidney disease certainly hasn't slowed her down. At least not at this moment. She walks like a true New Yorker—with a purpose. Not looking around. Paying no attention to anyone or anything except her destination.

It's how I walk too, just not at such a brisk pace. When I first moved here, I was so worried about being viewed as an impostor that I studied the locals and mimicked what they did. Walking fast and with a purpose was the first habit I adopted.

That thought hits me. I was worried what others would think, so I walked faster.

I have a real hard time occupying my own space.

I don't want to do that anymore.

I put a hand on her arm. "Let's walk slower today."

She looks confused, as if I just asked her to go stand in that fountain over there. She sighs but does as I've asked. I resist the urge to loop my arm through hers like we're two little girls on the playground. We round the corner, and I stop and smile.

Georgina looks at me. "What exactly are we doing?"

"We're going to eat," I say nonchalantly.

She frowns suspiciously. "Where?"

I nod toward the corner. "A New York staple."

"Zabar's?"

"Uh-huh."

She gives me a look, I'm assuming because my answer wasn't in the King's English. I try not to sound like a tour guide with a few facts about the famed deli, but I can't help a good story.

"The original owner escaped war-torn Ukraine in the 1920s. Did you know he came to America through Canada? And that Cossack soldiers ransacked his house and murdered his father?"

Georgina recoils. "Is that supposed to make me hungry?"

"Their story is amazing. Plus, did you know this is where Jerry Seinfeld first told his wife he loved her?"

"Ludicrous," she says.

"No, it's true," I say. "Love at first sight, over bagels and lox."

"The whole idea of telling someone you love them over bagels and lox—ridiculous." She scoffs. "And love at first sight is not a real thing."

"Okay, so where is a good place to tell someone you love them?"

She deadpans, "At their funeral."

I laugh. "Oh, come *on*, Georgina. I'm sure you've told someone *who's alive* you love them."

"Of course I have," she says. "I've been in love lots of times."

I stop. My brain goes into overdrive trying to picture it—Georgina holding hands with a man, musical-theatre style, and gazing into his eyes as they sing a song from *Carousel*.

"If . . . I . . . loved youuuu . . ."

I shake my head. "Okay, so . . . what's the deal there? Who was it? I mean, they. Who were they? Was one of them in high school? Like a sweetheart?" Georgina was married once, but knowing her personality a little, I suppose I thought it was a contractual arrangement.

I just can't picture Georgina in love.

"Oh no." She laughs ruefully, continuing to walk. "You're a romantic. I should've guessed."

I quicken my pace to catch back up with her. "What's wrong with that?"

"I suppose you think there's one person for everyone, don't you?"

I feel like I have to defend my position. "Well . . . yeah. There should be. Someone who's just as messed up as you are, who is willing to love you, even though you're weird."

"So what's your story? Haven't found your person?"

"Apparently not," I say, noting the twinge of disappointment in my own voice. Which is silly because I'm not looking for a relationship right now.

Georgina glances up at me (because I'm at least four inches taller than she is). "Is 'finding the one' part of your Summer of Yes?" Then, mostly to herself, she mutters, "Good grief, I hope not."

"*No*," I say, defensive again. "I'm not looking."

"Solid choice."

And I wonder, yet again, about Georgina's love story.

"My parents found each other in college, fell immediately in love, and they've been together ever since," I say, talking with my hands. "I want something like *that*. Something . . . electric. Something that makes you feel on fire from the inside out. I just want it, like, two years from now."

"Ha. I'm sure the Almighty is up there taking notes on how he can meet your every romantic whim." Her tone drips sarcasm.

We walk up to Zabar's, and I marvel at how the name is everywhere on this building—which takes up half a block. A vertical sign on the building's corner, "Zabar's" in chunky salmon-colored letters in a brilliant font under every brick arch. Windows covered in labeled pictures of *Homemade Grilled Panini*, *Parmigiano Reggiano*, and *Hot & Fresh Knishes*.

I pull open the door and step inside. I've never been here. It's the opposite of modern and minimalist. More cluttered and outdated, but in an oddly trendy way.

Georgina steps inside behind me.

"Have you been here before?" I ask.

She looks around, almost like she's remembering something, then faces me. "Of course I have."

"Great, then you can tell me what to get."

"There are no chairs at the tables," she says. "Whatever we get, we have to take it outside to eat it."

"Great, we can eat on the way to the park."

"On the way to the . . ." She stops herself with a huff. "I don't eat on the street. And I don't walk in the city."

"Huh," I say. "Sounds like it's time to say yes to both of those things."

She turns toward the door. "This is ludicrous. I'm going back to the car."

I grab her arm to stop her. She looks down at my hand, and I instinctively remove it.

"Sorry, it's just that . . . well, Eddie's gone." I wince. Have I made a terrible mistake?

She frowns. "Well, I'll call to get him back."

I pull a face. "I told him you were giving him the day off."

"You *what*?"

"I think he has a whole day planned with his daughter." I smile. "Let's . . . make the best of it? Come on, tourists in our own city! Subways and cabs and delis."

"If you say, 'oh my,' I'm going to call the police."

I chuckle nervously. I *was* going to say that, but she doesn't need to know. "It's going to be so much fun."

"Can I help you?" A man behind the counter has focused his attention on us.

Georgina glares at me, then looks at the man. "I'll have a hot tea." She looks at me. "You should get the bacon, egg, and cheese sandwich."

"Why?"

"Because it's to die for."

"Then why don't you get it?"

"I don't eat bread. Or bacon."

I look at the man. "*Two* bacon, egg, and cheese sandwiches. And an affogato for me."

I've *never* gotten one of those—but ice cream drowned in espresso sounds too good to pass up.

"How are we going to eat sandwiches and drink our drinks walking down the street?" Georgina sounds exasperated.

"We're incredibly smart, capable, modern women," I say, giving some attitude right back to her. "I'm sure we'll figure it out."

The man gives us our total, and before I can reach for my purse, Georgina has slapped her credit card down on the counter. "I don't know how you're surviving in this city on an assistant editor's salary. You're certainly not going to buy my food."

I'm tempted to protest, but instead, I simply say, "Thank you."

It's strange. Georgina does kind things in an unkind way.

I might be filling in the blanks—again—but it's as though she's created a persona for herself, not letting the real Georgina Tate show through. Like it'll mess with the public perception of her, even though technically nobody would know but me.

I wonder if that's why her family fell apart.

I wonder about a lot of things that aren't my business.

Chapter 14

KELSEY

I DIDN'T REALIZE just how stubborn Georgina could be.

She's *Good Will Hunting* purposefully-don't-talk-for-an-hour-of-therapy stubborn.

Once we have our food, we start walking toward Central Park. It's not a long walk, but Georgina was right—there's no way to eat and drink and walk, so we focus on walking. "We can sit and eat when we get to the park."

"And what are we going to *do* in the park?" she asks.

"Whatever we want," I say.

"Does one of those things involve me going back home?"

And that is how the day goes. It's tiring, me forcing Georgina to do touristy things in the city she's called home since she was twenty years old.

I'd hoped she might open up to me, but no such luck. She's tight-lipped and closed off all day long. And frankly, she doesn't seem to enjoy herself. Mostly, I feel like I'm dragging her around, like a cat on a leash.

We don't get to all of the places on my list because we're both somewhat slow-moving, but we do get in some people watching in Central Park, a ride on the carousel (which Georgina is quick to say she absolutely hates), lunch at the Stardust Diner, and a trip to the top of the Empire State Building.

We stand there, on the observation deck, looking out over the world. I'm thinking about *Sleepless in Seattle*, and I glance at Georgina.

I hope she's just pretending not to be amazed by the view.

I mean, how could anyone not be? Looking out over a city with so much life, so much energy, quieted only by the distance from here to the ground. Surely it's having an effect on her. Right?

I know I can't force Georgina to feel things, and it would be smart for me to stop trying, but something within me is demanding that I not let it go.

A young woman walks up to us, looking a lot like I feel in Georgina's presence half the time—timid and unsure.

"You're Georgina Tate," she says, a little breathless.

I expect Georgina to say something sarcastic like, *"Well, thank you for telling me, I had no idea,"* but she doesn't.

She surprises me with a gracious smile. "That's correct."

"Could we . . . take a selfie?" the girl asks.

Georgina balks at this. My notoriously private companion wants nothing to do with a selfie.

I give her an encouraging smile and say, "I can take a picture of the two of you?"

"Would you?" The girl's smile covers her whole face. She gushes, "We're studying you in school. I'm a business major, and there's, like, a whole course on you."

Georgina glances at me, and I raise my eyebrows as if to say, *"Told you so."*

"Oh my gosh, you're a rock star, Miss Tate," the girl says. "My professor's never going to believe this."

Georgina is visibly uncomfortable with the flattery, and I intervene before she utters something unintentionally off-putting. "Okay, scooch together." I motion for Georgina to step closer to the girl, who seems unsure where to put her hands.

She settles for clutching her bag in front of her, and I hold the phone up to put them both in the frame.

Georgina Tate, the tiny powerhouse businesswoman and one of the many, many young women who admire her.

The girl says a few more gushy things before scurrying off, and Georgina looks at me.

"I never would've agreed to that," she says.

"But you said yes," I say.

"No, *you* said yes." She groans.

"And you made that girl's whole year."

"I don't know why," she says. "I've done absolutely nothing for her."

I shake my head. "If that were true, they wouldn't be giving you a Lifetime Achievement Award."

She snaps her gaze to mine. "How do you know about that?"

I hold up my phone and give it a shake. "I have Google."

She looks away. "Ridiculous."

"It's not ridiculous, and I don't have to tell you why," I say. "I know you know that what you've accomplished is uncommon. I know you know it inspires young women everywhere."

"I know no such thing," she says. "There's a lot more to a life than a business." She avoids looking at me. "You should learn that now, before . . ."

"Before I turn out like you?" The words are out quicker than I can stop them.

For a moment, I see hurt and regret in her eyes. Just a flash, then it's gone.

"I'm sorry. I think that's what I *am* trying to learn," I say, softer, hoping to smooth the moment over. Then, after a pause: "You're going, right? To the ceremony?"

"I plan to send my regrets," she says. "Kind, gracious regrets."

"Georgina, you have to go," I say.

She scoffs. "I don't *have* to do anything. That's the joy of being me."

I go quiet. "Are you sure? Because I—"

"Can we change the subject?" she pleads. "This is boring me."

But I don't want to change the subject. Because this *isn't* boring me. I want to know why she would avoid a ceremony where people are begging to honor her. It's not like she's the old man in *The Holiday*, worried she won't be able to walk up the stairs to accept her award for herself.

Despite having some significant health issues, Georgina is faring pretty well. At least on the outside. She's in her early seventies, but she looks younger, and I've been the one trying to keep up with her all day long. She even approached this day off like it was her job to do so.

There's a brief moment, standing up here on top of the world, where I think maybe—just *maybe*—she and I might've found a bit of common ground.

But then she turns to me and says, "Can we go home now?"

I pause. She looks tired, and I might've pushed her too hard. Plus, I don't want to bully her into doing this with me. The truth is, I might be including her simply because I'm afraid to tackle something so out of my wheelhouse by myself. But I also wish she were a little more willing, because somewhere, deep down, I believe we were thrown together in that hospital room for a reason.

It's probably silly. It's not like I believe in fate, and yet I can't shake the idea that there was a reason for our meeting.

"Of course," I say. "Let's go."

We walk into the elevator and out onto the street, where I notice Eddie is standing beside the car, waiting for us.

"You called Eddie," I say.

"I have no interest in walking all the way back home," she says. "The taxi you made me ride in was filthy. And I make no apologies for saying a flat no to the subway."

Eddie opens the car door, and Georgina slides in. I make my way to the opposite side of the car and join her in the back seat.

"Look," I say, after we've been driving in silence for a couple of minutes. "I understand that you don't like people to fuss over you, but this is a huge honor. Are you worried accepting a Lifetime Achievement Award is like signaling the end of your career?"

"No, my kidneys are signaling the end of my career," she says.

I glance at Eddie, who seems unfazed by this, and I realize he's probably also signed an NDA.

"Okay, but isn't that more of a reason to go?" I ask. "Go out on a high note?"

"I have no interest in accepting an award in front of a bunch of strangers, many of whom have not wished me well on this journey. It's all so fake and pretentious."

"You could invite whoever you wanted," I tell her. "Make sure the front row is filled with people who love you."

"People who love me," she repeats with a scoff. "There are no people who fit that description. And frankly, I don't need a big ceremony to remind me of it." She turns away, staring out the window as dusk begins to shade New York City.

There's an early moon overhead that cuts through the buildings, appearing intermittently between each structure as we drive in silence toward her apartment.

And I hear what she's not saying.

She doesn't want to accept an award without anyone she loves there to cheer her on. And I get it. I wouldn't either. I think, and not for the first time, that Georgina is a cautionary tale.

This is a picture of my life if I stay on my current path.

Saying no to every single thing that scares me.

Maybe that is the only reason we were thrown together in the hospital. Maybe I'm trying to put too much weight on this coincidence when it's as simple as that.

Now, standing inside the entryway of her condo, JP meets us wearing the look of a parent who stayed up past midnight waiting for their teenager to come home when they said they'd be home at eleven.

Georgina passes by him and doesn't say another word to me, and when we're alone, her assistant glares at me.

"That was too much for her today."

"We took lots of breaks," I say, knowing that while it's true, it probably wasn't enough.

He presses. "I appreciate what you're trying to do here, but Georgina doesn't need to go gallivanting all over the city. Not in her current state."

I sigh. I think JP is right. Georgina needs something else entirely.

A thought hits me.

And JP isn't going to like it.

Chapter 15

KELSEY

JP OPENS THE door to usher me back into the hallway and out of his sight, but I don't move.

"Wait," I say. "I have an idea. And I need your help."

He pushes the door ever so slightly wider, tilting his head toward the hall.

I choose to ignore his not-so-subtle signal.

"Tell me what you know about Georgina's son."

He looks past me, as if I've just spoken aloud He Who Must Not Be Named. He lowers his voice. "We don't talk about . . . personal things in Miss Tate's house."

"Then let's go out into the hallway." I cross my arms like a petulant child, determined to get my way. "Come on, JP, I signed an NDA. I can't tell anyone. Just tell me what you know."

"I . . . can't," he says. He looks genuinely concerned.

"Look, JP, I think she has some serious regrets. I know they're estranged. I know she hasn't spoken to him in a really long time." I lean in. "What I don't know is *why*."

"Everyone has regrets," he says.

"But these are the kind of regrets that can be fixed."

He scoffs, and when his eyes return to mine, his face falls. "Oh, you're serious."

I frown.

"I can't help you," he says. "Now, you need to go so I can catch Miss Tate up on everything she missed today because you insisted on"—he says this next bit as if it's painful—"going to the park."

"She doesn't need to be working right now," I say. "Don't you think it's important they reconnect? Before . . . you know."

He sighs. "Attempts have been made." He says this like he's speaking in code.

"Okay . . . what does that mean?"

"He's made it very clear he does not want to reciprocate." He eyes me. "And it's really none of your business."

That is a fair point. And maybe I shouldn't prod, but once a story has piqued my interest, it's very hard for me to let it drop. I pause for a moment, then say, "I think I saw him."

"What? Where?"

"At the hospital," I say. "There was a man lurking outside her room."

"What did he look like?"

A model? A Hemsworth? My dessert?

"Um . . . he was . . . very, um . . . good-looking," I say, verbally tripping on my shoelaces. "He's the right age and, I don't know, he kind of looked like her."

JP looks away, dramatically this time, like this is news he needs to process.

I pause. "Help me find him."

He huffs, then pulls me out into the hallway, closing the door behind him. He looks around, comically so, like in the movies when someone thinks the room is bugged. Because I'm not sure what else to do, I join him, scanning the empty hallway.

"What are we looking for?"

He shakes his head, then levels with me. "What I'm about to tell you needs to be kept in the *strictest* of confidences."

I kiss three fingers on my right hand and hold them up. "Scout's honor."

He pauses. "That's the Mockingjay salute."

I am taken aback. "I actually love you a little more that you know that."

"I'm not a savage," he muses, then turns serious again. "Promise me."

I nod.

He takes a breath. "He lives in a beach town in North Carolina. His father moved him there when he was a child. He wanted to make sure Hayden grew up outside the city. And, I think, away from this life." Then, more pointedly, he adds, "He kept him from Miss Tate."

"Wow," I say, trying to take it all in. "How do you know all this?"

"I know *everything*, Kelsey."

"That's not shocking."

"I also know she's still married," he adds.

I widen my eyes at him. "Wait. Georgina? She's what?"

"They never actually went through with the divorce."

"That's insane—hasn't it been years?"

"Twenty-two, to be precise."

"What in the world . . . ?" My thoughts wander back to Georgina being in love. "Do you think she still loves him?"

He shrugs. "I think she loves her work." Then, after a pause, he adds, "But I also think you might be headed in the right direction."

"If you believe that, then you have to help me," I say. "I have an idea, but it's risky."

He eyes me. "How risky?"

"Well . . . maybe the less I say, the better." I also have an unrelated thought. "I found an invitation to an awards ceremony at the end of the summer, for a Lifetime Achievement Award."

"It's on my schedule to handle that this week."

"Can you accept it instead?"

"Absolutely not," he says. "I like my job and I need the dental."

"Come on. Can't you just trust me?"

He looks at me like I just asked him to hop on this magic flying carpet I just so happen to have. "I think you're in the middle of some weird postaccident pre-midlife crisis, and I don't want Miss Tate to get caught up in it."

"I am not," I say. "I'm just having . . . an awakening. I need to change my life."

"Do you know the definition of 'midlife crisis'?" He eyes me, then sighs. "How does nosing around Miss Tate's business change your life? What's in this for you?"

I shrug. "I can't explain it. I feel like we both landed in that hospital room on that day for a reason. It's like . . . I don't know, like fate. I feel like we're *meant* to do this together. Or maybe I'm supposed to help her or something." I sigh. "Nobody else will."

He shakes his head. "I think this is dangerous. She won't like being ambushed."

"Well, I'm not asking her permission," I say. "If you can find out what town her son lives in, that would help."

"I know what town he lives in," he says. "She'll never admit it, but she does keep tabs on him. And the lawyers have been trying to get in touch with him, given her . . . situation."

I smile. "Can you send me the address?"

He draws in a breath.

"Come on, JP," I say. "Let's do something great for her."

He makes a production of pulling out his phone, scrolling around in his Notes app, and locating the address for Georgina's son.

"Why do you have it on your phone?" I ask as he screenshots it, then AirDrops it to me.

"Because when she dies, I'm in charge of contacting her family," he says, as if I should've put that together.

The thought is morbid, and I hate it. "Is she really dying?"

"She's on the transplant list, but they're not hopeful," he says. "She's got a rare blood type—AB."

"Why doesn't she talk to her family about it?" I ask.

"She doesn't speak to them," he says, like I'm a complete idiot. "She's not going to ask for a *kidney*."

"Fair point," I say.

"She has her reasons," he says. "And those, you need to respect. Can you imagine how Hayden would feel if she showed up after all this time? 'Hey, kiddo, it's been twenty years, but could I bum a kidney off of you?'"

I do understand. I'm dangerously close to crossing a line, but a woman's life is at stake here, not to mention her legacy.

"Still," I say. "There is a chance that someone else will step up. I mean, I could be tested. Or you?"

He shakes his head. "Her doctor put her on the transplant list, but she has a very rare tissue type as well. And she will absolutely not go looking for a living donor. If there's one thing I know about Miss Tate, it's that she is a very proud woman."

"Yeah, well, that's all fine until she ends up six feet under."

He shrugs. "I've already told you way too much."

"Yeah, but I think secretly you loved it." I smile at him. "You care about her. It's pretty obvious."

His expression changes and he looks almost touched. And then Georgina calls his name from behind the closed door, and his expression changes back.

"I'll see you tomorrow," I say.

"Oh joy." His tone is dry. "You're coming back."

"*Summer* of Yes, JP," I say. "You'd better get used to me."

"I can't wait."

Chapter 16

GEORGINA

I'M ACHY, AND I hate it.

I'm old, and I hate that too.

Youth is wasted on the young, according to George Bernard Shaw. He also went on to say that the young people of his day were "brainless, and don't know what they have."

Some days I couldn't agree more.

The morning after my outdoor excursion with Kelsey, I move slowly. I'm exhausted. If saying yes to someone half my age is going to be this tiring, I'm going to have to set some ground rules.

I have no interest in ticking boxes off her bucket list. Especially when they are things *she* thinks are fun or important when I absolutely do not.

She's also perfectly content using up all her vacation time— unfortunately, I don't have the same luxury. I have a company to run. A successor to choose.

A funeral to plan.

I hope to wait on that last one.

I don't hear from Kelsey all day. I should be thrilled, but I find myself moderately disappointed.

I'm not sure what to make of that.

But early the next morning when I'm hooked up to the blasted dialysis machine, I hear the knock on the door followed by her much-too-chipper morning voice.

If Kelsey had a theme song, it would be "Walking on Sunshine," which I loathe.

And yet I can't ignore the fact that I'm a little relieved she's returned.

Not that I'd ever tell her that.

I know Kelsey is in the middle of some sort of awakening, and she probably sees me as a project of sorts, and I'll roll my eyes about that all day long . . . but the truth is, I could use a little awakening myself.

The machine I'm shackled to and my few stays in the hospital have given me too much time to think.

And "being alone with my thoughts" is hardly my favorite pastime. She is, at the very least, a distraction.

"JP, pack Georgina's bags," Kelsey is saying as she walks into the library where I'm sitting. Then, to me: "We're going on a trip!"

"There is no way—" JP is always a little neurotic, but right now, he seems downright worried.

"Pack her up for a week," Kelsey says, cutting him off.

"Kelsey, she can't be gone for a whole week," JP says, then nods to me. "Georgina has dialysis and—"

"I spoke with her doctor," Kelsey says. "He said she's fine to travel if she takes the machine with her. She can do dialysis a few times a week and it'll be just like being here. Only . . . out there."

"You spoke with her doctor?" JP asks incredulously.

"Uh-huh."

She looks at me. Despite her assault on proper English, I remain quiet, secretly amused by the way she pushes his buttons.

"I had to get him to speak in hypotheticals because he couldn't tell me anything specific about Georgina. And I had to pretend to be her caretaker, but yes."

"*I* am her caretaker." If JP had pearls, he would clutch them. "I've met with her doctor myself."

She grins, mischief on her face. "Apparently, you are utterly forgettable." Then, to me, "Are you ready, Georgina?"

"She hasn't even had breakfast yet," he protests. "Or her morning tea."

She holds up a brown paper bag with the Zabar's logo across the front of it. "And there's tea waiting for her in the car."

JP looks at me. "I'm sorry, Miss Tate. I'll find a way to get her out of here."

I detach myself from the machine and walk over to the window. When I peek outside, I see a blue Mustang convertible parked in front of the building. *My* blue Mustang convertible.

"Kelsey," I say calmly.

JP stops trying to push the poor girl out of the room and stands back, probably waiting for me to give it to her the same way I would any other employee.

But Kelsey isn't my employee. And I haven't seen that car in ages.

"How exactly did you get my car out of storage?"

She slides around JP and bounces over to the window where I'm standing. "Do you really want to know?"

"Yes," I say. "I need to know who to fire."

"Then I'm not saying a word," she says.

"Is that why you were here yesterday?" JP asks. "You snooped through the office, didn't you?"

She shrugs, but the cat-with-a-bird-in-its-mouth look tells me all I need to know.

Kelsey is resourceful.

I'm impressed. "JP, could you please pack a suitcase for me?"

"You can't be serious," he says.

I respond with a pointed glare.

"Should I pack one for myself too?" JP asks.

"Kelsey?" I ask. "Should he?"

She shakes her head. "Sorry, JP, this is a girls' trip."

He looks genuinely rejected, but he disappears, leaving me standing in the library with the girl. "I should have you arrested for stealing my car."

"I didn't *steal* it," she corrects. "I just . . . delivered it."

I turn to her. "I didn't ask you to do that."

"But you're happy I did." She points at me.

Maybe I am. But I would never tell her that. "Should I call Eddie?"

"Georgina, it's a *girls'* trip." Kelsey sits down in the armchair. "Do you know how to pack up that machine?"

"Where are we going?"

"Don't know. I thought we'd just pick a direction and drive," she says. "I've never done a road trip without my parents, so I feel like it's time."

"You really are a child," I say, knowing it's not true. Then, when she doesn't respond, I ask, "Do we have a map?"

"Nope."

"A plan?"

"Uh-uh."

"I don't do things without a plan," I say. "Especially not trips."

"Today you do."

I turn to the window to peer out at the car again.

The last time I saw it was when I put it in storage. After Dylan left, I didn't want to stare at it every day. I tried to get him to come and get it, but he claimed he didn't want it. Said it was a gift I gave him out of guilt.

And he was right.

I knew it was his dream car, and when the business started making money, I felt guilty for spending so much time at the office. So much time away from him and Hayden. So I bought it for him, like a shiny distraction to make up for the fact that I'd stopped putting them first.

People don't leave quickly, but they do leave suddenly.

It's the pot and the frog and the boiling water. You have no idea your relationship is slowly dying.

And then, suddenly, they were gone. And I was alone.

With a shiny blue Mustang convertible.

It went into storage not long after they left. I couldn't bring myself to sell it, but there was no sense keeping the reminder of my failure right out in plain view.

Still, as I stare down at it from the comfort of my condo, I don't feel sad. I can still hear Hayden's loud belly laughs as we took the car out on the rare occasion I found the time. I can remember long nights curled up in the back seat under a blanket, looking up at the stars, safe in Dylan's strong arms.

I lied the other day when I told Kelsey I'd loved many people in my lifetime.

I lied when I said I didn't believe in love at first sight.

I don't know why I do that. Like I'm protecting some truth about myself because if people found out I'm just like them, I'd be diminished in their eyes or something.

For me, the second I met that man, I knew I would never love anyone else.

And then I slowly but suddenly lost him.

The car is a reminder of that. And the feelings it conjures are ones I usually say no to. Ones I usually push aside. I don't like to dwell on the past or anything that didn't go my way.

But maybe I'm supposed to let myself feel some of these things.

Maybe it's the first time I've felt human in a really, really long time.

So that's why I say yes to Kelsey's proposed adventure. Because being human feels good, even though it simultaneously feels bad. Because it feels necessary. Because a part of me wants to carve my name in a giant, sturdy oak tree as if to say: *Georgina was here*.

About a half hour later, JP emerges with two packed suitcases and another bag, along with my dialysis machine and all the medicines I take to keep my body from staging a revolt. We pack everything into the trunk, and Kelsey slides into the driver's seat looking like an excited teenager with the keys to her parents' car.

"What am I supposed to do while you're gone?" JP asks.

"Take the week off, JP," I say.

His eyes dart to Kelsey, then back to me. "Miss Tate, are you going to fire me? Because I don't think Kelsey will be as good at my job as I am."

Kelsey laughs. "I don't want your job, JP!"

"Nobody is firing anyone," I tell him. "But you should take the week for yourself."

"Say yes to some things!" Kelsey says.

He shoots daggers at her, and she blows him a kiss.

"Yes," I say. "Do that, JP. And don't worry, I'll still pay you for your time. And I'll keep you posted on my whereabouts. Forward Kelsey all the emergency info, and we should be good for a few days."

He looks stunned by my instructions.

I admit, I'm a little stunned myself.

I get into the car, leaving him standing on the sidewalk, and face Kelsey.

"Are you ready to say yes to adventure?" she asks with a bright smile.

"Are you going to smile the whole time?" I retort.

"Maybe I am," she says with a crazed look on her face.

I bite back a smile of my own. She may be certifiable, but there is something to admire there.

Could just be that she's a lunatic.

I take a breath. I'm ready. Ready to feel alive again, for the first time in a long time. I don't know where we're going or what we're doing, but shockingly, I've decided to turn my hands up toward the sky and accept whatever this road decides to bring me.

I just hope Kelsey knows how to drive a stick.

Chapter 17

KELSEY

THANKFULLY MY PARENTS taught me how to drive a stick.

It turns out, too, that road trips are kind of boring.

Georgina fell asleep about forty-five minutes after we left.

It might be better this way, if she doesn't ask questions or interject. And while I drive, I think about the revelations that have struck me since my accident.

Some of the things I feel led to do—take time off work, for instance—are easy. Other things—waking up dreams I've let die—not so much.

Last night, after talking to Georgina's doctor, sweet-talking her car out of storage with a few little white lies, and packing myself for a weeklong adventure down the East Coast, I did pull out my laptop. And I tried. I tried to conjure words, stories, anything that might make me different from everyone else in the world. Any way to find my own voice on the off chance that the internal monologue that keeps showing up at the back of my mind is something other than lunacy.

But nothing came. I was hopelessly, utterly *blank*.

But now, as I drive, words form in my mind. Words that tell a story. Words that won't leave me alone. It's as if there's a voiceover to the memories I'm replaying in my head—the accident. The hospital. Georgina. The penguins. The Summer of Yes.

It's the story that's been brewing inside me ever since the accident happened.

It's the story I've been tamping down, and somehow it feels disrespectful to do that now, when it's here, on the surface, demanding to be told.

And it's mine.

Years ago, I used to process my feelings by writing them down. Almost as if nothing made sense until I saw it in ink on the page.

I abandoned that idea. I realized that the stories I told—real or fictional—were nothing more than the musings of a silly girl. I didn't need a career as a writer, baring my soul and exploring my emotions. I needed a diary.

But in time, I even abandoned that. I don't write anymore.

Whoever said words are powerful wasn't kidding. Words had the power to change the course of my life. Six little words, in fact.

"You don't have what it takes."

Words like that, when you believe them, change everything.

But with several years between me and those words, I have to wonder—could new words change my life now?

The words that race through my mind. Words that tell my story.

They don't have to be publicly consumed. They can simply be for me.

At the thought, my insides buzz. This is a revelation I must say yes to. Not because anyone told me I had to, but because *I* know, in the deepest recesses of my soul, that this is what I need to do.

I need to process what happened, what *is* happening to me. And I had forgotten the joy of doing that through my writing.

My writing. It's been years since I've had "writing." I've turned all my focus and attention to other people's words. Because while I may not have what it takes to craft them myself, I can recognize when they are brilliant. And because that has been a safer route.

Beside me, Georgina stirs, and the words go into a quiet scroll at the back of my mind.

"Where are we?"

It's been hours since we left New York City, and the traffic has been hairy. If I'm honest, it's the opposite of relaxing, and I'm starting to feel twitchy.

"We're in Virginia," I say. "But I need a break from driving."

"Well, I don't drive anymore," she says. "So you're on your own."

"You don't drive, as in, you don't know how?"

"I have Eddie, so I don't need to drive."

"But you do know how," I say, exiting the interstate.

"Of course."

"Good, then you can take a turn."

She lets out a groan. "Why don't we just stop for the day?"

"We can stop, but maybe after you drive."

"Kelsey," Georgina says firmly. "I'm not driving."

"Then I guess we're sleeping in the car." I grin over at her, and she rolls her eyes. I know nobody else in her orbit would ever give her an ultimatum, but for some reason, Georgina doesn't scare me anymore. Perhaps because I'm one of the few people who knows about her failing health. Or because I've seen her at her most fragile, hooked up to the machine she needs to keep her alive.

I get out of the car and put the top down on Georgina's convertible. She sits still as a statue in the front seat.

"You're like an eight-year-old who has to push every button in the car," Georgina says after I finish taking the top down.

"Come on, Georgina—don't you want to do something you haven't done in years?"

She doesn't say anything.

"Think about how fun it will be behind the wheel, feeling the warm wind blowing through your hair."

"I'm not in a Pantene commercial," she says.

"Look, I just white-knuckled it all the way through D.C.," I say. "I need a break."

After a pause, she says, "Fine, but I'm not going on the interstate."

I hesitate. "But . . . that's the route."

I pray I haven't just given everything away. I lied earlier when I said I had no map and no plan.

She gets out of the car and faces me. She might be tiny, but I still shrink a bit. She just has that kind of presence. "Do you really want to go on the interstate with someone who hasn't driven a car in years?"

"Actually, that's a good point."

The problem is that we have a schedule that Georgina doesn't know about.

We need to get to the tiny coastal town of Driftwood, North Carolina, where her son, Hayden, lives as quickly as possible to allow them time to reconnect.

This is the plan.

But it's a plan that included the interstate.

The old me, the story-weaving worrywart, switches on. What if we get way off course? What if we lose hours on these back roads? What if we break down next to some banjo-playing locals?

What if she gets fed up and demands to go back home and then she and Hayden never reconnect? This whole trip will have been for nothing.

"Not so sure about your detour now, are you?" She eyes me. "I don't know you well yet, Kelsey, but I do know that you like to overthink things. You're a planner, like me, and just like me, you don't like when your plans are disrupted."

"You're not wrong," I say.

"And don't think for a second that I don't know you have a destination in mind."

I swallow. "I don't know what you're talking about."

"You're a terrible liar." She shakes her head at me. "I might not know exactly *where*, but I do know we aren't just driving aimlessly."

She stands there, unnerving me.

"I'm willing to go along—for the time being—but if this place ends up being bungee jumping or parasailing or God-knows-what, I'm taking a flight home."

I breathe a sigh of relief. As long as she thinks I'm bucket-listing my way through this trip, my Driftwood plan is safe.

"The way I see it, you've been very content to upend my life, but taking your vacation time isn't actually you saying yes to anything."

"That's not true," I say. "I took the day to walk around the zoo. I went sightseeing with you—I'd never do that normally. And I went to Ravi's big, noisy family dinner."

"And yet you're still focused on me. This car, this trip, me driving." She almost seems to be issuing a challenge. "I'll say yes to you if you say yes to me. No interstate."

"Fine, Georgina, but it's going to take longer," I say.

"Isn't that the point, Kelsey?" she asks, a hint of sarcastic teasing in her tone. "To take the long way? To enjoy the journey? Smell the roses and whatever other stupid cliché you want to throw at me?"

"Fine." I hold out the keys. Her eyes land on them quickly, then back on me.

"Good."

"Good."

"Fine." Georgina wraps a scarf around her hair. Her big, round, black sunglasses remind me of a 1960s movie star. Her driving reminds me of a very nervous fifteen-year-old working on her permit with her mom in the passenger seat.

And I am the mom.

We start out onto the smaller highway, and after a bumpy start, muscle memory kicks in, and Georgina begins to relax.

So I begin to relax.

And we just . . . drive.

There's something much more interesting about the highway, and while being off the beaten path and letting go of my agenda feel unnatural to me, I try to tell myself that Georgina's snarky reminder is true—this is the point.

But then Georgina goes even more off schedule, following signs to a completely unplanned stop—Colonial Williamsburg.

"What are we doing?" I ask as we pull into town.

"Saying yes to a billboard back there that said, 'Don't you want to see history?'" Again, her tone mocks. I'm not sure why she's put up with me this long when she clearly isn't buying into any of this, but here we are. "I'm also saying yes to my bladder."

"But nothing will be open," I tell her. "It's getting late."

"That's where you're wrong," Georgina says. "I don't listen to most of what JP says, but I do like to eavesdrop when I'm hooked up to that boring machine." She stops at a red light. "Two weeks ago, he was talking to his sister about her trip to Colonial Williamsburg."

"I didn't peg you for a history buff," I say.

"I'm fascinated by history," she says. And I'm noticing there's a different tone to her voice.

It's brighter.

She adds, "Especially when it's haunted."

"Wait, what?"

"JP mentioned Haunted Williamsburg." The light turns green. "I thought it could be fun."

"Fun?"

"Are you nervous?"

"No!" But after I answer and see Georgina's reaction, I realize that I said it too loudly. I try to save face. "There's no such thing as ghosts."

"You don't sound so sure." Georgina grins, a bit evilly. "You're scared, aren't you?"

"Pshh. Not at all," I lie. I am nervous. I don't like haunted anything.

Once, when I was twelve, Ravi and I went to a fall carnival where we made the stupid mistake of wandering into a haunted corn maze.

The people dressed as scarecrows and zombies and serial killers jumping out and terrifying me stuck with me for years. One guy followed me around, crawling on all fours, making low-pitched groaning sounds, and I'm pretty sure I actually died for a few seconds that night.

If I thought about it long enough right now, I would wet my pants.

I would never *intentionally* put myself in a situation like that again.

It's the Summer of Yes but the Halloween of No Thank You.

"Maybe we could just, you know, find a good hotel, eat dinner, get some sleep," I offer. "Then we can be fresh for the morning."

"Well now, that sounds an awful lot like a no to me." She smiles. Not to me but to herself.

The tables have turned.

Crap.

Georgina is giving me a dose of my own medicine. I've been bulldozing her into saying yes to everything that pops into my head, and now she's taking back the control.

I don't stand a chance.

As soon as I see the tagline for the candlelit tour—The Fun Doesn't End When the Sun Goes Down—my whole body puckers.

Five minutes in, I'm chilled to the bone without even the slightest jump scare. Story is the quickest way to grip me, and these actors on this ghost tour easily do their job.

It's spooky and eerie and fascinating. And, yes, terrifying.

When it's all done, Georgina looks unfazed. "That was fun, but you look terrible."

"I don't like scaring myself," I say.

"How about that," she counters. "Just like I don't like leaving the comfort of my beautiful condo overlooking Central Park."

I roll my eyes but find myself smiling. "So this was payback then?"

"Absolutely," Georgina says, then drops the keys into my hand. "You're driving us to a hotel. And not some dumpy one either. I'm not sleeping on a glorified cot."

That night, after Georgina dozes off, I stare at the ceiling, willing myself to sleep.

It's at this point that my creative brain starts to wake up.

It's been so long since I've written anything down—but ever since the accident, it's like the Great Gum Machine in Wonka's lab, churning out seven-course meals in bite-sized pieces.

Getting hit by a car while walking on the sidewalk wasn't on my to-do list today. I don't think it's on anyone's to-do list, but for some reason, it rammed its way onto mine, ironically between "Get Coffee" and "Go to Hospital."

The words keep rolling through my mind, sentence after sentence, recounting my entire experience thus far, and something inside me thrums.

Write it down.

But I don't write anymore.

Just say yes, Kelsey.

Fine, brain. You win.

I slip out of bed, drag my laptop into the bathroom, and write down the words that have been nagging at me all day.

I conjure all the fears, real and imagined, and roll them around in my mind. My fingers fly across the keyboard, recording the thoughts of the story I'm living like a court reporter and adding comedic prose like a stand-up comic. Some of these sentences are absolute darlings, and it's been ages since I felt that way.

The next time I glance at the clock, an hour and a half has gone by.

I scroll through the pages I've just written, unsure of what this even is. I don't have an interesting enough life to write my own memoir, so what is the point? Why would anyone care about my Summer of Yes?

As before, a mental cog falls into place and things fit.

Maybe this is something I need to write for myself.

It's processing things the best way I know how. Nobody will ever see these words, so it's safe to write it all down any way I see fit.

Not for public consumption. Not to be judged. Just for me.

Now, with the words out of my brain and onto the page, my mind's machine whirs to a halt and goes quiet.

And for the first time in *years* . . . I feel like I'm alive again.

Chapter 18

KELSEY

Beep. Beep.
 Click. Drip.
 Whirrrrr.
 Click. Drip.

I'm stirred to that moment between sleep and wakefulness, where the best dreams happen and you slowly become aware of how the blanket feels.

The sounds become clearer, a *whir* and then something like *flip-click*, repeating rhythmically as if on a wheel, and I sit up, unsure of where I am or what time it is.

I force my bleary eyes to focus, and I see Georgina, quietly sitting next to her dialysis machine.

She's got her iPad out, glasses on, and I'm guessing she's not watching *The Real Housewives of New York*.

It's clear after just a day on the road with Georgina that while JP thinks he's irreplaceable, she doesn't really need anyone but herself.

"Are you okay?" I ask.

She doesn't look up. "Good morning to you too."

"Sorry," I say. "The noises of the machine reminded me of . . ." I shake that train of thought to a stop. "Good morning."

She draws in a breath. "I need tea."

By Georgina's request, we ended up in a very fancy hotel. Much fancier than I'm used to. Thankfully, she paid for it. Perks of a wealthy traveling companion.

I get to reap the benefits of a five-star suite.

I throw off the covers—and the memories of the hospital— and use the in-room Keurig to make myself a cup of coffee and Georgina a cup of tea.

"There's probably a coffee shop close by," I say. "Or the hotel has a restaurant. We can get some breakfast before we hit the road."

"Fine."

"How long do you have to sit there?" I ask, handing her the tea. "Doing dialysis, I mean."

"Four hours," she grumbles.

My eyes go wide. "You sit in the same spot for four hours?"

"Three days a week. I can't stand it. I've already got three hours in. I have to get up before the sun and sit here. Thinking."

I frown. "You don't like to think?"

"I don't like to dwell."

I get that.

But since the conception and implementation of the Summer of Yes, I've been *wanting* to think. And dwell. And create, and write, and dream.

Maybe I should get up before the sun.

Before I get coffee in the morning, I tend to have no filter. A thought hits me, and it's out of my mouth before I can stop it. "Do you ever feel like you're not really living?"

Georgina sighs, a bit melodramatically, and sags her head back against the chair. "This again?" she asks. "Didn't I already tell you I don't want to be a part of your pre-midlife crisis?"

"You did," I say. "But you've got an hour left and I haven't fully woken up yet, so . . ." I raise my mug in a mock toast.

"Great," she grouses.

I take a sip. It's actually not bad for hotel coffee. Maybe this is what five stars gets you.

"I know you and JP talked about me," I say, remembering his reference to my "awakening."

She shrugs. "Yes. We did. He wanted to warn me you're going through something, and I told him I wanted nothing to do with it."

"I am," I admit. "Going through something. It's not a crisis, and it's not crazy, but it is something. I feel like I'm waking up." I take another drink. "I'm looking at what I've been doing, what I've been working toward, and I'm realizing that none of it really matters. None of it excites me."

She clicks her iPad off, folds the cover, and sets it down. Then something on her face changes. The frown goes away; her shoulders relax.

"Listen," she says. "I think you have to find the things that fulfill you. Energize you. No matter what life you make for yourself, find some margin for those kinds of things."

I already know what that is for me.

The familiar worry spiral starts spinning. "What if you're not good at that thing?"

Her brows knit together in a straight line. "Who says you have to be good at it?"

"What's the point of doing something if you're not good at it? And what if people think you're crazy for trying?"

She laughs. "You're asking the wrong person," she says. "I've never much cared what other people think."

Oh, if only it were that easy.

The Summer of Yes is great for trying new things and discovering new places, but can it answer this question: *Can I stop worrying about what others think?*

After a sip of tea, she adds, "I believe if something makes you happy, it's not a waste of time. Nobody says it has to make you money. People do have hobbies."

"Do *you* have hobbies?"

She looks out the window. "I did. Not anymore."

"But you used to?"

She sighs. "When I had time. It seems I'm not so good at following my own advice," she says ruefully.

My mind flashes a bunch of different diversions and leisurely pursuits that Georgina could gravitate toward, each one becoming increasingly more outlandish and bizarre.

Georgina, taking up archery, but with her competitors' faces as the targets.

Georgina, spearfishing sea urchins off the coast of Hawaii.

Georgina, live-action role-playing on the open, expansive fields of Norway, dressed as a Tolkienesque dwarf, decked out in body armor and weapons.

"I used to paint."

Yeah. That makes more sense than larping.

I'm intrigued. "You did?"

She smiles a nostalgic, faraway smile. "Years ago. My word, it's been ages."

"Why'd you stop?"

She looks a mix of serious and forlorn. "Time."

I sit with that answer for a moment, then say, "You should pick it up again."

She tilts her head at me as if to say, *"Come on."*

"I'm serious. If it's what made you happy, at least at one point in your life, you should do it. Now makes the most sense."

"Now makes the *least* sense." She holds up the thin, clear tube attached to her side. "I'm trying to tell you things that *you* should do, not things that *I* have done. I wish I made more time for that kind of stuff, if I'm honest."

A cautionary tale. She does have regrets.

She shifts in her chair. "And what about you?"

"What about me?"

"Why don't you write more?"

Now I frown. "How do you know I write?"

"Please, your pecking on the keyboard kept me awake until midnight," she says. "What are you working on anyway?"

"It's nothing," I say, suddenly protective and a little defensive. "Just . . . you know. Some thoughts."

"Ah." She looks out the window again. Without looking back at me, she says, "And who told you that you were no good?"

Wow, she just read my mind. I don't answer.

"Was it someone important to you? A teacher—someone in a position of authority?" she asks.

I hesitate, but decide that Georgina just might understand, even if it's hard to imagine anyone ever criticizing her.

"My favorite professor," I admit. "He was sort of my mentor all through college."

"So you quit, just like that, because someone told you you should."

"I didn't quit," I say. "I just . . . pivoted."

"You quit." Georgina turns her iPad back on, as if to dismiss me. "You'll never be happy if you listen to what everyone else says about you, Kelsey. It's what *you* say about you that matters."

"My parents would say it's what God says about you."

Her eyes flick to mine. "What does God say about you? That you should quit?"

"Doesn't sound like God, no."

"It's a wild and precious life, Kelsey. If you have something that sets your soul on fire, you have a responsibility to chase that thing."

"You sound like my mother." This is the second time someone has said that phrase to me. Maybe I need to pay attention.

Georgina nods once definitively. "Smart lady."

I pause, then ask, "So what sets your soul on fire?"

She goes still, then looks at me. "You're not writing my memoir, are you?"

I frown. "Of course not."

"Okay, because that's strictly forbidden by that little legal document you signed."

"I know, Georgina," I say. "I'm not asking you this so I can write a tell-all. I'm asking as your friend."

The machine clicks and whirs and hums, and there's silence between us for several seconds. I expect her to correct me, to remind me that we're not friends, but instead, she seems content to ponder my question.

"It used to be my business," she says. "There was nothing like climbing that ladder. Proving people wrong. I set big quarterly goals for my company, and when I reached them, I set more. It was exhilarating. I don't regret that."

I sit on the edge of the bed, facing her. "But you do have regrets." I know this because she told me she did.

"Some."

"Personal ones."

She's back to looking out the window. "Some."

She's still again for several seconds, the silence filled only by the noise of the machine. "We used to have this old boat. It was my dad's. Nothing fancy, but we worked on it together to fix it up like new. He named it the *Georgina*." Her smile is tinged with sadness. "My dad was a good man. A down-to-earth, blue-collar kind of guy. Everyone loved him, but he almost never knew how he was going to pay the bills."

I conjure a picture of him. Warm smile, rough hands.

"In the beginning, he was the reason I worked so hard. Because I wanted him to be able to retire. And I wanted to thank him for taking care of me for so many years. In those days, when I was newly married and barely making it, my husband, Dylan, and I would take that boat out on the weekends. No agenda. No plan. We'd just go out on the water."

And then she disappears in her memory. I see the moment it happens. My mind fills in the blanks left by her wistful silence, and she's back there, on the water, filled up by the sound of laughter and the smell of fresh, salty air. She's basking in the warm sun on the deck of the *Georgina*.

She's *alive.*

"This was before Tate Cosmetics went public, before all the pressure and the stress and the thrill and the rush. Those days out on the water are the ones that filled me up and kept me going. I don't know why I ever let myself stop . . ." She trails off.

"I don't know why I ever let myself stop." Those words wind themselves around my soul.

I feel the same way about writing.

Why did I ever stop?

As many regrets as I have, not prioritizing my friends and family is at the top of the list. I imagine it's ten times worse for Georgina.

Which is the whole point of this trip, even though she doesn't know it.

"I'll shower quick," I say. "And then we can get you a real cup of tea."

"Good," she says. "This tastes like minty pond water."

Chapter 19

KELSEY

On the road again. Thanks, Willie Nelson, for that earworm.

We spend another day driving. We're off course, but I choose not to mind.

We drive with the top down, and I relish the way the sunshine hits my face. When we get close to the coast, the air changes, and my senses are hit with delicious salt-tinged oxygen.

According to JP, all of the paperwork that was sent to Hayden went to a PO box in a small town right on the water called Driftwood. He has a phone number for Georgina's son, but there's no way I'm calling it. The town doesn't have a website, and there were limited photos online, so I have no idea if we'll even be able to find a place to stay. Or if we'll be able to find Hayden once we arrive.

But I have to try.

Thankfully, Georgina dozes off again, and when we finally get close to Driftwood, the sun is sparkling on the ocean. I pull off to the side of the road to take it in.

To *pause.*

That word is not usually part of my vocabulary.

It's nice.

When the pressures from work or the rigors of life disappear, there are still plenty of other things rushing in to try to fill that void. Normally, for me, it's worry.

When did that happen?

How did that happen?

It's almost as if I tilted my childhood creativity away from discovery and cleverness and inspiration and focused it directly on adult what-ifs and anxiety and fear.

I stopped seeking wonder and started seeking stability. I leaned into a practical, logical side, one that needed a steady paycheck and a stable job.

All because someone laid out how impractical the dream I'd held for so long really was.

I stare out over the water, thinking of how I don't like the ocean.

I grew up inland, and boats make me nervous.

Big ones, like the Staten Island Ferry, make me feel a little more secure, but the thought of going overboard, of drowning—it's kept me landlocked most of my life. Even New York City doesn't *feel* like an island. I'm surrounded by buildings, not water, and that's comforting.

But I'm not sure why. New York City has plenty of problems to worry about. Curb-jumping cars, for instance.

As far as my fear of the ocean, though, it seems logically unfounded.

Nobody I know has ever drowned.

I know how to swim.

I can handle a pool.

But oceans and lakes, where there are currents and creatures— these are things that scare me.

Because I can't touch the bottom.

Because these things are out of my control.

My phone buzzes in my back pocket, so I pull it out and see a text from JP.

> **JP:** I see you're in North Carolina.
> **Kelsey:** Are you stalking me?
> **JP:** Don't flatter yourself. I'm paid to keep tabs on Georgina. She's not going to be happy.
> **JP:** And she's really not going to be happy when she finds out I'm sending you this . . .

JP drops a pin to what looks like a business. I click on it, and a web page opens for Driftwood Restoration. A boat restoration shop.

> **Kelsey:** What's this?
> **JP:** It's where you'll find her son.
> **JP:** You're not the only one who wants to see them reunited.
> **JP:** But if you tell her I helped you at all, I'll deny it and throw you under the bus.
> **Kelsey:** She's smart.
> **Kelsey:** She's probably going to figure it out.
> **JP:** Well, figure out a way to make sure she doesn't fire me, okay?
> **Kelsey:** As if she would ever listen to me.

I plug the address into my phone and head back to the car. Georgina stirs as I start the engine, and I wonder if there's a way to lull her to sleep until after I locate Hayden.

"Just stopped to look at the ocean for a minute," I say, not going into why or what I thought about while I did.

I pull back onto the highway and head toward Driftwood, concerned about how much Georgina knows about where

Hayden lives. My thoughts go into overdrive before I can stop them.

She has people to handle many aspects of her personal life, but does she permit them to tell her what they find? Or does she do any digging herself?

Will she recognize the name of the town?

Does she know he restores boats?

Did she tell him about her kidneys?

Calm down, Kelsey. Part of this Summer of Yes is saying yes to not worrying so much.

I glance over and find her resting her eyes again. Good thing, because we just passed a sign for Driftwood in five miles.

Five miles.

I look at the speedometer and try to do the math in my head to figure out how long it will take but give up because I can never figure out what the ratios work out to be. All I know is that if I were going sixty, this would take five minutes. But I'm going thirty-five.

Five miles.

Soon I'll know if this was the best—or worst—idea I've ever had. All at once, I'm filled with nervous energy.

I might be making a *huge* mistake.

I navigate to the address JP sent me, a business literally on the beach. It's a large building with two big garage doors. An industrial kind of workshop. There's a big wooden sign outside that says "Drift-wood Restoration" in blocky painted letters.

I park the car in the lot next door, facing the front entrance, feeling unsure of this plan I was so certain of only hours ago.

Georgina opens her eyes. "What are we doing now?" She looks up, and instantly I see the recognition on her face.

"What are we doing here?" It's more of an accusation than a question.

I face her. "I know I didn't tell you, and I know this feels like manipulation—"

"Get back on the highway." She is terse and her tone is firm.

I hold up my hands. I haven't thought this completely through. "Okay, just hear me out."

"You have no right," she says tightly.

"I know," I say, a bit desperate to get ahold of the moment and aware that I've overstepped. "And if you really want to go, we'll go. But there's something you should know before you decide."

"Nothing you can say right now will make me change my mind," she snaps. "This is not your business."

"You're right," I say. "And I'm sorry." I really am. I thought I was doing something good. "But, Georgina, I think I saw your son at the hospital."

Her shoulders drop. "You . . . you what?"

"I can't be certain, but . . ." I have no proof that man was Georgina's son—nothing but my gut to back me up.

"But what?"

"He was standing outside your room, just hanging around. I spoke to him briefly, but it seemed like he wanted to come in and see you."

She shakes her head. "Not possible. You're mistaken."

I gently say, "I . . . don't think so."

Her face tightens. "He hasn't responded to my lawyer. Not once. It must've been someone else."

I study the door of the building across the parking lot, chewing on words I'm not sure I should say . . . but say anyway. "Maybe he didn't respond because he didn't want to reconnect with a lawyer."

She looks at me, then down, like the thought has never even crossed her mind.

"Maybe he wanted *you* to be the one to reach out," I say.

She stiffens.

"I don't know what happened, obviously," I say.

"No. You don't."

"And not for lack of trying to find out. You're a very private person."

"For a very good reason."

I frown, not in frustration but because I'm hesitant about saying this next part.

"Maybe this is a big part of the Summer of Yes."

She looks at me like I just tried to high-five her with a hand that's growing out of my forehead.

"Is this why you came up with this whole plan? To throw all of your vacation time into ruining what's left of my life?" She watches the building as she says this.

She's watching the building. Huh.

"No," I say honestly. "This really is about me."

She whips around and stares at me.

"Partly, anyway," I admit.

She huffs. "Changing me isn't going to change you."

Now I'm the one who goes still.

"Stop pouring all of your attention into my life and what you think is wrong with it and start facing your own."

She has a point. It's like fixing her regrets will somehow prevent me from ending up with the exact same ones.

"Georgina," I say after a pause. "We're already here. You might as well go say hello."

I see her head tilt down and shake a small no. "It's not that easy, Kelsey."

"Why not?" I ask. "You said you have regrets. This is your chance to make them right."

She turns to me, and the look on her face is something I've never seen.

Fear, hurt, uncertainty.

"You have no idea what you're talking about," she says through half-gritted teeth.

I tap my thumb on the steering wheel and peer out over the parking lot. Seagulls call out in the distance, and a light, warm breeze blows through the car.

"I'm sorry," I say. "I didn't mean to upset you."

"What exactly *did* you think would happen if you brought me here?" Her gaze holds steady out the window, and her tone softens slightly. "Did you think I'd just walk up to him and say, what? 'Hey, it's me. I haven't seen or spoken to you in two decades. Want to go get ice cream?'"

"Has it really been that long?"

"Yes," she says. "So you can understand why I might expect a chilly welcome."

In spite of the heat, my hands are cold. I get it now. "You're afraid."

"Of course I am!" She raises her voice as she says it, but then, more quietly, more controlled, she repeats, "Of course I am."

"I understand," I say.

"You don't," she says. "You couldn't possibly."

"I do. Maybe not this, exactly, but I know that every choice I've made up until this point—*every single one* in my adult life—has been out of fear."

Her jaw is clenched, and I can practically see her wrestling with this impossible situation I've put her in.

I am such a jerk.

"You know what? You're right. This was a horrible idea. I didn't think it through, and I didn't think about how you would react." I start the car. "We can go. We can drive straight back to New York today—"

"No," she cuts me off quietly. "I'm tired."

"Okay," I say. "Let's go find a place to stay, and tomorrow morning we'll grab breakfast and hit the road. Pretend none of this ever happened."

I put the car in Reverse, realizing how badly I miscalculated.

I look at her. "And for what it's worth, I really am sorry."

She flicks a hand in the air, either to reject my apology or to clear it away, I'm not sure which.

Before I can pull out, I see the garage door of the building is opening. I keep my foot on the brake and glance over to find Georgina watching. It's almost like she's holding her breath as a boat backs out of the garage and onto the lot. A man—tall, muscular, tan—appears.

Georgina exhales, and I hold my breath.

I don't even have to think about it. That's the same man.

"Hayden." Georgina says his name on a whisper. Then, without looking at me, she asks, "Was he the one at the hospital?"

As if I could forget. His silhouette might've been burned onto my brain.

It's not like I don't notice attractive men, but Georgina's son is next level. Watching him now, even from a distance, I'm reminded of that all over again.

"Well?" Georgina says, waiting for me to confirm this very important detail.

I nod. "It's him."

Georgina's big sunglasses hide her eyes, but given her full attention on the man who is maneuvering around the boat with a casual ease, she's processing this information, and it's emotional.

"Do you want to go talk to him?" I offer.

She waits a beat, then shakes her head. "No. I . . . I can't. Not like this." She clears her throat and shifts in her seat. "Let's go to a hotel. And tomorrow we start back to New York."

"Are you sure? He's right—"

"Kelsey," she snaps. "I said let's go."

"Right." I back out, still watching Hayden as I pull out of the parking lot and onto the road. When he glances up, he pauses, and I hit the gas a little harder, spinning the wheels on the sand-covered pavement.

"Subtle."

When you feel stupid, Georgina has a way of ratcheting up the embarrassment another tick or two.

She's quiet for a minute. Then she lets out a small chuckle. "He looked good, didn't he?"

"Uh, *yeah*," I say way too quickly.

She looks at me, and I know I'm talking about her son, but facts are facts. Hayden is a very attractive man.

I can't help it—I crack a smile. "I wouldn't have a problem saying yes to anything that man asked."

Chapter 20

KELSEY

WE'RE ALL CHECKED into the hotel, and Georgina is in bed by seven. I doubt she's sleeping, but she's made it clear she is not to be disturbed.

I take this opportunity to touch base with JP. It's kind of fun because I feel like I have a secret contact.

I'm Kelsey Bourne, Jason's fun-loving younger sister, but apparently, I've received none of my brother's training because I botched this up so badly.

Kelsey: This might've been kind of, sort of a disaster.

JP: I told you. At least I don't have to worry about her liking you better than me.

Kelsey: She likes me WAY better than you.

Kelsey: She told me.

JP: 😳

JP: Did you see him? Hayden?

Kelsey: Yes.

Kelsey: We saw him, but she wouldn't go talk to him.

Kelsey: And now she's set on leaving in the morning.

JP: Sounds like Georgina.

Kelsey: I need help!

Kelsey: What do I do?

Kelsey: We can't leave without even talking to him.

JP: She's the boss.

JP: And she's stubborn.

Kelsey: That's a fact.

JP: You can't spring things on her. She doesn't like it.

JP: And really, can you blame her? You totally
  bamboozled her.

Kelsey: I applaud your use of the word "bamboozled."

JP: 😑

Kelsey: Look at us joking with each other.

Kelsey: Are we friends now?

JP: No.

Kelsey: We'll work on it.

Kelsey: I guess we'll be seeing you in a couple days.

Kelsey: Sigh.

JP: You're so dramatic.

JP: And you can't fix someone else's life in a single day.

Kelsey: Yeah, I know.

Kelsey: I guess I just hoped I could do something
  good.

JP: You can.

JP: Make sure Georgina isn't planning to fire me for
  helping you.

Kelsey: I'll work on it. No promises.

Kelsey: But I'll do my best.

I set the phone down, hoping I'm winning him over.

I take a breath and look around the suite. I have a whole room to myself, and I'm not used to free time. It's always work time. Or planning time.

Or go-get-things-for-my-boss time, which, in retrospect, is totally not my job.

With hours to myself, I'm not sure what to do. Up until now, all of my plans for this trip have centered mostly around Georgina and her son and my grand goal of reuniting them.

It went much differently in the scene I wrote in my mind.

Hayden (moving in slow motion, of course, with a short depth of field throwing everything in the background behind him into a blur) stands up from behind a boat, maybe a little dirty, maybe a little sweaty.

Maybe I'm a little sweaty.

He wipes his brow and looks over to our car, sees Georgina, and with a "Mom?" answered by her with, "My darling boy!" they come together for an embrace with a swell of music (and for some reason it's Taylor Swift singing on the soundtrack).

In a slightly different version, he pushes right past her and plants one on me.

Forget Taylor—in this version, a Marvin Gaye song plays on a boom box nearby.

My writer-brain is really out of control.

I stand and walk out onto the balcony, which overlooks the ocean. It's beautiful. There's a sliver of daylight left, and I start to feel antsy. Like sitting up here alone, in this quiet room, is stifling me somehow.

It's a new feeling. I normally crave alone time. I even have a wooden sign in my apartment that says "Let's Stay Home." But I don't want to be old Kelsey.

I want to go. Out. Somewhere. And do something.

Just say yes, Kelsey.

So I leave.

I justify it by telling myself if I'm only going to be here for one single night, I'm going to enjoy it. I'll most likely never get this opportunity again, so tonight it's *indulgence*, not *isolation*.

Never mind that I'm not sure what kinds of things constitute "fun" for me anymore.

Most days I work. Most nights too. I have no social life, and even if I did, I'm pretty sure I'd still choose staying in with takeout and Netflix over going out and socializing.

The very thought of that normally gives me hives.

But . . . now, for some reason, it's not. I actually want to go.

I exit the hotel through the back and make my way over to the wide boardwalk I saw from my balcony. I'm used to maneuvering around New York on my own, so it's not like I'm a total tourist. I'm not afraid to go out by myself, and yet this is uncharted territory. I don't know this tiny town or anyone in it.

It's early enough that there are still people out here, milling around. Up ahead, I hear live music streaming out onto the beach and then see a simple sign in a window for "Dolly's Saltwater Taffy."

I stop in front. I like saltwater taffy.

Say yes, right?

I go inside, and after looking around for a few minutes, I purchase a big fat bag full of candy. As I'm paying the teenage cashier, I take out a pink one, unwrap it, and pop it in my mouth. A burst of strawberry flavor ignites my taste buds, and I walk back out into the warm, salty summer air.

I keep walking, grabbing a blue taffy and chewing it like I'm a toddler and need to shove it in quickly before someone takes it away.

I don't eat nearly enough candy.

This is something I will have to remedy.

I pass by a cute little surf shop, geared toward actual surfers and not people like me. Actually, this whole town is that way. There's something wonderfully uncommercialized about it, and I start to think it might be North Carolina's best-kept secret. Plenty of little businesses to hold one's attention, but no golden arches anywhere to be seen.

I could live here.

The stray thought is, of course, ridiculous. Probably what everyone thinks when they're vacationing somewhere quaint.

But then it occurs to me that where one lives so often determines *how* one lives.

Am I living in the right place?

It's a shame we have to leave tomorrow, because I could spend a whole day on this boardwalk and not experience everything I want to experience. I don't want to simply "pass through." I want to see Driftwood the way a person who lives here sees it.

I have an odd longing—I want this view to become familiar. Which makes no sense because I don't even like the water. I don't want to live where the ocean gets to roam free.

I like skyscrapers. In a city. Not high tides and sea monsters and hurricanes.

Right?

There's an oyster bar with free deep-fried samples out front. I've never tried them, and I've always said I don't like them just because I *think* they'd feel squishy and weird in my mouth.

I walk over, smile at the guy behind the bar, and snatch one. Then, without thinking, I throw it in my mouth.

It's hot, deep-fried, lemony, and ocean fresh. *And utterly amazing.*

I've been missing so much.

I'm still savoring the buttery goodness when I see an ice cream shop with Blue Moon Smoothies and, nearby, a driftwood artisan creating whole carved worlds with elves, dragons, and fairies.

It's all so different and all so alluring.

I walk around without an agenda, paying attention to scattered families and couples and groups of teenagers strolling the board-walk. After a moment, I realize I'm walking slowly and with my head up.

Not like a New Yorker at all.

However, a cursory glance around the area tells me I'm the only one walking by myself.

I follow the music and take a seat on a wooden bench across from the outdoor patio of a bar called The Grotto. The band is playing a cover of "The Joker" by the Steve Miller Band, while a good-sized crowd of people drink and mingle and smile and laugh.

It's so rare that I get to people-watch. I used to do it all the time, trying to guess professions, making up backstories . . .

When did I stop doing that?

Usually, when I'm out of my apartment, I'm on my way to work, and I'm head down, no eye contact. I don't even look around. But here, everything is wider and more open, including my eyes.

So I watch.

There's a blond girl in a pink tank top and white shorts, dancing around a table of college kids. They must've gotten a head start on the drinking because they're loud and rowdy and she's singing the wrong lyrics at the top of her lungs.

There's an older couple holding hands, more engrossed in each other than in anything happening around them. She's tall and tan and wearing a black off-the-shoulder dress and a large turquoise necklace. He's got a Hawaiian-style shirt on with a pair of khaki shorts, and he's wearing one of those straw beach hats. The way he's looking at the woman makes me wonder . . .

Who are they? Where did they meet?

Is it a renewed-vows honeymoon, after twenty years of marital bliss?

Or maybe she's his mistress . . . or maybe he's *her* . . . what's the male version of a mistress?

Why is there no male version of "mistress"?

All I can think of is "mattress," but that's way off.

I feel like this is somehow an affront to the whole of the female species, as if only *women* can be secrets, but before my imagination can snag on that, it snags on something else. The crowd parts and there, sitting alone at the bar, is someone I immediately recognize.

Hayden.

Beautiful, broken Hayden.

I actually have no idea if he's broken. I'm adding that to his fictional character arc.

He could be perfectly fine, living a happy life out here in paradise, without his mother. But now that I've opened up the writing tap, like a backyard hose hooked up to a sprinkler, I'm helpless to resist running through it.

My imagination is a runaway train.

My curiosity is like a toddler's eyes peeking over the counter at a plate of cookies.

My words are back. With a vengeance.

I'm getting obsessed with stories all over again. Stories that aren't my own. Stories I really have no business inserting myself into.

But . . . I'm probably going to anyway.

It's a big red button that says "Don't Press This Button."

A very attractive big red button.

Another guy, I'm guessing about the same age as Hayden, sits down next to him and orders a drink. They chat for a few minutes, and Hayden interacts with the waitress, the bartender, and a woman who seems to be flirting with him. I would've pegged him for brooding when I saw him at the hospital, but I'm starting to see that's not who he is.

At least not here, in his own environment.

Here he gives off strong "everybody's friend" vibes, and I find myself wishing I were closer so I could hear what he's saying.

It's been a long time since I've even let myself look at a man in a way that wasn't strictly platonic.

This has always come to the great dismay of Ravi and Sasha, who are perpetually trying to set me up with their supersmart academic friends. Every time I saw Sasha, she had a new photo of some guy to show me, and every time, I responded to it with a resounding, emphatic *no*.

Always no.

Romance is not in my ten-year plan.

And now, sitting here outside this bar, watching a man who's captivated me in a way no one else ever has, I realize maybe I've been missing out.

But that is not why I'm here. No matter how much I wish it were.

Before I can tell myself not to, I stand and cross the boardwalk, entering the bar as the band starts playing the Beach Boys classic "Kokomo."

White lights are strung all around the edge of the ceiling of this outdoor space. It's not quite dark enough for them to make a difference, but I'm betting after the sun goes down they provide the perfect glow.

The table of college kids lets out a collective cheer so loud it startles me.

Not a single person seems to notice me as I walk over to the bar and take a seat, leaving one stool between Hayden and my-self. I catch a quick glimpse of my reflection in a mirror behind the bartender and quickly smooth the stray hairs that refuse to stay back in my dark, I've-been-traveling-all-day ponytail. I'm not going to be making a great impression with Georgina's son looking like I just woke up, that's for sure.

Running into him here, hundreds of miles away from home . . . it has to be fate, right?

Or divine intervention?

A sign that even though what I did to Georgina was manipu-lative and probably wrong, maybe it wasn't completely off base. Maybe I shouldn't give up just yet.

That's how I'm taking it anyway.

The guy behind the bar is almost as handsome as Hayden. Almost. He's got dark skin and even darker hair, and I'm pretty sure his eyes are the color of a moonless night.

Good grief, have men like this been out here all this time?

The bartender smiles at me. It's a very nice, very bright, very "let me get you a drink, even though you look like you got dressed in a gas station bathroom this morning" kind of smile.

I smile back, wishing I'd taken a second to consider the way I looked before I left the hotel room.

"What can I get you?" he asks.

I glance around. I don't really drink alcohol, and that's not something I'm interested in saying yes to, regardless of revelations. I never saw the appeal. I've been to office parties where my coworkers made fools of themselves after drinking one too many, and I don't feel like I'm missing out.

"Can I get a Sprite with grenadine?"

He looks amused. "A Shirley Temple?"

"Yeah," I say. "I have an early day tomorrow."

"Sure thing, babe."

Babe? He just fell a few notches on my attractiveness scale.

"I'm so sorry, but . . . do I know you?"

I feel my whole body tense.

I slowly turn to find Hayden looking at me. He's squinting, like he's trying to place my face. This is when I realize maybe it was also divine intervention that I happen to look like a first-class disaster right now. Because I really don't want him to know that the woman who was visiting Georgina in the hospital has driven for two days straight to meet him.

He holds up both hands. "I promise, it's not a pickup line." He chuckles. "I just really feel like I've seen you before."

"Oh, I have one of those faces," I say, playing it off and praying he has a really bad memory.

He turns his body to face me. "Yeah, maybe." He's still trying to work it out in his head, I can see it.

He turns back to the bar, and I hate awkward silences, so I jump in headfirst, still not sure what I'm doing sitting here next to him.

"Some people say I look like Emma Watson . . . so . . . maybe you're just a Harry Potter fan?"

He turns back and smiles. "Oh, I hope not."

I scrunch up my face. "Why?"

"I've always thought of her as the most terrifying character in those books."

He read the books.

"Oh my gosh, me too! She can cast practically anything, and she was just handed over the means to *travel through time*? I mean, what the heck?"

"I know, right?"

We laugh together—like friends do—just for a moment.

The bartender slides my drink toward me. "Your . . . Shirley Temple. Hope you're not driving tonight." He winks at me.

Now he's moved into the negative numbers on the attractiveness scale.

"Uh, thanks," I say. I turn back to Hayden—and I get a better look at his scar. I want to reach up and touch it, to ask him how he got it. To tell him it gives his perfect face character.

Just the right amount of imperfection.

"I'll watch out for her," he says to the bartender.

Please, dear Lord, let that be true. Make sure I get home safe, and when he walks me to the door, let him . . .

"You're not from here." Hayden smiles, then takes a swig from his bottle.

Get it together, Worthington.

"Good eye. I'm actually from Upstate New York."

"Really?" he asks. "What are you doing here?"

Stalking you.

"I took some time off work," I say. "And I just picked a direction and drove."

"That's . . . actually really cool."

I feel myself blush. "I'm working on saying yes to more things, so . . . here I am." I lift my kiddie drink in a salute.

He nods as if this is an acceptable explanation. "Well, you can't go wrong with Driftwood, though most people don't find themselves here on vacation."

"I'm just passing through."

"On your way to . . . ?"

I smile. "I'm not sure."

I feel weirdly cute in this moment, and think I'll try to do the thing in the movies where the girl drinks through a straw and looks up coquettishly at the guy with her big eyes and mischievous smile.

I sip my drink through the tiny straw, and the little paper umbrella catches on the end of my nose. I try to shift the glass and use my nose to move it out of the way, and the top of the umbrella goes up my right nostril.

I have the flirt game of a potted plant.

I move the glass away and find him watching me, an amused look on his face.

"I know I look like a toddler," I say.

"No, not at all," he says. "I see a lot of grown women drinking Shirley Temples with umbrellas sticking out of their noses."

"The umbrella was not my choice," I say, removing it. "It was the creepy bartender's."

Hayden lets out a laugh, almost like the comment caught him off guard.

"Creepy?" He laughs again. "Diego?"

I shrug and take another drink. "He called me 'babe.'" I glance at him, but he looks unconvinced, so I add, "Plus, he winked at me."

"Oh, okay, yeah, that is a little creepy."

I lift my shoulders. "Right? Winking? At a grown woman?" I almost laugh as I say this because most days I don't feel like a grown woman. I don't even usually refer to myself as a "woman." Usually I'm still "just a girl."

The conversation has lasted longer than I had hoped, and now it's settled into that moment where the feeling-each-other-out and small-talk icebreakers are slowly dissolving.

It's here when two people who just met start actually talking to one another.

"So . . . just passing through . . ."

I spin my stool slightly so I'm angled toward him. "Yep."

He clicks his tongue. "Shame."

"Why a shame?" My heart sputters. *Please let him say because he wants to marry me and live out the rest of our days in a small cottage with a stunning ocean view.*

"This is a really cool town. You'd miss a lot if you're just passing through." He looks around the bar, open to the street and the beach. "It's my favorite place in the world."

When he says this, I believe him. He's earnest and honest and down-to-earth. Likable.

I can't help but think how different he is from Georgina. He's kind and inviting, and when he talks to me, he looks me in the eyes.

It would be unnerving if it didn't make me feel so warm inside.

"Did you grow up here?" I ask, even though I know the answer.

He shakes his head and moves over to the empty stool that I'd positioned between us. I'd done that to protect myself, and now that he's so close to me, I realize that was wisdom on my part. His knee bumps into mine, and that simple point of contact makes my hand inadvertently shudder, clinking the ice in my glass.

This close, I can see that Hayden's eyes are icy blue. Almost gray. In certain lighting, I bet they even look green. And when he focuses them on me, the strange desire to run and hide meshes with the strange desire to hold his gaze for as long as humanly possible.

"I grew up in New York City, but my dad and I moved here when I was about eleven," he says.

I see an opening. It would be so easy for me to ask, *"What about your mom?"* But I don't. I can't. It feels wrong. And I'm a quick learner.

"You don't get bored?" I ask. "I mean, the boardwalk is great, but it doesn't seem like there's much to do around here. You know, for fun."

He lifts a hand at Diego, and within seconds, he's got another drink in front of him. "I find ways to pass the time."

"Ways like . . . ?"

He smiles. "Want me to show you?"

"Ooh. I don't know," I say, angling my body back toward the bar. "Your pickup line was 'Do I know you?'" I joke. "Not exactly A-tier material."

He laughs. "Yeah, that was pretty lame. But it wasn't a pickup line—you do look really familiar."

I try to steer the conversation away from who I am or where he saw me, inwardly chastising myself for bringing it back up. "There's *really* a lot to do here? Other than the beach?"

"Oh gosh, yeah. A ton. I'd be happy to show you around."

"Really?" I ask, and I hear the hopefulness in my own voice. I don't *want* him to be the guy I pegged him for, the guy who takes home a different woman every weekend.

Besides, it's Tuesday.

Also, I look like a shipwrecked sea wench.

"I could ask Diego to come with us," he says. "To chaperone."

"That's okay," I say. "But we need to stay somewhere public because you could turn out to be some serial killer."

A tall, blond waitress is walking by, and she overhears what I've said. She claps a hand on his shoulder and laughs. "Honey, this guy wouldn't hurt a field mouse."

"I don't even know your name," I say over the din of a very poor rendition of "Don't Worry Be Happy."

He sticks out a hand in my direction. "Hayden. Quinn."

Quinn. So he's not using Georgina's last name.

I slip my hand in his, noticing the roughness of his skin on mine. "Kelsey Worthington."

He squeezes my hand and smiles, and that gives an extra zap to my midsection.

"It's nice to meet you, Kelsey Worthington," he says, releasing his grip.

I don't care if this is the dumbest idea in the world.

I don't care if I'm being foolish or brazen or impractical.

Those eyes and that smile and the story of a scar waiting to unfold are the only things I can think about.

So I say yes.

Chapter 21

KELSEY

Is your car parked nearby?" Hayden asks.

"Oh no, I walked from my hotel," I say, pointing in the general direction of the only hotel in town.

"Ah, the Driftwood Sands."

"There weren't many options." I laugh.

"Yeah, we don't get many tourists," he says. "The bulk of this town can be seen along this stretch of beach."

We're back out on the boardwalk, and the sun is more than halfway through its glorious descent, dipping lower and lower on the horizon, casting everything in a soft orange glow.

It's probably stupid for me to be out here with a relative stranger, in a place I don't know, but the backstory I've concocted about Hayden is working to counteract that.

And I still have so many questions. Somehow, I feel drawn to him, and I'm not even sure that's because of Georgina.

When I realize we're headed in the direction of a dock, I stop walking. "Wait, are you taking me on a boat?"

He stops moving and faces me. "Oh shoot. That's a total serial killer thing to do. I'm so sorry . . ."

I chuckle nervously and shake my head. "No, no, it's not that, it's fine, it's just . . ."

He winces. "Are you afraid of the water?"

I scrunch up my face.

I glance down at the shore and see four boats parked at a small dock.

My whole body is tense. It's like that feeling when live actors in a show come off the stage and try to pull you out of the audience to act something out.

It's weird—this isn't a flight-or-fight kind of thing. I don't sense any danger from Hayden, though I do wonder why he's showing me around when he doesn't even know me. I've already ruled out "because he's attracted to me," knowing what I look like right now, so why is he wasting his time? I'm sure he has a girlfriend or maybe a wife or a *somebody* he'd rather be spending time with.

I glance at his left hand. No ring. No white tan line.

I won't pretend my heart doesn't do a roundoff back tuck at that realization.

I walk a bit forward and stand side by side with him, facing the dock, the sand, and the boats. The breeze off the water is sublime—a little cool and crisp. I relax a bit and realize I feel like it's okay to open up.

"I'm a *little* afraid of water," I admit.

He watches me.

I try to justify it. "I know that makes me sound like a baby, and I've always had a healthy interest in the ocean, but only from the safety of dry land. I guess . . ." I pause. "I guess I don't like things being out of my control."

He nods. "I totally get it. It can be scary. But . . . didn't you say something about saying yes more often? To things that you wouldn't normally do?"

Well, crap. I really need to stop telling people about this plan. It has a way of coming back to push me.

"If it helps, it's a short ride," he says, looking out on the water. "And I can stay near the shore. That way, if the boat capsizes, you won't have far to swim."

My eyes go wide.

"I'm kidding," he says, laughing. And then, probably seeing that I'm not laughing with him, he says in a more serious tone, "It won't capsize. You'll be fine. I'll make sure nothing happens to you."

A Yes Test. Like Ravi's family dinner.

Like the day off at the zoo.

But this isn't a fun trip to see penguins. Or spicy food with a side of self-reflection.

My mother was right when she said the accident was a disruptor. And not a single area of my life has been unaffected.

I tentatively start walking toward the dock, and he falls in line next to me.

"There are probably sharks out there," I say.

"Definitely," he says.

"What?!"

He waves his hand at the horizon. "They're way, *way* out there."

"But they do come into the shore sometimes, right? I mean, you hear about that all the time, and with global warming, they're probably changing their feeding patterns, which means people are on the menu, and—"

He bumps his shoulder into mine in a show of casual familiarity that I very much like.

The wind whips up briefly and straight through my hair, pulling more of it from the elastic doing a horrible job of holding it in place.

"Hey. In all seriousness, I've lived here twenty-two years, and I've never seen one come near the shore."

"You moved here when you were eleven," I say. "So you're thirty-three." I calculate that Georgina had Hayden when she was in her early forties.

"Fine math." He nods. "You?"

"You're asking a woman her age?"

"I think it only fair," he counters.

We stop at the front end of the dock, and I can hear the boats gently knocking against the tires fashioned around the posts.

I smile and look back out over the water. "Thirty-two."

"What do you do?" he asks.

"I'm an associate editor," I say. "At a publishing house."

"Oh, nice," he says. "In Upstate New York?"

My cheeks heat. I didn't lie. I *am* from Upstate New York. The fact that I don't live there now never came up. Until now.

I feel like I've just been caught.

"You promise you haven't seen any shark attacks?"

If he notices my change of subject, he doesn't let on. At some point, I'm going to have to come clean, begging the question: *What am I doing?*

He looks at me and puts a hand over his heart and nods. "I promise."

I look down at my feet, still in the sand.

"One more step, Kelsey; that's all it takes."

He said my name. And for some unknown reason, it gives me wings.

Say yes, Kelsey.

I take one more step, and I'm on the wood planks. We walk down toward the boats, each one neatly tied. He stops in front of a small green boat with gold letters that spell *Mirabelle*.

My eyes flick to his. "Mirabelle?"

He looks away. "She was my dog. Just the best girl. A sweet old boxer."

"You named your boat after your dog?" I ask.

He shrugs. "She was a lot more loyal than any woman I've ever known."

"Ouch," I say. "Someone did a number on you."

He shrugs as if to say, *"Yeah, well . . ."* but doesn't say anything.

I stare at the *Mirabelle*. Normally, I wouldn't have even walked down this dock. I look at my feet again, firmly planted on the cracked, weathered decking below. One wrong step, and I'm in the water. Plunging to my death or getting eaten by a giant octopus.

"You promise I won't go overboard," I say sternly.

He laughs. "Yes. But if you're not up for it, we can go rent some bikes or something. Honestly."

Beyond where he's standing, the sun has dipped even lower. Daylight is fading, and I know that if I say no to this, I'll miss a spectacular sunset on the ocean. I also know that if I say no, there's a chance I won't see Hayden again.

And this plan to reunite him with Georgina goes straight out the window.

That *is* still the plan, right?

"What do you say, Kelsey Worthington?" he asks. "Is it a yes?"

I pause for a few long seconds, then bring my gaze to his and blow out a long breath. "Yes."

"Good." He steps into the boat and reaches a hand toward me. "The boat will be a little unsteady underneath your feet, but I'll hold on to you."

For as long as we both shall live.

Good grief, Kelsey, you've known this guy for all of five minutes, will you calm down?

I reach out and take his hand, then take a cautious step, my foot landing wobbly inside the boat. I squeeze Hayden's hand so hard I'm surprised I don't cut off the blood flow. He uses his other hand to steady me, placing it on my waist and helping me into the boat.

Then we stand still for a moment, and he just . . . looks at me.

And I look at him.

And . . . there's a moment.

This is not in the plan.

I don't know Hayden, but already I can tell he is *not* safe. Not for my heart. No, I don't think he's trying to break it . . . I just know I'm at great risk of falling hard.

Somehow, when he looks at me, it's like he already sees more of who I am than anyone else in my life, and for a fleeting moment I think it would be nice to be known, truly known, by another person.

So even though I want to keep staring into the depths of these bright blue-green eyes, I look away.

"You good?" he asks.

"Living the dream," I quip.

"Ha," he says. "You'll see. I think it will change your whole relationship with the water."

He moves across the small boat, slips behind the steering wheel, and starts the engine.

"Where should I sit?" I ask.

"Here, next to me," he says, indicating the cushioned seat to his left. "There's a life jacket under that seat." He points, and I move gingerly over to it and lift it up. Stowed underneath are two orange life vests. I pull them out and hand one over to Hayden.

He looks at it, then at me. "I'm good."

"What if we hit a giant wave and it throws us off the boat?" I ask.

"The water's pretty calm," he says. "I think I'll be okay."

I shove one of the vests back under the seat, then affix the other one over my shoulders. "If that's the way you want to die, you know, you do you."

He laughs. Then looks at me funny.

I glance around the boat, then back at him. "What?"

He reaches for me, and I tense up. "You, um . . . you have it on backwards."

I make a face. "Of course I do."

He stops just short of reaching around me. "Can I . . . Do you mind if I . . . ?"

Act cool, be cool, it's cool.

"Yeah, sure, no problem."

He reaches to my side and unclasps the buckle on the side of the life vest. He's so close I can smell him, and all of a sudden, my Summer of Yes seems like a *really* good idea.

I count the times he brushes up against me—five, and one felt on purpose—as he pulls the vest up and over my head, spins it around, and pulls it back down.

I reach to the side as he does, and our hands both grab the buckle at the same time.

A nervous laugh, him putting his hands up and me pushing the clutch strap through.

Click.

He smiles. "You ready now?"

I move to the seat, and I feel more secure behind the windshield, but not so secure that I don't slap a death grip on the rail of the boat.

He unties it, moving around so easily. Then, using a foot, he pushes us away from the dock.

"Do you always take your boat out in the evening?" I ask.

"Any chance I get," he says. "I mean, I have a truck, but I rarely use it. What's the point when it's so much nicer out here?"

As we start down the coastline toward the sunset, I appreciate that Hayden is driving slowly. I'm pretty sure that's for my benefit. All along the coast, there are houses and businesses and restaurants, and I see how quiet and peaceful Driftwood really is, which is likely what Hayden loves about it.

After a few minutes, I look over and find him watching me.

"Everything okay so far?" he asks.

I nod. And . . . I actually am okay. "I'm . . . good."

He points. "You can let go of the side," he says, smiling.

I release my grip, and my knuckles are hilariously stiff. I didn't realize how tight I was holding the rail.

I'm thankful there's no mirror in his boat, because between the orange vest and the disheveled updo, I'm certain I look ridiculous right now. I settle into my seat and try to tame my hair. It's like I brushed it with a rake.

"Hey. Kelsey."

I look up and see him looking off to the west.

"Look."

I turn to see something that I almost can't describe. The explosion of colors, the crisp horizon, the undulating ocean . . . I'm rendered speechless.

I hear the smirk in his voice from next to me. "Told ya."

I smile in the moment, fully aware that saying yes brought me here.

"Are you one of those 'up before dawn' kind of people?" I ask.

The wind cuts through his hair, blowing it off his forehead and away from his face.

"I am," he says. "I love mornings. Best time of day."

"Until sunset?"

He laughs to himself. "Okay, maybe the *second* best time of the day."

"A morning person *and* a night person? Good grief."

He frowns over at me. "Mornings are great because they're quiet. I can think."

I wonder what he thinks about in that quiet.

"I always get at least ten minutes of sunlight first thing. Usually a run on the beach with my dog, Coco."

"Who is naming your dogs?" I tease.

He looks like he agrees with the just-okay name. "She's a rescue, so not me."

"And you *run*." I make a production of cringing.

"It's less about the run and more about the mood," he says. "It's . . . nice. Still. I can set my mind before the world wakes up. Then I have coffee on the deck."

"Well, at least you're a coffee drinker," I say. "Bonus points for that." Then I casually add, "I don't trust anyone who doesn't like coffee."

"Me neither! Heathens." He laughs, then slows the boat down, and I try to figure out where we're headed, but nothing about this place is familiar to me. "What about you?"

"What about me?"

"Mornings?" he asks. "Do you have a ritual?"

"Yes. Alarm goes off at 6:20. I hit Snooze until 6:52. Then I rush to get ready, race out the door, stop for coffee at the Starbucks near my apartment, and get to the office five minutes late."

He shakes his head. "Sounds hectic."

"It is."

"You ever try getting up earlier? To protect your sanity?"

I scoff. "Did you hear the part where I said I snooze my alarm?"

He starts turning the boat toward the shoreline.

"I don't know how you do that," he says. "I couldn't live like that."

Before I can defend my indefensible position, I see he's pulling next to a dock behind a big building.

A building I cased earlier that day with his estranged mother in tow.

I'll have to act surprised when he shows me around.

He doesn't need my help to tie up the boat, and when I stand, it rocks back and forth, and I stumble slightly, knocking straight into him.

He doesn't so much catch me as block me—it's not one of those meet-cute moments. It's probably me getting a bruise.

I'm in no danger of going overboard, but he still takes me by the arms and gently rights me. "Okay, maybe you were right to be a little worried. You're kind of clumsy."

I smooth my mane and half of it falls in my face, which I try to blow out of the way.

As I regain my footing, I say, "I am. But I blame that on the waves."

I unbuckle the life jacket, and he glances out over the very calm water, then smirks at me. "It's a regular hurricane out there."

There's always a moment in every new friendship or relationship where you, pun not intended, "test the waters" by gently insulting the other person. It's good-hearted ribbing, but if you move on this too soon, you're in danger of seeming like you can't take the joke.

I take a calculated risk.

"Shut up," I say, chucking the life jacket at him.

He grins at me, then tosses the life jacket right back at me.

Worth it.

"Where are we?" I ask because I'm not supposed to know.

"You'll see."

"Is this the spot for underground raves or something?" I laugh.

He chuckles softly, and I feel proud for having made him smile.

It would be nice to make a habit of that, even though I know that after tonight, I may never see him again.

I follow him up the dock and onto the sandy shore, a small patch compared to the shore by the bar. The sun has fully plunged below the horizon, and the air has turned brisker, and thankfully there's still the faint blue light of dusk to lead the way.

We hike up a narrow staircase, and as we round the front of the building, the recently familiar wooden sign comes into view: "Driftwood Restoration."

"Is this where you work?" I ask.

"Yeah," he says. "But it's also where I play."

"I'm listening for the dance music," I say with a teasing smile.

"You have a warped idea of fun."

He opens the door and flips on the light. The space is large and open with a tall ceiling that houses several boats in various states of disrepair.

"You fix boats?" I ask, turning to him. "Like a mechanic?"

"Not really," he says. "I restore them."

"Like a historian," I say.

"I never thought of it that way," he says. "But yeah. Kind of like that."

"Okay, but this is where you *work*, right? Aren't you supposed to be showing me what you like to do for fun?"

His eyebrows shoot up. "Follow me."

He turns around and walks toward the back of the shop. I hesitate again, checking for any stranger-danger warning bells to go off at the back of my mind. When none appear, I take a few steps toward a space in the shop that's been sectioned off. Here, there's a completely different kind of boat. Smaller. Wooden.

Beautiful.

It's up on a platform off the ground and seems to be half finished.

"*This* is what I do for fun," he says.

I glance up at him and find him looking at the boat the way a proud parent might look at a child. "Wow. Did you build this?"

"Yeah." One corner of his mouth twitches up in a half smile.

"That's impressive."

"I restore all kinds of boats, but the old ones are my favorite. I got to work on one from the landing in Normandy last month, and it was incredible."

"Whoa, really? Where is it now?" I ask.

"In a museum over in Beaufort," he says. "I do demonstrations there sometimes."

A ridiculously good-looking guy who reads, is great with people, loves history, and works with his hands.

He might be a little *too* perfect. *I'm doomed.*

"There's a wooden boat show coming up in a couple of weeks. I'd invite you to come, but I'm guessing you'll be long gone by then."

I do a double take, hopefully not too noticeably. "You'd . . . invite me to come?"

He shrugs. "Well, yeah. Sure."

"Why, though? You just met me, like, two hours ago."

He makes a face. "You seem nice. And you're not like everyone else who lives in this town. Plus, you seem like the type who'd appreciate it."

The Georgina part of this plan is fading further and further into the background.

"How'd you get started restoring boats?" I ask. "It's such a unique thing to do."

"My dad," he says. "He loves the water, and he taught me everything I know." He looks a bit nostalgic, wading through fond memories. "It's funny—whenever something was bothering me, he'd make me come out to the garage and help him with whatever boat he was working on. I hated it because I don't love being told what to do . . ."

"What teenager does?" I laugh.

"Right? But somehow, after a few minutes, I always found it easier to talk about things. To say whatever I needed to say. It didn't feel as intimidating having a conversation when my hands were occupied."

"For me, it was my mom and the garden," I say. "She'd insist she needed my help, and before I knew what was happening, I was spilling my guts while pulling the weeds."

"Brilliant parenting," he says.

"Your dad sounds like a good guy."

"He is."

It occurs to me that Georgina may have unfinished business with Hayden's dad too.

I peer around the space and notice a large, old boat sitting up on a platform. "What about this one?" I walk over to it.

"Oh, that's a work in progress."

As I move around to the end of the boat, I see the faded red letters in a neat cursive: *Georgina.*

This is the boat Georgina told me about. Her charging dock.

"Did you name this one too?" I ask.

He looks away. "No, she's also a rescue."

Georgina should see this. She needs to see this. If she gave it to him, he kept it, and that says something—doesn't it?

"When do you head back to New York City?" Hayden asks from behind me.

"Tomorrow," I say.

A pause, and then, "And what will you tell my mother?"

My mouth goes dry.

Oh no.

Chapter 22

KELSEY

He knows.

It would be stupid of me to try to pretend I don't know what he's talking about. And it was dumb of me to hope I could carry on this little charade. It's dishonest, for one thing, and I really don't want to be dishonest with him—and that has nothing to do with Georgina.

"That's why you agreed to hang out with me tonight," I say, realizing. "Because you recognized me." And not because we had some crazy, electric connection.

"Immediately," he says, crossing his arms.

"Not because of my stunning beauty?" I joke.

He shrugs and smiles. In spite of having every right to be angry with me, he still smiles.

"You're not . . . mad?"

He shakes his head. "I probably should be, right? I don't know if you were sent, or if you're trying to get some information out of me, or if you're just spying."

"It's none of those things, I swear."

He tilts his head. "Then what is it?"

I feel embarrassed, but not sure why. I truly believe my reasons were altruistic in wanting Georgina to reunite with Hayden—and

I know in my core that she and I were put together for a reason. Some reason.

I look down. "It's . . . complicated." And then, after a pause, "You're really not mad?"

He smiles. "No. I mean, initially when I saw you, I had my suspicions, but you unfortunately turned out to be really nice."

I laugh despite feeling caught.

"You were the only person I spoke to the entire time I was in New York. Plus . . . you're kind of hard to forget."

I feel the heat rise to my cheeks and desperately try to find a way to kick this conversation in a different direction. Off of me.

"How long did you stay?" I ask. "In New York, I mean."

"Three days."

"But you never saw your mom."

He smirks. "It's complicated."

"Touché."

The Google search. Georgina's reaction. The look on Hayden's face right now. All of those things scream "complicated."

"So."

I grit my teeth in a fake smile. "So."

"What *are* you doing here?" he asks. "And why were you driving my dad's car?"

I'm taken aback for a moment. "She said that it was . . ."

"That blue Mustang was a gift from my mom *to* my dad," he says.

I'm confused. "Then why does she still have it?"

He shrugs. "Dad didn't want it. When we left, he said he didn't want anything to remind him of the business that destroyed our family."

"Ouch," I say.

"It was pretty ugly."

"I'm sorry," I say. "And I really shouldn't be prying. It's none of my business." It *really* isn't.

Unlike Georgina, Hayden isn't mean to me for overstepping. He acknowledges it. He doesn't try to pretend that's not exactly what I've done. But he also doesn't lash out at me.

I'm thankful.

"Do you work for her?" he asks.

I shake my head. "I don't. It's . . . it's a long story. Is there somewhere we can go to talk?"

He looks around. There are literally no chairs in the entire space. "Yeah, follow me."

We walk away from the wooden boat and the *Georgina* and over to a very large, much newer boat in the middle of the shop. There's a ladder at the side of it, and Hayden motions for me to climb in.

"Up there?" I ask.

"You're not afraid of ladders too, are you?"

"Ha-ha." I start up the ladder, and when I'm a few steps up, I glance back down and find him watching me.

I take another calculated risk. "Don't look at my butt."

He laughs, and I'm so glad to hear it.

"I just want to make sure you don't fall. You nearly killed me just stepping out of a boat."

I turn around and keep climbing. "A likely story."

He follows me into the boat, which is surprisingly roomy. For a split second, I imagine taking this out on the water. Once I get over my fear of boat-eating sharks and shrieking eels, I bet this would make a pretty nice day on the ocean.

"This is incredible," I say.

"You should've seen it when the guy brought it in," he says. "I'll spare you the details, but we've done a complete overhaul."

I know talent when I see it. "You're good at your job, aren't you?" I ask.

He looks away, a shyness washing over him. "So I'm told."

Oh no.

I like him.

And not just because he's good-looking. He's got this quiet confidence, the kind that's not cocky or arrogant. Sure of himself, but still humble.

But I don't need to say yes to this. I can't. For a hundred reasons, just off the top of my head.

Number one on the list? He's the estranged son of the woman I dragged here.

Bad timing, Kelsey.

We sit down on the back bench of the boat, and I dream about what it would be like to have enough money to own such a vessel.

"So . . . ," he repeats.

I look over at him. "So . . ."

"You were going to tell me why you're here."

"Oh, right." I smile, feeling sheepish. Because while he was searching for answers, I was searching for a way to stop this whole night from feeling like the best date of my life. "I should probably just start at the beginning."

"Probably."

"It's kind of a crazy story actually," I say. "And it starts with me getting hit by a car."

"Right," he says. "You mentioned that. Did you know my mother before your accident?"

I shake my head. "We ended up in the same hospital room, which she really was not happy about."

I pause. The NDA.

Intuitively, he guesses, "She made you sign something, didn't she?"

I wince through gritted teeth and nod.

"Well, I don't think it applies to me, right?"

That makes sense. I hope.

I tell him the whole sordid tale. From waking up in the hospital, to meeting Georgina, to going back to work, to walking out a day later. I tell him about the penguins, about Ravi and the spicy food, and then I tell him how, for some inexplicable reason, I felt drawn to go back to the hospital.

"And that's when I saw you."

"And that's when I saw you too," he responds. "Hard to forget . . ."

My breath hitches.

". . . because of the pretzels."

Right. The pretzels.

Then I tell him about the Summer of Yes.

When I finish, he honestly looks impressed.

"Crazy?" I ask.

He shakes his head. "No, I think it's cool." A pause. "You just say yes? To everything?"

Georgina's example when she asked me that same question races through my mind. *"So, going to bed with a stranger?"*

"Yes . . . but within reason. I'm not going to rob a bank or punch the pope or something."

He laughs.

"It's yes to everything within certain boundaries. Like commonsense stuff. I'm not going to violate my own moral code or anything."

"But you'll go out on a boat with a strange guy you met in a bar."

"Yes," I say. "Because I actually knew who you were."

"I could still be a creep," he says.

"True. But you're not."

He nods. "I'm not."

"Plus, you never winked at me."

He laughs. "I guess that's good, that I don't give off creepy vibes." A pause. "But you still haven't explained what you're doing here."

I shrug. "Your mom says I'm obsessing over her life so I don't have to focus on my own."

"Are you?"

"Probably," I say honestly. "But her life is *way* more interesting than mine. And mine is a lot more confusing. Plus, she told me when we were in the hospital together that she has regrets. I can only assume she meant your relationship."

Over. Stepping.

"Ah, so you're here based on an assumption."

"Is that bad?" I ask, looking at him. "I really have no right . . ."

He shrugs. "I guess maybe I hoped that some part of this was her idea."

There's a pause, and for a flicker of a moment, I feel his pain. I imagine what it must've been like to be a little boy who lost his mother, his fully living, breathing mother. How abandoned does he feel?

"You obviously want to talk to her," I say. "You were there, in New York."

"Like I said, it's complicated."

"I get it," I say. "But she's here."

He meets my eyes. "She is? In Driftwood?"

I nod. "Yes. She was with me this afternoon, in the Mustang. You didn't see her?"

He shakes his head.

"Well, she's very small, so . . ."

His smile is sad. "How'd you get her to agree to come here?"

I look away. "I didn't tell her where we were going."

He laughs. "That's a bold move, Kelsey. How'd that go over?"

"Not very well, if I'm honest."

He clicks his tongue. "Yeah. That's my mom, for sure."

There's a pause. It's not awkward; it's nice—like when older couples at restaurants just enjoy each other's company without saying a word.

Then he brightens. "Hey."

I make a face at him. "Uh . . . hey."

He sits for a split second, looking like he's deciding to say something. Then, "Have you ever been night swimming?"

I frown. "What are we talking about here, in a pool? A large bathtub? What?"

He laughs, and I love it. "In the ocean, weirdo."

We've already progressed to fun name-calling. This casual familiarity and the way it makes me feel is going to be a problem.

"Do you want to go?" When I don't respond immediately, he screws up his face. "Ah. Maybe not," he backpedals. "Maybe it's a bit soon for that. Never mind. We just met, and it's a bit forward, and . . ."

But before he can take it back, I blurt out, "Yes."

Chapter 23

KELSEY

I'M LITERALLY WALKING a plank.

Sure, some people call it a dock, but whatever. It's a plank.

I start talking to myself. "What am I thinking? I don't have a suit, I'm terrified of the ocean, I'm not even really supposed to be here . . ."

"It's a full moon!" Hayden shouts from the end of the plank. "It's perfect!"

Perfect. For death. Sharks bite more humans when there's a full moon. It's a fact. It's called the lunar effect.

Thanks a lot, Shark Week.

Moments later, I'm off the plank and onto a sandy patch, looking at the rhythmic waves of the ocean. We're standing on the shore near where we docked the boat, and Hayden pulls his T-shirt off and tosses it aside. He glances back over his shoulder. "You're still coming, right? Is your yes bigger than your fear of the water?"

"Who said anything about being afraid?" I'm shocked I get these words out because my eyes are full of shirtless Hayden in the moonlight.

He wades into the water backward as gentle, lapping waves slap quietly at his heels, then his calves. "Aren't you?"

"Yes. Yes, I am. I'm afraid that if I go out into the ocean—in the dark—I'll get swallowed whole by a giant sea creature."

Or, at best, emerge with wet clothes that will take forever to dry because it's nighttime. And also afraid that this whole night could have serious repercussions because, while it's not, it really still feels like the best date of my life.

But it is warm out here. And I do feel sticky. And I did say yes. I take a few steps toward the water, slipping out of my sandals.

Hayden, up to his waist now, turns and dives straight into an oncoming wave, coming up seconds later with a joyous shout. "You don't want to miss this."

"It's cold!" I holler.

"It's refreshing!" he hollers back.

I look around and then pull off my top, leaving me standing there in shorts and a plain white cami. No way I'm taking off any more than that, and I can feel everything inside me tensing up, trying to find a way out of this. Trying not to partake in the fun.

Trying to say no.

I toss my shirt over on top of my sandals and take a few more steps into the water, letting it rise up to my knees. I can feel the sharpness of the shells and rocks beneath my feet, but as I inch out farther, it slopes into softer, smoother sand.

"It's better if you just get in," he calls out. "Don't think, just do."

Don't think. Just do.

Just say yes, Kelsey.

"You do know how to swim, right?" he asks, moving closer.

"I know how to swim in a pool with no fish and no sharks," I say, getting slightly knocked around by the surprising power of these small waves.

"This is just like that." I catch his smile in the moonlight.

I smile back. "You're a liar."

"I'm not going to let anything happen to you," he says.

And again, I believe him.

"I'm thankful for that," I quip, shivering a little from the cold water. "I don't much feel like dying."

Twice, I'm sure there's an eel or a jellyfish or a *something* trying to attack my feet, and both times, he's at my side to scare away what is more likely a harmless fish.

He's not at all what I imagined. And I *did* imagine.

After I saw him at the hospital and pieced together who he was, I definitely daydreamed about him. He's exceeding my expectations. I just never thought he'd be so . . . kind.

"You promise you're not mad at me?" I ask.

He frowns, moving out to where the water is not quite deep enough to require us to tread to keep above it. "Why would I be mad at you?"

"Because I came here without asking," I say. "And I brought your mom, who is a perfect stranger to me."

"And to me." His eyes crinkle at the edges in what looks like his best "I'm okay with this" smile.

"Do you still want to talk to her?"

He dunks his head under the water—without holding his nose, which is impressive to me—and when he comes up, he pushes his hair off his face. The moon *is* full, maybe the fullest I've ever seen, and there's enough light for me to make out his expression.

"I think the better question is, does she want to talk to me?" he asks, wiping the dripping water from his face and eyes.

We're out a ways—at least, a ways for me. I didn't realize how far away the shoreline was. We've also drifted a bit to the left of where the dock is. The waves must be pushing us in that direction.

I bob on my tiptoes a little closer, and the second my foot loses contact with the sandy floor of the ocean, Hayden reaches over and puts a hand under my elbow, just to let me know he's there.

Just in case.

I tread water for a few seconds, reaching down and finding the floor again.

Normally this would be terrifying . . . but it's not so much.

Normally I would never be in this situation . . . but here I am.

There's something about Hayden that allays my fears. Makes me feel okay with the unknown depths around me.

Still, we're drifting out a bit far.

"Can we move a bit closer to the shore?"

He lets a swell lift him up slightly, then back down. "Of course."

"I would normally *never* do this. *Ever.*"

He pushes off the ocean floor backward toward the shore, and the wave carries him a little. "I'm glad you said yes."

I turn around and mimic him, pushing off and letting the wave carry me. It's exhilarating and unnerving, losing my feet, but the feel of the water around me, the sensation on my skin—the moon and the mood and the movement—it's something I can't believe I've denied myself up to this point.

Saying yes to simple pleasures might be even more important to me than saying yes to big things. After all, it's the little moments that make a life.

"I think she's afraid," I say.

He frowns over at me and then realizes I'm revisiting our previous conversation. "My mother?" He shakes his head. "She's not afraid of anything."

"She's afraid to admit she was wrong," I say with more authority than I have. "Maybe afraid of her worst fear coming true."

"What's that?"

"You not forgiving her." I go silent, still pushing the water away. "I mean, I'm guessing."

Am I, though? She basically admitted to it earlier today. Besides, even her silence speaks volumes. She does regret losing

Hayden. She maybe even regrets losing her marriage. And maybe she's been able to convince herself it wasn't her fault or that it didn't really matter, but with her current diagnosis, surely she is coming to terms with the fact that she's been kidding herself.

Again, I remind myself I'm interfering. And yet it feels gravely important to fix what's broken in Georgina's life. For her, of course, and for Hayden. But also because if her life is a picture of my future, I want it to look different.

We're close enough to shore now where we can stand waist-deep in the water.

"Maybe let's talk about it later," he says.

"We're leaving tomorrow," I say.

"Yeah." He goes quiet for a moment. And then, "I do understand why you did what you did."

"Really?" I ask with a slight laugh. "Because Georgina's totally mad at what I did."

"I think life's too short to get angry about little things," he says. "Especially when someone meant well."

"I did mean well."

"I know," he says, then grins. "You lasted a lot longer than I thought you would."

I splash water toward him, then turn and trudge toward the shore. I tiptoe over the spiky shell layer, then up onto the beach, wet sand clinging to my feet and ankles. "We should've grabbed some towels."

"Yeah, next time I'll make sure to plan better." He laughs.

Next time . . . ?

"I actually have some towels in the boat," he says. "Come on."

I'm shivering as I pick up my shirt and my shoes and follow him over to the dock. The air is warm, and there are insects singing in the trees that line the beach. He gets into the boat and pulls two towels out from under the driver's seat, handing one over to me. I use it to dry off, then wrap it around my body.

He reaches a hand up, then helps me down into the boat. I assume he's going to take me back to the boardwalk, but instead, he moves to the back and sits down on the leather bench.

"All right, spill," he says.

I'm standing there wrapped in a towel, still dripping and clutching the only dry piece of clothing I have. "Spill?"

"Tell me about you," he says.

"You can't possibly be interested in my life story," I say. "It's utterly boring."

"I am, though," he says.

"Why?"

He shrugs. "We don't get many new people in town."

He seems sincere, which is strange. It's been ages since anyone asked me to share anything personal about myself. "What do you want to know?"

He pauses, as if to consider my question. "Something nobody else knows."

I laugh. "What makes you think there's anything nobody else knows?"

"We all have secret stuff, right?"

Oh man, do I want to know his.

It's not lost on me that this conversation is swiftly veering into uncharted territory. This is the part of a new relationship I usually don't have time for.

I look for convenience, not connection.

Ravi always says I'm hard to know. I'm starting to think it's because I never really spend the time to let people in.

Closing myself off. I wonder if that's more fear?

Fear of getting hurt? Fear of being known?

Fear of a real relationship?

This—Hayden and me—definitely isn't the start of a relationship.

This is simply two people who happen to have his mother in common. There's no reason for me to tell him anything about myself.

And yet there's no reason *not* to either.

What am I afraid of? That he'll use it against me? That he'll hurt me? That someone else in the world will know me—the real me—and maybe not like what they see?

If I'd made a true bucket list, having a heart-to-heart with a handsome stranger wouldn't have been on it. But the point has been to stay open to whatever comes my way.

And now *he* has come my way . . . even if I did orchestrate our meeting.

Say yes. Say yes. Say yes.

"I want to be a writer." The admission comes out in a blurt.

"Oh yeah?" He leans back and watches me, like this isn't really that big of a deal. A drop of water hangs on the top of a hair at his forehead, then falls onto his lap. "Like, write the Great American Novel?"

"No, actually," I say. "And I guess that was my problem."

The boat rocks back and forth gently, in a way that could probably lull me to sleep in seconds after my long day of driving.

"Why was that a problem?"

"I wanted to write fun stories," I say. "Romantic stories. Comedies. Things that move people. The kinds of stories that make people laugh through tears."

"What's wrong with that?" he asks.

"It's not what 'serious' writers write." I shrug. "My parents are both theatre professors at a college in Upstate New York, and when I was growing up, anytime my sister and I had a bad day or felt down about something, you know how they cheered us up?" I look at him. "They told us stories."

"They sound cool," he says. "And I bet they do killer accents."

"They do." I laugh. "I used to write plays and make my sister act them out after dinner. Sometimes my dad would add these silly songs to the stories I made up. In our house, my stories were celebrated. Performed."

"Do you know how lucky you are that you can say that?" he asks.

"I do actually," I say. "I really do. It's not lost on me how supportive my parents were—and still are." And before I can stop myself, I add, "I'm guessing it was a bit different in your house growing up, huh?"

He stiffens.

I feel terrible. "I'm sorry, I shouldn't have . . ."

He holds up a hand. "No. It's okay. You're right. It was . . . different."

And that's all he says about that.

I wonder if his childhood was all broken or if there are still some good memories lingering. After all, the *Georgina* is sitting in his shop. Did he keep it to remind him of better times?

I don't try to talk him into saying more.

Which is good because he changes the subject. "So are you keeping a list of all the things you've said yes to?"

"No, but I should! That's actually a great idea," I say.

"You should add 'night swimming' and 'having a conversation with a stranger at an oceanside bar' to that list." He smirks.

It's funny. He doesn't feel like a stranger at all anymore.

And thinking about it, I realize he never did.

The theatre curtains of my mind pull back, revealing two people.

A man and a woman stand hand in hand, center stage, with a small cast of people around them. Behind them are racks of costumes, and in an assembly line of sorts, they put on and pull off different outfits on the couple.

The racks are pulled in front of the couple, and each time they pass by, they're in a different outfit, quick-change style.

A set of gray wigs and reading glasses for both, an apron for her and a tweed cap for him. He holds a newspaper and she holds a book. Elderly.

The racks pass by, those costumes are whisked off and replaced with a flannel for him and a dress for her, and a twentysomething cast member stands next to them in a cap and gown, college diploma in hand. Middle-aged.

Racks roll. Costumes are removed and replaced with a pregnant pillow for her (which she puts under her shirt) and a brown paper bag for him (which he breathes in and out of comically). New parents.

Another pass, and this time we see them dressed in more modern clothes—her in a smart black dress and him in a casual tie. They're holding wineglasses, clinking them together. First date.

Several more changes, all aging backward, until the last one is the two of them dressed like kindergartners—him with a Peppa Pig backpack and mismatched socks; her with fun pigtails and a Barbie T-shirt.

Through all of this, they never let go of each other's hands.

I fade back to the real world, and as I do, I'm reminded of what Georgina said about love at first sight. How it was the most inane, ridiculous idea she'd ever heard of. Impossible. And it probably is all of those things.

Still, for some reason, here I am dreaming about a theatrical production of my imagined relationship with Hayden.

"Do you know anything about the stars?" he asks.

"I know I can hardly see them in New York." And that I haven't looked at them since I was a kid backyard camping with my parents.

I suddenly miss them.

I mentally add "visit home" to my plans.

He kicks his feet up on the side of the boat, angling his body over toward mine. Our shoulders are almost touching, and I don't even care anymore that I'm still soaked straight through.

I'm just happy to be here.

Happy.

Such a departure from stressed, or frantic, or overwhelmed, or any of the other feelings I normally feel on the daily.

He points. I look. He explains. I fill in the blanks on some of the Greek mythology (because I *love* Greek mythology) and he surprises me by already knowing almost all the stories.

For as much as I feel pulled into my imagination lately, I make a deliberate choice to remain present in this moment.

I focus on the fact that I've not only ridden on a boat in the ocean but also *gone swimming* in it. And now I'm stargazing with a new . . . friend.

This is huge.

Chapter 24

KELSEY

You know what I'm *not* planning to repeat after my Summer of Yes is over?

Staying out until all hours of the night on a boat next to a guy I'm pretty sure I'd be perfectly happy to spend the rest of my life with . . . *when I'm supposed to be back at a hotel with his mother.*

I might not have even noticed, but then Hayden shifted and I yawned and sleep tried to come for me.

"What time is it?" I ask.

He shifts and looks at his watch. "It's almost four."

"In the morning?!" I'd laugh if I weren't so shocked. How did it get to be 4:00 a.m.?

"Do you have a curfew?" he jokes.

"No, but . . . your mom!"

He calmly starts the boat and spins the wheel opposite from the shoreline.

"You're not going to tell me to calm down?" I ask. "Or tell me I'm overreacting?"

His brow furrows. "Should I?"

I stand, tipsy from the way the boat moves beneath my feet. "No." I pull the elastic from my hair and shake out my long waves.

"Whoa," Hayden says. "I wish you could see yourself right now."

I scrunch my nose and turn away. "Yeah. It's a hot mess."

After a pause, he says, "I think you look beautiful."

I stop and look at him, and he shrugs and smiles. "Sorry. But you do."

He says this so earnestly, it stuns me. In a world where people dance around what they think, Hayden speaks it out loud. It's refreshing.

I went swimming in the ocean. I probably smell like halibut. What was left of my makeup was washed away by salt and water.

But Hayden still said I was beautiful.

Beautiful.

And I feel the compliment all the way to my toes.

I stumble over a "Thanks, um, so do you," because I'm aspiring to be a writer.

He laughs to himself as he pushes the throttle, and the boat tips down at the back end, starting to move through the water with more speed. "I'll get you back to the hotel."

"No," I say, realizing that Georgina is getting up in a half hour and has probably already made plans to go back to New York without me.

"You don't want my mom to see you," he says.

I shake my head. "It would add fuel to the fire."

He angles the boat. "Then I'll drop you close by."

I nod and settle in for the short ride back to the boardwalk.

When we arrive, Hayden jumps out and ties the boat to a dock, then stretches out a hand to help me up. And he doesn't let it go, not even when I'm safely standing on the dock right in front of him. Instead, he holds it and looks me straight in the eyes.

"It was really nice to meet you, Kelsey Worthington."

Wait. This is goodbye.

I'm not ready for goodbye.

How can I not be ready? I just met him. It should be easy to walk straight up that dock and out of his life forever. And that's exactly what I *should* do because we're leaving today.

So why am I still standing here wishing he'd kiss me?

He reaches over and tucks my disobedient hair behind my ear. It feels familiar, comfortable, safe, like we've known each other for years.

Something in my mind, like a cog in a wheel, slips in and clicks.

Suddenly I want to tell him *everything*. All the things I bottle up. All the things I keep to myself, the things I never had time for before. I want to be known. And that feeling is as unfamiliar as swimming in the ocean.

I reach up and point to the scar above his right eye. "What happened there?"

"I got hit in the face with a golf ball," he says.

"For real?"

He rubs the scar with a few fingers. "For real."

"Ouch."

The corner of his mouth twitches up in a soft smile.

I linger. "Thanks for the night swim. And the boat ride."

He nods. "Anytime."

And then, because I like to ruin things, I say, "Why don't you meet us for breakfast? Me and Georgina?"

He deflates so slowly, it's like watching air drain from a tire. "Oh, um . . . I don't think that's such a great idea . . ."

"I know it feels awkward, but we're leaving today," I say. "And I really don't want to leave."

"I really don't want you to leave either." His eyes flick to mine. Am I imagining the war going on there? Is it just wishful thinking?

"But I should get going," he says. "Coco always has access to the yard, but I need to go feed her and—"

"I'm going to take your mom to that little café next to our hotel," I say, cutting him off. "I passed it on my walk last night.

Just in case you change your mind." I reach out and he offers his hand—which I take in both of mine. "She *should* be the one to make the first move, Hayden. But that doesn't mean you can't."

He slowly looks at me, eyes dipping to my lips, then back. "I really like you, Kelsey."

I smile. "I really like you too."

"And normally, I'd do anything for anyone." A pained look washes across his face.

"I get it," I say. "I hope to see you around."

But I won't, will I?

Because this is where this ends.

I take a step back, away from him, wishing I could conjure a reason to stay, but I know there isn't one.

Maybe Hayden was simply meant to help me realize I want a real relationship. That I want more than someone to pass the time with. I want a *love story*.

And I suppose I should be grateful that I know it now.

I walk up the dock, and when I reach the boardwalk, I turn around to wave at him. He watches me with a quiet intensity I'm not sure how to process. He lifts a hand in a silent wave, and then he steps back in his boat and drives away.

As much as I want him to know everything about me, I want to know everything about him even more. And my curiosity has nothing to do with Georgina.

Somehow, he feels like a part of my story too.

And that's when I remember.

She's probably up.

Doing dialysis.

Thinking.

Definitely going to want to know where I've been.

Welp.

Chapter 25

KELSEY

IT's NOT EXACTLY a walk of shame, but boy is it close.

Oh, sorry, G, don't worry about me, I was just falling for your son whom you haven't talked to in, like, a million years. But yay me! I swam! In the ocean! At night! Aren't you proud of me?

I come into the suite, and I can hear her machine whirring in the other room, but the door is closed, just like it was when I left last night.

There's a slim chance she has no idea I didn't come back here.

I rush over to my bed and mess up the covers. Then I think, *It's not even five o'clock in the morning—why would I be up now?*

Then I think, *Maybe I can say her machine woke me up and I couldn't fall back to sleep*, and I mess the bed up a little more.

I frown. I'm a writer. I should be able to make up a good story. But unfortunately, writing and lying are two different things. I happen to be very bad at the latter, much to my parents' delight.

I pull out a change of clothes, my toiletries, and my toothbrush. I hurry into the bathroom and try to turn on the shower as quietly as possible, which is ridiculous because showers don't have volume control. The water shoots out in a cold stream and splashes loudly against the tiled walls.

If she didn't hear me when I came in, she hears me now. Oh well.

I strip off my still-damp clothes, shower, and then get dressed. By the time I'm finished, Georgina is sitting on the little sofa in the main area of the suite with her packed bag at her feet.

"Oh, hey," I say, avoiding her watchful eye.

"Hey?"

"Hello." I glance at her. "Good morning, I mean. Your, um, machine, it . . . um, it was loud, and I couldn't go back to sleep, so . . ."

She doesn't say anything. Just sits there with her lips pursed.

"So . . . yeah. I'm up. Early. Up early with my thoughts." My lame explanation falls flat. I clear my throat because this is a tough room. "How did you sleep?"

"Fine. *Where* did you sleep?"

Well, crud.

My throat goes dry like cotton balls are blocking my airway. "Oh, I went out."

"Obviously," she says. "Did you have a change of heart about that whole 'going to bed with strangers' plan?"

"What? No!" I face her. "I didn't 'go to bed' with him!"

"Him?" She narrows her eyes.

I scramble. "I mean, *anybody*. With *anybody*." Controlling this conversation is like trying to wrangle a wild boar. "And nobody calls it 'going to bed' with someone."

"What do they call it?"

I frown. This is awkward. "I don't know," I say. "Other things."

"I don't really care," she says. "Are you almost ready to go?"

"Now? It's so early."

"You have a reason to stay?"

YES.

I sit. "You still want to leave, huh?"

"Can we have a conversation about your terrible use of the English language? You're an editor. Don't use words like 'huh.' And don't say things like 'hey.' You're not in college anymore."

"Okay," I say. "This doesn't feel like much of a conversation. This is just you berating me about the way I talk."

She gives her trademark hand flick and looks away.

"I saw a cute breakfast place on the boardwalk," I say. "We can stash our bags and grab some food, and then, if you really want to, we can get on the road."

"Why would you say 'if you really want to'?" she asks. "You already know my feelings on this subject."

"I was hoping maybe you'd had a change of heart."

"My heart doesn't change," she says.

"Fine. Before we go, I'd like to grab some breakfast. And before that, some coffee. And before *that*"—I point at her with both fingers—"I think I just need to lie down for a second."

"Lack of sleep will do that to you, you know."

I conjure boldness and flick my hand at her the same way she does to me. "Just give me about an hour and a half, and I'll be ready to go."

She harrumphs back into her room, then reaches over to grab a book out of her bag.

I set my alarm to wake me in an hour, then lie down. And I don't remember anything until I hear the soft tones of my phone waking me back up.

....

We check out of the hotel and stash our bags in the trunk of the car. Then we walk toward the café. The sign above the door simply says "Family Diner," and I half expect Georgina to give the owner a lesson in branding. But then we walk in and find the place is full, and the only conclusion that can be drawn is that they're doing just fine.

A waitress whose name tag says "Shelby" leads us to a table right in the center of the room.

"Oh, good," Georgina says. "Because I love being on display when I'm eating."

Shelby frowns.

"It's perfect, thank you," I say, smiling at the poor girl. After she walks away, I glare over at Georgina. "Could you just be nice?"

"What?" she asks. "I'm perfectly nice. I simply do not understand why she didn't seat us over there." She points to a table near the window. "Actually, let's move." Now she stands.

"Georgina, maybe there's a reason she—"

"Waitress!" Georgina says this so loudly everyone in the restaurant looks at us. Me and the crazy, rude lady who's dressed like she's going out for a day on the town—not like she's about to have breakfast at a casual café on the beach.

So much for not wanting to be on display.

"We're going to sit over here!" She motions for me to follow her, and because I clearly have no other choice, I stand up and move to the other table.

I look at Georgina, who is utterly clueless.

"See?" she says. "Much better. Look, you can stare out the window at the ocean and everything."

"Since when do you like to stare at the ocean?"

She doesn't respond.

Unfortunately for me, Georgina is busy on her phone, which means I'm stuck sitting here, staring out the window and at the door every single time someone walks in. It's ridiculous for me to hope that Hayden will change his mind, but I can't help it.

I hope he changes his mind.

"What are you doing? You're so antsy," Georgina says without looking up.

"I'm not antsy."

"You are, actually."

Shelby brings our food out, and I push mine around on my plate. I want to ask Georgina if she can drive herself home so I can stay here and have another wonderful not-date with her son.

I wish I could put her on a plane and drive the car back in a week or never, but that's not going to fly either. And I know it.

She gets a phone call just as Shelby sets the check down at the table. It's JP, and I tune out.

I think my intentions have changed regarding my reconciliation plan, and I don't know if that's good or bad.

Georgina hangs up the phone, and I make a face at her—a hopeful one, trying to ask without asking if she's rethought her position.

"Please tell me that look on your face isn't about me," she says.

"What look?" I ask, feigning innocence.

"That 'kicked puppy' look," she says. "Guilt has never worked on me."

"Oh, I'm not trying to make you feel guilty," I say. "I'm trying to make you feel bad."

"I don't feel either."

"Not even a little bit?"

She presses her lips together. "Like I said before, this is none of your business."

"I know." *So why can't I let it go?*

A memory of last night scrolls through my mind. Hayden's smile. His kindness. His promise not to let anything happen to me. But more than that, the obvious, if guarded, hurt he feels when thinking about his mother.

And I know exactly why I can't let it go.

"We should get on the road." Georgina picks up the bill and starts rummaging through her purse. She'll insist on paying, but she'll make me handle the transaction. I've learned this about her after a couple days of travel.

She pulls out her card and slides it across the table. "Can you . . . ?"

I pick it up, along with the bill, and when I stand, I turn toward the cash register to find a freshly showered and *very* conflicted-looking Hayden Quinn.

I say his name on a slow exhale.

Georgina looks at me, then follows my gaze toward the door.

Their eyes meet, and I hold my breath. He glances at me, and I give him the slightest smile. At that, he moves toward our table.

They're quiet for a moment, both of them frozen, and then Hayden draws in a deep breath. "Hey."

Georgina's face softens. She smiles at him and her voice cracks slightly as she says, "Hey."

Chapter 26

GEORGINA

I'm dreaming.

I'm dreaming, and I don't want to wake up.

Is my son actually standing in front of me?

I stand, or try to, mouth agape, staring. Marveling. Wondering how that little boy grew up to be this strong, handsome man.

I remember the last time I saw him. He was thirteen. Just two years after Dylan took him out of the city, a move I didn't even protest because I believed it was the right one.

Also a move I regret more than anything.

What mother lets her son go?

One who was too selfish to ever be a mother.

He was an angry boy. He knew I'd abandoned him. No matter how many times I protested, claiming the opposite, I'd chosen my work over my family.

There's no undoing that now. I've made my peace with that.

I smooth my pants and press my lips together, then realize I'm still staring. "Please, sit."

Kelsey moves out of the way, and when Hayden passes by her, they make eye contact, and that's when I realize what's happened.

"You two have met," I say as Hayden slides into the booth across from me.

Kelsey looks like I've just caught them making out under the bleachers. She holds up the check and shakes it at me. "I'm going to go take care of this."

I watch as she scurries off, then I turn toward Hayden.

He's here, in the flesh, making the first move. And whether Kelsey got him here or not, he actually came. Regret heaps on top of regret. I'm the mother. I have things to apologize for. Things to explain. I should've made the first move.

The thought shames me.

"You came."

He smiles. "I did."

I have so, *so* many things to ask. To say. And one huge thing to apologize for.

"How are you?" I ask.

"Today or for the last twenty years?" He folds his hands on the table in front of him, then looks away. "Sorry," he says.

"I deserve that."

The memory of my only trip to Driftwood before now resurfaces. Dylan let me know that Hayden was competing in a regatta. It was the kids' division, and he was sailing solo, and *"it would mean a lot if you could be there."*

I tried to get there in time, but I missed the finish by about an hour, and when I showed up, Hayden was so angry, he finally said all the things that must've been accumulating in the two years since I let them leave. I still remember every word he said to me that day, but the most important takeaway was, *"I never want to see you again!"*

He was a kid. Kids get angry at their parents. I thought it would blow over. But in the years that followed, every attempt to reach out went unanswered. After a few more years, I finally stopped trying. No more invitations to New York City. Our relationship dissolved, and eventually Dylan stopped cashing the checks I sent for childcare.

I started a trust for my son with that money, and I still deposit funds into it monthly. Hayden may not know it, but even without taking over any stake in Tate Cosmetics, he's a very wealthy man.

He might've been young, but he never wavered in his decision. He did not want a relationship with me. Some days, thinking about it hurts. Some days, it makes me angry.

But always, it makes me sad.

"What are you doing here?" I ask, and I mean it as, *"What made you come to see me?"* but it comes off as *"Why did you show up?"* judging by the look on his face.

As if *he's* the one who needs to explain. I know as soon as the words are out of my mouth that they are the wrong words.

"I live here," he says. "What are *you* doing here?"

I flick a hand in Kelsey's direction, surprised she hasn't come back to the table to insert herself into this awkward conversation. "She made me come."

He scoffs a little and looks away. "I suppose I should be glad you're not pretending the trip was your idea." He pauses, giving me a moment to study him. It's been ages since I've seen his father, but Hayden looks just like him. Same intense eyes. Same jawline. Same broad shoulders. My goodness, he reminds me of Dylan.

I don't want to relive the past or any of my mistakes. I just want to tell him one thing: *I love you.*

What's stopping me?

Fear.

The word enters my mind, and I reject it just as quickly. Unlike Kelsey, I've made a point of living a life without fear.

I'm certainly not afraid of my own son.

But that's not quite true.

The fear I felt yesterday sitting outside his shop made me realize how much I want his forgiveness.

I want to apologize. To admit that I made a mistake. I'd trade my entire company for more time with Hayden. Judging by the look on his face, I'm lucky to have even these few, fleeting, awkward moments.

It's too late.

"You look good," I say, choosing surfacy small talk over anything meaningful. I don't *do* emotions.

"You . . . don't." His eyes meet mine. "You're sick."

I'm caught. And I nod.

"How serious is it?"

"My lawyer called to discuss this with you," I say, because it's the only thing I can think of.

"I don't want to discuss it with your lawyer," he says coldly. "I want to hear it from you."

I fold my hands on the table and lift my chin. "I didn't think you wanted to hear from me at all."

I can't stop myself. Why is this so hard?

He draws in a slow breath, and there's a little voice inside me begging me to *stop acting like a child. Be the bigger person. Tell him you're sorry already.* And another one reminding me: *This may be your last chance.*

I ignore them all. Because I'm stubborn and getting older and not used to apologizing. If I wasn't already set in my ways by now, the concrete is certainly hardening. And I know these things will cost me what precious little time I have left with him.

"Do you want to have dinner?" Hayden asks, stunning me silent before I can say a word. "I'm not a bad cook, and . . . you could see where I live. Maybe come into my work instead of hiding outside in Dad's car."

I glance at Kelsey, who has seated herself at the counter. At least she's not eavesdropping. She quickly looks away. "We're supposed to leave this morning."

He nods, and while it's only there for a breath, I see the sadness as it passes over his face. He extended an olive branch, and I grabbed it, broke it in half, and dropped it back in front of him.

He starts to slide out of the booth. "Okay, then I——"

"Wait." I cut him off.

He stops and looks hopeful. I see the boy in him still.

"I can see if that's okay with Kelsey," I say, searching for justification. "She's the one who's driving."

Hayden raises his eyebrows. "Okay."

I wave Kelsey over, and she rushes at us like this is what she's been waiting for. "Hey, guys." Her tone is too chipper, and I suspect what I'm about to ask her is going to make her entire year.

I know I need to change my heart. I *know* I do. He's not an employee; he's my *son.*

And he deserves the truth. All of it.

Time is running out, and I have to stop running away.

"Hayden has invited me for dinner tonight," I say. "Are you okay if we stay another night?"

"Of course," she says, like it's the best news she's ever heard.

"Both of you," he says. "You can both come."

Her cheeks turn pink, and I narrow my gaze at the two of them as she responds, "Are you sure you don't mind?"

He shakes his head. "Not at all. Besides, don't you have to say yes?" His eyes flick to mine, then he gets out of the booth. He hands Kelsey his phone. "Put your number in, and I'll send you the address."

"I know the address," I say.

He and Kelsey both snap their heads to look at me. "You do?" he asks.

I nod. Of course I do. I've known it for years, which makes it all the more horrible that it's taken this long—and a perfect stranger kidnapping me—for me to get here.

He looks at Kelsey. "Can you still put your number in my phone?" Then glances at me and adds quietly, "In case she changes her mind."

Kelsey does what he asks, handing his phone back after adding her number to his contacts. The first time I met Dylan, he asked me to write my phone number on his hand, but the only thing he had was a permanent marker. He later told me that number didn't wash off for eight days.

I said it was a sign.

I was so foolish then.

"All right. It's settled then." Hayden faces me. "It looks like I've got some shopping to do. I'll see you both tonight."

Kelsey mutters something I can't make out as he walks past her and out of the café, and I turn my full attention to her.

"Kelsey," I say. "Did you spend the night with my son last night?"

"What? No!" Her eyes go wide, and she sits back down with a sigh. "Well . . . not on purpose."

Chapter 27

KELSEY

I FOLLOW GEORGINA out onto the boardwalk, where we stand near the railing looking out over the water for too many silent minutes.

"I didn't seek him out," I try to explain. "I went for a walk, and I saw him sitting there in the bar. I . . . just took it as a sign."

"You and your signs." Georgina rolls her eyes. "I'm starting to wonder if you're interested in Hayden for my sake or yours."

I guess I don't have a very good poker face. Because the truth is, when I saw him standing in that diner, I was thrilled.

Partly for Georgina, partly for me.

Wishful thinking.

Stupid thinking.

This is *not* the kind of woman I want to be. And yet . . . I'm discovering I *am* the kind of woman who could get lost in his blue-green eyes. The kind that could do the whole "weak in the knees" thing every time I'm in close proximity to that man. Nobody, in all of my thirty-two years, has ever had this kind of effect on me.

But first and foremost, the priority here is *their* relationship. Not my fantasy.

"No response," Georgina says after what I'm guessing is a solid twenty seconds of me silently having a full-on conversation with myself in my own head. "Interesting."

Her phone rings, and she steps away to answer it, leaving me standing on the boardwalk, the warmth of the morning sun beating down on my shoulders. It's humid today, and it makes me think of my night swim with Hayden.

Pre-accident Kelsey never would've done that. Pre-accident Kelsey wouldn't have stepped in that boat.

I'm struck by just how much pre-accident Kelsey has missed.

My phone buzzes in my back pocket, and I pull it out to see a text from an unknown number. When I open it, I find:

> **Hayden:** It's Hayden. This is my number.
> **Kelsey:** 👍
> **Kelsey:** Adding it to my contacts now.
> **Hayden:** Great. Do you eat seafood?
> **Kelsey:** As a rule, no.
> **Hayden:** But since that's not a word in your vocabulary anymore . . . will you eat seafood?
> **Kelsey:** I'm starting to think I shouldn't have told you about my Summer of Yes.
> **Hayden:** You absolutely shouldn't have.
> **Hayden:** So . . . seafood?
> **Kelsey:** A very hesitant yes.
> **Hayden:** Trust me. I'm going to make you a fish lover.
> **Kelsey:** In any other context that would sound weird.
> **Hayden:** 😊
> **Kelsey:** I'll try it. But you'd better have a big salad around, just in case.
> **Kelsey:** And by salad, I mean pizza.
> **Hayden:** You won't need either.

Hayden: I'm glad I get to see you again.

Kelsey: Me too.

Kelsey: And I'm proud of you for taking that step. I know it wasn't easy.

Hayden: You made a strong argument.

Hayden: And I guess I wanted to try saying yes to something I'd normally say no to.

Hayden: You inspired me.

Kelsey: I'm very persuasive.

Hayden: You have no idea.

"You're grinning like a lunatic."

I turn and find Georgina staring at me. I snap my face back to neutral and tuck my phone away. "What should we do today?"

Georgina glances down the boardwalk, then back to me. "We can go back to the hotel, secure a room, work for a few hours."

"Okay, so, let's *not* do that," I say.

"There's not much else to do here," she says.

"Hmm, give me a minute." I pull out my phone and open my text thread with Hayden.

Kelsey: Any suggestions on how we should pass the time today?

Hayden: You're just waiting around until you see me again, huh?

Kelsey: Pretty much . . . but I do have a cranky old woman to entertain.

Hayden: You could come to the museum in Beaufort? I'm doing a demonstration today.

Kelsey: About boats?

Hayden: About boats.

Kelsey: Sounds fascinating. Send me the details.

I tuck the phone back in my pocket. "I have the perfect plan for the day."

"Oh, you're telling me what we're doing now instead of just springing it on me?" Georgina crosses her arms over her chest. "How novel."

"I would say I'm sorry for that, but I honestly don't think I am," I say. "Now that you've spoken to Hayden, some of the awkwardness is gone, and maybe you can find a way to reconnect."

"In the few hours we're here, you think we're going to undo twenty-plus years of awkwardness?"

I shrug. "It's a start."

She thinks for a moment. I really hope she's deciding against her normal knee-jerk nature. "What's your brilliant plan for the day?"

Wow. She did.

"Hayden is doing a boat demonstration," I say. "He makes and restores boats."

"I know that, Kelsey."

"Right. Of course. You saw the shop." I feel nervous, but I'm not sure why. Maybe because my little mission is no longer *just* about reuniting Georgina and her son. Maybe it's a little bit about me now too.

"So, what? We're going to watch his demonstration?"

"Yes," I say. "At a museum in a nearby town."

She appears to be considering this, maybe playing out some scenario in her mind. She steels her jaw and looks at me. "I'll pass."

I frown. "What? Why?"

"I don't like museums."

"I know that's not true," I say. "I read that you're on the board for three different museums in the city."

"This is hardly the city."

"Don't do that, Georgina."

She starts to walk away. I have no idea where she's going, since we don't currently have a hotel room, but I follow her anyway.

"He took the first step," I say. "That has to count for something." When she doesn't respond, I add, "I know it was hard for him to come to the café this morning. Hard for him to invite you to dinner. But he did it. You have got to meet him halfway."

Georgina is so unmovable, she might as well be a grand piano.

After a few seconds of silence, she stomps off. "How far away is this museum?" she asks, loud enough for me to hear.

I want to point out that she's acting like a child.

I shouldn't.

But I do.

"You're acting like a child," I call after her.

She whips around and does something completely unexpected.

She sticks out her tongue at me.

I gasp, a real one, and say, "You did *not* just do that!" I start toward the car as she hurries into the passenger side and slams the door.

"Okay, old woman, I see how this is going to go," I scold her to myself as I reach for the handle.

We start the drive toward Beaufort. I've got the museum address plugged into my phone, and according to Google Maps, we're about a half hour away. And Georgina is a captive audience.

"You know, I hate to say it, but you've got to do something about your attitude," I tell her once we're on the road.

"Don't start preaching at me like one of those insipid twenty-five-year-old motivational speakers you see all over the internet," she says with a huff. "They think they know everything until they hit an age where they realize they actually know nothing." She crosses her arms and stares out the window.

"All I mean is, Hayden is a good guy," I say.

"Yes, it's obvious what you think of Hayden." Then, after a pause, she adds, "What about you?"

"What about me?"

"What are you doing to fix your own life?"

I stare at the road in front of me. "Yesterday, I said yes to a bunch of things I'd normally say no to."

"Like the no-dating thing? What did that take you, a whole forty-eight hours to switch that one around?"

"I didn't—" I let my heavy sigh finish the sentence.

"You like him," she says.

"I'm not talking about this with you."

She turns away, silent.

She thinks she's just won because she turned it around on me. Again.

Without thinking of the risk, I launch.

"I do like him. Are we dating? No. We just met. Would I like to date him? Yes. Absolutely, I would. Will I? No, because right now I care more about you and him figuring your crap out. Do I hope it happens? Yes, because then you just might stop treating me like some stupid millennial intern who doesn't know better!"

My voice steadily increased in volume through that whole diatribe, and it ends a bit louder than I anticipated. I glance at Georgina, half expecting her to chastise me for my rudeness, but instead, I find her watching me.

"Well, now." She folds her hands in her lap. "It's good to see you do have a voice of your own."

Chapter 28

KELSEY

When Hayden told us he was doing a demonstration, he failed to mention it was for a group of about fifty kids.

From the second we get out of the car, it's clear the museum is overrun with children on a field trip from a local summer camp.

And Georgina isn't having it.

"You have *got* to be kidding me," she says, extra grumpy on account of two young boys knocking into her on the way through the doors to the museum.

I try to ignore her and lead her inside. As we enter, I see the group gathering off to the side. There are a few young camp leaders trying to calm them down, but someone must've given them a double dose of sugar on the way here because nobody is listening.

And then there's the sound of four loud claps. The chatter softens as the kids' attention is drawn to the front of the room. And there, standing up on a bench, is Hayden. He claps again, four times in rhythm, then points at the kids. A call-and-response type of activity, and they catch on immediately, clapping back the same rhythm.

They go back and forth a few times, and then Hayden starts to make the rhythm more difficult, making goofy faces at the kids as they fail to keep up and then finally ending with a loud "Shhhh!"

And everyone is quiet.

"Wow," I say. "That was impressive." I glance over at Georgina, and I see undeniable admiration in her eyes.

"Good with a crowd. He gets that from his father."

I don't need to go back in time to get a clear picture of their family dynamic. Georgina, the powerful, driven, ambitious businesswoman and her husband, the nurturing, bighearted, fun parent.

And Hayden, the result of that pairing. The best of both.

I glance over at him and catch him looking at me. His smile widens, and then he turns his attention back to the kids. He does a brief presentation, all about something called a dinghy boat, which, I'm gathering, is a very small sailboat, big enough for just one or two people.

He lingers on the word "dinghy," and the kids lose it, laughing and chattering.

He gives a brief lesson on the terminology, which I find strange since it has nothing to do with wooden boats and how to restore them, but the kids are actively engaged in everything he's saying.

I'm less engaged because I'm trying not to let myself daydream about Hayden, which is nearly impossible. The way he's captivated this entire group of once rowdy children is impressive, but not surprising. He's captivated me, too, though in a completely different way.

At one point, Georgina looks over at me and whispers, "Quit drooling."

"Shut. It," I hiss.

She responds with an uncharacteristic smile, and for the first time since we left New York, I feel more than just duty toward Georgina. I feel genuine affection. I'm starting to think she's a lot like an onion, and if I can keep peeling back layers, maybe I'll find there's something wonderful waiting inside.

Or maybe just something that will make me cry if I poke too deep.

"All right! Who is ready to sail a boat?" Hayden calls out to the group.

The kids let out a loud cheer. Georgina and I look at each other.

"I thought he would be teaching about boat restoration," I say.

"He's wearing swim trunks," Georgina says.

Maybe I should've paid closer attention.

"Hayden is apparently full of hidden talents," she says with a knowing glance back toward the front of the room. The young camp leaders have begun the process of herding the kids through the room and out a door in the back, which is a lot like herding cats, it turns out.

Hayden turns his attention to us.

He could point out that he's seen his mother more in the span of two hours than he has in twenty or so years, but he doesn't. He simply smiles and asks, "Are you ready to go sailing?"

"I thought you were doing a boat demonstration," I say.

He grins. "Yep. I'm demonstrating boats by actually going on a boat." He quips, "It's a new concept."

I smack him on the arm.

"Interesting job," Georgina says.

"Oh, it's not a job," he says. "I volunteer."

She frowns, like this is the strangest concept she's ever heard of. "They don't pay you?"

His smile is almost pitying, but he says, "I love it. I can't think of a better way to spend my time."

"And your job lets you do this?" Georgina asks.

He grins at her. "I own the restoration shop, so yes, I let myself do this."

She raises her eyebrows in surprise. "You own it now?"

And it's clear Georgina has been keeping track of Hayden. Maybe more than he knows.

"I bought it last year," he says. "It's a small business, but I have everything I need. And I get to teach kids to sail in the middle of the week if I want to." He looks at me. "And that's better than money."

I know he doesn't mean for this to be a dig against Georgina, but her jaw tightens and she looks away.

"What do you say?" he asks, unfazed. "Sailing lesson?"

Georgina lifts a single manicured hand. "I know how to sail."

"Right . . ." His voice trails off, and he looks away. My heart squeezes at the sight. He's trying so hard, and Georgina is giving nothing back.

There's a horrible lull, and I want to fill the space, but there are no words in my head.

And then, by the grace of God, Georgina asks, "Can I watch? I don't think my body is cut out for choppy waters."

"We'll be in the protected waters around Beaufort, and it's a very calm day." He starts off in the same direction the kids went, and we follow. "But yeah, you can watch."

"You can take Kelsey," Georgina says. "She can't stop staring at you, so you might as well give her a reason to do so."

I gasp. "Georgina!"

Hayden laughs a shy, boyish, "I'm embarrassed for you but flattered at the same time" laugh, and I swear I'd follow him straight into the shark-infested waters if he asked me to.

"What do you say, Kels? Wanna give it a try?"

He just nicknamed me. And I want him to call me that forever.

"No sharks, I promise."

I wince. "Right, but it's still the ocean."

He leans a little closer and whispers, "Don't think, just do."

Pre-accident Kelsey would never do this. She wouldn't wear the little helmet Hayden is strapping on my head. She wouldn't listen to him outline the basics of dinghy sailing or desperately try to commit every bit of that lesson to memory to keep the boat from rolling over.

But this Kelsey is going to tackle it all. It's an experience, and I want to have it. I don't want to wish it away, so I make a point to pay attention.

I'm going to learn to sail a boat.

Eat your heart out, Hemingway.

I glance at Georgina. She's sitting off to the side in the shade, and I get an idea. A quick search on my phone, followed by a short phone call, and I put it into motion. She'll probably get annoyed with me, but I don't care. I'm probably going to be dead from a capsized dinghy in an hour anyway.

We start on land. The kids are more adept at this than I am, which is obvious from the start. But according to Hayden, he can have us sailing in an hour.

After all the "boring stuff," according to a kid named Landon—who could do with a very long time-out—Hayden announces it's time to put what we've learned into action.

I notice there are several other instructors in matching trunks and tops to help get the dinghies in the water, and all at once, I want to hop out of the boat and run away.

What am I doing? I can't sail a dinghy! Before today, I didn't even know what a dinghy was!

But I don't hop out, and I don't run away. I start toward the water with the rest of the class.

I'm just one of the kids, don't mind me.

I'm about to step into my boat when a delivery guy shows up with two large bags. He glances around and finds Georgina, then hands over the art supplies to her just as I asked.

She looks up and finds me staring, so I quickly look away, suddenly feeling safer in this tiny boat than I would if I were standing over by her.

"Are you ready?" Hayden is at my side, and I look up, squinting from the sun.

"That's a funny question," I say. "Maybe I should just watch?"

"You want to watch all the ten-year-olds sailing around like they own the ocean while you stay here?"

I ponder and pout and process.

He gives me a look that communicates exactly what he's thinking—that I'm full of it. "Stop overthinking this," he says.

"Fine," I say.

"Great." He grins. "I'll get you started."

"Or you could just get in the boat with me?"

"Nah," he says. "Where would the fun be in that?"

He helps get my dinghy situated on the water, giving me a last-minute rundown of everything I need to do to keep my boat doing what it's supposed to.

"Don't worry, Kels," he says. "I'll be here the whole time."

And he is.

While managing the kids, who all have clearly had more than just this one lesson, he talks me through what to do to launch my boat onto the water. And I quickly learn that the point of this first sail, in the protected and very calm waters, is to acquaint myself with this little boat, to get comfortable with easy maneuvers, and to barely move away from the shore.

After a little while, I settle in, feeling safe and almost—but not quite—comfortable.

Out here, on the water, I start to realize I'm capable.

I'm capable of more than I think—and definitely more than I've let myself do up to this point.

I'm not saying I'll take up water sports anytime soon, but it's fun to try something I've never done before and wonder if I could ever become proficient at it. To the point where every accidental wobble doesn't scare me.

I glance back at the shore and see Georgina has finally pulled the canvas and paints from the bag.

I hope she might discover something new about herself out here too.

Chapter 29

GEORGINA

KELSEY IS A meddler.

Really. Art supplies.

I stare at them.

And they stare right back.

I open the bag, expecting to find subpar watercolors or cheap Walmart brushes—but they're not.

They're pristine. Paints and colors I would actually use.

I have no idea how she got them out here. But I'm not going to *use* them. It's been ages since I've picked up a paintbrush.

I turn my attention to the scene in front of me. Watching my son interact with kids in a way I never could stuns me.

And I find something about it inspiring.

Hayden moves his way through the little boats, helping not only Kelsey, who is lucky she's still dry, but everyone out there on the water. The other leaders wade out to troubleshoot, and there are, of course, kids who want to show off. He handles it all in stride.

This thing I could never master is what he was born to do.

Connect.

I pull the package of canvases from the plastic bag and look over what Kelsey ordered for me. I begin to unwrap the supplies and simply feel them between my fingers and in my hands.

My eyes drift out to the shore where Hayden is standing in the water next to Kelsey's boat. He says something, and she laughs and splashes him with her paddle.

Something inside me shifts.

It's been so many years of keeping myself *to* myself, I'm not sure how to act any other way.

She bought me this incredibly thoughtful gift, and my first thought is to criticize it. Was I always like this?

What if I simply said thank you?

What if I simply said yes?

I unwrap the two-pack of canvases and set one up on a small easel that the delivery boy said was "on loan." I scan the shoreline, the horizon, the tiny boats bobbing around in the water.

I pull out the small bottles of acrylic paint, open them, and set them in a neat row on the picnic table where I'm sitting.

Another look up tells me Kelsey is watching. I pretend not to notice as I dip my brush in the blue paint and tap it onto the canvas.

And I start to feel a tiny spark of something way down deep. Something familiar, but lost.

Something that feels a lot like joy.

....

Kelsey

When we come in from the water, I'm sunburned but exhilarated. The words are back, narrating the story of how the entire experience made me feel. I pull the helmet off as I make my way to Georgina, who is packing up her art supplies.

"You got my gift," I say. "I'm glad you used them."

She angles the canvas away from me so I can't see what she's been working on. "What else was I going to do? Go bird-watching?"

"One of these days you're going to be nice to me," I say.

"Don't bet on it."

I ignore her. "Show me what you painted."

"Absolutely not."

"Georgina!" I put my hands on my hips like a bossy toddler. "Show me!"

"Mind your own business," she says. "You really should go do something about your helmet hair."

Hayden walks up just in time to hear her say this, and he chuckles to himself as he gives me a once-over.

I try to fluff my hair, which does nothing. I still feel a defined crease midway down my scalp.

Nobody can say he's only hanging around me for my looks, that's for darn sure.

"Are you up for another adventure?" he asks, looking at both Georgina and me.

"That depends," I say. "What is it?"

"It's a surprise," he says.

"I think I'll stay here," Georgina says.

There's a flicker of disappointment on Hayden's face, but then he brightens as he turns to me. "You?"

I glance at Georgina.

"You go," she says. "I can drive myself back to Driftwood. Hayden, you can bring Kelsey when your little excursion is finished."

"Are you sure?" I ask. "You feel comfortable driving the car?"

She slowly turns toward me. "Kelsey, I do not need to be mothered. I'm fine."

"But what will you do?"

"Gosh, I don't know." Her tone drips with sarcasm. "However did I survive before I had you as my entertainment director?"

I give her a "yeah, yeah" look and barely keep myself from rolling my eyes.

After Hayden has walked away, she puts a hand on my arm. And in a completely different tone, she says to me, "Go. Have fun."

Then she leans closer to me and pats me on the arm. "Say yes."

And with that, she picks up the art supplies and walks away.

Hayden watches her, and I watch him, wondering how he feels being around Georgina for the first time in years. I want to ask, but I'm not sure she is what I want to be talking about right now, which might make me a very thoughtful or a very selfish person.

I'm just not sure which.

He glances over at me. "Ready?"

I take a breath. "Yes."

A few minutes later, we've boarded a ferry, and when he asks if I want a life vest, I glance around. "It's safe, right?"

He nods. "It's safe."

"Then I think I'm okay."

He smiles.

We walk over to the side of the ferry, and I stay close to Hayden, watching as the shoreline grows farther and farther away.

"Still okay?" he asks, probably sensing my hesitation.

I nod. "I am. I feel a little safer on a larger boat."

"Good," he says.

There's a pause, and then I say, "I'm sorry Georgina didn't come with us."

"It's okay." His jaw twitches, the wind catching his messy, sand-colored hair and pushing it back off his forehead. This windblown look is a good one for him.

Any look is a good one for him.

"I didn't expect her to come," he says.

"You didn't?"

He shakes his head. "I don't remember her being as into saying yes to surprises as you are."

I grin. "I know, right?" I bump into him. "I'm getting really good at it!"

He glances at me and smiles. "Yeah, but have you said yes to anything you really don't want to do yet?"

"Uh, yeah. Everything on the water."

"Really?"

"Yes, really. I'm *terrified* of the water. If you weren't there, I wouldn't have done any of these things."

"Oh, so you're just doing them to get close to me . . ."

My jaw snaps shut, but I resist my no. "Pretty much."

He laughs. "So my mother was right. You've been drooling."

I shoot him a look. "I mean, come on. You own a mirror."

Another laugh. And it feels good to flirt. To say the things that pop into my head without censoring myself. Especially when the reward for doing so is Hayden's smile.

He points in the direction of an island. "We're almost there."

"What is this place?"

The ferry begins the process of docking, and people start to move toward the exit. Hayden stays still, watching the commotion around him.

"Should we get off the boat?"

"We will," he says. "I don't like to rush."

I scoff. "You'd hate New York."

"I *do* hate New York."

I need to remember this. It's a very important difference between the two of us, and reason number one that I should stop imagining the exact moment when I can pledge my undying love to him.

Our lives are different, and unless one of us is willing to make a huge change, there's no future here.

We watch as people scurry past us, each racing toward the exit like there's a prize.

"I prefer to soak it all in," he says. "I mean, look at this place."

I follow his gaze back to the island in front of us.

"Where are we?"

"Shackleford Banks," he says. "It's a barrier island. Largely undeveloped."

I stare out across the beach in front of us as passengers scurry off the boat and onto the vast stretch of sand. "What are they going to do all afternoon?"

"Shelling, fishing, hiking . . ." Hayden starts walking toward the exit of the boat.

I follow. "I've never done any of those things."

He turns back and grins at me. I feel the heat of it from my toes to my shoulders. "Then you're in for a treat."

We turn and walk in the opposite direction of the rest of the group, something I'm thankful for. It's nice to go against the fray. To make our own path, regardless of where everyone else is headed. There's something wild and wonderful about all this open space.

I've learned to love New York—there's energy there that makes me feel alive.

But there's a peaceful mood here that accomplishes the same thing in a completely different way.

"Are you up for a hike?" he asks. "It's about a mile."

"Yes," I say, but what I really mean is, *"I'd follow you anywhere."*

My crush on Hayden seems to be getting worse, which is an unexpected side effect of going on this adventure. I like how calm he is. I like that he can take a day off in the middle of the week to volunteer with kids. I like that he's willing to show me a world I barely knew existed. His whole approach to life is what I've been trying to achieve, and seeing it in action makes me think maybe it's not completely unobtainable.

Still, despite the excellent company, it turns out hiking isn't my favorite thing to say yes to.

I'm not wearing the right shoes. I manage to find every uneven footfall and stumble every fifteen steps or so. Plus, it's *very* buggy.

After about ten minutes, I'm ready to turn around.

I don't want to be a killjoy, but it stands to reason that some new things I'm trying aren't going to jibe with my personality.

And this is one of them.

The mosquitoes are out in force, and apparently, I'm an all-you-can-eat buffet. I smack myself in the neck, and the noise pulls Hayden's attention. He turns and looks at me.

I give him a chagrined smile.

"You hate this," Hayden says.

"Mosquitoes really like me."

"Wait." He frowns, then steps toward me. "How many times did you get bit in the face?"

I touch my cheek and feel a welt forming. Some people have perfectly normal reactions to mosquito bites. I am not one of these people. When I'm bitten, I swell. A lot. So much so that in about five minutes, I'm going to look like I just went eight rounds with the welterweight champ.

"I might have some Benadryl," he says, going for his backpack.

"Is it nondrowsy?"

He stops digging in his bag and frowns at me. "I don't think it is. Maybe we can save it for the boat."

I can feel my face swelling already. I nod. "Okay."

"And we can catch an earlier ferry back," he says, and if he's horribly disappointed to learn that I'm an excellent meal for mosquitoes and don't really love hiking, he doesn't let on.

"I don't want to ruin this," I say. "You wanted to come here for a reason."

"I did," he says. "But maybe we can come back another time when it's less infested."

"Was it the lighthouse?" I ask. "I saw it on the way in."

When I saw it, I'd conjured a story of a lightkeeper, living alone up inside the black-and-white lighthouse. One night, he finds a woman in a half-wrecked boat that's washed up on the shore.

He nurses her back to health, and even though she doesn't speak his language, they manage to have deep, meaningful moments almost without saying a word.

It stoked my imagination because there's just something about a lighthouse. A single light can cut straight through the darkness and guide a lost sailor home.

How powerful.

Also they just look cool.

"No, not the lighthouse." Hayden takes a few steps away from me, like he's looking for something, then turns back. "Do you have two more minutes in you?"

There's something wonderfully mysterious about the way he asks this.

"Say yes." At that, he lifts his eyebrows and grins at me.

"Even though I'm five minutes away from looking like a dog who tried to eat a bee?"

He laughs. "Is your face going to blow up like that? Is it that bad?"

I smack my neck again. "Yes, but how can I say no now?"

He grabs my hand and helps me across the rocky terrain, and after just a couple more minutes of hiking, he stops.

I look at our hands, hoping he doesn't notice they're still clasped together.

I *like* the way his hand feels in mine. I like how he simultaneously assures me that I can do anything while also telling me he won't let anything happen to me.

I like a lot about this man.

The logical part of my brain sends up a flare.

He hates New York.

He's Georgina's son.

He lives in North Carolina.

He's Georgina's son.

I don't fantasize about marriage often, but if I did, I wouldn't be imagining *her* as my mother-in-law.

Oddly, none of these reminders is enough to stop me from relishing the way my hand feels in his.

He must notice I'm looking at the wrong thing because he squeezes my hand and says, "Kelsey, look."

I glance up, and there, about fifty feet away, are ten horses. "Oh my goodness! Are they . . . Do they belong to someone?"

"No."

"What are they doing here?"

He seems to be marveling at them. "Living their lives."

"*Wild* horses?" I never even knew there was such a thing in this country. I take a step, but he pulls me back.

"Yes, so you have to keep your distance."

"How did they get here?" I ask, watching as another five horses run across the beach in the distance.

"One theory is that they swam here after a Spanish shipwreck in the 1500s," he says. "They're called Banker horses."

I watch the horses as they roam freely in the open space in front of us. They're graceful and beautiful and . . . "They're amazing."

Beside me, Hayden presses his shoulder into mine. I like his nearness.

"I thought you'd like them."

I pull out my phone and snap a few photos of the wild horses.

"Worth the bug-infested hike?"

I nod. "Worth it."

"I guess sometimes you gotta wade through uncomfortable things to get to the payoff."

"We should get that on a T-shirt," I tease.

"Oh, I'm very profound." He wags his eyebrows, and I grin at him.

I turn back and watch the horses, making myself pause and take in this moment, thankful to be here. I've never seen wild horses before. Or been on an uninhabited island.

My mind whirs with words and feelings and thoughts, all demanding to be written down. My dormant writer-brain has been unlocked, cracked open, and woken up. I'm no longer on autopilot, and it feels good.

What doesn't feel good, however, is the itching. I feel another bite at my ankle, and yelp at the sting of it.

Hayden chuckles. "Okay, let's get going. There should be another ferry soon."

"I'm sorry." I turn toward him. "I don't mean to be a baby."

He looks at me, and his face falls. "Oh man, you weren't kidding about the swelling."

I reach up and touch my cheek. "Is it bad?"

He grimaces. "It's not good."

I turn away, clicking on my phone and flipping the camera. When I position the viewfinder on myself, I immediately wish I hadn't. "Oh my gosh!" I'd been kidding about the dog eating the bee comment, but it turns out, I wasn't that far off.

"We should find you some Benadryl." Hayden has his backpack off and is rummaging through it with a reckless lack of concern for where his possessions land.

"I look like something out of a horror movie," I say, completely embarrassed that I seem to be sporting at least three bites on the left side of my face, one above my eyebrow and two on my cheek. It's blown up like a tight, fleshy balloon. And here I thought he'd already seen me at my worst.

Surprise!

"Okay, I found it," Hayden says, unwrapping a little pink pill. "Take this."

I do as he says, hoping this yes doesn't lead to my death.

"How do you feel?" He takes my hand and leads me out of the clearing, away from the horses and hopefully back to the ferry.

"Itchy," I say.

"No other symptoms?"

"A little nauseous."

He presses his hand to my head. "You don't seem to have a fever."

I can't bring myself to look at him.

"And somehow you still look cute. I mean, for an orc."

A smile cracks through, and my gaze falls to the ground. "I don't think hiking is going to become a permanent fixture on my Yes List."

His hand has moved to my cheek and is now lingering there. I want to press a kiss to his palm, but knowing that I look like an inflated blowfish takes away the romance of the moment.

When we get back to the beach, we find another ferry docking.

Hayden nods toward it. "We can jump on that one and head back to Beaufort."

I'm starting to feel drowsy already, so I simply nod and follow him. About fifteen minutes later, I'm sitting on the boat, waiting to go back. Hayden is talking to someone and I'm struggling to keep my eyes open.

When he returns, he's holding a bag of ice, which he presses gently to my cheek. It feels like heaven.

"I'm so sorry, Kelsey," he says. "Banker horses are cool, but not worth this."

"It *was* worth it," I say, my eyes still closed.

He moves into the seat next to me, positioning the bag of ice between my face and his chest, letting me rest my head on him. I like the way it feels to have his right arm draped around me, and even though we've been out hiking, he still smells good. He could give my coworker Daniel a lesson in how to properly apply cologne or aftershave or whatever it is I'm smelling.

Daniel's "cologne plunge" method is highly offensive.

Hayden laughs, and I realize I've said all of this out loud.

The noise of the boat fades in and out as I struggle to keep my eyes open. I should've told Hayden that I don't take medicine very often because it usually has a very strong effect on me, but I suppose he's about to figure that out.

And as the drowsiness begins to take over, darkness flickers before me and I think, but hopefully don't say, *You are a very attractive man.*

And then the world fades to black, just like it did in the hospital.

Chapter 30

GEORGINA

I TOOK A chance coming here.

And maybe it wasn't the right choice, but when I turned the knob on Hayden's door and found it open, I let myself in.

Technically, I've been invited. I'm just several hours early. And about twenty years too late.

I stand in the entryway of the cottage, looking around at the space where my son lives. On a table near the front door is a wooden bowl that looks like it was crafted from some washed-up driftwood found on the beach. In it, a couple of keys and a small seashell. Next to it, a framed photo of Hayden and his father.

I pick it up and study the faces frozen in time. They have the same eyes. The same defined cheekbones. The same strong jaw. There isn't a trace of me in my son, neither in his looks nor in his personality. Dylan was born to be a father.

But my strengths lie elsewhere.

I have mixed feelings about that.

It's been years since I've spoken to Dylan. For months after he and Hayden left, he tried to keep me involved, and then, after one too many missed birthdays or regattas or soccer games, I ran out of chances. They stopped responding to my half-hearted apologies, and I exited their lives for good. For *their* good.

At least, that's what I told myself.

His last card to me contained a few school pictures of Hayden inside, and on it, he'd written the words "Come home anytime, Georgie."

The words always shamed me. Because Dylan might've been the one to leave New York, but it was my choice to walk away from them through my actions.

A memory struck me on the drive back to Driftwood from the museum. A scene so vivid it practically jumped out in front of my car and forced me to pay attention.

I've never been the domestic type, but there was one meal my mother taught me to make—lasagna. She swore that every woman needed to know how to make a homemade lasagna "for the times you need to drop off a dish to a sick friend or a new mother."

I've never dropped a lasagna off to anyone, but that's beside the point.

It was a Sunday, and I'd been working a lot of long hours. I felt the unraveling of our family unit even then, and I knew I had to do something to keep us intact.

Or rather I had to make an effort to reconnect.

I planned a big, homemade family dinner, and we made a day of it. We started with a trip to the farmer's market, picking up fresh vegetables for a tossed salad and a big loaf of homemade bread. Then we came home and all of us spent the afternoon in the kitchen, singing along to the oldies station as we cooked dinner.

I still remember Dylan coming up behind me while I got a pot of boiling water started, wrapping his arms around me and spinning me around to the rhythm of "My Girl." Hayden sat on the opposite side of the counter, stacking raw lasagna noodles, and when Dylan kissed me, he shouted, "Ew! Gross!" and we all laughed our way through the best night we'd had in a very long time.

In my life, I've been to galas and awards shows. I've been to movie premieres and stayed in private villas. I've seen and done exciting, notable, photographable things.

But none of those compare to that memory of lasagna night with my boys.

Hindsight is always twenty-twenty.

I was too young and foolish to realize what I had in those days. Sometimes I wish I could've started my life with the wisdom and knowledge I have now that I'm nearing the end. I would've done so many things differently.

I'm proud of what I've accomplished, but I don't love what I had to sacrifice to get here.

Wrapped up in the warmth of that memory, I navigated to a nearby market and picked up all the ingredients to make that meal again.

Will Hayden remember it too?

Which is how I ended up here, in my estranged son's cottage, holding shopping bags containing more food than three people could eat in a week.

I walk the bags over to the counter, then return to the car to grab the rest. When I come back inside, I close the door behind me and turn to see a man standing on the patio out back, staring at me through the sliding glass door. I drop the bags and scream, frantically looking around for something to use as a weapon, when the man lifts his hands up in surrender.

I stop moving, but I'm frozen, my pulse racing, as I squint to see the man moving toward the door. As happy as I am that Hayden left his front door open, I'm equally as angry that he did the same for the back door.

The man slides the glass door open and steps inside, and that's when I realize this isn't an intruder at all.

"Georgie?"

"Dylan." I straighten.

He frowns. "What are you doing here?"

How do I even answer that question? "It's a long story."

"Does Hayden know you're here?" he asks.

"Yes," I say, avoiding his eyes. "But no. Not here, in his house, here." It's like he's turned me into a tongue-tied teenager, smitten once again by his good looks and his tan skin. I'm not sure how it's possible, but Dylan's looks have only improved with age.

How unfair.

"Does he know *you're* here?" I ask.

"I live here," he says.

"You live with Hayden?" I frown. "I thought he bought his own house."

"He did," he says. "And then I sold my house and started renting out the pool house. I was spending more time traveling, and it just made more sense."

"I can go," I say. "I didn't realize."

I also didn't realize how it would feel to be in the same room with him. Like all of the oxygen has been sucked out of the windows.

Dylan has this quiet, easy charm. He was born to live at the beach. Looks better in swim trunks and an open button-down than in work attire. Why I ever thought he'd be happy in the city is a mystery.

"No," he says. "Stay."

Stay. My mind lingers on the word. It's not the first time he's asked. But it is the first time I'll agree.

I move to pick up the bags, and he crosses the living room. "Let me."

I'm very much a capable, independent woman, but even I can appreciate when a man is being chivalrous, so I step back and watch as he picks up the groceries and walks them into the kitchen.

I follow, feeling like an outsider invading his space.

"What is all this?" he asks.

"Groceries," I say. "Hayden invited us for dinner."

Dylan's face falls. "Us?"

"My . . ." I'm not sure how to describe Kelsey. She's a nuisance. A pest. And possibly my saving grace. "A friend."

"A . . . male friend?"

I raise a brow. "Would it matter?"

He leans back against the counter and crosses his arms, and all at once, I'm eighteen again, spotting him on campus for the first time. My insides flutter, a feeling I forbade a whole lot of years ago.

"Well, yeah," he says. "It matters. I'm not sure I like the idea of some other bozo trying to date my wife."

I look away to keep him from seeing my smile. There's too much history between us for this to be anything other than what it is—a reunion of two people who *used* to love each other.

But if that's true, then someone had better tell it to my heart. Because it's beating wildly, and I'm full of questions, namely . . . *How did I ever walk away from this man?*

"A female friend," I say, noting the relief on his face. "There are no male . . . *friends.*"

A smile skirts across his lips. "Good. I ruined anyone else for you anyway."

Hasn't lost his charm either.

"So he invited you for dinner, but you're not letting him cook?" Dylan begins unpacking the groceries.

"I thought it would be nice if I made something."

"He's a pretty good cook," Dylan says. "And unless you took a class, you're . . . not."

I fight to keep the smile from forming. "I'm not completely incapable."

He pulls the box of noodles from the bag and holds it up. "You're making lasagna?"

"It's still the only thing I know how to make."

He laughs. "Some things never change."

Almost to myself, I add, "And some things do."

I take a step toward the counter, pulling items from the bags and setting everything in a neat stack on the counter while Dylan does the same. I can feel him looking at me every so often, but I avoid his eyes, trying to orient myself to a kitchen that's not mine and a man who used to be.

"I heard you're sick," he says.

I'm standing at the refrigerator with my back to him when he says this, and I stop moving. I should've known the small talk wouldn't last long with Dylan. It never did before. He hates small talk. The night we met, he told me he saw no point in conversation if it didn't say something real.

I'm pretty sure I told him every single one of my hopes and dreams that night, and I think he did the same. One conversation was all it took for me to fall madly, completely, head over heels in love.

How did I ever let you go?

"Georgie . . . is it serious?" he asks.

The question hangs there. So much history and hurt between us, and yet I can still detect the concern in his voice. It's palpable how much he cares for me, how much he's always cared for me, and I'm angry with myself all over again for believing the lie that he was better off without me.

Or maybe I'm angry with myself because that wasn't a lie at all.

I close the refrigerator and face him. "It is."

He steps toward me and pulls me into his arms. Here, I'm not the stiff-necked, tightly wound businesswoman I am at the office. Here, I'm a girl in the arms of a boy, and he is taking care of me at my worst moment. Here, I can melt into a puddle and Dylan will be there to mop me up—even though I've done nothing to deserve it.

He never asked me to be anything other than who I am. Why didn't I recognize what a gift that was before it was too late?

He holds me, his strong arms pressing my body into his, my cheek lightly resting on his chest. But after only seconds, I pull away.

I can't get lost in him again.

Not now, not with this prognosis and so little time left.

I didn't come back here to break his heart all over again. It's better if I keep him at arm's length. It would be selfish of me to wish for anything more.

I busy myself with the ingredients, searching the cupboards for the necessary dishes, leaving Dylan standing behind me, looking a little lost and confused.

I glance over at him.

"I see you still don't like feelings."

I clear my throat, pushing any emotions way down.

"But, Georgie, you must have *some*. You're here. I can't imagine what you're dealing with, being here with the situation what it is," he says.

I fill a big pot with water and set it on the stove. "I'm trying not to."

"That's my girl."

The words hang there between us. As true as the first time he spoke them, and yet completely false. Because I'll always be his . . . and I never will be again.

Thankfully, my train of thought is interrupted when the door opens and Hayden walks in, carrying Kelsey over his shoulder like a rag doll.

At the sight of Dylan and me in his kitchen, Hayden stops moving and frowns. "Well, chalk this image up to one I never thought I'd see in my lifetime."

I frown back, nodding at Kelsey. "I could say the same."

"Allergic reaction plus Benadryl," he says. "I'll go put her down in the guest room." He starts up the stairs, then turns back and looks at us. "And then you guys can explain whatever the heck is going on here."

I glance over at Dylan, whose eyes are trained on me. He grins, arms wide. "Welcome home, Georgie."

And even though I scoff and turn away, I have to admit . . . I like the way it sounds.

Chapter 31

KELSEY

I keep waking up having no idea where I am.

I'm groggy. Foggy.

I focus enough to know I don't know this place. I'm in an unfamiliar bed in an unfamiliar room. There's a tall dresser on the opposite side of where I'm lying, and I'm covered with a cream-colored afghan.

I glance around and don't find a single photo or personal item anywhere. I sit up, trying to land on a memory of how I got here.

Horses. Bugs. Benadryl.

My head is spinning, and after about two minutes of mental swimming, I remember the ferry ride back. I touch my face and find the swelling has gone down a little bit, but I'm still covered in itchy welts. My legs, especially my ankles, are on fire.

I slip out of the bed and see my bag sitting by the door.

The last coherent memory I have is of ice on my cheek. Resting my head on Hayden's chest.

Everything after is a blur.

I crack open the door and the welcoming aroma of garlic wafts into the room. It's a delicious smell, and my stomach loudly reminds me it's been hours since I ate.

I start down a staircase, recognizing both Hayden and Georgina's voices as I get closer.

At the sound of movement, they stop talking, and when I reach the bottom, Hayden is standing there. He greets me with a smile. "You're awake!"

A multicolored dog is curled up in an armchair. She glances up at me, then lays her head back down, disinterested.

"Is it morning?" I glance outside. Looks more like evening.

He touches my cheek. "The drugs knocked you out. This looks a little better. Does it hurt?"

I like the way his hand feels pressed against my skin. "It's okay." I close my eyes and savor the moment.

"We're getting ready to eat. My mom made lasagna."

I snap my eyes open. "She . . . made . . . what?"

I follow him into the kitchen, where I see Georgina in an apron.

In an apron.

This alone is enough for a mental hiccup, but when I see she's standing next to an attractive older version of Hayden, I'm sure I've entered the Twilight Zone.

Before I can grill her about the fact that she's cooking, she frowns at me and says, "What happened to your face?"

"Mosquitoes."

"Wow," the man next to Georgina says. "They really got you."

"Why didn't you use bug spray?" Georgina asks.

"I did. It didn't work," I say. "But that's not really the headline here." My eyes flick to the man standing beside her. "You're wearing an apron." I pull out my phone and snap a picture. "Definitely going to need proof of this."

Georgina points a wooden spoon at me. "Delete that."

"No way."

"Do you want something to drink?" Hayden walks over to the refrigerator.

"Just water, please," I say. "And I might just hold it on my face. Where am I?"

"My house," Hayden says. "And, Kelsey, this is my dad."

The older man extends a hand to me. "Dylan."

"Nice to meet you."

"Dad lives in the pool house," Hayden says. "But he wasn't supposed to be back for another week."

"Well, well, well," I say, with a pointed look at Georgina, "it's like fate."

She ignores me.

"And that"—he points to the dog—"is Coco."

At the mention of her name, Coco perks up a little but still makes no effort to move.

"You have a pool house?" I ask.

He shrugs like it's no big deal, but it's obvious by the space that Hayden has done very well for himself. I hope it makes Georgina proud.

"Can I get a tour?"

"Can you see through that eyeball? Your face looks like a bounce house," Georgina muses.

"She still has one good one," Hayden says, and then he winks at me.

I shake my head, pointing at him. "Uh-uh. No. No way. No winking, you creep." Never mind that he totally pulled that off.

He laughs. "Let's start out back. It's my favorite part of the house."

I follow him through the living room and out a sliding glass door. There's a stone patio with lounging chairs around an in-ground pool, and off to the side, an outdoor sofa and two chairs positioned around a fire feature.

"Whoa," I say. "You could Airbnb this place."

He laughs. "It was a mess when I bought it. Dad and I have been renovating it for five years."

"For real?"

He nods, leading me toward a small pool house at the back of the property. He opens the door, and I follow him in. The little house is the perfect vacation oasis.

"I had a designer help me," he says. "I can build a kitchen, but I have no idea how to make it look good."

"Well, they did an incredible job." I face him. "*You* did an incredible job."

"I'm glad you like it."

There's a pause, and then I say, "Hey. Thanks for taking care of me today."

His smile is polite. "Of course."

"Did I"—I make a face—"say anything embarrassing?"

He scrunches his nose.

"Oh no. What did I say?"

"You might've told me you want to marry me," he says, grinning.

I cover my face with my hands. "Please tell me that's not true."

He shrugs, then goes still. "And you also told me you really want to quit your job. Be a writer. And I think there was a 'We'd make beautiful babies' in there somewhere too."

"There wasn't." I'm mortified.

"There was." He grins.

I shake my head. "I should've warned you about 'Kelsey on meds.'"

"Yeah, sure," he says. "Let's blame the meds."

"Let's," I say.

Or not.

"It was cute," he says. "But maybe next time I'll give you half a pill."

"Hopefully there's not a next time," I say. "I don't think I'll be going on more hikes anytime soon."

His laugh is soft. "That's fair."

I absently wonder if this is how relationships are *supposed* to start. I have so little practice, I genuinely have no idea. Love isn't something I usually say yes to.

"Can I ask you something?" I say.

"Sure."

"You don't seem angry." I realize it's not a question. "With your mom."

He sits down on the edge of the white couch and takes a breath.

"I was angry for a long time," he says. "A part of me still is. She hurt me. Us. Badly. But . . ." He pauses. "I don't know, I guess knowing she's sick and there's not much time left . . . it doesn't seem worth it to hold that grudge."

I sit near him and listen.

"Don't get me wrong," he says. "I wish things were different. But I've had a really good life so far. And my dad always said that my mom was great at just about everything she tried—except parenting. It's hard for someone like her not to be good at something."

I sit with that for a moment. "And you're okay with that?"

He draws in a breath, and then, on an exhale, he says, "No, not really. She doesn't quit at anything . . . except our family."

I reach over and cover his hand with my own. "I'm sorry, Hayden."

His shrug is so soft it's nearly undetectable. "It's fine."

"It's really not," I say.

"No." His eyes meet mine. "It's not. But I really don't want to waste time staying angry."

I nod. After a slight pause, I ask, "Is your dad angry with her?"

Hayden shrugs. "I think he's proud of her, for all the things she's accomplished. And I think he's sad he didn't get to be by her side when she accomplished them."

"Do you think he still loves her?" I ask.

"One hundred percent yes," Hayden says emphatically. "You know they never got divorced."

I nod. "I did hear that, yeah."

"And he's never been with anyone else all these years," he says. "He's never even looked."

"Wow. Never?"

He shakes his head. "And it's not like he didn't have prospects. The women around here are pretty free with their phone numbers."

I exhale, pondering the sadness of this situation. "Why didn't they ever try to work it out?"

"I don't think he wanted to stand in her way," he says. "She's really driven, and he never wanted to be the reason she didn't go after her dreams. But he didn't fit in the city." He pauses, and what he says next seems difficult to say. "We didn't fit in her life."

I think about what Georgina told me about having regrets. Surely she'll tell Hayden how she feels while we're here . . . right? He should hear it from her. He should know that there's a part of her that knows she missed out.

"But yeah, he loves her," he says quietly. "Love's a funny thing. It doesn't always let you choose."

I watch him as he says this, wondering how many people Hayden has loved in his lifetime. Wondering if he still loves any of them now.

"I'm betting she still loves him," I say.

"You think?" he asks.

I shrug. "I did some digging about her before I convinced her to go on this trip. She was never linked to anyone romantically. No headlines. No tabloids, even. And you know her—if she wanted to end it, she would've ended it. Legally."

"Hmm." He stands. "Are you hungry?"

I stand. And while I'm slightly confused by the abrupt change of subject, I simply say, "I'm starving."

We go inside and find Dylan setting the kitchen table and Georgina tossing a salad in a large bowl on the counter. If I didn't know any better, I would think these two are like any other married couple making family dinner.

But I do know better. And there's tension in the room.

As we sit, I begin to see the polite conversation for what it is. Years of hurt pushed to the side. Hayden says he's not angry, and maybe he's not—maybe he *has* forgiven Georgina—but the fractured past is like a fifth person at this table.

There are glances between Hayden and his dad that I tell myself not to read into but do. There's Georgina, who seems like a person unable to relax. Like she's trying to act out a role she doesn't actually know how to.

And then there's me.

Puffy, still a bit itchy, and a stranger by all accounts.

"Hey," Hayden says to Dylan, "the *Rutherford* is ready to go back."

"Oh, good, good. I'll be ready."

Hayden glances at me. "Once the boats are restored, my dad drives them back to their owners. This one is a day's sail down the coast."

I notice that he's done this several times—turned to me to include me, inform me, keep me a part of the conversation.

Just like steadying me on the boat, holding my arm when I lost my footing in the ocean, and paddling around me with the kids at the museum, he's making sure I'm okay.

I take a bite of the lasagna and blurt out, as I'm chewing, "Wow. Georgina, this is really good!"

"Well, it's the one thing I know how to make, so I'd better be good at it by now." She's brusque, per usual.

It's like she can't break out of her habits. How can I take a sledgehammer and crack that exterior?

"So you're leaving?" Georgina looks at Dylan from across the table.

Dylan swallows his bite of food and meets Georgina's eyes, smiling. He has the confident look of a mongoose staring down a cobra.

In other words, he's not going to get bit. He's too quick.

Hayden is right—he *does* still love her.

Dylan takes a sip of water, then says, "Only for a few days."

Georgina goes back to her plate, but Dylan's eyes are trained on her.

"You could come," he says.

She sets her fork down. "On a boat."

"It'll be like old times." He smiles nonchalantly.

Georgina scoffs. "But in much older bodies."

I think of that dialysis machine. Would she be safe out there on the water?

"Oh, come on, Georgie," he says. "You used to love the water."

Georgie? She has a nickname?!

"You should go," I say.

"Oh, should I?" She points her attention at me. "And what will you do while I'm gone?"

"She can help me," Hayden interjects, scooping up another huge piece of lasagna and putting it on his plate.

"I can?" I frown over at him.

"Sure," he says. "Haven't you always wanted to learn about boat restoration?"

I look at him, and he widens his eyes just a bit.

"Uh . . . yes," I say, trying to pick up on his nonverbal lead. "Totally. I'm even thinking about . . . writing a book on that subject."

Georgina stares. "Oh, really."

I wave her off. "Oh. Yeah. I've been thinking about it for a while."

"You have." Her eyebrow lifts ever so slightly.

My imagination bursts open, and I start spitballing. "I'm thinking it's a rom-com. The main girl—we'll call her Chelsea"—Hayden laughs at this—"is involved in a freak car accident and gets amnesia, but then this *sweet*, beautiful, talented, distinguished woman"—I indicate Georgina, who sits, unmoving—"who she meets in the hospital takes her on a road trip to try to spark her memories. They visit all her old haunts, stay in a swanky hotel, even run into an old boyfriend, but nothing works."

I'm on a roll, and I start talking with my hands.

"But the boyfriend, after proposing, turns out to be a total dud, who she doesn't remember anyway, and after stopping off in a small seaside town, she meets this guy who restores boats, but also works with kids, and who is not bad looking—"

Hayden chimes in, "*Thank* you."

"Wait, I thought she was talking about me," Dylan wisecracks.

I point at Dylan. "Who *also* has a hot dad, a total silver fox—"

Dylan fist pumps. "Yes!"

"This no longer feels appropriate," Georgina says.

But I ignore her. "And Chelsea, the older lady, the not-bad-looking son, and the hot dad all get together over lasagna." I pause. "That's as far as I've gotten."

Mock applause from Hayden and Dylan, an eye roll from Georgina. I wave like the queen, accepting their accolades.

Dylan beams. "Heck, I'd read it. Any chance the silver fox hooks up with the sweet, distinguished older woman?"

Georgina coughs a bit and has to take a drink. I notice Dylan grinning.

Man, he's got her number. It's fun to watch.

"So, yes, Georgina, you should go," I say. "We will be totally fine."

"We'll find something fun to do," Hayden says. "I promise."

Oh, the things that creep into my mind at that comment . . .

Dylan sets down his fork and leans back in his chair. "What do you say, Georgie? Are you up for a little trip?"

She presses her lips together and takes another sip of her water. "I don't think so."

"Georgie," I say pointedly. "Say yes."

"We should go." She sets her napkin to the side of her plate. "And you don't get to call me that."

"But . . . I'm still eating," I say, my voice bordering on a whine.

"Then you can meet me at the hotel," she says.

"Actually, I thought you could both stay here," Hayden says, doing his best to smooth things over. "You two can have the pool house and Dad can take the guest room."

"Oh no, we don't want to put you out," I say.

"Then you can take the guest room, and these two can take the pool house." Hayden glances at Georgina. "There are two bedrooms."

She stands. "We can go back to the hotel."

"Why?" Hayden stands. "It's comfortable here. And it's free."

I hear a twinge of desperation in his voice, and I want to take Georgina by the arms and shake her. *Choose him, Georgina. Say yes to him.*

"Thank you for letting me cook," she says. "It was . . . fun."

Hayden's shoulders drop, and Dylan stands up next to him. Georgina walks off to the kitchen, seemingly oblivious to the way her actions affect her son.

It makes me mad. And sad.

She rinses off her dishes and puts them into the dishwasher. Hayden sits back down and goes back to eating. My eyes land on his dad, and I can see the pain on his face.

For her part, Georgina has chosen no.

And whether it's my business or not, I'm determined to help her change that choice.

Chapter 32

KELSEY

I walk into the kitchen and stand on the opposite side of the counter from Georgina.

"Can I talk to you for a second?" I ask, knowing that while Hayden and Dylan are too polite (or too afraid?) to say anything, I am not. Not anymore.

She barely acknowledges me.

"Georgina."

"I'm cleaning," she snaps.

"You can't multitask?" I snap back. This isn't how I want it to go. I've learned, in the short time I've been with her, that confrontation doesn't work.

She hesitates, then wipes her hands on a towel and walks out the front door and into the driveway. Outside, she crosses her arms over her chest and glares at me. "I hope you're not here to lecture me."

I feel heat rise up my neck. "I'm not. I'm just . . ." I pause. "I don't know what I am, but it hurts to see you like this with him."

She just stands there, defiant. Why is she being so stubborn?

I think over how to best approach her and decide I'll take a page out of her playbook. "I'm here to tell you that you're being an idiot."

It feels wrong to be so pointed, but it works. Her eyes widen, and she's offended. But at least she's listening. "I'm *sorry*?"

"Don't you see what you're doing to them?" I plead, pointing back at the house. "It's so selfish!"

I know it's the wrong thing to say as soon as it's out of my mouth.

She bristles and rises up. "How *dare* you. You have no idea, no *clue* about this family. What, you're a writer—actually not even that, but a wannabe writer—so you fill in the blanks with assumptions and backstory?" The gloves are off now.

"They want you to stay." I will myself to stand my ground. "And I think *you* want to stay. What is wrong with you? Why are you running away?"

"As usual, you have no idea what you're talking about."

"No, I actually do," I say. "I know that you feel guilty for choosing your company over your family."

"How could you possibly—"

I cut her off. "Because I do the same thing."

She folds her arms and looks away.

"I work. All the time. I push everyone away. I don't call my friends, I don't spend time with my parents, and you're the same."

She shakes her head. "Do you also know that it would be completely cruel for me to come back now, trying to make everything right, with such limited time left on this planet?"

"No, Georgina," I say. "That's the kindest thing you could do."

She laughs sardonically. "You're so naive." A beat. "If I die tomorrow, they'll barely even notice. But if I spend what's left of my life here, reminding myself of everything I walked away from, weaseling my way into their lives, and *then* I die? That's cruel. Heartless." She shakes her head again. "I'm protecting them."

I take a step toward her. "No. You're hurting them. You haven't even told Hayden you're sorry."

She scoffs. "Why would I do that?"

"Because . . . you're sorry?!" I can't fathom how she doesn't get it. "Aren't you? Even a little?"

"What good would it do to say it? Words are meaningless. They can't change anything."

"You're wrong," I say. "Words change *everything*."

She steels her jaw. "This from someone who hasn't written a *thing*."

That stings, and I go still.

She glares at me. "You came up with this grand Summer of Yes idea, a huge revelation, but you're not even saying yes to the one thing you really want. You have all these big opinions about *my* life when all you're doing is hiding from your own!"

She's angry. And hurt.

And right.

"You don't know what you're talking about." Anger pricks the back of my neck.

"Oh, that's where you're wrong," she says coolly. "I know *exactly* what I'm talking about. Get your focus off of me, and my family, and put it back on yourself!"

Hot tears pool in my eyes, but I will them not to fall.

"If you want to be a writer, and you really believe your words can have meaning, then stop talking about it and do it."

I lift my chin to meet her eyes.

Now she takes a step toward me. "Do not ever preach to me about apologies and choices and selfishness." Her voice trembles a little. "I know what I am. And I know what I've done. I don't need you to point it out to me."

There's a lull.

It's that point in an argument when all that needs to be said has been said, and the kicked-up dust is starting to settle.

"Maybe all of that is true," I say. "Maybe I've been using your life as a way to avoid living mine. Maybe I've even convinced myself I was having a breakthrough because I went on a boat and got eaten by a swarm of mosquitoes. But that doesn't mean I'm wrong about apologies. Or words. Or those two men in there."

She straightens.

"So, yeah, I have more work to do," I say. "But so do you. And I meant what I said. You'd be an idiot to walk away."

I go back inside as Georgina pulls away.

I'm keenly aware that I have no right to be here. I'm just a Post-it note on this family.

Hayden is standing in the kitchen, and his dad is no longer in the room.

He looks at me, and his face wilts. "You look like you need ice cream."

I nod, a bit in a daze, endorphins racing through me from that heated exchange. Georgina is right, and I hate that she is. I've tried some new things and had some memorable experiences—I won't let her take their value away from me.

But the one important thing is still waiting for me to make a move.

The words I write in the late-night hours are always meant only for me. I told myself I was processing. Not writing. I told myself that was enough.

But maybe it isn't anymore.

Safe relationships have been my routine. Work and worry have always trumped wonder and wanting.

Maybe they shouldn't anymore.

Am I willing to take the risks required to go after the things I really want?

Am I really strong enough to silence the fear that's been my ever-present companion for all of my adult life?

Hayden walks over to where I'm standing and pulls me into his strong arms. "You okay?"

He should not be the one comforting me right now.

I wrap my arms around his torso and press my cheek against his chest. I could stay here forever.

"What did she say to you?" Hayden pulls back and looks at me.

I shake my head. "It doesn't matter."

"It does, obviously."

I turn away. I have nowhere to go. Georgina took the car.

My mind races, replaying her accusations, and Hayden must sense that I'm processing something I can't talk about yet.

"Maybe you just need sleep," he says. "You'll feel better in the morning."

I nod. "But first . . . ice cream."

Chapter 33

GEORGINA

I'M IN THE same room at the Driftwood Hotel, unpacking my toiletries and thinking it's time to get back home.

I pull out my phone and text JP.

> **Georgina:** Book me a flight back to New York as soon as possible.
>
> **JP:** Two tickets?
>
> **JP:** Shall I arrange to have the car brought back?
>
> **Georgina:** One ticket. And I'll leave the car.
>
> **JP:** What about Kelsey?
>
> **Georgina:** She's an adult. She can find her own way home.

I click my phone off when there's a knock at the door.

If that girl thinks she's staying here with me, she has another thing coming. I stomp over to the door and pull it open. But it's not Kelsey standing on the other side.

"Dylan."

His hands are stuffed in his pockets, and he's looking at me like he did the night we met. "Georgie."

I straighten, wearing the truth of our situation like a suit of armor. "What are you doing here?"

"Came to convince you to come with me."

I leave the door open but walk away, back to my suitcase, which is flung open on the bed. "I can't."

He's right at my side. "Can't? Or won't?"

I turn toward him, our bodies so close we're practically touching. "Both."

"Stop running away from me," he says. "It's been long enough."

I close my eyes as he says, "Come home."

I harden, scoff, and walk away. "This was never going to be my home, Dylan."

"It could've been."

I shake my head. "It couldn't have been."

"We could've made it work," he says.

"It wouldn't have been fair to you," I tell him. "And staying here isn't fair either. I never meant to disrupt your lives. My plan was to make a quiet exit so nobody would be upset."

"You really think if we'd found out you died that we wouldn't be upset?" His face holds the pain of a thousand years. "We love you, Georgina."

"Words change everything."

I shake the thought away, trying not to let my mind or my heart snag on that word: *love.*

But Dylan knows me so well, he can probably see me trying to push it away. He forces my gaze. "I love you. I never stopped."

I love you too. The words are right there.

Just say them!

The only problem is, in this moment, I'm starting to question what the kinder option is—telling Dylan the truth or walking back out of his life, this time for good.

"Spend a few days," he says. "Let's take the boat back. It'll be like old times, you and me, out on the water."

My brain runs through a list of reasons I can't go with him. It starts with: *My board will have me replaced by the end of the week,* and ends with, *It'll hurt too much when I have to say goodbye.* And in the middle is just how tired I am these days, thanks to my failing kidneys.

I look away. I don't want my face to betray my feelings. But I want to go with him. More than anything.

He takes my hand. "What are you afraid of?"

Losing you again. But I don't say that. I don't say anything. I simply walk to the other side of the room and busy myself packing items that don't need to be packed.

"At least tell me what you're thinking?"

I stop moving and look at him. "Why are you doing this?"

"Doing what?"

I start to wade into emotional waters I've avoided for years. "You . . . must hate me," I say.

He comes closer. "I think I did, for a long time."

"And now? Now that I'm dying, it's water under the bridge?" Even as I say this, I wonder why I'm saying it.

Why is my default to push him away?

He takes a step toward me, but I stop him with an upheld hand. "Don't."

"Are you really?" There's a line of worry etched into his forehead. "Dying?"

"Everyone is dying."

He glances at my dialysis machine. "Is there anything they can do?"

I shake my head.

There's a reason I avoid these kinds of feelings. They hurt. Deeply. They cut through memory and emotion like a jagged blade.

What makes them compound exponentially is the fact that everything, *everything* is completely my fault.

I can't stand the sorrow in his expression, so I huff away, trying to busy myself with my toiletries, taking them into the bathroom.

"What about a donor?"

I stop. I've thought about this many times. I walk back into the room but don't meet his eyes. "In business, you want to be original and utterly unique in every way. When it comes to other, more important things, like kidney donation, the opposite is true. My tissue type is apparently very rare."

He pauses. And then, "We could—"

I know where he's going, and I hold up my hand again. "Absolutely not."

"He would do it," Dylan says. "In a heartbeat."

"I know," I say, because in just a few short interactions with my son, I've seen enough to know that he inherited Dylan's goodness. His kindness. And if he knew this was a possibility, he would get tested without a second thought. But it's *too* selfish. Even I can see that.

But that's not what I want to discuss. I look at him. "Why aren't you angry with me?"

"I already told you—"

"Please talk to me like I'm not dying," I say. "Tell me the truth."

Even from where I'm standing, I can see his lower lip quiver. I can see him trying desperately to let grace be the only thing he feels when all it's done is cover the truth.

I take a step toward him. "It's okay to tell me that you're mad at me."

"I'm not," he says so earnestly I almost believe him. "But I am sad. We missed out on a whole life together, and it could've been so beautiful. I know you loved me, and I know you loved Hayden."

I stand quietly, still clinging to the idea that my brand of love never would've been enough for them.

I didn't try hard enough to be the wife and mother they needed. I failed.

"And I admire the heck out of what you've done," he says. "I don't begrudge you that success."

"But . . . ?"

"But I do wish you'd chosen us," he says. "I won't lie about that."

I close my eyes and two words race through my mind like the crawl at the bottom of a news program.

I'm sorry.

I'm sorry.

I'm sorry.

For all my pride and justification. Sorry I missed out on a life with this man. A man who would've loved me on my worst day. I was so blinded by my own ambition I failed to see what really mattered until now.

Life can't be lived in reverse.

And now it's too late. And I'm dying.

I glance down and see the ring on his finger.

I pick up his hand and turn it over in my own. "You're wearing your ring."

He presses a sweet kiss to the inside of my palm. "You're not wearing yours."

I reach under the neck of my blouse and pull out the long gold chain that never leaves my neck. There, dangling from the end, is my wedding ring.

The corner of his lip quirks. He meets my eyes. "I'll be at the dock behind the hotel at seven in the morning," he says. "I hope you're there too."

And with that, he walks away.

The empty room, a physical reflection of my heart.

Chapter 34

KELSEY

AGAIN WITH THE waking up and it taking me a second to realize where I am.

There's a metaphor about my life there, but I can't quite put my finger on it.

Georgina's speech about me not saying yes. The way that made me feel. My lingering hug with Hayden. The way *that* made me feel.

And then . . . the writing.

I stretch my eyes open, and they fight me.

I wrote last night.

Hayden sent me to bed with a bowl of cookie dough ice cream and his promise that I would feel better in the morning.

I do feel better, although I have a sort of curdled ice cream taste in my mouth. Blech.

I wrote last night. A lot. The words just poured out, and I don't actually remember falling asleep, but I . . .

I sit straight up.

I sent an email.

Wait.

Did I actually send it?

I pull my laptop from the bag I've been carting around with me and flip it open, squinting through the sleep in my eyes as the screen comes to life. There in front of me is my work inbox with a new email reply from Charlie.

Holy heck, I sent it.

I click on the email.

> *Kelsey,*
> *Got your email. Will review and be in touch.*
> *Let's hope you found a winner.*
>
> *—Charlie*

It all rushes back.

Writing for three hours straight. Editing my own words. Seeing a chapter outline. Not pointless ramblings but a book. *An actual book.* Not a memoir about Georgina but a story about *my* experience saying yes. A story that's still unfolding, but one that I feel, deep in my bones, might be important.

I worked it into a proposal, which I could've done with my eyes shut since I've read so many over the years. I saved the first three chapters as a separate document, and then I sent it off to Charlie with a note that read:

> *Stumbled upon a new project I thought would be perfect for us.*
> *Debut author, but with a fresh new voice. What do you think?*

I cover my mouth with my hand. "What have I done?" It's like waking up the morning after a drunken night of poor choices with only spotty memories and a horrible sense of dread.

Only my drug of choice wasn't alcohol. It was creativity. I was desperate to prove to Georgina that I could take a bold step, and I turned my *I'll show her* into a horribly irreversible and impulsive decision.

And now an overwhelming fear takes hold of me.

I scan the proposal, and contrary to how I usually react when I reread my writing, I'm shocked to discover it's not garbage. It's coherent and smart and I'd definitely request a full manuscript based on the synopsis. But I wasn't ready to send this. I'm not ready to hear Charlie's thoughts on my work.

I can't undo it. It's already in Charlie's inbox. He responded.

What's done is done.

But hey . . . that burst of creativity felt *good*.

Like, really good.

I've shut off this side of myself for so long that letting it run free was invigorating, even if it was a little like a rambunctious child running around with an open gas can and a sparkler.

I'm a creative soul who needs to be creative.

I'm down with saying yes to that.

I get out of bed, brush my teeth with the spare Hayden has in his guest room, splash some water on my face, and take my hair down from my messy ponytail.

It's early, and the house is quiet. I remember what Hayden said about spending mornings out on his patio, and I make my way downstairs. As I come into the kitchen, I see him sitting in a chair next to the pool. The sliding glass door is open, and I can hear him talking to someone. As I get closer, I see that it's his dad.

"Are you sure?" Hayden says. "I thought it wasn't something they could fix."

"It's not," Dylan says. "Not without a donor."

My stomach drops. They're talking about Georgina. And they know about her kidneys. I'm frozen in place, my bare feet chilling on the cool wood floor. I should escape back to the quiet of the guest room and not insert myself in any more of Georgina's business, but the truth is, I *want* to talk to Hayden about this.

I clear my throat, and he turns around in his seat, then looks at Dylan. I walk over to the door and smile at them through the screen. "Good morning."

"Morning, sunshine. Did you sleep okay?"

I scrunch my shoulders and stretch. "Yeah, I think so. Swelling's gone down, so that's a win."

"Did you know a kidney transplant could save my mom's life?" Hayden asks.

I open the door and step into the humid air, sitting in the chair next to Hayden, aware that he's trying to process this news with what I can only imagine are very conflicting emotions.

"I did know, yeah," I say.

"Why didn't you say anything?" he asks.

"Because she doesn't want anyone to know," I say. "She even had me sign an NDA when I was in the hospital with her."

Hayden groans. "She's got so much pride," he says.

"It's not just that." Dylan takes a sip of coffee and leans back in his chair. "She doesn't feel like she deserves it. Especially not from you."

"I'm surprised she told you," I say.

"We spoke last night." Dylan looks away.

"Well, there's definitely more to *that* story," I muse.

Dylan just lifts his mug in a mock toast, wagging his eyebrows, and Hayden responds, "Okay, I'm all for you two figuring things out, but . . . that's gross."

"We just talked. Some." Dylan pauses. "But we haven't done that in a while. She's still stubborn as all get-out, but I think I'm wearing her down."

"So did she say I can get tested?" Hayden says. "See if I'm a match?"

"I don't know if she'll accept a kidney from you," I say. She'd said as much.

"What are the odds another donor will come through?" Hayden asks.

"Slim," I say. "Georgina has this rare tissue type, and I don't think she's holding out hope they'll find her a kidney in time. Most people are on that list for years. Some never get the transplant they need."

Coco whimpers beside Hayden and he pets the top of her head. "She can't stop me from being tested though, right?"

"I did some reading last night," Dylan says. "If you want to, you can get tested anonymously. You can even donate the kidney anonymously. Georgina would never even have to know it was you."

I frown. "She won't like that."

Dylan shifts. "Well, we don't like the thought of her dying. Especially if she doesn't have to. *Especially* because this is the first time we've seen any sign she might be ready to let us back into her life."

The pain of that last sentence is palpable. She has a chance to reprioritize, and both Hayden and Dylan seem willing to give her a second chance.

Why can't she see how lucky she is?

"She doesn't always get to call the shots." Dylan says this under his breath, but his frustration is clear.

"Do you want some coffee?" Hayden is looking at me, and even though I haven't known him long, I can see pain in his eyes. There's forgiveness, and then there's this. Saving the life of the woman who walked away from you when you were just a child? That's Jesus-level goodness.

"I'd love some, thank you," I say.

He walks inside, sliding the door shut behind him.

I look at Dylan. "Is he okay?"

"He will be," he says. "It's just a lot. He's worked hard to get to a place of peace where his mother is concerned."

"He's a lot kinder than I would be," I say.

"It hasn't been easy." Dylan shifts back in his seat.

I study his face. It's a weathered, handsome face, full of laugh lines that seem to tell the story of a good, good life. "For either of you, I'd imagine."

"She wasn't always like this, you know." He smiles kindly. "She used to be so fun."

I scoff. "Georgina? Fun? I'd pay to see that."

He laughs. "You have no idea. She *loved* being out on the water. She loved to laugh, and dance, and paint. She always had these big dreams, you know? I knew I needed to give her space to go after them, but now that she's met every goal, I just want to know if it was worth it."

"I asked her that exact question," I say. "The day we met. She didn't answer really."

Now his smile is sad. "There's a trace of the girl I used to know in there somewhere. I'm just not sure we have time to coax her out."

"I should do the test." Hayden is standing in the doorway, holding two steaming mugs of coffee.

"No, Hayden, that's not what I meant . . ." Dylan leans forward.

"I know. But I have questions for her too, and a few weeks or even a few months isn't going to be enough time to get answers. And it's definitely not enough time to have any kind of relationship with her."

"And you want that?" I ask. "Even after everything?"

He considers this, and after a moment, he nods. "I do, yeah." He looks steadfast, resolute. "She's my mom."

His willingness to forgive is inspiring. "Georgina thinks she's protecting you both by walking away. She thinks that getting close to you now would be cruel." And I don't feel like I'm violating her privacy saying so, because they both deserve to know what lies she's telling herself.

"She couldn't be more wrong," Dylan says. "And I'm hoping I convinced her of that last night." He stands, and only then do I see a bag on the opposite side of his chair. "I invited her on the trip with me. I guess I'll know in"—he looks at his watch—"about thirty minutes if she's accepted."

He looks at Hayden. "You don't have to get tested."

"I know," he says.

"But if you do, she can't know it was you," I say.

Hayden nods.

"All right, kids, I'm off." Dylan slings the bag over his shoulder. "Hayden, I'll let you know when the boat is delivered."

"Sounds good."

"Kelsey," Dylan says. "Thank you. Because of you, maybe our family can start to heal."

He squeezes my shoulder and walks around the side of the house, leaving me sitting there with Hayden and Coco.

"So," I say. "That's a lot."

But he must not want to talk, because he says, "Do you want to go for a walk?" He stands. "Coco needs some exercise." At that, the dog jumps up and starts turning in circles. Hayden looks at me. "You have to say yes, right?"

I laugh. "You're interpreting my Summer of Yes a little too literally."

He holds his hand out to me, and I take it. He starts to walk inside, but when I don't move, he turns to look at me. "You okay?"

"I don't want to run away."

His eyebrows pull, and a smile inches across his face. "Okay. Then don't."

"I always run away from my feelings, but I don't want to do that anymore."

"What feelings are you talking about?"

I smile. "I like you, Hayden. I'm worried how much I like you. Especially since I've only known you for a few days."

"Well, shoot," he says, feigning disappointment. "I like you too."

"No, but . . . I *really* like you," I say. "Not like 'oh, he's a nice guy.' More like 'I want to know everything about him.'"

He laughs. "This is new for you, isn't it?"

"Admitting how I feel? Yes. It's weird. But good." Embarrassment washes over me. "I haven't been good about prioritizing people or relationships, and this whole experience has shown me I need to change that." I try to hold his gaze, but I have to look away.

I try to drop his hand, but he doesn't let go.

I look up at him and see his eyes dipping to my lips, then back again.

"And to be honest, I—"

He takes my face in his hands and kisses me.

I was midsentence, but I have no idea what I was going to say.

I step in closer so our bodies are touching, and mentally proclaim an emphatic *YES*.

This is the kind of moment that usually makes me uncomfortable, the kind that makes me want to run away. Because right now, I swear he can see straight through me—through all the things I'm not saying. But I still don't want to run. I want to soak up the weight of his attention. I want to revel in it. And I really, really don't want him to stop.

He pulls back slowly and opens his eyes, brushing his thumb across my cheek.

"Hmm, I can't *quite* get what you're saying. It's not *totally* clear yet," I whisper with closed eyes.

I feel him lean in close again, and he presses another soft kiss to my lips. I inhale that same woodsy smell from yesterday and decide it's my new favorite scent in the world.

And Hayden is a really, really good kisser.

Coco jumps up, and when Hayden pulls back, she's turning a circle next to us, leash in her mouth.

"I love that dog, but not right now," he says.

"I guess we'd better go, huh?" I glance down at myself, only just now realizing that I'm still wearing pajamas. "I'm going to run and change real quick."

I turn to go and, after only a few steps, turn back around, run up to him, and kiss him one more time.

Just to make sure what just happened wasn't a scene I made up in my head.

I race upstairs, pull on a pair of jean shorts and a sleeveless shirt, throw my hair up into a ponytail, dab on some lip gloss, shrug at myself in the mirror, and call it good.

It occurs to me how different my mornings have been since I left New York.

Maybe it's because this is sort of like being on vacation.

Or maybe it's because there's a whole other way to live.

Either way, I think I could get used to it.

I meet Hayden outside and fall into step beside him. At the back of my mind, I keep thinking the same thing: *Hayden kissed me.* There's only excitement over what could come of this. Not fear, or worry, or what-ifs. I feel more hopeful than I ever have.

If I close my eyes, I bet I could even convince myself I don't have to go back to New York at all. Which would be crazy, considering that's where my life is.

I choose to ignore these thoughts for now and focus instead on Hayden. His dog. His town. The ocean.

I might be falling in love with all of it.

It's fast. Almost *too* fast. But for once, maybe it's okay to let myself get swept up in emotion. Especially after keeping it inside for so many years.

I follow him down a sandy path that leads to the beach, and before I know it, we're walking along the shore. I take off my shoes and venture to the edge where the water darkens the sand. I let the waves wash over my feet, the wet sand squishing between my toes.

In only a few days, my fear of water has subsided, like low tide. It's there, but not nearly as deep.

I wonder if doing things when I'm scared, if saying yes in the face of those fears, will always have that kind of result.

Facing these things head-on seems to take the mystery out of them. It's like seeing a dark, scary shape on the wall of your childhood bedroom and then turning on the light—only to find out it was your sweatshirt on a hook.

Not so bad when you see the truth of things.

We've been gone about fifteen minutes when I realize where we are—near the boardwalk. Hayden has stopped and is now staring in the direction of the shops and cafés.

"Are you looking for something?" I ask.

"That's the boat Dad's taking back," he says, pointing to the big, beautiful yacht. "He'll haul it down the coast, back to its owner, then rent a car and drive back."

"So what's he doing there?"

Hayden watches, so I watch, though I'm not sure what I'm watching for.

"He's waiting."

I glance at him. "For your mom."

We stand there in silence for several long seconds, and finally, Hayden turns to me. "I don't think she's coming."

I'm unsure what to say to untangle this complicated mess of emotions.

"I thought if she showed up, it was a sign she wanted us back in her life." He kicks at something on the beach. "Probably stupid."

"It's not stupid." I quietly slip my hand in his. "She's a complicated woman."

He glances over at me. "It's not complicated to fight for the people you love."

I nod. I can't speak to his pain. It's beyond me. I can't pretend I understand it.

"We can head back," he says.

Beside him, Coco sniffs at a seashell. We're about to turn back, and then . . . I see her. Tiny frame. Perfectly dressed and looking like she's walking into a photo shoot with instructions to "look like you're going sailing."

Her white linen pants are tailored to her petite frame, and she's wearing an open, white button-down shirt over a navy blue tank top. She has her big sunglasses on, there's a bag over her shoulder, and there's a man wearing a Driftwood Hotel uniform following behind her, carrying her dialysis machine.

"Hayden," I say, nodding toward her.

He follows my gaze, and we both watch as Georgina reaches the dock and stops. Dylan walks out onto the deck of the boat, and they look at each other for a few seconds before he holds out his hand to help her inside.

Even from here, I can see the history between them. The tension. The familiarity. The care. The hesitation. And so much love, just under the surface.

I *might* be reading between the lines a bit, but I'm sure it's all there.

At my side, Hayden is still watching, and there's a trace of that little boy in his eyes, standing in the doorway, watching his mother, this time with a quiet curiosity. I lean in, pressing my arm against his.

His gaze stays locked on his parents, together for the first time in years, and I can only imagine what he's thinking.

But then he glances down, steels his jaw, and says without a single trace of hesitation, "I'm going to give my mother my kidney."

Chapter 35

GEORGINA

THAT SMILE.

It's not the smile of a man holding a grudge; it's the smile of a man who's happy to see me. The smile of a man I absolutely don't deserve.

I stand at the end of the dock, my overnight bag on my shoulder and my dialysis machine by my side, thanks to a young man from the hotel. I instruct him to set the machine beside me, pay him his tip, and send him on his way.

Being alone with Dylan might be the worst thing I've ever said yes to.

He steps off the boat with all the ease of a man who's been doing that his entire life and walks out to meet me. "I'm glad you decided to come."

"Don't read too much into it," I say. "I didn't have anything else going on."

His smile is so genuine. I'm taken back to the day I fell in love in the first place.

And then I remember the day he left.

We had an argument. A fight that ended us for good.

I remember the moment I thought staying would only do them more harm. That they were both better off without me.

A part of me now still thinks I was right. Hayden is who he is because Dylan raised him. Away from the luxuries of my life.

Away from me.

Dylan slings my bag over his shoulder, then picks up the machine and starts back for the boat.

"This was a bad idea," I say.

He doesn't even turn around to look at me. Instead, he calls out, "Too late now!"

I hesitate a long moment, then finally make my way down the dock. He's standing inside the boat, holding out a hand in my direction. I look at it, then at him.

"Let me help you in."

I hesitate a moment, then finally slip my hand into his, and after stepping into the boat, I break contact with him immediately.

Not because I don't love the way my hand feels wrapped in his, but because I do.

I've missed his touch.

I look around the yacht. It's beautiful. Lavish, even. Nothing like the *Georgina*, which was a modest boat, best used for a simple afternoon on the ocean. A person could live on this boat and not miss any of the comforts of dry land.

"How far are we going to be sailing?"

"To Charleston," he says. "It takes about twelve hours."

"Twelve hours?!"

"And you're stuck with me." He grins, his eyes catching the glimmer of mischief I loved once upon a time.

But all it takes is a glance down at the machine to remember I'm not in some kind of fairy tale.

Unlike me, Dylan wasn't—and isn't—driven and ambitious. He never cared about having a big life. He wanted the opposite, really.

Simple, peaceful, calm.

At first, I loved the way he could relax me. If I'd had a bad day, he always knew how to make it better. Rest was as important to him as eating, and I often criticized him for that.

It felt lazy.

I'd been too quick to judge.

In the weeks after he and Hayden left, Dylan called me every day or so. He flew to New York to try to persuade me to see reason. He fought for our marriage, even though he was the one to move away.

I was the one who let it all go.

How selfish and misguided.

And now, sitting on this boat with him, I feel all of that regret like a knife.

I remember the words he said to me as he walked out after what ended up being his last attempt.

"I'll be waiting when you're ready."

I sobbed the second the door closed behind him. Because I didn't want him to leave. I wanted to run after him and figure out a way to make it work. I didn't really want to lose him.

But I had made my decision. And I was wholly convinced it was the right one.

I was too afraid my ambition would irrevocably wound the only two people in the world I loved.

"Do you want anything to drink before we head out?" Dylan asks now. "I made some coffee."

"I'm okay," I say. "But thank you."

Things between us feel calm and polite, but under the surface I'm anything but.

Dylan takes his place behind the wheel, and I settle in the seat next to him.

And we head out to sea.

It's a beautiful day, perfectly temperate, the breeze keeping the sun from being too warm. It conjures memories of all those weekend trips on the water. Of Hayden as a little boy, laughing with every bump of the boat. Of Dylan's long, meaningful embrace.

I used to think it was the sun and the water that refueled me, but now I'm wondering if I had that wrong. Maybe it was my boys.

I took for granted the way Dylan anticipated exactly what I needed. Sitting here with him now, it seems he still has that superpower.

I stand and move out to the deck and into the sun. I sit down and close my eyes, savoring the way it feels on my skin.

It's been so long since I've felt the sun not filtered through an office window or the blinds of a hospital room.

Dylan has never been a man of many words. He doesn't talk to fill the space, which is why we've been sailing almost an hour before either of us speaks.

He walks over and blocks my sun, and when I open my eyes, I find him holding a bottle of cold water and a tube of sunscreen. "You need both of these."

"I'm fine," I say.

"No, you aren't. The sun's different out here." He sets the sunscreen down and opens the bottle of water. "Drink."

"Don't boss me around," I say.

He smiles. "Believe me, I know nobody can tell you what to do."

I hold his gaze for a three-count, then take the bottle. I take a sip and hand it back. "Are you happy?"

"Drink the whole thing," he says. "And put some sunscreen on your face—you're already pink."

He's right. Nobody can tell me what to do. But I still listen to Dylan because somehow this feels less like bossing and more like caring. And nobody's really cared for me in years.

He returns to the wheel, and the quiet returns.

A couple of hours later, I stand and announce it's time for lunch.

"Galley's below," Dylan says. "Feel free to look around."

I go down into the living area, and I see there's a folder on the table with the Driftwood Restoration logo on the cover. I open it. Inside are photos of the renovation. What the boat looked like before. Renderings of what it could look like, and now, the final product.

It doesn't even look like the same boat.

Restored.

I glance around the cabin. The space is a blank slate for the owner to decorate to their liking, but the bones of this yacht are now solid and beautiful.

Somehow, my husband and son took an old, rotting, dead ship that could've easily been discarded and brought it back to its original, beautiful nature.

I feel a slight dip from the boat, and I step to keep my balance. The motor is slowing, and eventually it shuts off completely.

We've stopped.

When I hear Dylan coming down the stairs, I quickly close the folder, aware that my vision has blurred. I blink back the tears, annoyed and betrayed by the emotions of it all.

"The galley is through there," he says when he reaches the bottom of the stairs.

I turn to face him. I force myself to smile, but I can tell by his expression he can see through it. "You okay?"

I nod.

Because of my condition, I've been feeling this ticking of time in the back of my mind. Like when, for some people, the day hits seven in the evening and they just waste time watching television or reading until it's an acceptable time to go upstairs to bed.

Time is undefeated, and mine is running out.

I want to close the distance between us. I want to step right into his arms and let myself be held. To let myself be loved.

I want to tell him the truth—that I miss him.

And that I don't want to die.

But there is something within me that won't let it be said.

And I know exactly what it is.

It's shame.

I'm ashamed of what I did, the decisions I made, the hurt I caused.

Opening up and talking about it feels like cutting myself open. I simply can't force myself to do it.

Besides, it would be cruel to pretend we can go back. Not wanting reality to be real doesn't change it. I *am* dying. I remind myself of this over and over, and I'll keep reminding myself every hour we're together because that's what it's going to take to keep myself from falling right back into his arms.

But then he takes a step toward me. I know I'm no longer beautiful and full of life, the way I was when he fell in love with me, but he looks at me like he still sees me the same way.

Instinctively, I take a step back, and he stops moving.

"Georgie . . ."

I hold up a hand. "I shouldn't be here."

He offers a soft smile.

I look away from him. "I shouldn't have come."

"I disagree."

I respond with knee-jerk defensiveness and anger. "Why?"

"Why what?"

"Why are you doing this?" I demand. "Why are you being kind to me? You and I both know I don't deserve it."

"I disagree," he says again.

I shake my head, and he comes around in front of me, forcing me to look up, straight into his stormy gray eyes. He reaches a cautious hand out, letting it rest on my arm. At his touch, something inside me begins to melt. "Don't push me away again."

Tears fill my eyes, so I look at the ground. "I shouldn't have come."

All I can think about is my stupid kidneys and my stupid machine and the fact that if I get close to him again and die, I'll be leaving him all over again.

It feels unfair and cruel. And too hard.

I walk away, away from talking about my massive, looming diagnosis. Away from facing him, or this, or any of it.

While the boat is a nice size, there's nowhere to go.

I find the galley, and I busy myself with making lunch. I open the small refrigerator and find two sandwiches inside, along with containers of salads Dylan must've picked up in preparation for the trip.

After a few moments, he follows me in here, watching as I search for plates and silverware in an effort to avoid his eyes.

"You're still so stubborn." It sounds like an observation, not an accusation.

"And you're still infuriating." It's not true, but I need it to be, so I say it.

"And you're still beautiful."

I scoff. "I'm old. *You're* old, but for some reason men get better looking and women shrivel. Such cruel irony."

"Thanks for that," he jokes.

If I turn around and see him looking at me, I know my resolve will crumble, so I don't move. "What are you doing?"

At the shortness of my tone, I feel Dylan flinch. "I've missed you, Georgie."

I've missed you too. Just say it.

Instead, I spin around to face him. "Did you think you'd get me out here and, what, everything between us would go back to the way it was? When we were young and dumb?"

"I think we need to talk," he says.

"Fine," I snap, as if I have a right to be mad. "Let's talk. What did you want to talk about?"

"I know what you're doing," he says.

"Really?" I spit out. "What am I doing?"

"You're pushing me away so you don't have to confront these feelings."

I stew.

He steps back and folds his arms. "I still know you, Georgina. Can anyone else in the world say that?"

"No, they can't. And you don't know me, Dylan," I say.

"Oh, I think I do," he says.

He used to do this before too—this nonchalant attitude when I'm angry. It feels condescending.

"Not anymore," I snap back.

"Maybe not. Maybe you've changed. But one thing that hasn't changed is the fact that you still think you have to do things all on your own."

He unfolds his arms and leans forward.

"But you don't, Georgie. I'm here. We're still here."

The lump that forms at the back of my throat threatens to choke me. "I don't want you here."

"I don't believe you."

"I'm not sure how much clearer I can make it," I say, purposely goading him. Purposely trying to wound him so he'll give up and walk away, so I can stay safe from hitting the shame and fear head-on.

"Oh, you've made it clear, all right," he says. "But something doesn't add up."

Now I fold my arms, defiant.

"You never do anything you don't want to do," he says. "And yet you're here, on this trip with me. You can say whatever you want, but I'm listening to your actions. Not to your words."

A small crack forms in the dam I've built to hold back the years of guilt and regret.

"And another thing," he continues. "You never filed for divorce."

I didn't. Mostly because I didn't want it to be true.

"Why didn't *you* file for divorce?" I challenge.

"You know why," he says.

I shake my head. "No. I don't."

"Yes. You do."

Another crack. A few more and this dam is going to fail. My anger isn't going to be strong enough.

"You have to be mad at me," I say, willing myself not to cry.

"Why?" His smile is lazy and flirty and *sexy*. "Because you said so?"

"Because you deserve to be!" I shout at him. "It's *my* fault, Dylan! Mine! I knew it wasn't working, I knew I was hurting you and Hayden, I *knew* it." My hands are trembling. "So I made a decision. I decided to walk away. I thought I couldn't do both—I thought I couldn't achieve what I wanted to achieve and still give you what you needed. This is *completely* my fault, and now I'm . . ." My voice fails me for a second as I choke on the emotions that are pouring out like a river. "I'm dying. I'm dying because this stupid body isn't working, and there is no way I'm going to get close to you and my boy just to leave you again. I'm . . . I'm not . . ."

The tears have been building, but they surprise me nonetheless. With the dam broken, I burst into sobs. The catharsis of letting all of that go is too overwhelming, and my knees buckle, and I fall into a seat behind me, my body wracked with grief.

Dylan immediately comes to me and pulls me to him, and I just can't resist any longer.

I weep.

I weep for the mountain of shame I've bottled up.

I weep for my boy, who grew up without me.

I weep for the years I've lost.

I clutch his shirt, apologizing over and over, and he just sits there and takes it.

I rage against my situation, against the decisions I've made, and I cry and cry until there are no more tears.

Dylan's strong arms are wrapped around me, holding me to his chest, willing my deep breaths to sync with his. I tune in to the air entering and exiting my lungs, and I finally loosen my grip on his shirt and can feel the stiffness in my fingers as I do.

He holds me, here at my lowest, and without saying a word, he knew exactly what I needed.

Again.

Still.

"I forgive you, Georgie," he whispers.

I close my eyes, another wave of emotion pushing up, like waves crashing against a rocky shore.

He gently sits me up, and I feel odd—lighter somehow. He reaches up and wipes away my tears with his thumb.

"I need you to be mad at me."

"I know you're used to people doing what you say." He smiles. "But I'm not good at following orders."

I press my lips together to keep from smiling. I fail.

"I never stopped loving you." He leans forward and presses a sweet, tender kiss to my forehead.

I'm still shaking, trembling from the outpouring of emotion. "I hurt you. I hurt you so badly. And Hayden, he must . . ." I start to cry again. "He . . ."

"You did." He stops me. "And . . . it was hard for a long time. But that's in the past. What's best is for us to be together. Especially now."

I shake my head, trying not to choke on the lump that is still at the back of my throat. "I'm out of time."

"We're all dying, Georgie," he says. "And however many days I have left, I want to spend them with you."

"But why?" I whisper.

"I said I'd be waiting for you when you wanted to come home," he says. "I meant it."

"We don't even know each other anymore," I say.

He shakes his head. "I disagree."

I go still. "You still think of us as married."

"We *are* still married," he says simply.

I look away, trying to understand what he's saying. "You've really been waiting for me all this time?"

"Crazy, right?" He laughs. "But I love you, Georgina. I've always loved you."

My muscles tense. I do not deserve this kind of love.

He must feel it, because he says, "Can you just drop it for once? Drop the stubbornness, drop the pride, drop it all and let me love you?" He takes my face in his hands, and I try not to think about how much older and more wrinkled I am these days. I resist the urge to push him away. I simply close my eyes and welcome his soft, tender kiss.

It's familiar and brand new all at once, and the last pieces of the wall I built around my heart wash away.

I lay my head on his chest, spent, and he holds me, then presses a soft kiss to the top of my head.

"Welcome home, Georgie."

Chapter 36

KELSEY

WE NEED TO go to New York."

Hayden has been on the phone all morning, talking with Georgina's doctors, and now he's back out on the patio, full of purpose.

"We do?"

"They have a way to do all the preliminary testing and get results in a few days," he says. "The process can take months in other hospitals."

"We might not have that long," I say.

"Which is why we need to go to New York."

"Okay." He just stares at me. I start. "Wait, like today?"

He clicks around on his phone, then turns the screen to face me. "I already booked two tickets, and I have an appointment at the hospital tomorrow."

"That was fast," I say, surprised.

"They were anxious to get me in," he says. "It sounds like my mother's situation is dire, and it probably doesn't hurt that she's one of the wealthiest women in the country."

"That's a horrible commentary on the healthcare in this country . . . and you're not wrong."

He sits. "I should've asked if you're okay coming with me."

"I'm not super excited to get back to the city," I say, feeling like my happy bubble has just been popped. "But she's more important."

And you, I think. *You are more important.*

A few short hours later, we're on the way to the airport, and a few short hours after that, we're seated inside the cabin of a Southwest flight, thankfully next to each other. Hayden gives me the aisle seat, which lands him between me and a large man who is, unfortunately, a mouth breather.

I send Ravi a quick text to let him know I'll be back in town, then I send my mom a series of photos along with a text that simply says, Looking for what sets my soul on fire.

A voice tells us to put our electronics away, so I tuck my phone in my bag and prepare for takeoff.

"Maybe while we're there, you could show me around?" Hayden asks after we're at cruising altitude.

"You hate New York," I say, trying not to dwell on the fact that this makes our fledgling relationship pretty much impossible.

"I do. But I want to see what you love about it." He slips his hand in mine, and I shove aside thoughts of how these euphoric feelings I'm basking in are bound to wane. I don't want to think of how different we are, of how our lives don't work together, just like Georgina and Dylan's.

I don't doubt that they loved each other, or even that they still do. But ultimately, they couldn't make it work because Dylan didn't belong in New York any more than Georgina belonged in Driftwood.

If Georgina is a cautionary tale, I should pay better attention.

When we land, we make our way outside at JFK Airport, and I call an Uber. It's late afternoon, and the city is as alive as ever. We drive toward my apartment, and I glance over at Hayden, who's watching out the window with the same wonder I imagine anyone who doesn't live here might have.

I let my head rest on the back of the seat of the SUV and try to see the city through his eyes. It's busy and noisy, but there is an undeniable creative energy here that I've never found anywhere else.

It's exactly the opposite of Driftwood. Not better. And I have the same thought I had before . . .

Where you live determines how *you live.*

How do I want to live?

Ever since I was in high school, it was my dream to live in New York, but now, for the first time in my adult life, I'm starting to question if maybe there's something different out there for me.

New York is scary and challenging, but I'm comfortable here—kind of like a hamster is "comfortable" in a cage. It's a familiar pain, living in New York. Anything other than this city and my job feels foreign and slower.

The Uber driver drops us off in front of my apartment. We grab our bags and slide off the sticky, not-quite-black seats onto the sidewalk. Hayden looks up at my building—a tall, nondescript dwelling with a bunch of tenants who don't know each other living inside.

I think of how friendly he was to everyone we saw at the bar and wonder if I'd even like to know my neighbors. Mostly, I'm content to do my own thing.

"This is it, huh?"

I nod. "This is it."

I hadn't thought about this part. Showing him my apartment. Putting him up on my couch. Letting him into my neutral-walled world. Pieces of myself that I typically hide.

He must sense my hesitation, because he pulls out his phone and says, "I'm going to find a hotel. I got so caught up in getting to the airport, I forgot."

I put my hand on his. "No, it's fine. My couch turns into a bed." Never mind that I'm using an unpacked cardboard box as a bedside table. Or that he's about to see just how very unsettled my life really is.

We walk upstairs as a text from Ravi comes in.

> **Ravi:** Free tonight? I have news.
> **Kelsey:** News? Is it what I think?
> **Ravi:** 😄

"You're smiling," Hayden says as we reach the third floor.

"I think my best friend is getting engaged," I say.

> **Kelsey:** Tell me everything!
> **Ravi:** I'm having a party tonight . . . say you'll come?!

With Ravi's parties, there is always dancing. And mingling. And people. For a math professor, he's surprisingly social. Not to stereotype math professors.

I've certainly never been his fun friend.

> **Ravi:** There might be some dancing. But I need you there,
> K.

Called it.

I stare at the words on the screen, then glance over at Hayden. "Do you want to go out tonight?"

He smirks. "Are you asking me on a date?"

My lips crawl into a smile. "I guess I am."

"Then yes. Count me in."

The backs of my knees tingle when he says this.

He smiles at me, but my focus shifts to the backdrop of the city behind him—and to reality.

This isn't going to end well.

·················

Hayden and Ravi instantly hit it off.

We walk into Ravi's apartment, he greets us with his usual joyfulness, and Hayden's charming "I'm friends with everyone" personality latches right on.

Ravi and his roommate, Brian, are throwing an '80s party, and Ravi is dressed like he just stepped out of a Wham! video. Sunglasses, tight jeans, frosted tips in his hair (how did he do that?). It's appalling. But he's not the only one committing fashion crimes tonight. The whole place is crawling with big bangs, blue eyeshadow, leg warmers, and popped collars. Brian looks like he's auditioning to play the lead in a *Miami Vice* remake.

I would feel out of place in my normal clothes if it weren't so hilariously hideous.

I stand off to the side as the bass vibrates through my shoes. Ravi bounces as he sips his drink, and Hayden stands casually beside me, garnering more than his fair share of double takes from women walking by.

I take his hand, to claim him for myself. I try to remind myself that Hayden and I aren't dating, that this is just a passing attraction, but then I think of why we're here—because he's dropped everything to try to donate his kidney to a mother who basically abandoned him—and I know I'm lying to myself.

It's more than attraction. It's respect. Admiration. Infatuation.

I bet I could love him.

The words enter my mind without my permission, and I'm helpless to remove them. Reality is no match for my imagination.

My thoughts are quickly silenced when the song changes, and the familiar opening notes of "The Safety Dance" by Men Without Hats comes on.

"Ravi!" I shout over the noise. "Tell me you aren't proposing here."

He grins, then directs his reply to Hayden. "I met Sasha at a party like this. She's going to love it."

"Right, but this is your *engagement*," I say.

"I know." Ravi waggles his eyebrows. "It's perfect, right? I'm going to have the DJ play 'Total Eclipse of the Heart,' and I'm going to drop down on one knee and pop the question." He pauses. "Too predictable?"

"Not at all, man." Hayden claps him on the shoulder. "Sounds fun."

I start to worry that I've failed him as a friend. I don't know any woman who wants her proposal to happen at an '80s party.

But then I spot Sasha walking toward us. Her hair is crimped, like Whitney Houston in the "I Wanna Dance with Somebody" video. She's wearing ripped stockings underneath a black skirt and black heeled boots, and there's a neon-pink top under a black jacket that's had the sleeves ripped off.

And she's owning it.

Now I get it. This *is* the perfect spot to propose.

With parents like mine, you don't escape childhood without costumes. We had a whole trunk in the attic that we rummaged through daily. Crowns and swords and capes and princess dresses—we had it all.

And then I grew up. And costumes felt a little silly and impractical. But seeing Ravi and Sasha makes me wish for a little silly and impractical.

Ravi gives Sasha an admiring once-over. "You look so awesome, babe."

"Thank you!" She brightens at the compliment, then turns to me. "Kelsey! You're back!" Then a look at Hayden. "With candy."

Beside me, I hear him chuckle, and I put a hand on his arm. "This is Hayden. Hayden, Sasha."

She raises her eyebrows in approval, then latches onto my arm and pulls me off to the side. "You leave for a week and come back with a runway model?"

I laugh. "Hardly. He's the son of a friend. He's here for some medical stuff."

She frowns. "He's okay, right?"

"Oh yeah! It's not him. He's fine," I say.

She raises her eyebrows again. "Yes, he is."

I laugh.

"So what's the rest of the story?"

I frown. "There is no 'rest of the story.'"

"Whatever," she says, clearly not believing me. She blinks, and I catch a glimpse of the glitter on her eyelids. I have to hand it to them: she and Ravi know how to go all in on a party theme.

Ravi rushes toward us and grabs Sasha's hand. "Let's dance."

She lets out a loud "Woo-hoo!" and races off to the living room, where all the furniture has been cleared away to make room for a makeshift dance floor. Here, they proceed to let go of every inhibition, taking the whole "dance like no one's watching" thing to heart.

I move back to Hayden's side and smile. "This isn't really my scene."

"I guessed." He smiles when he says it.

It's hard to swallow that he's already got me pegged, even though we haven't known each other very long. In spite of the Summer of Yes, I'm really still the same stick-in-the-mud I've always been. And I don't want to be.

"Do you want to dance?" I ask.

He looks surprised. "Do *you* want to dance?"

"Yes," I say emphatically, trying to convince myself.

"You don't." His smile is sweet. "And that's okay. Do you want to get some air instead?"

I sigh in relief and take his hand, leading him through Ravi's room and out onto the fire escape. We crawl through the window, and once we're outside, I let out an embarrassed laugh.

"I'm not great at saying yes to things that pull me out of my comfort zone. Like the hiking. Or the mosquitoes."

"Or dancing."

"Right," I say. "Not good at dancing."

At the mention of the hike, he points to my face. "At least you don't look like Sloth from *The Goonies* anymore."

I burst out laughing. "I *love* that you know that movie."

"Know it? I could quote the whole thing to you." He grins.

"My mom thought it was important for us to know all the movies she grew up on," I tell him. "I'm not sure she realized how inappropriate some of them are."

There's a lull, but it's not awkward or uncomfortable.

After a beat, he says, "I think your Summer of Yes is brilliant. You know that, right?"

I nod half-heartedly because it sounds like a compliment, and I'm not sure how to take it.

"But you do have to leave room for the idea that you aren't going to love everything you do. Like hiking or dancing." He leans over the railing, and I wish our view was pretty, but we're basically just staring at another building. "I think there's room for you to still be yourself."

I stand next to him so I'm also leaning over the railing. "I'm pretty boring."

"Not wanting to dress up like Madonna doesn't make you boring."

I smile to myself just as the crowd lets out a loud cheer. Through the window, I can see Ravi, down on one knee, holding a ring box up to Sasha, "Total Eclipse of the Heart" playing in the background, countless friends capturing the moment on video.

Sasha covers her face and nods her answer, and my heart doubles in size. Ravi slides the ring on her finger, stands, and pulls her into a tight hug. The music kicks back up—Bonnie Tyler's raspy voice belting through the speakers—and the whole room starts singing, dancing, or playing the air guitar.

"Look at them," I say.

"They look happy," he says.

"They *are* happy. It's the real thing." They're ready to pledge their love to each other for the rest of their lives. I've never had that.

My body becomes keenly aware of Hayden standing next to me, watching through the window with an amused curiosity, and then watching me the same way.

I bet I could love him.

I'm conflicted.

I'm worried that this can never work. Legitimately.

It's not some book on a Barnes & Noble shelf, where you know three-fourths of the way through the story that the guy and girl are going to end up together, regardless of the third-act misunderstanding that keeps them apart—we live in different places. We have different lives.

Maybe, ultimately, it can't work out. And maybe it's not supposed to. Maybe Hayden isn't *the one*.

But that doesn't change the fact that I've never felt as strongly for anyone as I do for him. Am I really doomed to know he's out there, living his life without me?

Why do I have such a hard time believing a love like Ravi and Sasha's or like my parents' might exist for me?

And why am I just now realizing that I might be the one thing standing in the way of me finding it?

Later, after a couple more hours of music and dancing, I find my best friend restocking the snacks in the kitchen. He looks up and grins at me.

"She said yes," I say.

He gives a boyish shrug, then says, "I *am* a catch."

I hug him, trying not to think of all the ways this could change things between us. Ravi is moving on with his life.

"You really are." I pull away and clap him on the sides of his arms. "What made you decide to pull the trigger? Did your family finally wear you down?"

He gives me a trademark crooked smile. "You, actually."

I raise my eyebrows in surprise. "Me?"

"Your Summer of Yes."

"Shut. Up." *I* inspired this?

"It made me realize I've also been holding back because I was afraid," he says. "And when I started thinking about it, I realized that was a dumb reason not to propose to the love of my life."

"What were you afraid of?" I ask.

He shrugs. "Change, I guess. Not being all she needs me to be. Not being able to provide. All the things guys think about before proposing." He laughs. "But you helped change all of that for me."

"I think you're giving me too much credit."

"And I think you're not giving yourself enough," he counters.

I sigh. "I'm not sure I'm doing a very good job with my own plan."

Ravi glances at Hayden, standing across the room with Sasha. "Because you're still scared?"

I shrug, not wanting to admit it out loud.

"It's okay to still be scared sometimes," Ravi says.

"But you're not," I tell him, as if I know the inner workings of his mind.

"Are you kidding? I'm terrified," he says, laughing. "There's still a lot of stuff freaking me out. But I'm doing it anyway because I know it's the right thing."

"And because you're in love." I smile.

"And that."

At that moment, "Walk Like an Egyptian" starts to play, and Sasha, from across the room, lets out a loud, "Ravi! It's our dance!"

He grins, lifting a finger as if to say, *"One second!"* Then, back to me: "We have a dance to this one."

"Like choreography?" I tease.

He responds by flipping his arms up in the "Egyptian" pose from the Bangles music video, moving his head back and forth as he crosses the room to meet Sasha just in time for the chorus.

I stand in my quiet spot, off to the side, watching, thinking about what Ravi said.

I inspired this.

He did it—but that doesn't mean he's not afraid.

My eyes drift over to Hayden.

And I wonder if I could do the same.

Chapter 37

KELSEY

I DREAM IN technicolor.

I've heard some people don't, and I can't imagine what that looks like.

I've been dreaming wildly of late, and last night's didn't disappoint.

I'm on a boat—a big one—with my parents, and we were having some kind of celebration. I was supposed to give a speech, but as I was walking to the front of the bow, where a microphone and podium were, I looked off to my left to see clouds in the sky and a huge wave barreling down on us. I shout for everyone to hold on, and I grip the railing like I'm on the tipping Titanic *as the wave crashes over me.*

But it's not destructive, it's not horrific, and I find I can breathe under the water. I look up and see waves from underneath, a curling geometry of rolling bubbles. I let go of the railing and see that all the guests are swimming about underwater, like nothing is wrong, and I wonder how I could get swept up and still be peaceful.

I wake with a start, the afterimages of the dream still lingering.

It's the morning after Ravi's proposal party. I come out of my room to find Hayden already dressed, having folded and stacked the bedding at the end of the couch.

He really is a morning *and* evening person. An all-day-long person. I didn't know those existed.

I'm grateful we have somewhere to be, because otherwise this whole day would've started out on an awkward note. As is routine,

I have to hurry to get ready—and after a NASCAR-style pit stop of makeup and toothpaste, I walk with Hayden out the door to get to his appointment on time.

We're standing in the crowd on the subway, en route to the hospital, and I glance over at Hayden just as the man sitting next to him reaches over and pats his hand. He looks at me, a quizzical expression on his face, and I motion for him to follow me. We move toward the door of the subway, and I pull hand sanitizer from my bag.

"New York is full of . . . uh . . . colorful characters," I tell him as I squirt the gel into his open palm.

He rubs his hands together. "It sure is."

I can tell by the way he says it that New York isn't charming him.

I sense the disappointment of that in my body. I want him to love it here, or at least tolerate it like I do, even though I know he never will. He doesn't yearn for the city any more than I yearn for a small town.

Just like Georgina and Dylan.

When we reach the hospital, Hayden turns to me. "Thanks for getting me here. I'm not sure if you can come back with me, because . . ."

"Yeah." I finish his thought. "I'm not family."

"I'm sorry about that."

"It's okay. I'll find something to do."

"Like?"

"I'm not sure," I say, feeling odd with a whole day off in the city when everyone I know is at work. "I guess I'll spend the day with myself. And I'll be back at the end of the day to meet you."

"I'm sure I can find my way back to your place if it's out of the way."

"Oh no, I don't mind."

His eyes lock onto mine, then dip to my lips and back again.

"You want to kiss me, don't you?" I give him what I hope is a flirty look.

He raises an eyebrow. "Maybe."

"Good." I inch up on my tiptoes and kiss him—quickly, even though I'd very much like to do that all day long. When I pull back, I catch something in his eyes that makes me ask, "Are you nervous?"

He nods. "Yeah. I am. A little."

"About the tests?"

He shakes his head. "No, not that. Just wondering, what if I'm not a match?"

I slide my hand into his. "I know. But you're trying anyway. You're saying yes."

Yes to a relationship with the mother he's never gotten to know.

Yes to another person's life.

Yes to potential disappointment.

"It's a big deal."

He kisses me again, a little longer, a little sweeter, a little more lingering, and I feel it all the way to my toes.

"Do you want me to stay?" I ask when I pull away. He told me the doctor told him they'd need him the entire day. Around fourteen hours. But I'd spend it in the waiting room if he asked me to.

"No," he says. "You should go do something fun."

At the moment, I can't think of a single fun thing I want to do, but I nod anyway, pretending I love this idea. "Good luck," I say, dropping his hand.

He nods, then steps away from me, disappearing through the entrance of the hospital, leaving me standing on the sidewalk, and all at once, I know exactly how I want to spend the day.

I make my way back through the city and over to the very familiar building where I spend most of my time. I get in the elevator, get off on the floor where I work, and instantly smell Daniel, so I know he's nearby.

It's a weird feeling. It hasn't been that long since I've been here, but it has the same feeling as when you revisit your elementary school as an adult.

It all feels a bit smaller.

I walk through the room to my cubicle and take stock.

Have I missed it? No.

Do I wish I were back from my little leave of absence? Also no.

Can I imagine my life without this job . . . ?

Before my head can answer, I hear Tess call my name from behind me.

"Kelsey! Are you back?" She rushes over.

"Not totally. Still using up my vacation. I just stopped in to talk to Charlie."

"You're not quitting, are you?" She looks panicked.

I frown. "Why would you think I'm quitting?"

"I don't know," she says, starting her normal free-association style of talking. "You look . . . *great*. Refreshed. Brighter. Maybe because you're not here? But it seems like you might need a change. Or something. I'm not sure. Ignore me. I'm just so glad to see you."

"What have I missed?"

Tess begins to unload all the latest office gossip, and it seems like a lot, even in the short time I've been gone. Who's dating who, which clients Daniel's been after, all the drama with Chase Donovan . . . and as she talks, I find myself drifting from paying attention. I'm thinking about the boardwalk. The saltwater taffy. The boat. My night swim. Ravi's engagement. Putting on plays in my parents' backyard. Furiously writing. Hayden. Georgina. Driftwood.

And I realize I don't really care about what I've missed. What I've found seems so much more interesting.

Charlie walks out of one of the conference rooms and spots me standing there with a dumb look on my face. He raises his eyebrows in acknowledgment.

"Hold on, Tess," I say, sidestepping her to catch Charlie before he goes to whatever meeting is next on his schedule. "Charlie!" I race over to catch up to him. "Can we talk quick?"

"I've got five minutes."

"Early tee time?"

He gives me a side-eye, and I clamp my jaw shut.

"Sorry." I clear my throat and summon every ounce of bravery I have. I mentally acted out this scene on the way over here, and this is my first line.

"I wanted to talk about the proposal I sent you," I say.

Normally, I wouldn't do this. Like ignoring nagging symptoms and avoiding the doctor, I just grin and bear the pain and don't speak up or ask pointed questions.

This is me seeing the doctor. Taking the test. Forcing myself to deal with results.

We walk into Charlie's office, and he sits behind his desk. He's shuffling papers and barely paying attention to me as I stand there awkwardly. Waiting.

"So . . . ," I say dumbly.

He looks up, as if he's only just remembered I'm standing there. "Sorry, Worthington. Busy around here." Then, with a bit of snark, he adds, "We're a little short-staffed."

Instant guilt pricks at my edges. "Sorry about that."

I'm not sorry. I earned my time off.

"Did you have a chance to read through the proposal I sent?" I feel beads of sweat forming over my upper lip, and my face beginning to flush.

He pauses for a split second, as if trying to remember. "Yes, I did. Didn't I email you back?"

I nod my head.

"Debut author, right? But not someone famous."

"Right."

"Then why do I care what this person has to say?"

I'm struck dumb for a moment. This wasn't his line in the scene in my head.

He's going off script.

"Well, I . . ." I'm stumbling for a reply. "I . . . don't think a person has to be famous to have a valuable story to tell or opinion to share."

"Seems like everyone's got an opinion about everything these days," he mutters.

"Right, but this is something unique, don't you think?"

"Not really." He shrugs. "It's not original. The writing is okay, I guess, but it didn't dazzle me. Didn't make me care about the story at all."

I think back on the night I sent the proposal. I remember feeling inspired. Moved. Like I cut myself open and bled all over those pages. And he's saying he didn't care?

He stops shuffling papers around and looks at me. "Is that all?"

"You really don't think there's something there?" I ask gingerly, trying to lead the witness. "I was moved by the chapters. The whole idea of the book spoke to me."

He shrugs. "Sorry, not for us." He looks at his watch. "Unless this author has a hundred thousand TikTok followers or something. *Then* I'd be interested."

I don't respond. I don't know what to say. This is not how this is supposed to go.

"Do they?"

"What?"

He frowns. "Have a hundred thousand TikTok followers?"

"Uh, no."

"Keep looking, Worthington. This author isn't worth our time."

Gut punch.

I give Charlie a quick nod, then take a few steps back. "Right."

Rejected.

It follows me out of his office, past Tess, who tries to talk to me, into the elevator, and all the way out the door.

Rejected.

It's not the first time someone said I don't have what it takes, and now that it's been repeated in such a blunt fashion, I hear the message loud and clear.

Summer of Yes. Yeah, right.

It was so stupid of me to get wrapped up in this ridiculous idea that I've got anything important to say. What did I think I was going to do? Inspire a new generation of fearless women? With my *words*?

How arrogant and misguided.

But then I think of Ravi, saying he was inspired by me to finally take the step he'd been avoiding.

I think of Hayden, saying yes to something big and difficult and uncomfortable.

I think of Georgina, out on the ocean somewhere with the love of her life, hopefully giving herself permission to admit what she wants.

And I even think of my mother, who's been saying yes for as long as I've known her.

I think of how this whole journey has affected me, what it's taught me, how it's already changed me.

Maybe those things are enough.

And maybe they're not.

I failed. Again.

At least now I know, right? At least now I can go back to work saying I gave it a solid try. This is the healthy dose of reality I needed to pull me back. It's not like I was going to quit my job and write a book that would make me millions. Or leave New York in favor of some sleepy little town on the coast. That's not me.

I got caught up in the fantasy of, well, everything, and this is good. This is the reality check I needed to plant my feet back on the ground. Firmly.

Like cinder blocks in the ocean.

Now I know.

My professor was right. Charlie is right.

I don't have what it takes.

Chapter 38

GEORGINA

I HAVEN'T CRIED like that in years.

Maybe ever.

After our heart-to-heart in the galley, the mood on the boat changed.

The tense small talk disappeared, and it was . . . well, it was just like old times.

I took a turn behind the wheel while Dylan stood behind me, his hands on mine, teaching me how to steer a ship of this size. We ate and talked and laughed and reminisced. He told me stories of Hayden as a boy, as a teenager, and while it hurt to hear them, it was good too.

Cathartic.

He held me as we watched the sunset over the ocean, and he kissed me so fully it felt like oxygen.

I wondered how I ever survived without him.

"I'm stepping down," I tell him as we approach Charleston.

"You are? From the company?"

I nod. "I have to choose a successor soon."

He looks out over the ocean. "Mighty big shoes to fill."

"Maybe I could spend a little bit of time with you," I offer.

Now that we've crossed this line, there's no going back. I can't fathom a world without him in it.

I know it's not as simple as all that. I know the heartache of our past *will* return. I know he's giving me more grace than he should because who knows how much longer we'll have.

His smile is so clear, so genuine. "Well, heck, I can't think of anything better."

I smile . . . and then wince.

Something doesn't feel right. In my side.

Oh no.

An uncomfortable, unsettling throbbing starts to radiate from my side through my stomach.

Something is wrong.

I've been fortunate up to this point. Things have gone smoothly, I've done all of the protocols, eaten the proper diet, followed every procedure and precaution to a T.

A ball of pain expands on my left, almost doubling me over. I let out a small gasp.

I look over and find that Dylan, thankfully, didn't hear. I brace myself with one hand and arch slightly against the pain, which is making me slightly nauseous.

I'm panicked. And afraid. *We're miles from help. What am I going to do?*

I hold my breath and let it out slowly. I take another . . . and another.

Gradually, the wave of nausea eases—and the pain dulls but remains.

Dylan turns to me and smiles, then quickly looks concerned. He must see my distress.

"Hey. Hey, you okay?"

I hold up a hand and nod, making it sound way less serious. "I just got a bit nauseous; it's nothing." I weakly wave him off.

He frowns at me, but I straighten and smile. It hurts, but I don't show it. "It's probably your driving."

He relaxes his shoulders. "Funny girl. Drink some water—it might help the sickness."

The pain lingers, like hidden dangers under the surface of the water. I feel like I'm speeding right toward them. And I'm running out of time.

We return the boat to its owner—a wealthy, particular man, who despite his best efforts can't find a single thing to criticize about the job Dylan and Hayden have done. Once that's settled, we take a cab and pick up the car he reserved.

Thankfully, things inside my body have settled down. I have no idea what it was or what caused it.

"How are you feeling? Are you hungry?" he asks as he takes my dialysis machine and tucks it into the trunk. "We haven't eaten since lunch."

"I could eat, yes," I tell him. "But we aren't exactly dressed for a dinner out."

He grins. "Let's get a pizza and take it back to the hotel. Find a movie to watch."

"That sounds like a date," I say. "For two teenagers."

"Exactly." He opens my car door, and I get inside, and as I watch him walk around to the driver's side, I realize the fear and anxiety I felt on the boat are being replaced with . . . excitement.

About not having any responsibilities except what toppings to get.

About the prospect of retiring. Of leaving my company in good hands.

About the possibility of moving to Driftwood to live with Dylan and Hayden.

About getting to know my husband and son.

I imagine days out on the ocean, just like old times. And summer nights of burgers on the grill and walks on the beach at dawn.

Such a departure from who I've been for more than twenty years. And I feel oddly at peace with the idea.

"So . . . you still like garbage pizza?" he asks.

"It's the only way to eat pizza," I say. "But I haven't had it in *years*."

He frowns. "Has your life been all about restriction and duty? I think I need to remind you what it's like to have fun."

I laugh. "Fun isn't really a part of my scheduled activities. There's work and . . . more work." And diets and protocols and regimens. But I don't mention those because I don't want to be reminded. Besides, will eating pizza once actually make a difference?

He shakes his head and starts the car. "Oh, Georgie. You've missed so much."

A deep regret curls inside me at that thought.

I try to push it away, but it, like the dull pain, lingers. The choices I made all those years ago reach out, like the twisted, bony fingers of a villain, flashing what could've been in front of my face.

The car Dylan rented is a convertible, and he's quick to put the top down. Then he pulls away from the small rental building and out onto the highway. The air is warm, and in spite of the cocktail of feelings welling up inside me, I settle in for a calm, easy drive.

He reaches across the front seat and takes my hand, stroking the back of it with his thumb.

I always liked Dylan's hands.

They're strong and secure and protective and capable. I'm aware in this moment how lucky I am that he's chosen to focus that love on me.

We find a pizza place and order a large garbage pizza and a salad with bread to go. As we sit side by side in the lobby, waiting for our food and inhaling the smell of garlic and tomato sauce, Dylan picks up my hand and kisses it.

"What if you move to Driftwood?" he asks.

I glance over at him, wondering how he read my mind.

"What if we give this a real shot?"

My other hand moves unconsciously to my side, where the catheter is now a permanent fixture of my small frame. "Dylan, I—"

"I know about your kidneys," he says. "I know it may not be for long. But what if you spend whatever time you have left with me and Hayden?"

Before, I thought it would be cruel to do that.

Now, I think it would be crazy not to.

"What will we do all day?" I ask, honestly wondering. I've spent every day of the last several decades in the office—I thought I'd die there one day. I expected JP to come in after lunch and find me keeled over across my desk.

I used to think it would be the best way to go. *"She died doing what she was best at."* But now I realize it's not at all what I want.

For a person who usually knows exactly what she wants and doesn't refrain from speaking her mind, I've taken a long time to reach this conclusion.

"I can think of a few things." He raises his eyebrows and tosses me a boyish grin.

I can't help it—I laugh. I feel like a whole different version of myself when I'm with him. He makes me feel young. And *alive.* "I'm serious."

"So am I," he says.

I turn and face him. "Why would you want to do this? Knowing how much it'll hurt when I'm gone?"

He shrugs. "It's going to hurt either way. I'd rather have you here."

"If we spend the next however many months together, as a married couple—that would be more painful, wouldn't it?"

"That's not a reason to stay away," he says.

"I think it's the kindest reason to stay away."

He shakes his head. "You're trying to protect me, Georgina, but you really can't. The day you leave the earth will be the worst day of my life, whether you come back to Driftwood or stay in New York."

Slowly, I lean against him, my cheek resting on his chest, and he wraps an arm around me.

The restaurant isn't busy, and there's hardly anyone around, so the moment feels intimate and private. And I realize that maybe it's not only his heart I've been trying to protect—it's my own too. Because up until this trip, it was easier to come to terms with the end of my life because there really wasn't anyone I would miss.

Now, though, I realize I was kidding myself.

He's right. This is going to hurt either way. And all at once, I don't want to go.

"I'll do it," I say.

He inches back and looks at me. "You'll do what?"

"Move to Driftwood with you. Well, not with you. I'm going to buy us a house right on the water. I don't want to live in Hayden's pool house."

His face lights up. A kid on Christmas morning who just got news of a trip to Disneyland couldn't compare. His smile is so genuine, I feel it in my soul. Without hesitation, and not caring about where we are, he leans forward and kisses me. He's given me a reason to want to live, and I'm suddenly struck with the sadness I've been running from.

"You're coming home?"

I nod. He kisses me again, and the man behind the counter clears his throat. "Pizza's ready."

"Hey, buddy," Dylan says to him without taking his eyes off me. "I'm kissing my wife here. I'll be right with you."

I laugh softly, mortified, and he kisses me again.

I love it as much as the pizza guy doesn't.

We take the pizza back to the hotel, and as we're standing in the lobby waiting to check in, Dylan turns to me. "I got us two rooms. I thought it would be better."

I slip my hand in his. "I disagree."

I see the slightest raise of his eyebrows, and he freezes.

I only smile. *I feel young. Alive.* What if I say yes to these feelings? *Even if it hurts later.*

We check in and make our way up to the room, then spend the next half hour devouring pizza and drinking soda, both of which I haven't had in ages and shouldn't be having now.

And then, after we've changed into pajamas, we settle into the bed and find a movie to watch. It's like we're newlyweds all over again, and I wonder how I got lucky enough to have a second chance with the only man I've ever loved.

"Georgie, I need to know if we're doing this for real," he tells me as I search for a movie we can both agree on.

I set the remote control down and look at him.

The look on his face is so earnest it twists something inside me. "I know it's a big change, but if you're willing, then I'm all in. We can figure out the logistics later."

"Are you sure that's what you want?"

"I'm sure." He takes my hand in his. "All I want is you."

Maybe it's crazy, but everything about it feels right. *He* feels right. And after a few long moments, I finally nod my answer.

"Is that a yes?"

"It's a yes," I say.

If he says this is what he wants, I believe him. Because this is what I want too.

The movie plays, and we pretend to watch, our feet finding each other under the covers, his hands pulling me into his side. We spend the night remembering what it was like to be married, and the next day, we decide to extend our trip by a day or two.

We walk around Charleston, holding hands, escaping real life for a while. We take our time. Shop. Eat. He sits with me while I do dialysis and tells me stories about people they've met restoring boats, what Hayden was like when he was younger, how they renovated his house and the pool house together.

He starts filling in the gaps that I have missed, and it all feels like a precious gift.

They're close, he and Hayden, and I'm thankful for that. Maybe I'll have enough time left to get close to our son too.

Hopefully.

The only thing to focus on here is each other. We have no agenda, and it's . . . nice.

The next morning, Dylan calls Hayden to let him know we're going to take our time getting back, and we spend another day doing almost nothing that means everything, and I realize this is exactly how I want to live out the remainder of my life.

With Dylan. Like a real married couple.

He's attentive and thoughtful and kind, and I can feel the armor I've been hiding behind begin to fall away.

It only took a hard conversation and a couple of days for me to get used to this. To him.

I was such a fool all those years ago.

....

I wake up on the third day in Charleston, thankfully to no more pain. It only flared up one other time while walking, but I've been able to push those looming thoughts of my life's deadline out of my mind and focus on the moment.

I roll over to find his side of the bed empty. I'm not alarmed because he's been slipping down the block for scones and coffee (tea for me) very early each morning, returning to the room before I'm awake.

It's been lovely to have someone bring me things I like because they want to, and not because I pay them to.

I'm slow to get up, but I'm pulled out of bed by the sound of a squeaky horn on the street below.

The hotel we're in is an old building where the windows actually open, and our room has a balcony overlooking the street.

I walk outside and peer down, where I see Dylan sitting on a Vespa. At the sight of me, the beeping stops, and he lifts a hand in a wave. "Morning."

I smile at him. "You're going to wake the whole block!"

"It's nine o'clock!"

I gasp. "What? Why didn't you wake me?"

"You looked so peaceful," he calls up. "When was the last time you slept in?"

When was the last time I slept in? Have I *ever* slept in?

"Get dressed and come down! Let's go for a ride before we hit the road!"

My knee-jerk reaction is to tell him no, then hand him a list of all the reasons why. But I can practically hear Kelsey's voice in my head: *"Say yes, Georgina!"*

"Give me ten minutes!" I can't remember the last time I got ready in ten minutes, but somehow I manage.

The slower, easier, less fussy pace suits me, which surprises me, but I think I can get used to it. This will be my new normal. Easy mornings. Sleeping in. Exploring new-to-me cities. I've loved our trip to Charleston—we could visit Savannah next or Tybee Island. Take the Mustang and drive down the coast.

In this moment, it's clearer than ever how I want to spend my days.

As I pull the door closed behind me and head out to the lobby, my phone rings. I fish around in my purse as I step out onto the sidewalk, catching a glimpse of Dylan across the street.

He's sitting on a red Vespa, and parked beside him is a baby-blue one. My favorite color. How he managed to get them both here, I have no idea, but knowing him, he charmed somebody and now we get to go out for a leisurely ride before heading back to Driftwood.

"Hello?" I say into the phone, stopping on the sidewalk.

"Miss Tate?"

I glance over at Dylan and think, *Mrs. Quinn,* but I say, "Speaking."

"Miss Tate, this is Roberta, Dr. Schneider's nurse."

"I don't have a Dr. Schneider," I say.

"He's the surgeon, ma'am, and I'm calling to inform you that we've found a kidney donor."

My heart stops.

I hitch my breath and hold it.

I turn away, pressing the phone harder to my ear, as if I heard incorrectly. "I'm sorry, Roberta, could you repeat that?"

"We found a donor, Miss Tate," she says, and I can hear the smile in her voice.

"I don't understand," I tell her. "I was told the odds of that happening were almost zero."

"It's rare, but it does happen," she says. "We're all really excited for you!"

"So do I need to get to the hospital immediately? I'm in Charleston."

"No, not immediately. There are still a few things we need to set up here. We'll schedule your surgery," she says. "This is a unique situation. A living donor."

I stop and turn toward Dylan, who mouths at me, *"Who's on the phone? Let's go,"* and I hold up a finger and mouth back, *"One second!"*

I say into the phone, "A living donor?"

"Yes, it's pretty amazing. A perfect match."

"Who is it? A random stranger?"

"The donor has chosen to remain anonymous, and while it is exceedingly rare, it does happen, ma'am," she says. "Possibly someone who knew another affected by kidney disease, or whose loved one passed away waiting, that sort of thing."

"I don't know how I feel about this," I say. "I don't think it's right to take someone else's kidney."

"All due respect, Miss Tate, but this isn't the kind of thing you want to pass on," Roberta says. "If all goes well, your life will return to normal, and you'll have many more years to live it."

My skin is tingling, like it's being pricked with a thousand tiny needles. "No more dialysis?"

I can hear the smile in her voice again. "No more dialysis."

I let out a breath of relief so heavy I nearly collapse. I tried to convince myself that I was okay with dying, but my body's reaction to this news suggests otherwise.

"You should be able to return to life as usual after a few months," Roberta says. "We'll need to get you in here as soon as possible to get the ball rolling, but congratulations, Miss Tate. Everyone here is thrilled!"

She hangs up, and I hold the phone against my ear for several seconds, frozen.

Return to life as usual. In New York. At my company.

I'm not going to die.

My whole life doesn't have to change.

"Georgina?" Dylan has crossed the street and is now standing beside me. "Are you okay?"

I pull the phone away from my ear and meet his eyes. Tears well up in mine.

"Honey, what's wrong? Who was that?"

I tremble as I reach for his hand. "They found a match, Dylan. A match."

He immediately reaches for me and pulls me into him, burying his face in my hair. "Georgie!"

Through the whiplash of emotions, a thought hits me.

"Tell me you didn't have anything to do with this," I say while he's still holding me.

He pulls back, eyes wide. "I've been here with you this whole time."

"And Hayden——"

"Has been working," he says, cutting me off. "And he's with Kelsey, I'm sure."

I take a step away.

"Georgina, this is a good thing," he says. "A *great* thing! We should celebrate."

The news is hard to process. For months now, I've resigned myself to this unbearable death sentence, and now, everything has flipped.

"Why don't you look more excited?" Dylan asks. "This is great news."

I nod, still shell-shocked and unsure. "She said if the transplant is successful, I can return to my life." I look at him. "Nothing has to change."

His face falls.

Seconds ago, I was so certain of what I wanted. Dylan. Hayden. This easy, peaceful existence. That hasn't changed. But this complicates things. Nothing feels quite so certain anymore.

I'd made my peace with giving up my company because I had to, but now? Now it would be a choice.

Something I'd have to say yes to.

"Is that what you want? For things not to change?"

"I don't know." I shake my head and turn away.

He takes my hand and forces my gaze. "Someday, our lives *are* going to end, Georgina. Kidney transplant or not. And when it's all winding down, I don't want either one of us to be full of any more regrets. This is our chance to be together. Please don't run from that."

I reach up and touch his cheek. "Let me think, okay? I just need time to think."

He nods. "Fine, but I'm coming in for your surgery, and I'm going to be the one to help you recover."

I smile, but my heart is sad. Now I'm faced with this impossible choice.

The same exact choice that presented itself all those years ago.

Chapter 39

KELSEY

A PERFECT MATCH.

It's not like it was a test one could study for . . . but Hayden came back a *perfect match*.

After hours of extensive testing for two days straight, Hayden and I returned to Driftwood. Georgina and Dylan, however, did not. Dylan called to let us know they were staying in Charleston for another couple of days, and I wish I could get the scoop on *that* story.

I haven't spoken to or heard from Georgina since she left, so I'm not expecting a rundown of everything that happened while she was away. It's not like she's big on girl talk.

They'd expedited Hayden's test results, either because of who Georgina is or how sick she is; I didn't ask which.

Finding out the miraculous news almost took the sting out of Charlie's rejection.

Almost.

It also means that I'll be heading back to the city. Soon. That all of this is coming to an end.

My heart aches at the thought.

Since we got back to Driftwood, we haven't had a single break from each other, and I don't want one. We've worked at his shop, strolled around town, eaten a lot of really delicious meals, walked on the beach, had coffee on the patio, and stolen kisses like teenagers every chance we've had.

And I've loved every single second of it.

Maybe a little too much.

I've gotten attached. Not only to Hayden but to this small, sleepy coastal town that settles something in my soul.

I'll be sad to leave it.

"You okay over there?" Hayden's voice pulls my attention.

I'll be sad to leave him too.

"I'm good." I fake a smile. "Just thinking about how amazing it is that you're doing this for your mom."

We're out on the highway, driving back to his house after a day of working in his shop. He keeps his eyes on the road and taps the steering wheel with his thumb. "It's the right thing to do."

"But not everyone would do it," I say. "I'm not even sure I would."

"You would." He smirks at me.

I go quiet, thinking back on our day. He's getting the wooden boat ready for the show, and I spent most of the day writing in a notebook I picked up. Ideas, phrases, thoughts, musings, scenes, all of it.

There's something about *not* typing something out. It makes it more . . . real, in a way.

And somehow, despite Charlie's harsh words, I haven't been able to silence the voice inside me that begs me to write. I want my own voice to be louder than anyone else's.

It was a simple day, like many of our days have been—but a day I want to repeat. Because I know that soon I'll be back at work, wishing I were here.

This can't last forever.

"Hayden, I really like you." The words are out before I give them permission to be.

He turns, a quizzical look on his face. "I really like you too."

"But you hate New York."

"I do."

"And I live in New York."

"You do."

"So . . . what is this? A summer fling? A fleeting crush because we were cast opposite each other in the musical?"

He laughs. "I would never be cast in a musical."

I press. "Is this just a fun little distraction?"

We're nearing his house, driving slowly through neighborhoods that all make me ache for a life like these people are living.

"I don't know," he says. "But I don't think of you as a distraction. You're really fun, Kelsey. You're different, and even though your methods are a little misguided, your heart's in the right place. You care about people. A lot."

I fold my hands in my lap and stare at them, realizing I shouldn't feel this attached to him already. It's barely been a week. Heck, I might as well be in a musical—those people fall in love in the space of one act.

I can't explain why my feelings for him are already this strong—maybe it's the pre-midlife, postaccident second-chance crisis.

And as sad as it makes me, I know it's smarter to say this hard thing out loud.

"I don't want to get hurt." Not what I mean to say, but definitely the honest truth. "I mean, the more time we spend together, the more attached I'll get. And I'm leaving. Eventually."

Just like Georgina.

"So what are you saying?" He turns onto his sleepy street, and I stare out the window. The houses are set apart from each other, giving each one its own space. I crave that space. My apartment is the size of a shoebox, and I never take the time to get out of the city to see anything green. My life is all brick buildings and obstructed views.

"I love New York," I say, realizing. "I love the energy and the buzz. It makes me feel so alive. And Driftwood"—I close my eyes wistfully—"it makes me feel alive in a completely different way."

"I get it," he says quietly. "I get that this—whatever it is—is problematic."

"Yeah," I say. "You don't up and leave your whole life just because you met a cute boy." I shake my head.

"You think I'm cute?" I'm grateful for his flirty grin, not only because it cuts through the tension, but because it's so nice to see.

"Yeah, like stuffed animals are cute. Don't get a big head about it." I smile at him, then groan. "I wish we had all the time in the world to get to know each other."

I bet I could love you.

"But we don't." He looks away.

I shake my head. "Why couldn't I be a surfer or a boatswain or something? Or unemployed?"

"A boatswain?" he interjects, but I'm on a roll and don't stop talking.

"Or a nomad? Nomads move all the dang time."

"Never mind. I don't like you anymore." He grins.

I throw up my hands. "I'm serious! Right when I'm so close to figuring things out, right when I'm ready to say yes to an amazing guy, it has to be, 'No, sorry, you live different lives in different cities at different speeds.' What the heck."

"Yeah," he says. "It's not ideal."

I stare at my hands, folded in my lap. "Besides you, and my newfound love for the beach, there's nothing for me here."

"And nothing for me in the city." He pulls into his driveway and turns off the engine, then reaches over and takes my hand. "So what happens now?"

I hate this. I grit my teeth, because I want everything but can't figure out a way to have it. "I don't know. I guess . . . we part as friends?"

"Friends who keep in touch or friends who keep touching each other?" He laughs as he says it.

I know he's trying to keep the mood light, but my smile is laced with sadness. "It might be harder to keep in touch. It'll hurt more."

An overwhelming sadness washes over me. "I shouldn't feel like this." I smile at him through tear-filled eyes. "We just met."

He reaches over and touches my cheek. "It felt special, though."

I turn into his hand and press a kiss to his palm, hating that he's now referring to us in the past tense.

"My mom is going to have to get back to the city, probably right away," he says. "So why don't we enjoy one last night together? Pretend you're not leaving tomorrow."

I nod. "That sounds like a plan."

"A Yes Plan? Because I've got an idea for seafood you might not want to try."

Everything about us feels right. But we just happened at the wrong time.

We walk down to a tiny little market, where Hayden buys steaks, fish, scallops, and mussels, along with tons of vegetables to cook on the grill. I want to slide my hand in his, but instead, I keep my distance. I feel myself trying to detach from him, anticipating the moment we'll have to say goodbye.

We take the food back to his house and find Georgina and Dylan unpacking the Mustang in the driveway. As we reach them, I take the groceries from Hayden so he can help Georgina with her bags.

"You're here," she says.

"Where else would we be?" Hayden asks.

She narrows her eyes. "You didn't . . . go anywhere?"

Hayden looks at me, then back at his mother. "Like . . . Beaufort?"

"Like New York." Georgina's eyes flick from Hayden to me and back again.

Dylan comes around the car to stand next to Georgina, a perfectly benign expression on his face.

I frown, pretending I have no idea what she's talking about, even though I could've guessed that she would assume Hayden is her anonymous donor. I pray there's a way to get her off this theory, because honestly, if she confirms it, she might not go through with it, and then this fractured family will never get the time it needs to heal.

Hayden's right. Despite my misguided methods, I do care very much about them.

"Why would I go to New York?" Hayden says. "I have way too much work to take off."

"That's good to hear," Dylan says. "I was worried you were going to let *this* one distract you." Dylan nods at me with a grin.

This only makes Georgina turn her attention my way. "So what did you do while I was gone?"

"Helped Hayden at the shop," I say. "Or really just kind of pretended to help. I don't know anything about restoring boats."

"She did use the sander, though," Hayden says.

I look at him wide-eyed, praying Georgina doesn't ask me anything about this tool when all I really did was admire Hayden and scribble in my notebook.

She squints at me, clearly not buying this story. "You spent the whole time at the shop?"

"Of course not," I say. "We didn't sleep there."

Her brow quirks. "Where did you sleep?"

"Good grief, what is this, the Spanish Inquisition?" I say with an exasperated sigh. "In the guest room, Georgina. I know you aren't happy unless your days are jam-packed with stuff to do, but we just sort of hung out." I look at Hayden. "It was really nice."

To my surprise, Georgina glances at Dylan. "I understand that, I suppose."

And there's a whole story in those words.

"Your mother is just suspicious because she found out some news while we were away." Dylan follows behind Hayden.

"It's no big deal," Georgina says as we walk into the house. I'm slightly panicked because I'm not sure I can believably pretend to be surprised by what Georgina is about to say.

"It's a huge deal," Dylan says.

"Are you going to clue us in or . . . ?" Hayden sets the suitcase in the hallway and turns to his parents.

Georgina straightens, clears her throat, then says, "It sounds like they found me a kidney."

Hayden's eyes widen, and he does a passable job of feigning surprise. Considering the mixed emotions at play here, nobody can fault him for having a complicated response. But then he reaches out and hugs her. "I didn't even know you were on the list."

Georgina stiffens, then slowly puts her arms around him, and the moment is so tender I have to look away.

It's the first time they've embraced in years—and Hayden has to pretend.

After a moment, he pulls back. "I'm really happy for you."

She seems slightly shaken at this rare moment of affection, and she looks away. "It's unexpected. I still haven't decided if I'm going to do it."

"What?" There's a slight shriek in my voice.

She shoots me a look. "I don't like the idea of taking someone else's kidney."

"Georgina, don't be ridiculous," I say. "This is a chance for you to *live*. How can you walk away from that?"

She eyes me. "Why do you care?"

"Are you serious?" I shake my head. "Because I don't want you to die! You're too proud to ask someone to help you, and now this magical kidney falls in your lap and you're going to reject it?"

"She's not going to reject it," Dylan says. "She's going back to New York tomorrow to do what she needs to do to get ready for this transplant." He steps forward and puts a hand on her shoulder. "Because she's got a lot more life left in her."

She reaches up and touches his hand, then looks away, and I wonder if that life will stay in New York.

Then Georgina turns to Hayden. "Are we going to keep pretending we don't know whose kidney happens to be a match to my very rare tissue type?"

His eyes flick over to me, then to his dad, then back to Georgina. I hold my breath.

He sighs. "Fine. Yes. I'm the match."

"I'm not doing it." Georgina walks into the kitchen, and Hayden follows her.

"Yes, you are." Hayden's tone is firm.

"I beg your pardon?" She spins around to face him. "I will not ask you to give me your kidney. Not after—" She stops short. "It's not right."

"You're not asking," he says. "I'm offering. And you're going to take it."

"Hayden, even I am not that selfish."

"And she *is* selfish, believe me," Dylan chimes in, and I see where Hayden learned to deal with conflict.

She shoots him a perturbed look.

"This isn't about you," Hayden says. "This is about *us*. *All* of us. This is about me and Dad finally having a chance to get to know you. It's about all of us getting to make this right. It's about a second chance, and it's about making the right decision." His voice gets louder as he continues, "And it's about time someone told you to do something and you actually listened!"

Dang.

"And I'm sorry if you disagree, and I'm sorry if you think it's a bad idea, or whatever, but you don't get a choice. We've been doing things your way my entire life. Now you're going to do something someone else's way."

In my mind, Hayden drops a mic on the floor.

Georgina softens, lifts her chin, and looks impressed. Heck, I'm impressed. Hayden has stood up to someone nobody else in the world stands up to. And he did it with gusto.

"Now. Can we eat?" Hayden asks. "I'm starving. And I promised Kelsey I'd change her mind about seafood, and I want to make good before you guys leave."

He walks into the kitchen and Dylan follows, leaving me standing there with Georgina.

"Sorry I yelled at you!" Hayden shouts from the other room. "I just don't want you to die!"

Georgina and I look at each other.

"I second that," I say. "You're annoying, you yell at me all the time, you correct my grammar, you make fun of my style choices, but I don't want you to die either."

She takes a step toward me and makes a face.

I fold my arms, then unfold them, then fold them again. And stand straighter.

She draws in a breath. "This is all sappy and a little dramatic for my taste, but I suppose it's nice to know someone cares."

"I do." And after a calculated risk, I add, "Though I don't know why. You're horrible."

"And you need to wax your upper lip," she says with a huff. "Didn't anyone ever teach you about good grooming?"

Chapter 40

KELSEY

I'M SITTING ON another plane waiting to fly back to New York and thinking about the goodbye kiss Hayden gave me that morning before we left for the airport.

It was a proper goodbye, and I simultaneously loved and hated every second of it.

It's unfair.

I finally meet someone I might actually be willing to risk my heart on, and I have to leave him before I ever get a chance to see where it's going.

There's no sense dwelling on it. After all, nobody said life was fair.

So now I'm sitting here, feeling my lips tingle at the memory of that kiss and trying to tell myself that it was "fun while it lasted," and all those other dumb platitudes that only make people feel worse.

Georgina sits next to me, a little more tired and worn out than usual. She's quiet, and she's been quiet most of today. It occurs to me that this transplant might be coming just in the nick of time.

"Do you need anything?" I ask.

"Don't fuss over me." She goes quiet, but then, out of nowhere, she says, "I read whatever it is you're writing."

I spin in my seat and face her. "What?"

She flicks a hand in the air in a dismissive wave. "I figured if you're going to butt into my life, I might as well return the favor."

"When did you . . . ?"

"This morning when I was hooked up to that blasted machine," she says. "What else was I going to do?"

"Oh, I don't know, maybe *not* read my private thoughts?"

"Same way you didn't interfere with my private family business?"

I stop. She has a point. "Fine," I say. "I'll allow it."

"Good."

"But for real, I never wanted anyone to see my—" I stop short of calling it a *manuscript*. It's just pages and pages of senseless drivel.

Not good enough for publication. Or a hundred thousand followers.

"What are you doing with it?" she asks as the flight attendant does one final pass through the cabin, pushing on every overhead bin, making sure everything is securely fastened.

I shrug. "Nothing. I just had words in my head, so I put them on the page. No plans to do anything more than that." It's not entirely true. Charlie's comments were a setback, but my voice is still loud in my own head.

"So you *don't* want to be a writer," she says, folding her hands in her lap.

"Nope."

"You're a terrible liar." She lets her head rest on the seat and closes her eyes.

"It's not going to work out for me, that's all." I say this as if the case is closed, and I expect it to be because Georgina has never really taken an interest in my life up until this point—why would she start now?

"Why?" she asks. "Because you're afraid to show this to someone? You work in publishing. Surely there must be an editor or—"

"I tried that," I say. "It got rejected." A pause. "*I* got rejected."

"What?" She looks genuinely confused.

I shrug. "I sent it to my boss. Apparently it's not what they're looking for. 'Not original.' Basically, just not good enough."

She straightens her shoulders like she's personally offended by this, which surprises me because this is my humiliation on full display, not hers. "So that's it?"

I scoff. "That's pretty final."

"You sent it to *one* editor and that's final?"

Oh. Yeah. Fair point.

Now I understand why she's personally offended. Because unlike me, Georgina doesn't take no for an answer.

"If that's it, then you're not the woman I thought you were." She turns away from me and lifts a hand to get the flight attendant's attention. Unlike when Hayden and I flew to New York, Georgina has sprung for two first-class tickets, and even though I insisted I'd be just fine back in coach, she wouldn't hear of it. She told me that even though I dress like I belong in coach, she didn't want to have to keep track of me half a plane away.

I confusedly thanked her for the insult/compliment.

Kind things in an unkind way.

The flight attendant is at Georgina's side. "What can I get you, Miss Tate?"

"I would love some lemon water," Georgina says.

The flight attendant looks at me. "Can I get you anything?"

"I'm okay, thank you."

She nods, then disappears.

"Who is the woman you thought I was?" I ask.

She purses her lips at me. "I hoped you'd have learned by now that one person's opinion of you shouldn't hold that much weight."

"It's not just anyone's opinion, though, Georgina. This man is my boss. He's one of the best in the business."

"So what?"

"So . . . he knows what he's talking about."

"Kelsey, there are hundreds of men running companies who don't know what they're talking about."

I laugh. She's probably not wrong.

"This is what the world does," she says. "It tries to keep you down."

The flight attendant is back, fawning over Georgina with her lemon water and a hot towel. She hands a towel to me, and I have no idea what to do with it, so I set it on my armrest and cross my arms over my chest.

"The world is going to tell you all kinds of things about yourself. You're not good enough or smart enough or strong enough or thin enough or rich enough or talented enough. They'll come up with a million reasons you can't do the thing you want to do. The thing you were born to do." She takes a sip of water and looks at me. "They'll tell you, 'No, Kelsey.' Or 'Not at this time, Kelsey.' Or my favorite, 'Not good enough, Kelsey.'"

I'm tearing up thinking that I'm not doing the thing I was born to do. I'm tearing up at all the no's. I'm tearing up because I know Georgina is right.

"So what do I do?"

She sets her glass back down on the tray, picks up the warm, wet cloth, and wipes off her hands. And then, very pointedly, she looks at me. "You look them in the eye and tell them *yes.*"

The words land like a cog slipping into place. And when they do, I have to look away.

I've been saying yes at nearly every turn. Small yeses in comparison, but maybe those served as practice for ones that are bigger and more difficult.

"And you'll tell Hayden yes?" I ask when the lump begins to disappear from the back of my throat. "About the transplant?"

Georgina stiffens. "I will." She looks away.

I stare out the window, turning her words over in my mind, thinking that it's easy for Georgina to say this in her position when everyone practically falls all over themselves to do what she says.

But for me? It's terrifying to think about putting myself out there again. Setting myself up to fail again. Georgina has forgotten what it's like to be at the beginning of a career.

She doesn't say anything else about it, but her words follow me home.

Chapter 41

GEORGINA

Leaving Dylan and Hayden was the hardest thing I've ever had to do.

Because unlike the first time I left, I know now what I'm leaving behind.

I've been back in New York for a few days, and Dylan has called every night for an update on my transplant.

Tonight we're talking about the details of his arrival because he insists on fussing, and truly, there's no point in pretending I mind, because I really do like it.

I like his attention.

Even though I also like my freedom.

"Have you talked to Kelsey?" he asks. "Since you've been back?"

"No. I assume she's gone back to work, back to bothering people her own age," I muse. "I've never met anyone like her."

"We owe her a lot," Dylan says.

I frown. "We owe her for butting into our lives and sticking her nose where it doesn't belong?" I realize it's a harsh characterization, but that girl turned my world upside down. Though, even I can admit, it wasn't all bad.

"Yes, Georgie, we do," he says. "How many people do you know who would've bothered?"

"I wasn't looking at it that way," I say, pacing the floor of my bedroom and wishing he'd come back to New York with me. "I just thought she was nosy."

"I think she genuinely cares about you."

There aren't many people I can think of who do. Most people only want my money or my name. At first with her, it was a memoir, but even that now seems like she wanted to help others with what I had to say—which is ridiculous when I think about it.

What do I have to say? It's all common sense.

Kelsey didn't seem to want either money or notoriety, which makes me want to give them both to her.

Like Charlie Bucket being the perfect person to get Willy Wonka's factory, when he was the one who thought he deserved it the least.

I'm trying to figure out how I could do that when Dylan says, "Have you thought any more about what you'll do after the surgery?"

"Recover, I suppose."

"You know what I mean."

I do, and I'm not sure how to answer. It's all I've thought about. Do I abandon the life I've built for myself here in the city? Turn my company over to someone else and live out my days on the ocean with the man I've always loved? Or do I stick to what I know?

Only a few days ago, I was ready to walk away from Tate Cosmetics, but now? Knowing I could have years left on this earth . . . well, it's not so easy.

What if I move to Driftwood and all of the old stuff resurfaces? What if I get bored and become unbearable and Dylan realizes he's been romanticizing what we had all this time? What if I make him miserable?

"Georgie?"

I realize I've been contemplating silently.

"Tell me what you're thinking."

"I don't know," I say honestly. "It's a big change."

"Well, don't decide now," he says. "I'm not going anywhere. Well, except to New York to take care of you, which I know you're going to hate."

I smile. "I am going to hate it. I want no part of the fussing."

"Tough luck, you big baby." I can hear the smile in his voice.

I sigh. I miss him.

"I miss you," he says, echoing my thoughts.

I hesitate a moment, then decide not to hold back. "I miss you too."

There's a pause.

"And how is Hayden doing?" I ask. "Any second thoughts?"

"Georgie, you couldn't keep him from going through this with all the money in the world."

I'm shamed by this. Humbled. In awe.

I don't want to be the recipient of this because I don't deserve it. But Hayden isn't taking no for an answer. And that moves me in a way nothing else in my life ever has.

I hang up after promising to send over all the surgical details he needs in order to be in the city in time for me to get wheeled into the operating room, and I appreciate the space he's giving me to sort this all out.

Once again, he's put his feelings aside to let me figure out mine, and I think maybe it's about time that changes. It's time for me to put him first. This transplant doesn't change that, and I think deep down, I've always known it.

I stand in front of my vanity, staring at my own reflection. I'm not the same woman I was when he left, but Dylan was right— time hasn't changed everything we knew about each other.

I'm older, frailer, and more wrinkled.

In my heart, though, I'm still the same woman I was back then. A little colder and a little more jaded, perhaps, but maybe being with Dylan will change that.

Maybe there really is more to this life than climbing ladders and shattering ceilings. I'm proud of what I've done, but I've done it. And maybe it's okay if I move on.

I reach around my neck and pull the necklace out from inside my shirt. I undo the clasp and slip the wedding ring off and into my hand. I slide it onto my finger and exhale a quiet breath.

No swelling. It fits. And it feels right.

I call for JP.

When my assistant appears in the doorway, I turn to him. "I need you to schedule a meeting with my board of directors."

He frowns. "Oh?"

"I think it's time we make a few changes at Tate Cosmetics."

Chapter 42

KELSEY

IT'S BEEN A week since I got back to New York. A week of ignoring the words that are still very present at the back of my mind.

Even though I'm back at work, this was supposed to be a *Summer of Yes*. A whole summer.

Summer isn't over, which means I'm still supposed to be saying yes.

So far, I've been failing at that.

But ever since I got back, I've mostly been avoiding my life, filling my days with Netflix and junk food.

Turning down Ravi and Sasha when they ask if I can go out.

Telling my parents it's not a good time for a visit.

I've been saying no to all the things I promised myself I'd start embracing.

And it's making me miserable.

I'm sitting in a meeting with Charlie, Daniel, Chase Donovan, and two of the sales guys when a text from Hayden comes in. I glance down.

Hayden: Thinking about you.
Hayden: How is it being back in the game?

I haven't stopped thinking about him since I got back to the city, despite my very concerted effort to do so. I told myself that once I got back into my normal routine, I'd forget all about him, but so far that's been a big fat lie. In fact, it's been even harder.

I've fallen asleep replaying that first kiss, that last kiss, and all the kisses in between.

I text back:

Kelsey: :/

I miss him.

I tell myself it was only a little fling. I try to convince myself that it's done, it was nice, but I've got to move on.

I know better.

This felt different. *We* felt different.

My phone buzzes in my hand again. It's a photo of Hayden at the wooden boat show, standing next to his finished boat, the one I absolutely did not help him build, and he's grinning. Underneath, it simply says:

Wish you were here.

And I realize I wish I were there too.

After Georgina's thirty-thousand-foot pep talk, I spent a lot of time considering what I want to do. I thought about quitting. I thought about sending my proposal around to other houses.

I thought about becoming a nun and moving to an abbey where the hills are alive.

But then I remembered Brigitta is a brat, so forget that mess.

Ultimately, I landed here, right back where I started, as if the Summer of Yes hasn't changed me at all.

I'm not sure why they asked me to come to this meeting, except that I'm supposedly "providing support" for Daniel as they put Chase's book into production.

Providing support? What am I, a sports bra?

I refocus my mind and tune in to what they're talking about, because even though Chase was technically my find, I've removed myself from her project and have done a very poor job of keeping myself in the loop.

"So, Chase, how's the book coming along?" Charlie asks.

It's not customary to bring authors in for meetings like this, but apparently Chase needs more hand-holding than most.

Chase, who has dyed her hair pink, flips a long strand behind her shoulder and smiles. "It's really hard."

We're all expecting her to elaborate, and when she doesn't, Daniel clears his throat, leans forward, and asks, "What's tripping you up? Maybe we can help."

She leans back in her chair. "It's just hard to get, you know, the words out. Like to make sense. I mean, telling my life story is . . . well, a lot."

I frown. Telling her life story? I'm confused.

"Do you know the level of creativity it takes to do what I do?" Her voice is whiny.

I've watched her TikTok videos, and let me just say, her makeup tips are magic. I tried her highlighting technique, and my eyes really did pop.

There's the occasional fashion idea. Turning a garbage bag into a dress or putting her own spin on the previous night's *Project Runway* challenge. What she does requires creativity, but what she said has me wondering what kind of book we're publishing here.

"I thought we were working on a book of your top tips?" I ask. "A pictorial with fan favorites?" Wasn't that the idea we discussed?

"Didn't you get the email I sent out?" Daniel asks. "The update on Chase's project?"

I stare at him blankly. "I did but I didn't read it," I blurt. I kind of like this "saying what I'm thinking" thing. Georgina's influence.

"Chase wants to do more of a . . . a memoir of sorts," Daniel says.

"A memoir?"

"Yes, her life story."

I feel my forehead wrinkle. "Her life story? That wasn't the plan."

Daniel shifts in his seat. "She's decided to switch gears—which we love, just love it, Chase—and that's why we brought you in here. We wanted you to help spruce it up."

"Spruce it up?" I stare at him.

"Yeah, you know, take her words and make them shine. You're really good at that, Kelsey."

"But that's not my job," I say. "Chase is your client, Daniel."

"True, but this kind of project is right in your wheelhouse, Kelsey," Daniel says, shooting me a pointed look. "You're so good at helping other people find their story."

Helping other people find their story.

I am good at that. I chose this path because when my professor told me I didn't have what it takes to write, I realized I didn't want to find out. I was scared. I realized that putting my own thoughts and ideas into the world for everyone to judge wasn't something I could do.

Because I wanted to be liked.

This path I'm on felt safer. I could still work with words and stories, but I didn't have to see if my own were any good.

Safer isn't always better. And I've done myself a terrible disservice.

In the back of my mind, I hear Georgina saying, *"You tell them yes."*

And all at once it hits me.

Sometimes a yes has to start with a no.

No, I'm not okay with this.

No, I don't want to spend my life doing this.

No, I don't agree with this.

And the kicker: No, this is not the kind of story I want to tell.

"Kelsey, do you need to step out?" Charlie leans forward in his chair, like a teacher trying to make a point.

"No, I don't need to step out," I say.

The final cog falls into place, and in my mind, the creative machine is completed.

I don't want to sit in this office anymore. I want to explore the world. To search for stories. To find people whose lives are extraordinary and write about them.

And in my free time, I want to write stories that make me laugh. Romantic comedies that will make the world feel a little lighter because the world can be heavy and hard. I want to bring people joy.

And it's risky because it's not stable. And maybe people won't love what I write. And I'll probably never win awards or hit lists, but at least I'll be doing what I love.

It's time for me to say no. To the things that are keeping me from feeling alive. And if I have to get a job at Starbucks to fill in the gaps, I can do that. I have money saved up. I can move somewhere less expensive.

Somewhere on a coast . . .

"I quit." I stand.

"What?" Charlie stands.

"I can't do this anymore," I say. I look at Charlie. "I'm sorry, I just haven't been doing what I really love."

"Kelsey, is it your accident or . . ." Charlie frowns.

I think about what my mother said. The accident was a disruptor, just like my sister and I were for her. *"The very best disruptors."* I smile. "Maybe it was. But I think I have my own stories to tell, and if I stay here, in my safe little job, I'll never tell them."

Living life gave me a story.

And that story isn't finished.

I pick up my notebook and phone. "You'll have my resignation letter in your inbox this afternoon."

And with that, I turn around and walk out.

Chapter 43

KELSEY

I'm shaking and a little out of breath.

No is my new yes.

The Summer of No.

Or maybe the Summer of No More.

I'm standing at my desk with a box in my hand.

Tess watches as I pack things up. My guess is that she's trying to piece together what the real story is—there's only so much you can hear through the wall.

My whole life here is going to fit into this tiny box.

That's telling.

"Daniel said you got fired." Tess stands rigid and tense beside me.

"I did not," I say, rolling my eyes. "I quit. I sent my resignation letter to Charlie."

"You did?" Now she looks even more concerned. "Are you okay? You really haven't been yourself since you got back."

"I'm actually really good." I'm holding a stapler, which I now realize doesn't belong to me. I set it down and sit. "I want to see more than the inside of this office." I look at her. "And I realized there are other things I want to do." I pause. "I want to write."

I'm expecting some sort of reaction from her, but then a strange quiet comes over the entire office. The room, full of cubicles and chatter, is rarely quiet.

Tess drags her attention toward the elevator. "Oh my gosh."

"What's going on?" I stand.

"It's Georgina Tate."

At the sight of her, I freeze. I haven't spoken to Georgina since our flight home. Since her big, grand pep talk. Will she be proud when she learns that I've quit my job? Or will she tell me it was really impulsive and stupid to do that since I have nothing else lined up, which is honestly what's racing through the back of my mind right now.

I'm standing there, expecting Georgina to stop at my desk, and surprised when she walks right on by without looking at me, JP trailing behind.

"What the . . . ?"

She seems to know exactly where she's going, which is odd because I don't think Georgina has ever been here before.

The entire office watches as she walks straight through Charlie's door, closes it, and sits down in the chair across from his desk. I can't tell from where I'm standing if Charlie is surprised to see her, but what I wouldn't give to be a fly on that wall.

....

Georgina

"Uh, Miss Tate . . ." The man across the desk is fumbling over himself, which is exactly the reaction I was hoping for.

It's why I didn't let him know I was coming until I was already in the building. I want him to feel a little off his game.

I sit, and JP closes the door and stands off to the side.

"Mr. Goldfarb."

"It's such an honor to have you here," he says. "We didn't expect you."

"I want to discuss a proposal that was recently submitted to you by one of your editors. Kelsey Worthington."

He frowns.

"It was a proposal for a book about saying yes—do you know the one I mean?"

"Uh, y-yes," he stutters. "I do, but what do you have to do with—"

"You rejected it."

He stammers. He's probably trying to piece together how I know.

"I, um . . . yes, we, uh, did"—he clears his throat—"reject it."

"Why?"

Charlie tugs at his collar, squirming a little under the weight of my gaze. "Uh, I didn't feel the project was right for us."

Now I scoff. "Well, I suppose you're right about that."

His smile is unsteady.

"I did a little research on what you've been publishing lately," I say. I lean in for effect. "It was quite eye-opening."

"Publishing is a hard business, Miss Tate," he says. "We've found our niche is in—"

"Pure and utter trash," I say. "I know."

More squirming. "Uh, well, now, there have been some worthy projects—"

"There absolutely have not."

He's at a loss for words.

"I read that proposal Miss Worthington sent you," I say.

"Oh?" he asks. "Are you in publishing?"

"I'm in the book."

He frowns. "I don't understand."

"The 'older woman' she talks about. The one she goes on the trip with."

Realization washes over him. "The manuscript didn't mention—"

"No, because before now I didn't give Kelsey permission to use my name," I say. "But after reading it, I think it'll be fun to collaborate with her on this project. It's a good story. An interesting story. And full of revelations that I think many young people will be able to relate to. Things I wish I'd known when I was her age."

"Well, if I'd known—"

"That's just it, Mr. Goldfarb," I say. "It shouldn't matter. The story is good. The writing is stellar. Do you agree?"

He looks away, metaphorical tail between his legs. "Yes, I suppose so."

"But you told her the opposite, didn't you?"

He looks at me. "I did."

"And now, because of you, because of *you*, Mr. Goldfarb, she believes in her heart she's not good enough to be a writer." I narrow my gaze. "Do you know that your words have power, Mr. Goldfarb?"

He frowns. "Kelsey isn't a writer."

I raise a brow. "Isn't she?"

"She's an editor," he says. "And as of about an hour ago, she's not even that."

"I don't follow."

"She resigned this morning. She's out there packing up her things as we speak."

Behind me, I can practically feel pride radiating off JP. I know because it's radiating off me too. "Good for her."

Not that I advocate quitting a decent, stable job. Unless misguided bosses are making you miserable. Then I'm all for it.

"I'd be happy to take another look at the proposal," Charlie says. "With this new, uh, development, I think we'd be very interested in working with you and Kelsey."

"I'm sure you would," I muse. "But I'm afraid I'll have to . . . reject your proposal."

He physically gulps. I'm enjoying this a bit too much.

I press on. "I have friends in the industry who I think are maybe a better fit." I hold his gaze. "I don't think you're right for this project. I'm not sure we can trust you to do right by it."

"I can assure you, I will put my best people on it," he says.

"And I can assure you, your best person just quit."

He stutters, then replies, "Surely you of all people can understand the need to make *money*, Miss Tate."

I sit up straighter. "I can. But I've also learned recently that there's a lot more to this life than that." Standing, I continue, "I'm going to lend Miss Worthington my name for her book. And help her get it published. And then I'm going to hire her to help me write my memoir. And I'm going to get that published too."

He stands. "I see."

"Do you?" I inch my chin up to look at him. "Hmm. A little too late, I think."

And with that, I nod toward the door, which JP pulls open, and I walk out.

The office goes quiet again, and I spot Kelsey, standing off to the side next to a boring cubicle that would suck the life out of any creative soul. I walk over to her and see she's packed her things into a small box.

"Well?" I say. "Are you coming?"

She looks around the office, then at JP, then finally at me. "Yes."

I start off toward the elevator, and Kelsey half jogs to keep up. When we reach it, JP hits the button, and we wait.

"How you walk says a lot about you," I tell her. "You should walk with a purpose. Always with a purpose."

"Okay."

I stare at the light above the silver doors, waiting for our floor to illuminate. When it does, there's a ding, and the doors open. We get inside and JP hits the button to take us down to the lobby.

"Georgina," she finally says. "What are you doing here?"

I give her a quick once-over. "You look like you haven't slept in a week."

She frowns. "Uh, thanks?"

"It's not a compliment."

"I'm aware," she says dryly, then asks again, "What are you doing here?"

I stare straight ahead and draw in a slow breath. "You can use my name."

She's blank.

"In your book."

"Oh." A pause. "Oh!" A realization. She shifts the box, and a stapler falls over inside it with a clunk. "But I'm not—"

"I've sent it to two of my friends who are in publishing. They both want to see more," I say, cutting her off. "I'm hoping we can get a bidding war going."

"Oh?"

"And you're going to help me write my memoir," I say.

Another pause. "I'm sorry, what?"

"I spoke with a friend in publishing, and she agrees it's a good idea. I figure if I'm getting a new kidney, I should have some time. But you cannot make me the villain." Then, absently, I add, "No one is the villain of their own story."

"But I just quit my job," she says.

"I'm not hiring you to edit it," I say. "I want you to write it."

"You want me to write your story?"

"Yes," I tell her. "It's not boring."

"No, I know, I just—" She fumbles her words. "You're offering me a job?"

The elevator dings and the doors open. I walk straight out and hear Kelsey and JP scramble into step behind me. "Please keep up, Kelsey."

"I'm sorry, I just—" She's still behind me, fumbling with the box, and she just shouts, "Stop!"

I stop. I turn.

She looks disheveled. Unkempt. Homeless, by the hair. We'll work on that.

Luckily, beyond all of that, I can see one of the most caring, teachable, brilliant creatives I've ever come across.

"Why?" she asks plainly. "Why would you do this?"

I level my gaze. "You're a good writer, Kelsey. I don't need to be a professional editor to know that. Your words are moving. The way you're turning this experience into a compelling story—" I look away, as if it's physically painful to say the next part. But then I remember what Dylan said about Kelsey caring enough about me to intervene in my life. "I can recognize talent anywhere, in any field. And you're one of the most talented I've seen. Ever."

I pause because I want her to let that sink in.

"And there's one important thing I forgot about being a young woman with dreams."

"What is it?" she asks.

I draw in a breath. "We all need someone to believe in us."

Chapter 44

KELSEY

IN HER TYPICAL Georgina way, the woman says nothing else to me.

We're standing on the sidewalk outside of my former office building, and JP has just helped her into the car. Eddie tips his hat at me, and I flash him a smile.

My life has changed dramatically since the first time I met him. I barreled into Georgina's life and practically forced my Summer of Yes idea on her, but look how the tables have turned. Now she's the one barreling, and I'm so, so thankful she is.

"JP," I call out, as Georgina's assistant starts around to the other side of the car. "What has gotten into her?"

He smiles. "*You* did."

I make a face. "Shut your mouth."

He gives me a proper JP frown. "I will not, thank you very much. I think it was you who got to her. And Dylan. And Hayden. And Driftwood. I'm not sure what kind of spell you cast, but it's been a wonder to behold." He raises his eyebrows and widens his eyes. "She's actually been"—he leans in and whispers—"nice."

I feign a heart attack and fainting, clutching at my chest. He smiles and nods, mouthing, *I know!* and opens the door to get inside. Before the car pulls away, I tap on Georgina's window. She rolls it down but doesn't look at me.

I want to shower her with my utmost thanks. To tell her this is the chance of a lifetime, and I'm not going to let her down. But instead I say, "I'm going to ask you hard questions."

"I know," she says.

"And I'm not going to take scripted stock answers that some random PR person wrote up for you."

Slowly, she looks at me. "I'm counting on it."

"If we're going to write your memoir, it's going to be required reading in business classes at universities across the country. We have to get it right."

She nods.

"And I want my name on the front cover."

Now her brow quirks. "Smaller and underneath mine."

"Same size font, but still underneath."

She tilts her head in approval. "Fine."

"Fine."

I grin.

She looks away.

"When do we start?"

"After my transplant. It's tomorrow. Unless my donor backs out. Then this whole deal is off."

"He won't back out."

She eyes me again. "I'm bored. Are we done *chitchatting?*"

"Yes," I say. "I'll come visit you in the hospital."

"Please don't," she says.

I step back and point at her. "Doing it!"

"Fabulous," she says dryly, rolling up the window. "I'm giddy with anticipation."

"Thank you, Georgina," I say.

In response, she ignores me and taps on the seat so Eddie knows it's time to drive away, leaving me standing there with a box of all my professional possessions and the overwhelming feeling of endless possibility.

I pull out my phone, desperate to tell someone about everything that's just transpired.

Hayden. Of course it's Hayden.

It's scary and exciting and exhilarating and fear-inducing, but I'm doing it, and I want him to know. I realize that I might see him tomorrow if I go visit Georgina. I realize that he's probably in town for the surgery. I realize that it'll be every bit as difficult to leave him as it was back in Driftwood.

And then I realize I don't want to.

Instead of dwelling there, I open up a new text to Ravi.

Kelsey: Quit my job.

Kelsey: Working with Georgina Tate on a new book project.

Kelsey: Missing Hayden.

Ravi: Well, that's a lot to unpack.

Ravi: We need to get coffee.

Ravi: But I'm at a convention in Columbus.

Kelsey: A math convention?

Ravi: It's fascinating.

Kelsey: Nerd.

Ravi: Unemployed.

Kelsey: Too soon!

Ravi: The first two items on your list will need further explanation, but if you're missing Hayden, why don't you just call him?

Kelsey: It's dumb, Ravi. He lives so far away.

Kelsey: Why couldn't he be a guy from my building or something?

Ravi: I'm glad he's not a person from your building.

Ravi: I've seen the people in your building.

Kelsey: This is so dumb. I just met him.

Ravi: I knew the day I met Sasha that I loved her.

Kelsey: And it still took you years to propose. 😊

Kelsey: . . .

Kelsey: I bet I could've loved him.

Ravi: Don't kid yourself, K. I think you already do.

·················

That night, I'm sitting on my couch in my pajamas and eating ice cream and missing Hayden. He's like a drug I'm trying to wean myself off of, and the withdrawals are nearly unbearable.

Twice I've opened my phone to text him, and twice I've tossed it aside.

Is Ravi right? Is distance a stupid reason not to pursue a relationship with Hayden? Are our fundamental differences really not something we could overcome?

Could I be happy living anywhere else?

The thought gives me pause.

Wait. I don't have a job here anymore.

I could move.

Do I want to move?

I think of Driftwood. The sands, the water, the ease, and the sun. Could I be happy there?

Who am I kidding? God probably vacations there.

A knock at my door pulls me from my thoughts and my ice cream. It's late, and the only person I know who might show up unannounced is my mother, and according to a text I received this morning, she's in the middle of a theatre workshop for incoming freshmen.

I stand and walk to the door, my breath catching as I peek through the peephole and see Hayden standing on the other side.

I look about as presentable as I did the first day I found him in Driftwood, but I don't even care. The second I see his face, I pull the door open and stare at him.

"You're here." I can't help it. I'm smiling. There's no point in pretending I'm not happy about it. "You're making it impossible for me to forget you."

He takes a step closer. "Then my plan is working."

"What are you doing here?" I ask.

"Can I come in?"

"Of course." I move out of the way, and he looks around my apartment. It hasn't changed much from the last time he was here, though I did practically strip naked out of my work clothes today when I got home, and they're still strewn across the living room floor.

He sees the mess, then looks at me, brow quirked. "Naked dance party?"

"Naked dance *celebration*," I correct. "I quit my job today."

His eyes go wide. "Wait. You quit?"

I nod. "I realized it's not where I want to spend my days."

"Wow," he says. "That's huge."

He looks so handsome standing here in my living room, and I wonder if he's nervous about the surgery. I wonder how things have been since I left. I wonder if he's been working on the *Georgina*. In just a matter of days, I've amassed a million more questions for him, and I want all the answers.

Instead of bombarding him, I ask, "Do you want some ice cream?"

"You know I'm not going to turn down ice cream," he says.

I walk into the kitchen and pull the carton from the freezer. "So what are you doing here?"

He follows me. "Came to thank you."

I scoop a generous amount of ice cream into a bowl. He gives his head a little shake, and then, like I'm a blackjack dealer, he taps the counter.

I add more.

Another tap.

Another scoop.

"Do you just want the whole carton or . . . ?"

Finally, he holds up his hand as if to say, *"That's good."*

"Thank me for what?" I slide the bowl over to him and return the carton to the freezer.

He takes a bite of ice cream, then says, "Because of you, I get to save my mother's life tomorrow."

"Don't give me credit for that," I say.

"Wouldn't be happening if you hadn't brought her to Driftwood," he says. "You gave me a second chance. You're saving her life."

"*You* are saving her life," I say.

"We're equally to blame, I think."

I walk around the counter and stand in front of him. "You could've told me that on the phone. Or in a text."

He shovels another huge bite of ice cream in his mouth. "Yeah," he says, mouth full. "I could've."

"So why didn't you?"

He swallows, sets his bowl down, and looks at me. "Because then I couldn't do this." He wraps an arm around me and pulls me closer, then kisses me so fully I can taste the cold mint on his lips.

His lips search mine, and I reach my arms up his back, feeling like I can't get close enough. He turns us around so I'm standing against the counter, his body pressed into mine, giving me all the attention I crave.

I've missed this. I've missed *him*.

I think of what Georgina said about not being able to fall in love over bagels and lox. I think of what Ravi said—that he loved Sasha the day he met her. And I think briefly about my past relationships and how this, the way I'm feeling right now, was never in the cards for me with anyone else.

Hayden pulls away, and I'm a little out of breath. My heart is pounding like Jumanji in an antique trunk.

"You're lucky I like mint chocolate chip." I smile.

He returns the grin. "I know it doesn't make logical, practical sense with you here and me there, and I know we're supposed to be just friends." He kisses me. "And I know I'm supposed to let you walk away." Another kiss. "But even if I wanted to, I don't think I can."

I reach up and trace the scar above his eye. "But what if you get hit by another golf ball? How will I ever carry on?"

"You're so weird."

"Hey, you should know what you're getting into here." I step back and indicate my whole body. "You get *all of this*, baby. I'm a catch."

"You have no idea how cute you are."

I smile. He thinks I'm cute.

He pushes a hand through his hair, leaving it messy and sexy. "So what do we do? Long distance? Trade off weekends?"

I scrunch up my face. "There's no future in that."

A pause. And then he asks, "What if you come back with me?"

"What, and leave all this?" I motion to my blank-walled, neutrally decorated apartment.

"You could find someone to sublease it, just for a couple months?" He picks up his bowl of ice cream and takes a bite. "You quit your job—what's keeping you here?"

Nothing. Nothing is keeping me here.

"Say yes, Kelsey." He smiles at me.

I smirk back. "That's not fair."

"You have an out if you end up hating it," he says. "Dad can take the guest room, and you can have my pool house for free. You can write."

"I would pay rent."

"Uh, no," he says. "Absolutely not. You could work on this project you and my mom are doing. She told me about it yesterday."

"Yesterday, as in the day before she told me about it?" I grin. "That's so Georgina."

"She's very sure of herself."

I can't keep myself from smiling. "It does sound perfect." Like a sabbatical. A working vacation. A chance of a lifetime.

He grabs the belt of my robe and pulls me closer. "It would give us time to figure out what this is. It would give us a chance."

"I like the way that sounds."

He leans in and kisses me again. "Then say yes."

I smile against his lips. "I'll think about it."

"Don't think," he says. "Just do."

"There are logistical issues," I say. "Like, what if your mom is here and I'm there?"

"That's what email and Zoom are for." He presses a soft kiss to my neck. "But maybe she'll surprise us both and move to Driftwood."

I pull back. "That would be amazing, but . . ."

"But?"

I frown. "But I don't want you to get hurt. You know, if she doesn't."

He looks away. He probably doesn't want to consider that he will go through this huge ordeal to save her, only to have everything go back to the way it was. But I'm nervous he's setting himself up for heartbreak.

The same way I'm nervous that that's exactly what I'm doing with him.

"I'm still going to hope," he says. "Hope is never a bad thing." He shovels another bite of ice cream in his mouth and grins.

I shake my head at him.

"Let's watch a movie." A fan of the non sequitur. I like him even more. He walks away, leaving me standing in the kitchen, contemplating what he just said. The words are profound even though he didn't intend them to be.

"Hope is never a bad thing."

I watch him as he settles himself on my couch, and I realize hope is something else that's been missing in my life.

He looks over at me. "You okay?"

Old Kelsey would think of every possible outcome, and they'd all start with "What if?"

Old Kelsey would try to plan for the worst-case scenario, then expect it to happen.

New Kelsey, though? She hopes now.

I choose hope.

And I start flipping the script on my what-ifs.

What if it's amazing? What if it's fun and exciting and inspiring? What if he's as sweet and kind and wonderful as he seems? What if this relationship doesn't lose its luster but only gets brighter and better over time?

What if he's the one?

I walk into the living room and sit down on the couch next to him. "I'll come with you."

He freezes, remote pointed midair at the television, and looks at me. "You will?"

I nod. "Yes."

He leans toward me and kisses me again, like it's the most normal thing in the world. "Good."

I nestle against his chest and smile to myself as he goes back to scrolling the movie guide. *What if it's wonderful?*

He scrolls to *Ferris Bueller's Day Off* and clicks Select.

Yep. It's wonderful.

Chapter 45

KELSEY

IT's THE MORNING of the surgery.

We arrive at the hospital, and a woman at the counter directs us to the fourth floor. As we walk down the hall toward the elevator, Hayden slips his hand around mine, and I'm so glad we aren't pretending we're just friends anymore.

We step into the elevator, and I glance over at him. "How are you feeling?"

He blows out a breath. "A little nervous now that we're here."

I squeeze his hand. "I think that's normal."

He nods, but he looks like he might throw up.

"You're brave," I say.

"I'm just doing the right thing."

"It's a big thing," I say. "It's a big deal."

He glances over at me. "I'm sure it'll be fine."

I slide my arm around his and lean into him. "I know it will."

When we reach the fourth floor, we check in at the nurses' station, and Hayden lets the nurse know he wants to speak to his mom before they get him prepped.

We walk into Georgina's room and find Dylan sitting next to her bed, holding her hand. They appear to be deep in conversation, and once again, I'm struck with curiosity about their story.

I want to beg her to choose Dylan and Hayden, but even I know it's not my place.

At the sight of us, they stop talking, and Dylan stands. "Morning."

Georgina's eyes drop to our hands, still clasped together. She raises a brow and I let go, but Hayden grabs my hand back.

"It's fine," he says, then to his parents, "We're seeing where this goes."

Dylan grins at us. "I approve."

"I'll reserve judgment," Georgina remarks.

Classic Georgina.

My eyes drift over to her, somehow looking fashionable in her hospital gown. Her hair is done, full face of makeup, and she actually smiles. It's faint, but I catch it.

"I wanted to see you before I have to put on one of those ugly gowns," Hayden says.

She quirks a brow. "I think it's very chic."

I giggle. We're all trying to keep things light, but there is heaviness in the room. This is no small event happening here today, and the doctors have made it clear to Hayden and Georgina that there are still risks involved.

But we're not thinking about those right now.

We're choosing to hope.

"Georgina and I were just talking about her plans for after the surgery." Dylan sits back down and takes her hand. I notice she's wearing her wedding ring and absently think she's going to have to take it off for the surgery, which is hardly noteworthy. In the weeks I've known her, I've never seen that ring on her hand.

That must mean they're back together, and somehow, this warms me from the inside out.

"What are your plans?" I ask.

"To work with you on the book," she says.

"Books," I say.

"Books." She gives her head a slight shake, clearly annoyed by my correction.

"We're partners," I say, beaming at the realization. Somehow, Georgina has made the whole idea of writing less scary.

Her belief in me has given me wings.

Georgina Tate.

"We're going to have to work remotely," Georgina says, "because I'm moving to Driftwood."

"Wait, what?" I admit, I'm shocked.

Beside me, Hayden exhales. "You are?"

She reaches a hand out to him, and he steps forward to take it.

"I'm very proud of what I accomplished," she says. "I built a multimillion-dollar company from the ground up. I reached all my goals. And that's no small thing." She presses her lips together, and they tremble. "But in order to do that, I had to sacrifice a lot. I had to sacrifice my relationships with the two people I love most in this world."

I take a step back, feeling like an intruder in this very personal family moment.

Georgina squeezes Hayden's hand. "Hayden. My beautiful boy." Her voice falters slightly. "I'm so, so sorry."

I can't see his face, but when he speaks, I hear him holding back tears. "It's okay, Mom."

She closes her eyes and shakes her head. "It's not okay. And both of you letting me off the hook so easily is not okay either. Your dad says this is what grace looks like, but you can't possibly know how humbling it is for me to receive it."

And then Georgina looks at me. "And you."

My eyes widen. "Me?"

"My husband pointed out that we have you to thank," she says. "For everything."

"I didn't do anything, Georg—"

"Yes," she cuts in. "You did. You forced me to confront what I told myself I couldn't change. My regrets. My failures. Because of you, I have my family back." A pause. "That's why I'm moving to Driftwood."

"What about your business?" Hayden asks.

"I told my board it's time I move on, and we're working diligently to find a new CEO. I'll still be involved, but on a much smaller scale. More of a figurehead, really. I'll still have a hand in the big picture. I'll still be able to walk into the building and tell all of the idiots in there to stop being idiots." She looks at Dylan and smiles. "But not the day-to-day operations."

They look so happy it squeezes something inside me.

"What will you do with so much free time?" I ask lightly.

"Aside from these book projects?" she asks. "Paint. Learn to cook. Go out on the ocean. Get to know my son. Admit that I'm in love with my husband."

"I knew you were," I say.

"So did I," Dylan says. "It just took her a while to catch up."

She swats him on the arm.

"And we're buying a house," she says. "So you'll have your pool house back in case anyone"—she looks at me—"wants to stay a long weekend."

I glance at Hayden, and when he looks at me, I see his eyes are glassy. "Actually, I'm going to sublease my apartment." I look at Georgina. "And move to Driftwood."

"You little copycat!" she barks out with a laugh. And then she reaches a manicured hand in my direction.

I take it, aware that this is a moment I need to fully pay attention to, the kind that won't come around again. After her surgery, I know her acerbic attitude will return.

But for now, I get to see a softer side of Georgina Tate. How lucky am I?

"Thank you, Kelsey," she says. "If you learn nothing else from my life, learn this. Don't wait to love the people you love. We aren't guaranteed a second chance—we're only lucky enough to seize one when it comes."

I squeeze her hand just as the nurse enters to finish getting Georgina ready.

"I'm sorry to interrupt," she says. "But it's time. I have to kick everyone out." Then to Hayden: "And we have to get you prepped."

When we say goodbye to Georgina, her expression changes, and for the first time since I've known her, I think maybe she's afraid.

I lean in to hug her, and I sense her hesitation, but eventually her hand pats my back, and I whisper, "It's going to be okay."

When I pull back, I see tears in her eyes. Her lashes flutter and she shoos us out. "No fussing!"

Hayden and I file out into the hallway, and once we're out there, I wrap my arms around him. "Your mom's coming home."

We stand like that for several seconds, and then another nurse interrupts. "Are you ready?"

He pulls away and looks at me. "See you in a bit."

"I'll be here."

Chapter 46

KELSEY

SIX WEEKS LATER

I'VE BEEN DREAMING. A lot.

I've been creating and writing and freelance editing and carving a new path. I've gone on adventures on the ocean and gotten to know the locals. I've learned to love (*some*) seafood and to use a few of Hayden's power tools. I've interviewed Georgina, who is blissfully alive after a successful transplant surgery.

And I've been letting myself fall in love.

It's not all roses. We've had a couple of arguments. I've discovered that Hayden has a moody side, and he's unfortunately uncovered that my insecurities run deep.

But we've committed to giving this a try.

Ice cream helps.

I haven't been back to New York in over a month, and I'm shocked to say I don't really miss it.

Charlie reached out twice trying to get Georgina and me to reconsider our publishing deal, but I politely explained we're very happy that we've found a home with one of Georgina's publishing friends, who understands the story we want to tell.

My life is completely unrecognizable because of the Summer of Yes, and I have a feeling this is just the beginning. I've dared to hope for the things I want, rejecting the worst-case scenario—that dreaded voice of doom that accompanies every exciting thing.

I haven't mastered it, but I'm learning.

Hayden and I spent a week at my parents' house, and I received high praise for "finally doing the thing I'm born to do." And I felt so grateful again to have grown up in such a creatively nurturing environment. And so foolish for ever thinking it hindered me in some way.

Ravi and Sasha are planning a spring wedding, and Georgina agreed to go back to New York to accept her Lifetime Achievement Award.

And we're all going to cheer her on. She'll have a front row filled with people who love her—not for what she can do for us but simply for who she is.

She had that all along, but the difference is, she knows it now.

She put us all up at the Waldorf Astoria hotel, and now, an hour before the ceremony, I'm meeting Hayden in the lobby wearing the first designer gown I've ever worn—on loan from one of Georgina's friends.

I never thought designer dresses had much appeal, but I'm starting to get it now. Everything about this dress makes me feel beautiful. When I slipped into the floor-length, midnight-blue gown, I was immediately struck by the sharp silhouette. With long sleeves and a high slit at the side, the gown has an asymmetrical neckline complemented by exaggerated shoulders.

It's stunning.

I told Georgina it was too much, but she waved me off and told me to stop being boring.

So here I am, exiting the elevator and approaching my *boyfriend*, whom I spot instantly across the lobby. He's leaning against a counter, wearing a tux and looking like he was chiseled from stone by some Greek guy with a hammer.

When he turns and sees me, he smiles, and I decide in that moment I'd be perfectly happy to make it my life's goal to warrant this exact expression from him.

He is, in a word, beautiful. But it's not even his looks that make him so.

I have to pinch myself to believe any of this is real. That he and I figured out a way to make it work, and that this so-called sacrifice I made in leaving the life I'd always known ended up being exactly what I needed to be happy.

I admit I didn't see him coming. But I'm so glad he's here.

I walk up to him, and he leans in and kisses me on the cheek. "You're stunning."

"I think it's the dress."

"A dress is just a dress," he says. "You make it come alive."

"Well, thank you." I pull back and fuss with his tie. "You're not so bad yourself."

"Are you ready? My parents are going to meet us there," he says.

I nod and follow him out to the car that's waiting on the curb in front of the hotel. He opens the door for me, and I slide into the back seat. He gets in next to me, takes my hand, and kisses it.

I glance over at him, and all at once I'm overwhelmed with the realization that he is what saying yes brought into my life. This man who's come to mean everything to me.

Him and *so* many other beautiful things. Things I can't display on a shelf. Experiences. Memories. Moments I'll carry with me for the rest of my life.

We ride in silence for a few minutes, and then he asks, "What are you thinking about?"

I let out a contented sigh. "You. Me. Us."

"What about us?"

I face him. "I like us."

"I like us too." He makes a face.

"I might even . . . love us."

He smiles. "I might love us too."

"You might?"

He smirks. "Well, I definitely love myself."

Now I'm the one smiling.

He takes my hand. "And you're not so bad."

"I agree. I'm not bad at all."

I lean in and kiss him, and when I pull back, I look him straight in the eyes and say, "I love you too." It's not only that I've let myself be loved. I've also let myself *love*. And that's no small thing.

He kisses me again, and even though I'd prefer to stay right here in the back seat of this car, I know Georgina is counting on us, so when we arrive at the auditorium where the awards ceremony is being held, we reluctantly separate and get out of the car.

Inside, we're surrounded by people we don't know—fancy people, the kind Georgina is used to. I would feel out of place, but somehow, I think Hayden and Dylan and I belong here more than anyone else. This is a night celebrating Georgina Tate, and for better or worse, she's a big part of my life.

She's changed my life.

She's shown me what saying yes can do. And she's proven that it's never too late to try again.

We meet her and Dylan and go into the ceremony, where JP is waiting for us.

Once we're seated, right in the front row, I turn to Georgina and smile. "I'm glad you said yes to this ceremony."

"Because you get to wear that gown?"

"Because I get to see your son in that tux." I grin at her and pump my eyebrows.

She shakes her head at me, hitting me with her program.

I'm pretty sure she's smiling.

"I'm kidding. I'm glad you came here because you deserve to be here," I say. "And because now, when you're standing up there, you get to look out here and see proof of how loved you are."

She side-eyes me. "Are you going to get sappy?"

"Probably," I say.

"Boring."

When her name is called, Georgina takes the stage. She's not fully recovered, but she's come a very long way since her transplant. She's living again, and it's clear that the time away from work has been good for her. Or maybe she's simply proof that love changes a person.

Georgina begins her speech with the appropriate thank-yous, and then she brings her attention to the front row. To her son. To her husband. And, surprisingly, to me.

"They say you can't teach an old dog new tricks, but I've recently learned that's not true," she says. "A young woman barreled into my life recently—a nosy, presumptuous young woman who may or may not be a criminal . . . the jury's still out on that one . . . but a girl who single-handedly changed my life."

I feel the weight of her gaze on me, and I wonder if my heart has stopped beating.

"Because of her, I've learned a few valuable lessons. About life." Her eyes flick to Hayden. "About forgiveness." Then to Dylan: "About love." Then, back out to the crowd: "And here I thought I knew everything."

A laugh ripples through the auditorium.

"That woman challenged me to say yes to things I really didn't want to say yes to," Georgina says. "Things like standing on this stage and accepting this award. I hate this garbage."

Another round of laughter.

"I honestly thought I could send my regrets and get my little plaque in the mail. Because it's easier. And because I wasn't sure the people I loved would want to celebrate this with me." Her eyes scan the front row. "But here they all are." She smiles.

Hayden reaches over and takes my hand. I feel like Georgina is giving me far too much credit, especially since she is the one who changed my life, but I still appreciate her kindness. I know it doesn't come easily for her.

"The other thing I've learned, and I want you all to listen closely," she continues, "is that life . . . is good. And wonderful. And horrible, and beautiful, and messy, and everything all at once. And that is the beauty of it. It's overwhelming, but it's never boring. And it should be lived to the fullest.

"And no, that doesn't mean the biggest car or the best condo. It doesn't mean a house in the Hamptons or a promotion at work. It means filling your life with the people you love, doing the things that make you feel the most alive."

As she speaks, I think about her words. I let them resonate. I let myself consider them. I think about how I've hidden myself away to avoid the emotional roller coaster of a messy life for so many years thinking it would keep me safe. It didn't keep me safe . . . it only kept me lonely.

Yes, it's risky to feel things.

And it's risky to hope for good.

And it's hard to say yes to the unknown.

And it doesn't always result in wonderful memories. But that's what it means to be alive.

"So thank you, Kelsey, for convincing me to say yes to things that scare me," Georgina says. "And thank you to my son, Hayden, for forgiving me and for saving my life. And thank you to my husband, Dylan, who loves me even though I am a terror to live with and obnoxiously bossy." She pauses. "I am utterly unworthy of his love." She glances down the row one more seat and smiles. "And thank you to my assistant, JP, who keeps my life in order."

I can practically feel JP beaming at the end of the row.

"And thank you all," Georgina says. "For recognizing my life's work. I appreciate it more than you know, and I hope that in this next chapter, I make a name for myself in how fiercely I love. Because that is the one goal that means the most to me."

She nods to indicate she's finished speaking, and the audience erupts in applause.

We all jump to our feet and cheer for this woman, who, I'm learning, is a little like a two-sided sponge. People are accustomed to her abrasive side, but when you flip her over, there's a soft, squishy side just waiting for you.

The ceremony ends, and Georgina meets us in the auditorium, looking a little tired but very, very happy.

"See?" I say. "Aren't you glad you came?"

Dylan wraps an arm around her. "I am. And I'm glad you all came. Thank you."

"I think we should celebrate." I grin over at Hayden, and we both say, in unison: "Ice cream?"

"I don't eat ice cream," Georgina immediately protests.

I hold up a finger to stop her. "Say yes, Georgina. It could change your life."

"Kelsey . . ." She glances over at Dylan, then at Hayden and me. "You are absolutely right."

THE END

A Note from the Author

DEAR READER,

Somewhere along the way, I discovered that I've been living my life afraid. Every single decision I made was run through the filter of fear. Fear that paralyzed me. Because "what if something bad happens?"

But one day, I woke up and realized that bad things can happen whether you're sitting in your living room or out exploring the world. And I didn't want to miss the things that life had for me anymore. I didn't want to keep saying no every time something came up and threatened my well-laid plans.

Oh, I could write about bold characters living out fantasies, and there have been a few times I've actually agreed to taking risks, but implementing this kind of behavior in my real life? Easier said than done.

It's easy to say no. It's easy to stay comfortable. It's much, much harder to do things that make me feel awkward or uncomfortable. And I wondered if maybe I'm not alone. Maybe readers would relate to a character who has a wake-up call that forces her to examine the way she's been spending her days.

And maybe, in writing about her journey, I'd be inspired to say yes more myself.

I'm a work in progress at saying yes. I still really love my comfort zone, but I *am* working at it. And I am learning along the way. That the good stuff of life is outside the four walls of my house. That being with people, even ones I don't know, often makes me feel happier. That we're all on this journey together, most of us feeling awkward at the same time, and it's okay to admit it out loud.

I genuinely hope something in Georgina and Kelsey's journey speaks to you. That you can relate to their story and maybe it inspires you the same way it's inspired me.

To get out there and feel the wind in your hair, the earth under your bare feet. To plan the trip. To go to the zoo in the middle of the day. To reconcile with a loved one. To forgive. To love yourself. To choose to build a different kind of life.

Say yes to adventure and love and *living*.

We only get to do it once, right? Make it count.

Eternally grateful to you, dear reader, for the time you spend with my stories. You make it all worth it.

LOVE,
Courtney

Acknowledgments

I've been thinking a lot about what a privilege it is that I get to write books. When I need time to meet a deadline, there are people in my life who give me the space (and the grace) to do so. I'm not always easy to live with when I'm working something out in my head, so this is no small feat.

I'd like to thank every single person who has ever read, recommended, or purchased one of my books. By name. Over a cup of coffee. But since that's not possible, I'll start with these:

Adam. Always my first reader and my most honest one. You make me better on the page and off. I'm inspired by your creativity and humbled by your love. Thank you for being my best friend and for loving me so well. Ours is the best love story of all.

My kids. Though why I'm thanking them here, I don't know . . . they will never crack the spine on one of my books. LOL. (But honestly, so grateful they cheer me on. What a blessing to raise humans you fall in love with daily.)

Becky Wade and Katie Ganshert. My favorites. Writing friends turned real-life friends. I'm so thankful for you both. For the hours of brainstorming, whining, cheering, sharing, encouraging, and loving. You two are a gift.

For the entire team at Thomas Nelson. Thank you for all the work you do to champion books and to help me make my stories the very best they can be. I'm eternally grateful to you.

For you, dear reader. What can I say . . . thank you. Without you, there'd be no reason to write. I'm thankful to you for taking the time to pick up this book, and it is my greatest wish that it will speak to some part of you.

I am forever grateful for this opportunity, to share the stories of my heart. Every character takes me on my own journey, and I know what an insane blessing it is to be able to explore life through the world of fiction. This is how I process pain and joy and grief and love . . . through the written word. And I'm so thankful to have the chance to do so.

Discussion Questions

1. The Summer of Yes begins when Kelsey is in a freak accident. This is what it takes to get her to realize what's been missing in her life. Have you ever had a "wake-up call" that set you on a different course?

2. Part of the reason Kelsey says no to things is because of fear. What has your own fear kept you from pursuing?

3. How do you keep your fears from overwhelming you so much you don't try new things?

4. Talk about a time you stepped out of your comfort zone. What did you learn when you did this?

5. Georgina sacrificed precious relationships because she was convinced the people she loved were better off without her. Have you ever believed a lie about yourself, and if so, what did it cost you?

6. What is something you often say no to that you wish you could say yes to?

7. What is preventing you from saying yes?

8. If you could go on a journey of self-exploration, who would you want to be your co-pilot?

9. Kelsey realizes that her to-do list was keeping her from making time for the people in her life. Do you find this to be true for you, and if so, how can you create more space for your relationships?

10. Who do you relate to more, Kelsey or Georgina? What is it about their journey that resonated with you most?

About the Author

Courtney Walsh is a novelist, theatre director, and playwright. She writes small town romance and women's fiction while juggling the performing arts studio and youth theatre she owns with her husband. She is the author of thirteen novels. Her debut, *A Sweethaven Summer*, hit the *New York Times* and *USA TODAY* bestseller lists and was a Carol Award finalist. Her novel *Just Let Go* won the Carol in 2019, and three of her novels have also been Christy Award finalists. A creative at heart, Courtney has also written three craft books and several musicals. She lives in Illinois with her husband and three children.

....

Connect with her online at courtneywalshwrites.com
Instagram: @courtneywalsh
Facebook: @courtneywalshwrites
Twitter: @courtney_walsh